Other books by E. R. Wytrykus:
    Novels:
        The King of Coins
        The Money Run

The Connections Trilogy:
        A Stone To Roll
        A Road of Your Own
        On My Way Home

        The Girls of His Dreams
        Family Ties

    Short Stories:
        By The Short Hairs
        The 9th Inning and Other Stories
        The Adventures of Rex and Lexi

    Screenplay:
        The Money Run

"A ROAD OF YOUR OWN"

a novel by

E.R.WYTRYKUS

"A ROAD OF YOUR OWN"

Wheat Field Publications
109 Kiwi Court.
Lincoln, CA. 95648
NDWY2@aol.com

ISBN: 978-0-9839338-0-9

While *A Road of Your Own* stands on its own as a novel, it is a sequel to *A Stone To Roll,* in which we first meet the main characters, Rock, Di, and Cheyenne. For maximum enjoyment it is recommended that the reader first read *A Stone To Roll.*

"You got a road of your own, your own
You got a road of your own." ---from the song, 'Roadaway', by John Stewart

ONE

If you are lost as in a dream and you
Cannot find your way
All the reasons you are lost will
Guide you on your way---from the song, 'Across The Milky
Way,'
by John Stewart

Dear Diary:

WHEN I FOUND CHEYENNE he was lying facedown on a cot in the back room of Mac's Cowboy Bar & Grill. The cot was an old Army castoff with busted springs and a soiled mattress that was no thicker than a pizza delivery box. It set in a narrow slot between stacks of cases of booze and beer. Cheyenne was asleep.

No, he was passed out, is what he was.

"I'm sorry, Mac," I said. I wasn't sorry for Mac, I was sorry for Cheyenne, and I was sorry for me, because I had to get him home.

Mac shook his head. He was a pot-bellied professional bartender, with a receding hairline, a forehead that always had a sheen of sweat on it, and a face so weary-looking I thought he might crash on the cot himself, and sleep for a month.

"I can't have this, Dinah. It's the third time. He started another fight."

I nodded. "I know, I know. War talk, eh?"

"I guess. I'm too busy to pay attention to all the conversations going on. But he's always raving about something Iraqi this, or Pakistani, or Afghani; gets people riled up."

"Not Pakistan," I said.

"What?"

"He's never been in Pakistan, Mac." No sooner were the words out than I thought, how the heck do I know? How do I really know where Cheyenne has been and what he has done? He comes and goes like a goddamn alley cat.

"Whatever, Dinah, but you need to keep him out of here for awhile."

"He's still fighting the war, I guess."

"Well, I can't have him fightin' it here. Was he really in Iraq, no bullshit?"

"Yeah, he was there, Mac. Sometimes I think he still is."

"What did he do there?"

I looked at Mac as if he were a moron, standing in a dirty apron, holding a bar towel in one hand, his mouth slightly open, showing off his cigarette-stained teeth, gaping at me as if Cheyenne was a child who I had allowed to run loose and disrupt his lovely bar. Not nice of me, I suppose, but sometimes I am not a nice person.

"He killed people, Mac," I said.

Mac helped me get Cheyenne into his car and I drove home. I couldn't handle the bum myself, dead weight that he was, so I left him sleeping in the back seat of the car. I cracked open the windows, covered him with a dusty blanket I found in the trunk, and slammed the doors, hoping it would wake him; it didn't. What I feared was that Chey would upchuck all over the interior of the car, the bleeping idiot. Tomorrow, if the fool sobers up, I'll have to get him to drive me back to Mac's to pick up my car, as I had no intention of hiking several miles in the middle of the night to retrieve it now. Nor did I care to pay for a cab.

I looked inside the car one more time to see that the dodo hadn't puked yet, but it'd serve him right if he did. His car anyway, not mine. Before I went inside the house I stared straight up at the sky and admired the stars for a minute. Not as many here as I was used to seeing when we lived in Dry Hole, where nearly every night millions, I swear, millions, of tiny dots of light would sparkle. Sometimes I still missed that dirt bag of a town. For some reason looking at the stars reminded me of Rock, and of when he first popped into my life. Rock was a good one for talking about the stars and wondering what they really were and whether they had planets with people living on them, and what the people, or creatures, looked like, and whether they made war on each other. And he'd talk about his favorite sci-fi movies, like *Forbidden Planet*, or The *Day The Earth Stood Still.* A lot has happened since Rock stumbled into Dry Hole. I wondered what he was doing right now. Well, girl, he's sleeping, at least, at the time I was thinking of him.

As if the sky were speaking to me, a flash of light tore across the sky, as brilliant as a light saber defending against the evil Emperor in some far off galaxy, yet I knew it was merely the dying throes of an icy rock, showing off for me, and me alone.

It's very late as I write this, or is it very early if it's past midnight?—because if I don't write my notes when they're clear in my head I won't remember to later, and anyway I'm too keyed up now to sleep...I also think I'm stalling, hoping Chey will wake up and drag his sorry bod in here and apologize to me, but he was so blitzed I'm sure he'll sleep straight thru the night...just hope he doesn't wake me up too early!

MORNING: THE SONOFABITCH is gone! You'd think he'd come in and thank me for getting him home last night, but he likely doesn't even know what happened. Probably thinks he drove himself home and fell asleep in the car. Or else he's afraid to face me. Tough soldier shoots bad guys all day long when he's in Iraq or Afghanistan or wherever he goes, but he can't face me in the morning after getting wasted. Why do I put up with him?

I had gone outside to check on Chey and to smell the fresh air and help wake myself up, and when I didn't see him or his car where I'd parked it last night I thought he might have gone to get those delicious cinnamon rolls I adore, as a peace offering. I smiled, just a tiny smile, and when I went back inside the house I found the note, next to the coffee pot. Don't know how he could have been in here, made coffee, and not awakened me. I guess it's his sneaky ways that keep him alive.

'Dearest Di:

I'm sorry for last night, and I'm sorry for leaving this way, but I figure you're madder than hell at me and you've got a right to be, but I don't want us to argue. So I'll get out of your way. I've only got a few days before I need to report for duty and I need to visit some people back East before I go. Take care, sweetheart; I'll call.

Chey'

I read the note twice, scrunched it into a ball and threw it as hard as I could. It bounced off the cabinet and back into my face. I swatted at it, knocked it down, kicked at it, and stubbed my toe on a chair.

"Goddammit!" I yelled. (Diary, I may have said something worse than that, for the record). Can you believe he called me 'dearest'? And 'sweetheart'?!

"Visit some people back East, my eye! He's gone to see her, I don't friggin' believe it!" (Honest, Diary, I was screaming out loud!)

But I did believe it. He'd gone to see the girl on the east coast, his 'dream girl', the sister of the guy he was in prison with when they were captured in Iraq. I should have known he wasn't over her yet. Diary, I sat down and sobbed, I must admit. Then I said some more bad words, poured a cup of coffee (that Chey had so kindly made) and drank it while I voided my mind of any thoughts, because I knew if I didn't I'd be thinking of ways to emasculate Cheyenne.

After my second cup of coffee I called Rock. He didn't answer, and I didn't leave a message. Why doesn't he answer his phone, I wondered; it's Sunday morning and he ought to be home. I considered the possibility he doesn't want to hear from me, a stupid thought but right here and now I wanted to feel sorry for myself. Maybe he's not home, I pondered; maybe he spent the night with a new girl friend. I mean, why can't he have a girl friend? He's not too old to get married again, tho he did say he didn't think he'd ever find anybody who could replace Mary Ann. Of course, he was still saturated in grief. Even so, that doesn't mean he couldn't spend the night just to have someone to cuddle up to. Why does it still make me jealous, dang it!

Oh, heck, I don't need a shrink to tell me. Rock to me represents stability, decency, loyalty, strong character...a real man who's not afraid to show his emotions. Not that Chey doesn't have all those same characteristics, it just that some times he seems like such a little boy. But then, like me, he's not half Rock's age, so he doesn't have the life experiences that Rock has. Still and all, the things Chey has to do, a little boy couldn't do.

I'd been building up to be mad at Chey ever since yesterday afternoon when he said he was going to Mac's for a spell. I didn't want to go, but I would have, except I got the distinct impression he didn't want me tagging along.

Why can't you stay with me, Chey, I asked. We'll watch a movie, or let's go to the Country Blues, (the new place that opened recently—they have good chicken dinners and a fantastic banjo player.) No, he said, he wanted to have a beer or two and bullshit with the guys and he'd be back shortly and then we'd watch a movie.

Horse-puckey—I could have gone to bed right then and there knowing he wouldn't be home until late. He goes for a few days with no problems, then there'll be several nights in a row when he wakes up in a sweat, or screaming at somebody. Like to scare me to death. Or else he goes drinking—just a beer or two, sure—and then, kaplooey!

Night before last he woke me calling for her—that girl, Susan. "Susan! Where are you?" he yelled out. I shook him awake and he stared at me for a second as if he didn't know me. He was probably looking for her. What'd I say, he asked. Nothing, I told him, and slammed my fist into my pillow. Go to sleep, I shouted. I wouldn't talk to him all the next day.

"It was just a dream," he said, repeatedly, in the morning.

"Yeah, well, dream about me next time, okay?" I said, the first time he tried to appease me. After which I ignored him.

He followed me around the house like a puppy's just been taken away from its mama until I told him to leave me alone for awhile before I socked him in his shootin' arm.

Guess that's why he went to the bar without asking me to go with him; so it's my fault he got tanked?

I guess it's just as well, since his leave time is almost over. But you'd think he would have wanted to spend the rest of it with me, not *her*! I hope the fool remembers to report when he's supposed to. I guess I could call and remind him, but shoot, if he's too busy sparkin' his other girl friend, let him go AWOL! Serve him right if they kicked him out of the Army or put him in jail—at least he wouldn't get shot or captured again.

I don't know, Diary, too much has happened. I remember the day I met Rock and Cheyenne came hobbling back from the dead. The same day, it was, so it must have been fate. But now Rock's in San Diego and I haven't even heard from him in weeks and weeks, and Chey is barreling down the highway somewhere running away from me. Is it me? Do I chase men away?

Chey's become like those wind storms we get in Dry Hole; they come in faster than you can snap your fingers, turning the sky black barely a minute after it was pure blue and the sun was laying golden blankets as far as the eye could see. Darn storm would blow down a few buildings, sandblast the ones still standing, and be gone before you could take cover, leave everybody spitting sand for a week. That's my Chey, blowin' in and out with the wind.

As he explained it to me, the few times he'd talk about his work in the Army, (which he said he wasn't supposed to talk about so I'd better be careful what I write, because sometimes the Army sends people out to check on their own people so they'd better not get a hold of this diary!) he was in this special outfit, Alpha Betas, or Deltas, or something like that, very secretive. Anyway, he'd go on these missions to kill some really horrible terrorist creature, like Osama bin Laden, (Chey says he never did get that bastard, tho he did come close, but when I asked him more about it he clammed up.)

Anyway, it sounds awful sneaking up on people and killing them, but Chey says it's an important job because the guys he killed were the ones who planted bombs and pulled off terror attacks all over the world, and I'm sure he's right—I keep up with the news, I just don't care to read about killings. Somebody's got to do the dirty work, so I guess it's good there are people like Chey who have the ability—and the nature—to take out the real creeps of the world. I'm thankful I don't have to be the one to do such an awful job. Even if he's good at it, (some skill, like, what kind of job will that get him in the real world?) I know it's begun to grate on Chey, all that killing and dying. I think that's why he's so volatile these days. Still doesn't excuse him getting drunk and leaving me for another woman. It's a darn good thing we haven't gotten married yet.

As I think on it, trying to imagine what goes on in Chey's mind, I guess if my job was to sneak around in the dirt and kill some bastard, murderin' snake tho he might be, and I had to do it over and over, I'd want to get drunk so I could drown the memories. But I don't think a few beers are strong enough to wipe away those awful thoughts running in Chey's mind.

Times past, when I felt so low, I'd go see Mom. She'd cheer me up. Of course, when she got sick, she didn't even know who I was. I could have been one of the nurses, or the janitor, didn't matter to her. Still, it was always nice to see her, and I'd talk to her as if she knew me and understood what I was yakking about. Now she's gone, and Aunt May's gone, and Chey's gone again, skip to my Lou, my darlin', and I don't even have the café anymore, since I sold it to Betty Ann and Jake.

You know, Diary, I like writing to you because it's like writing a series of short stories about my life. I'd forgotten how much I need to do this. I guess it goes back to growing up with so few people around to talk to. Nobody knows as much about me as you do, and I'd be down right fearful if anybody did! Even Chey doesn't know as much about me as you do, but that works both ways. He doesn't talk a lot about what happened when the Iraqis captured him and kept him prisoner all those months. You remember, that was when Chey was classified as a battle death, and I got the insurance money, and we had to go to Washington to straighten it out, and Rock's buddy, a general who said Rock saved his life in 'Nam, cleared it up, and Chey went back to the Army, etc. etc. I wonder if Chey talks to *her* about when he and her brother were prisoners?

Since it's Sunday I don't have to go to work...it's just a part time job, Diary, working for an accounting firm to give me some experience...you know I took several classes at the Jr. College in Lordsburg and I still help some of the small ranchers back in the Dry Hole neighborhood with their bookkeeping...not that I need the money.

I still have time to make it to church—there's one a ten-minute drive that I've attended a few times, and today seems like a good day for some salvation talk. I'll say a prayer for Chey, and for Mom, and for all those other guys who Chey knew when he was in Iraq. And Afghanistan, and Pakistan, or wherever he goes when he leaves me.

LATER: DIARY, LATELY I've been thinking I'm getting too old for you. Diaries are for teenagers, aren't they? That's why I haven't kept you up to date on the events of the last few months, after we got back from our trip east with Rock. Maybe it's time to cull through all the notebooks I've kept all my life and make a bonfire. What do ya think?

It's been a quiet, but busy, day...first I had to call a cab to take me to pick up my car from Mac's parking lot, then after church I came home and fixed breakfast for myself, read the paper and some magazines, took a long, long walk out to the creek, watched the ducks, picked up around the house and vacuumed, and then pampered myself with a hot bath with the bubble bath soap Chey gave me that smells so good...too bad the fool wasn't here; he missed out and it serves him right! I did call Rock again, but still no answer...again I didn't leave him a message...I wasn't sure what to say...I knew I'd end up telling him about Chey and I didn't want to talk about Chey...I wonder if the job Rock offered me is still available...probably not...I waited too long...I was all set to go when Chey called and said he was coming home...I thought for good but he was just on an extended leave...that's when I stopped writing regularly, I was so sick with fear for Chey and disgust that he was leaving me again.

You know I sold the café to Betty Ann and her husband Jake and moved to Tucson to stay with Mom and Aunt May. Mom was going downhill faster than an Olympic skier and I wanted to be near her for the last few weeks. Then Chey came home on leave and it started getting crowded. Chey said he'd for sure be out of the Army in a few months and he'd have a better chance of getting a regular job around Tucson than in Dry Hole, where there aren't any jobs for him other than to pick up his Dad's old business, and that wouldn't take us far...good thing we've got the insurance money, tho I'm still concerned some goon dressed in battle gear is going to show up at the door someday and ask for it back...then Mom died, the poor dear, and it really sucks to have your Mom die and she doesn't even know who you are as you're saying goodbye.

Then to top things off, Aunt May, after all the time she spent taking care of Mom, gets sick herself. She had a cancer...hadn't told me, and she put off treatments because she was afraid she couldn't take care of Mom...so, three months after Mom died, Aunt May passes away, talk about a poor dear. Me, now I have no relatives at all, none that I know of, except Mom did mention an uncle somewhere in the Deep South who I'd never heard of before, but this was when she was really lost in la-la land, about a week before she died, so I don't give the story much credence.

So I inherit Aunt May's house because she has no one else to give it to. I didn't even know I was in her will until shortly before she died and she took me aside and explained the facts of life. She left me the house (no mortgage) and over a hundred thousand dollars, and still had a healthy chunk left over to give to her favorite charities. So now I have two houses—Aunt May's, and the old family home in Dry Hole, the one I grew up in and where there are several volumes of you, Diary, sitting regally on the shelves in my bedroom. I don't know what to do with the Dry Hole house, as the real estate market practically doesn't exist there any more, but it's not a bad house, just needs paint and TLC, like everything else that's constantly bombarded by the wind and the sand.

Aunt May's late husband, Uncle Bobbie Joe, did pretty fair for himself—and Aunt May—in the A/C business, but they never did know how to spend money. Aunt May had several miscarriages, the way I remember hearing it, and eventually the doctor said it was dangerous for her to get pregnant again. So they never even had kids to spend their money on. They went on a cruise once and didn't like it—too much water, Uncle Bobbie said!

Guess I'm doing okay for myself, aren't I? I get a bundle from Chey's insurance, but I don't have Chey around much, now I inherit another nice sum from Aunt May, but she's not around either. So why do I deserve this? I don't understand...I need to get Rock to help me figure out how to handle my ill-gotten gains...

Chey has been non-committal about our getting married, but I didn't push him on it anyway because I wasn't sure it was a good idea myself, but oh, I think I told you all that already...I'm probably repeating myself...anyway, his additional three months in Iraq turned to six, then he was home again, and back and forth like a ping pong ball.

I'll send Rock an e-mail and tell him I'm coming to San Diego for a visit soon. Even tho my job is only part-time, I need to give them at least a week or two notice. This way Rock won't be taken completely off guard and if he doesn't want me to come to San Diego he can e-mail or call me and let me know before I show up on his doorstep like a lost kitty and find I'm not wanted. I won't say anything about his job offer...don't want him to think I'm desperate, because I'm not, but a girl's got to have something to do, if she's not raising kids. (And you don't see any kids running around here, do you?) So if there's still a job open, I may just take it!

Dear Diary:

It's been two weeks and I haven't heard a peep from Cheyenne, nor has Rock called or sent an e-mail. I feel abandoned. I'm thinking of getting a job on a tramp freighter.

I did send Rock an e-mail that I was coming soon, hoping it would be a pleasant surprise, but he hasn't responded; in fact, I haven't heard from him in weeks, and we usually exchange e-mails several times a week. I suppose he's absorbed in his business; gives him something to do now that Mary Ann is gone...poor dear. Maybe I better not go to San Diego without first hearing from him. Who knows, he may have sold his business and left San Diego and is on a tramp freighter himself, hey? On the road to Mandalay?

I've been busy, trying to keep myself from thinking about Cheyenne and where he is, and what happened to him when he went to see that girl; heck, maybe he married her! I finished up my part-time job, and now we, you and I, are going to Dry Hole for a visit, and then we'll see about San Diego—Cheyenne can come and go as he pleases, why can't I?

I know Dry Hole is the opposite direction from San Diego but I miss Dry Hole...well, I miss Betty Ann...and the Only Café. Dry Hole may not be home, sweet, home anymore, but living in

Tucson without Chey, without Mom, without Aunt May, certainly isn't.

When Chey returns from his latest adventure—if he does—he'll find a cold house and worse, a cold bed! I must remember to shut the water heater off and I'll do like he did to me and leave a note!

'Dearest Jerk, I'm not home. There's cold cuts in the frig.'

***

TWO

"Mid pleasures and palaces though we may roam,
Be it ever so humble, there's no place like home."...John
Howard Payne (1791-1852)

Dear Diary...

WE'RE BACK IN DRY HOLE. I'm snuggled in my old
bedroom of the house I grew up in with Mom & Dad. My stuffed
toys are still piled high in one corner, and mementos like my
pom-poms from high school and pictures of Chey and I at
various ages cover the walls. The bookshelves are loaded with
my personal history. I use to hide my diaries so no one would
read them, although now I sometimes wonder if it makes sense
to write words that no one will read.

After Dad died and Mom took sick, I put my beloved
ledgers on the shelf, and every so often I'd pick one at random
and read a page or two or three...I wasn't a kid anymore and
Mom never came into my room...it was fun to read excerpts
from my diaries, but sometimes I'd find something silly I had
written when I was nine or ten years old...I'd be tempted to rip
out those pages, but I never did...what's been writ, has been
writ, I told myself...if I wrote something that sounds silly now,
it's because it's the way I felt at the time. Who can say that
something I write today won't sound silly if I read it ten,
twenty, thirty years from now?

The room, in fact, the entire house, seems small now, as if it had shrunk from lack of warm bodies living in it, and I've only been away less than a year. But my room is comfy and the bed has a thick quilt that has kept me warm through many a cold desert night...I'd rather have Chey here to keep me warm, but, let's not go there. Let me tell you about coming to Dry Hole...

Diary, it's been nearly two weeks since I made an entry...I quit my part-time job, cleaned the house from top to bottom, haven't heard from Rock, the jerk, even a response to my e-mail (should I be worried about him?), took care of some last minute details regarding Aunt May's estate, set up my bill-paying on my new laptop (Yes! I am becoming technically savvy—spent an entire day learning how to use the thing. I can't decide if the money for it came from Chey's insurance or Aunt May's will!)

I hadn't thought what it would be like returning to Dry Hole as a visitor, not a permanent resident, until I came to that mutilated old sign, the one that reads:

'*Dry Hole, Arizona, pop.115*'

The word, *Arizona*, has been crossed out with chalk and the initials, N.M. for New Mexico, written in. It spoke to the confusion over the exact geographic location of the town. I never thought about it much until Rock mentioned it to me the day he first stumbled into Dry Hole. Officially, Dry Hole is in Arizona, but some wags insist it's in New Mexico, for reasons lost to history. Some of the confusion is because we are so close to the border of the two states, and because there's nothing much here except wind and sand, so who can tell where one state ends and the other begins? There are several ranches in the vicinity, some definitely in Arizona, others in New Mexico, but none of them care much what state they're in, as long as they get their mail. (That is, until it comes time to do their state tax returns.)

And the Post Office insists Dry Hole is in Arizona, so that's what counts. It makes for conversation at the Boot Hill Bar and the Only Café; both establishments where the unofficial state lines meet in the middle of a booth in the far rear corner of each.

"Where do you want to sit," one half of a couple might say, if they get that particular booth, "Arizona or New Mexico?"

Dad played along by putting a map of Arizona on the wall on one side of the booth, and a map of New Mexico on the other side. The maps have faded with age but they are still there, now looking like antiques from the days of the pioneers and the silver miners.

It long ago quit being a major topic of conversation in the town, except for passers-by, like Rock, and there aren't too many people coming through Dry Hole who don't already know the town unless they are completely lost. So other than strangers, no one makes an issue of it.

The number 115 on the sign had been marked over and 112 scratched in, and 112 had in turn been marked over and 109 scratched in. I guess the Mayor, Clyde Redfoot, is keeping track. Old Clyde, he's been mayor all my life, and long before I was on the scene. Somehow, some years ago, he got himself appointed, and no one else cares for the job, so he goes on being mayor. Gives him something to do, tho it's a mystery to me exactly what it is he does do.

There is only one decent road leading to Dry Hole (there's a couple dusty tracks that'll get you in, or out, from the north and one from the west, old Indian trails, they say, but you need 4-wheel drive and even then you'd better have plenty of water and a spare tire in case you get stuck), so I've come this way many times, and I'd see the sign, but never paid it any attention. Now I stopped and gazed at it as if it had suddenly fallen out of the sky. It was cracked and dented from rocks and BBs and buckshot. Crazy kids, they get a gun in their hands they've got to shoot something. Clyde wants to keep busy, he ought to make a new sign.

Seeing it now reminded me that I don't live in Dry Hole anymore, not really, even if I still have the house. I wanted to sell the house but there were no buyers, even though property is cheaper than a bucket of sand and I set a price so low I wondered why I bothered...but now I'm glad I didn't sell it...just in case.

I suppose I could come back, but what would I do? It doesn't matter, because I've no intention of living here again. I'd rather drive around in circles from one end of the country to the other than come back here and live out my days digging sand out of my ears.

Not that I mean to disparage the town I grew up in and lived in and played in and worked in... I guess I'm just angry...at Dad for dying too young, at Mom for getting that awful disease, at Chey for going back into the Army, at myself for not being able to figure out my own life instead of waiting on somebody else. Sure, I figured Chey and I would get married, have a couple kids, la-la, happy days forever. He'd work his late father's business—repairing saddles, boots, etc. and I'd run the café...and the kids would grow up here—and, aye, there's the rub. Yes, I could live here again, and for the rest of my life if I had to (as long as I'd get to go to Tucson or Santa Fe now and then), but I'd be a rotten Mom to raise kids in this forsaken desert and expect them to have a normal childhood. And it's not likely Chey and I could make enough money living and working here to send kids to college. And if Chey thinks I'd marry him and live here, or even in Tucson, while he's gone half the time chasing terrorists in places even more God-forsaken than Dry Hole, he's dumber than he looks!

What I have to remember now, what I need to pound into my head, is that the road that takes me into Dry Hole, also takes me out. I don't have to stay here; I can, if I want, but I have other avenues—don't I?

I sat staring at the sign for ten minutes, I believe, like in a trance, remembering days of yore, before I continued on into town. Everything looked strange to me; being a visitor gave me a different perspective. The road was in its usual crummy condition, with potholes big enough to swallow a herd of steers, dust kicking up in back of the car so thick that another vehicle could be on my tail and I wouldn't know it.

The first buildings on entering the town are the abandoned warehouses from the mining days. Old, empty buildings are great places to play in...hide-n-seek when we were kids, and when a bit older, in the attic of the former Silver Lode Mining Co., Chey first kissed me. Now there are signs warning against the danger of these buildings crashing down. So today's kids, can't, or aren't, supposed to play here. So what do they do for fun? Play video games, I guess.

Then there's the gas station, run by an Indian so old his teeth have wrinkles, and his grandson. The old guy claims he's Sitting Bull's grandson, and since the famous Sioux chief lived until 1890, and was only sixty years old or so when he died, and *our* Sitting Bull is surely over a hundred years old, he might not be full of horse-puckey. I've forgotten his real name because everyone got to calling him 'Bull', either short for Sitting Bull or because they think he's full of it. His grandson goes by the more common name of George and I waved to him as I drove by. George is one of our few entrepreneurs and added a grocery store to the gas station, and does a fine business with the ranchers when they come by to gas up. (After which they're just as likely to go to the Boot Hill Bar and get themselves gassed!)

Note, Diary, that I wrote 'our', as if I'm still a part of Dry Hole. Can I ever not be?

Then there's the hotel, the Grande, it's called, can you believe? I guess calling it the Dry Hole Hotel wasn't considered a name likely to draw customers. The Grande does a good business, mostly because of the ranchers who pass thru and occasionally don't feel like driving—or riding, because a lot of them are on horseback if they've been out in the boondocks looking for strays in places you can't even get a four-wheel drive into, or out of, even worse—the forty or fifty miles back to their ranch house. Not to mention the Grande has a nice old bar, a real wood bar said to have been carved by a fellow who made furniture for some of the finest hotels in Denver and San Francisco; who knows?

Two or three young ladies—or not so young, if we're going be honest about this, seem to show up when a bunch of them cowpokes come into town, but I wouldn't know about them, ha! ha! I even saw those acne-faced James brothers go in one evening and come out a couple hours later with big grins on their faces and I wondered if they'd been getting an education in the ways of the world.

Some of the old timers have complained about the noise on those nights when a whole passel of cowboys stay in town, but for the few businesses remaining in Dry Hole, the income is vital.

Now my place—I should say Betty Ann's & Jake's place, The Only Café, is the only place in town where you can get a decent breakfast or lunch, pardon me Grande, where they concentrate on liquid refreshment. (I didn't keep the Only Café open after late afternoon, so the Grande's the place to go for dinner, so I'll give 'em credit, and I must say they can fix a proper steak, though some of those cowboys like their steak so rare you just need to pass the it over a match as you carry it to the table.) But if you insist on medium rare, and that the darn thing isn't still mooing when it's served, the steaks are better than many places in the big cities.

Betty Ann insisted I give her my pie recipes and spend a few days showing her my technique, because the pies are a big seller and they even draw customers from towns as far as fifty miles away. Those cowboys love their pie and coffee.

I pulled up to the Only Café and was glad to see several pickups parked in front. Almost everybody drives a pickup in this part of the country. I think Clyde's wife still putts around in a Ford Fairlane that's older than me, but otherwise it's pickups and jeeps and SUVs, so my Range Rover fit in. One good thing, mine hadn't yet accumulated the dents and scratches that decorated most vehicles in this part of the country that were more than a month old.

I was also pleased to see that Betty Ann & Jake are keeping the place clean. The way the sand blows around here, if you don't sweep off the porch and steps every day, before you know it you'll have gophers building a community on your doorstep.

Being late in the morning, business was starting to thin out. The ranch hands and cowboys eat early, the old timers who live on social security, a meager pension if they were lucky enough to have worked for the lumber mill before it closed its Douglas plant, and cash from doing odd jobs, come and go any time of the day. Some of them will sit and sip coffee all day long if you don't boot them out. If they can't find anything to do, chances are they'll show up again in the afternoon. As long as they bought a piece of pie and coffee, I didn't mind. But three refills of coffee and out you go, was my policy.

Tim Miller and Jess Redfoot, the mayor's son, were sitting at one table, and they waved to me and called out my name when I came in. I walked over to say hello and chatted for a minute. Betty Ann had been in back and came out when she heard them call my name.

Big smiles all around, but guess what, Diary? I could barely give Betty Ann a decent hug, she getting so rotund! No, not too much pie—she is in the family way, if you know what I mean. I am so happy for her and Jake, and yes, just a teensy jealous. Or is it envious? I always get those two vices confused.

"Dinah! You should have told me you were coming!"

"Why? Would you have baked a cake?"

"No, dearie, pie!"

We laughed and hugged some more and talked about the café and business—she said business is good and some of the customers think I'm hiding in the kitchen still baking the pies (I'm not sure I like that—either I taught Betty Ann very well, or I wasn't as special a baker as I thought I was).

"Here, have a sample," Betty Ann said.

I sat at the counter while she poured coffee and served me a slice of apple pie. "See how you like it."

I would have said I loved it even if I didn't, but dang, it was good.

I looked around, feeling nostalgic about *my place,* and wondered, just for an instant, whether I'd made the right decision in selling it. Every time I think about it I decide yes, it was right because Betty Ann & Jake needed it more than I did, especially now that their family will be growing. And I needed to stay with Mom, and I had the insurance money.

Above the counter, in the corner, the TV was on, and I smiled to see that Betty Ann was keeping the tradition alive. Years ago my Dad set up a TV to play old movies, mostly westerns, his favorite genre. In Dad's day the fellows loved them and sometimes would come by just to watch the movies.

But they spent money, too. I kept the movies playing, tho the sound is usually muted or very low, and not too many people watch them, but it's part of the Only Café history, along with the décor of pictures of western scenery, the old Custer's Last Stand painting, and various Old West mementos, like rusty horseshoes and a display of spurs, most of which were found over the years littering the desert.

I watched a few minutes of *The 3:10 To Yuma*—the original, not the remake—while Betty Ann tended to two new customers. It was a pair of weathered cowpokes who I hadn't seen around town since before the last rain. They nodded at me and one of them said, "Howdy, Dinah", he not having seen me in so long he wouldn't know I wasn't running the café anymore. I smiled at them and sipped my coffee. I was feeling carefree but a bit sad at the same time.

On the TV—a newer one since Dad's original black and white set died shortly after he did, no coincidence, I believe, it began to rain as Van Heflin and his prisoner, Glenn Ford, watched from the open boxcar and their train chugged off to Yuma prison. I found myself eager to see what movie would come on next.

Betty Ann and I chatted like teenagers who had lost their cell phones and had been out of touch for hours, heaven forbid! She hustled to take care of customers and I offered to help, but at first she wouldn't let me. I think she wanted to show me she could do it on her own. I know Jake helps out sometimes, but he also works at odd jobs for various ranchers, depending on what needs doing. I felt bad that they were making payments to me for the café, because with the insurance money I didn't need their money. But one, I was still afraid the money would be taken away if the Army found out their mistake, and two, Betty Ann & Jake didn't want charity from me.

When she could we talked, when she had to attend to customers or work in the kitchen, I watched the TV, now enjoying *She Wore a Yellow Ribbon.* I'd seen it dozens of times, and it reminded me of one of the things Rock and I had in common, a love of movies, especially older ones, ones he had seen long before I had. He's introduced me to a lot of black and white films I'd never heard of, but because of my Dad I don't take a back seat to anyone when it comes to knowledge of western movies.

I decided to call Rock to see if he'd read my e-mail, but all I got was his voice mail. Where the hell is he, I wondered? Why doesn't he call me back? I was slightly miffed. I left a message this time but I think it came out kind of angry.

After Betty Ann closed the café we went to her house and continued to gab like silly teenagers until Jake got home. The three of us talked and laughed all thru fixing dinner and late into the night. Betty Ann finally caved in near eleven o'clock, reminding me she needed to get up again in less than six hours...how well I remember!

So I'm sitting in bed writing this, and I'm getting sleepy and my writing is getting worse. I need to make sure my penmanship holds up; if I want my great grandkids to read this 100 years from now, it needs to be legible. Of course, to have great grandkids you first have to have grandkids. And to have grandkids you first have to have kids! And it use to be that to have kids you had to have a husband first...fat chance!

I remember when I was just a tyke, no more than seven years old, and my folks took me on a shopping trip to Phoenix, I saw this newspaper in a grocery store; you know, one of those rags with bizarre stories like, *The Loch Ness Monster Ate My Grandmother For Lunch While We Watched!* There was this bizarre story about a five-year old girl, I think from Peru, who had given birth to a baby. And I was nonplussed ...of course, at that age I didn't know the word, 'nonplussed', but I was confused, to say the least, not because she was only five years old, according to the story, but because I wondered, how could a five year old girl be married, and you have to be married to have a child, right? I was so naïve, and maybe I still am. Anyway, do I want to look like I swallowed a watermelon? Goodnight.

Dear Diary:

I'M ON THE ROAD again, a week later, but first let's finish with my visit to Dry Hole. In the mornings, I insisted on helping Betty Ann get things started at the café. I had to be careful to not let her think I was checking up on her, so I let her take the lead, especially with the pies, and I helped out where she suggested.

She did good; doesn't need me at all...oops, I should be careful what I say...seems like nobody needs me these days but when I write that I realize I'm feeling sorry for myself. Another place I don't want to go right now.

After the morning rush I'd take a walk around town or borrow a horse from George and take a ride into the desert. My favorite horse, Sandy, died of old age a couple of years ago and I haven't had the time to go riding much, what with the café and visiting Mom and all. One morning I walked to the other end of town to the cemetery, or what passes for one out here, you know, the plot of land behind the old church building, the one that's been abandoned for years now, the church that is; they're still burying people here as long as there are plots to fill. Nothing grows here except for when an occasional clump of brush or an ambitious young weed gets a grip. It's so dry even the cactus die of thirst. It's not a long walk, from one end of town to the other, but it gave me the chance to reminisce and talk with a few people I met along the way.

It's actually one of the nicer times of the year in Dry Hole, not too hot, not too windy, not yet, anyway. Autumn is the best time of year, weather-wise...some times we even get an early rain, just a teaser to remind people that water does occasionally fall out of the sky.

I'm not a big one for visiting graves. I know in movies it's common to have the grieving spouse visit the grave of hubby or wife, and to talk to the ground as if the person was really there and could hear. Oh, I shouldn't make fun, because everybody has to grieve their own way...I'm just not a person who gets much comfort from cemeteries.

Having said that, it was nice to walk around, desolate as it is here, and kick at dirt clods and swat at tumbleweeds as they rolled by—those damn things are always around, as if there's a factory hidden in an old mine shaft deep in the desert pumping out tumbleweeds day and night, spring, winter, summer, fall, night or day; windy or not, there are tumbleweeds... and think about Mom and Dad and how much fun I had with them as a child growing up in this barren land.

We'd ride horses far into the desert, sometimes all the way to the town of Apache, not much bigger than Dry Hole, but enough so that you can find it on a map, and even to the Geronimo Surrender Monument, the site where the great chief surrendered to Gen. Miles, I think in 1886 (you can look it up); played games like dodge the tumbleweed, horseshoes, and as I mentioned, all sorts of games in the abandoned warehouses, like hide 'n' go seek...of course we were always told it was dangerous to play around the warehouses and to watch for wells and lost mines and scorpions and snakes, but we were kids and knew we were immortal...and thanks to the grace of God or an abundance of good luck, I don't remember any of us getting seriously hurt—plenty of scratched knees and bumps on the head sneaking around in the old buildings, but nobody ever got badly hurt.

Chey's tombstone is still standing, the one I had made for him when he was reported as killed in Iraq. Of course there's nothing buried underneath, but I guess I'll let the stone set there a while...what would I do with it anyway? A hundred years from now an archeologist may come across it and wonder, who was this guy? Besides, the lunkhead probably will get himself killed and then we already have the tombstone, isn't that great?!

Mom & Dad's stones are there too, side by side, Dad's a little weatherworn already, but Mom's quite readable. Hers may be the newest grave in town. Aunt May I had buried in Tucson, 'cause that's where Uncle Bobbie Joe and she had purchased plots. It's times like this I feel alone; no siblings, no cousins that I know of (or else they're hiding from me) no Cheyenne, and no real reason to stay in Dry Hole anymore.

I continued to walk and came to the only park in town, the one built over the spring. This was where everyone came to picnic, sometimes a planned town event, sometimes a family or two, or whoever showed up on a Sunday afternoon. I shouldn't say *was* because people still gather here, there just aren't as many anymore as there used to be. In fact, I saw a couple of the old-timers sitting on a bench and nodded to them.

"Love your pies, Dinah!" One of them called to me. I can see I'm really missed.

It was a nostalgic treat to walk around in one of the few shady areas in and around Dry Hole and remember the fun I had here. I recall one year, I must have been seven or eight, one of the wealthy ranchers from the area around Rodeo, a town in New Mexico just across the border a few miles, rented a carousel for the Fourth of July celebration. Had it trucked in from Phoenix. I must have ridden it a thousand times, round and round and round. I was so dizzy my head was spinning for three days after; my stomach, too.

I poked my nose in at Carrie's, one of my childhood friends, and now the home-school teacher for the handful of kids not old enough to go to the school in Douglas. She only has three kids right now—business is drying up in Dry Hole. Carrie seemed glad to see me and envious that I had moved away. But when she asked how Cheyenne was my face told the story. Then she wasn't so envious. After all, she has Jimmy, who being a truck driver is gone for days at a time, but at least he does come home on weekends.

"Di, you know that you and Cheyenne are meant for each other. You always were; it'll work out, you'll see. Just remember to invite me to the wedding." I rolled my eyeballs.

Eventually we ran out of things to talk about—actually, we ran out pretty fast. So I mentioned I was going to San

Diego to visit a friend, and she kept asking, "Who? What friend? A guy?"

"Yeah, but he's...an older guy."

"Dinah! Wow! Is he rich, you know, like a sugar Daddy? That kind of thing? Where'd you meet him?"

Eventually I lied and said that he *and* his wife were old friends of Mom and Dad and I'd promised to go visit them, blah, blah. It's difficult to explain about Rock and me.

I hate to admit it but after a few days of hanging around I was bored. On the day I intended to leave I planned on going after I had lunch with Betty Ann, and return to Tucson by evening to pack what I needed to take to San Diego and check my e-mail ...maybe Rock sent a message and for some reason I can't pick it up on my new portable.

But Betty Ann insisted I stay another night so we'd have more time to visit. She and Jake wanted to go to dinner to Rodeo Sal's in Lordsburg, and heck, why not, I haven't been there since the day Rock first stumbled into Dry Hole. He didn't actually stumble in, he smelled the aroma of my wonderful pies, but whatever...

I REALLY WANTED to hit the road early this morning but I slept later than I'd intended to because I stayed up until even the coyotes had gone to sleep, wandering through the old house and picking up knick knacks and looking at them, wondering what to do with them, and with the house itself—

39

Betty Ann checks on it once in a while, picks up the mail and sends me the utility bills to pay—and if I thought she and Jake wanted it I'd sell to them dirt cheap. I should gently pose the question—it actually is a roomier house than the one they're living in; I just don't want them to think it's charity.

Then I ended up helping Betty Ann at the restaurant because Jake has a job in Douglas for the next few days. I told her she should hire part-time help and she said she would soon, once she gets too big to move around as quickly as she needs to when the place is real busy, like it was this morning.

(I considered volunteering to come back for a few weeks when she has the baby, to help out, tho I didn't want to commit myself just yet, but it might be fun.)

It seems every rancher from fifty miles around was in today, so I ended up renewing acquaintances, and next thing you know it was noon. Top it off I'd had so much coffee I had to stop twice on my way to Tucson to pee. I even thought of spending the night at home and leaving early in the morning, but forced myself to drive a ways so that the next day the leg to San Diego wouldn't be so long.

I drove for about three hours and now it was getting late, so I opted on a mediocre-looking joint a little east of Yuma. It wasn't awful, truth be told, and the sheets were clean and the water hot, so what more could you ask for?

I took a leisurely, hot shower, put on my robe and turned on the TV. Then my stomach growled and I wished I had picked up something to eat so I wouldn't have to get dressed again and go out.

By the way, there's still no message from Rock and now I'm wondering if it's a smart thing to do, showing up on his doorstep when he might be trying to tell me he doesn't want to see me. Instead of going to his house I'll go to his business place, then if he throws me out he'll have to embarrass himself in front of his employees, ha!

Later...

I'M GETTING SKITTISH in my old age, Diary. I got dressed in plain ole jeans and a bulky sweatshirt Rock gave me, one with this funny Leprechaun character on it, and went to find something to eat. I didn't want to go far and I had noticed a pizza joint near the motel as I drove in. I figured I could walk there and get a couple of slices, and bring 'em back to eat in my room.

As I arrived at the pizza place there were two guys, nice looking young men, that is, my age, wearing boots and ten gallon hats and with holstered guns strapped on, standing outside chatting. That didn't surprise me; hell, you know, for some of these 'macho assholes' it's a point of pride these days to walk around wearing a gun. Arizona seems to be reverting to the days of the Wild West; Tombstone, the O.K. Corral, etc.

Before long we'll have shootouts in the street, just like the good old days. Most likely they'll shoot themselves in the foot.

It's not just Arizona; I read that in Texas they were considering legislation to allow college students to carry concealed handguns on campus. "Give me an A, professor, or I'll blow your brains out!"

It seems there's a groundswell to the idea that if everybody has a gun, no one will dare use it, sort of the Dodge City hypothesis. What these pseudo-historians forget, or didn't know, is that as the cities of the Old West began to get civilized, marshals like Virgil Earp established regulations to ban handguns from within city limits.

The cowpokes both smiled at me and as I opened the door to go in, one of them said, "nice jeans".

I guess I should be flattered, or at least my jeans should be. Maybe I bought them a size too small?

I ordered two slices of cheese pizza and a drink to go. When I nonchalantly looked outside the two guys weren't there. In a few minutes my order was ready and I started to walk back to the motel. As I neared my room I saw Wyatt Earp and Doc Holliday standing right outside my room, still chatting but having moved from the pizza place. Had they seen me when I came out of the motel, and were purposely waiting for me at my room? Why, because I have nice jeans? Not likely, Dinah Russell.

Now I wished I had brought one of my own guns. Hell, Diary, you know I can handle a gun pretty well; a rifle anyway. I learned from my Daddy and from Cheyenne, shooting at tins cans and cactus in the desert. Of course I was never as good as Chey, who could shoot a twig out the mouth of crow as it flew by a hundred feet up in the sky.

I always kept a gun under the counter at the Only Cafe, and thank you, never had to use it, because I can't hit the side of a barn with a handgun if I was standing ten feet from it. But I'm not in the habit of carrying a gun with me, for which Chey has often scolded me.

I stepped past them as if I was going to a different room.

"Hi, boys," I said with a smile as I walked by, those few steps a bit more rapid than the norm. I fully expected one of them to whack me on the ass.

I wasn't sure what to do; I didn't want them to see which room I was in. I decided to get into my car and drive away, and wait for them to leave. As I reached my car, now afraid they might kidnap me, one of them, a tall, lanky fellow with blond hair sticking out from under his hat, too handsome to be anything but a good guy, said, "See ya around, Bud," and walked in the direction opposite from my room. The other guy, shorter, built like a fireplug with a dark complexion and a villain's mustache, walked in my direction. My heart skipped and I slipped into my car and locked the door.

" 'Night, ma'am," he said as he passed by and doffed his hat.

I smiled at him and watched as he walked to the end of the building and took the stairs. He went to one of the rooms, unlocked the door, and went in without looking back at me. In the other direction the tall cowboy was still walking. I watched until he got into a car parked near the pizza place. After he drove away I got out of my car and briskly scooted to my room, feeling a little silly.

I undressed and put my robe on again and sat on the bed and for a moment I thought I was going to cry. What's with you, Di, I asked myself. Maybe it was because there were two of them; one I could've taken—Chey taught me how to wrestle, too, besides shoot. Of course, some of the holds he'd practice on me weren't ones you could use in competition, and I had to swat him a few times to remind him.

I nearly jumped out of my robe, underwear, and skin when there was a sudden pounding on the door. I held my breath, hoping they'd go away. Then I heard someone yell, "Sorry, wrong room!"

"Oh, good goddamn!" I gasped, Diary, shame on me.

I checked that the door was locked, pushed a chair against it, turned the TV on, and crawled into bed with the pizza and soda, which by now were cold and warm, respectively.

Oh, joy, joy, happy, happy: a special program came on about the use of IEDs—improvised explosive devices, in Iraq and Afghanistan. Just when I'd put Cheyenne out of mind for a few hours.

***

THREE

I stir, between life and dream,
As the black of the night
Meets the fog of the dawn,
*And I'm alone, again...*Nancie W., from 'The Bitter and the
Sweet'

*The worst loneliness is not to be comfortable with
yourself...*Mark Twain

IT WAS THE STILLNESSS that woke me. Dead quiet, isn't
that the term—so quiet you can hear the background hum of
the universe, the synapses sparking in your brain, and then, the
distant howl of a dog, miles away, who in turn has heard, or
more likely, smelled, the presence of a tomcat, sneaking
amongst the garbage cans of an alley. I was reminded of those
nights as a youngster when my buddies and I would 'camp out'
in our backyards, never getting much sleep, and pretending to
be terrified by the sounds of the night: an owl hunting its prey,
the spine-tingling yeow of a frightened alley cat, the yelp of the
police siren.

The longer I lay there, not moving, the more sounds I
recognized. The ticking of the grandfather clock in the living
room, the ripple of the fountain in the neighbor's yard, and
then, and this caused me to move, to look to my left, the
breathing of Helen, who slept next to me.

And then it struck me like a slap in the face, what it was
that had awakened me. It was the dream, the one where the

car slides off the road, me asleep, and Mary Ann, having dozed for an instant, a half a second, maybe a mere tenth of a second, desperately trying to regain control. She doesn't, she dies, I live, I despair, and now, over a year later, the dream comes back, not as often as it used to, but it comes with a vengeance, sharper somehow, more frightening when I'm with Helen.

It's probably my guilt at being with a woman who is not Mary Ann. But then no one can ever be Mary Ann, and Helen is the first, the only woman, I've dated since Mary's Ann death. The only woman I've slept with other than Mary Ann in over thirty years.

I smiled, remembering that wasn't entirely true. There was the night in San Antonio when Di crawled into bed with me, snuggled up and went to sleep, craving for contact and warmth. I hardly knew her then, but we ended up together when she and Cheyenne had been in an accident and Cheyenne was hospitalized for a few days. Di and I had adjoining rooms at a motel near the Alamo in San Antonio. I never have figured exactly what she was thinking, if anything, but I'm positive our relationship would have peaked then and there had I made love to her, and a friendship would not have developed. She can be a flirt, but at the time, having been shocked by the return of Cheyenne, who she thought was dead, then the both of them almost ending up on the coroner's slab when a truck sideswiped them, I can see where anybody might have acted a bit out of character, almost like being intoxicated.

Staring in the dark I reviewed my plan for the week. I would drive to San Antonio instead of flying, because I enjoying driving, especially deep into the country, and Helen will fly and meet me a few days later, in time to help with the trade show. She isn't happy about my going ahead of her; says I should wait for her. I explained that I need to arrange a few details ahead of the show, attend some pre-show informal conferences, plus I want to play a little golf with friends I don't see very often. "I guess somebody's got to take care of the plant," she countered. Sometimes I think she forgets whose company it is.

Then we'll drive together back to San Diego. And on the way back I want to stop in Tucson to see Di, and have her and Helen meet, so they can get to know one another.

Is that a good idea? Do I want them to get to know each other yet? All I ever mentioned to Helen was that I had these young friends, Dinah and Cheyenne, who I had met last year and helped them after they'd been in an auto accident. Not quite the whole story, and when I'd tried to explain how I came upon Dry Hole and the story of Cheyenne showing up the same day, like a zombie rising from the dead, and the accident Cheyenne and Di had, and about our misadventure with that slob of a sheriff who tried to scam us, it got too complicated for her. In fact, I think she didn't believe all of my story and was suspicious about exactly what my relationship with Di was.

Since I don't plan a long-term romantic relationship with Helen, why bother having her meet Di? Hell, I didn't *plan* anything! I never should have gotten involved with someone who works for me. The first rule of being boss, and I broke it because I was a bit lonelier than usual one night and Helen looked particularly fetching. Fetching; what the hell kind of word is 'fetching?'

Truth is, I'd love to see Di alone and catch up on things with her. And give her what news I have about Cheyenne. So what I should do is squeeze in the time to stop in Tucson on my way to San Antonio.

It's crazy that I am keeping these two women away from each other. And though I'm sleeping with Helen, I know Di is more important in my life, which is why I've haven't been answering Di's calls, or returning them—because I don't want to tell her about Helen, and if I don't tell her, I'll be lying to Di, be it by omission or commission. And if I do tell her about Helen, I'm afraid she'll be upset. And it's not like I'm sleeping with Helen as a daily way of life; I mean, this is what, the third time? No, the fourth, okay, big deal. I can end it any time. Yeah, that'd be great for company morale.

Anyway, why should Di be upset? Or why should I care if she is? I've got a right to have female companionship of someone my own age. Okay, Helen's several years younger, but it's not like Di, who's only as old as my daughter. So why should I care what Di thinks?

Di's like another daughter to me. No, that's not true; she's like a niece; no, a friend and a daughter, or a friend and a niece. In any case, I've told Janice and Chris about Helen, but can't get myself to tell Di.

The kids didn't exactly jump for joy, but they didn't seem overly upset. I don't know, they may have been too stunned to respond. Of course, if they lived nearby and had to actually see me with Helen, holding hands or hugging each other, they might gag. Guess I'll have to figure out what to do when they come to visit at Christmas.

I reached for my cell phone, which sat on the bedside table. I flipped through the messages, most of which dealt with business matters I could take care of in the morning. Then there were the ones from Di that I had saved.

The first two were empty. When I listened carefully it sounded like I could hear, or sense, someone on the line, but they—Di, decided not to leave a message. But it was her cell phone number.

Then there was one where she did leave a message, and it confirmed that she had called before. I'd listened to it but wanted to hear it again. I quietly slipped out of bed and went to my den, and played Di's message.

"Hi, Rock. I've been trying to reach you but, ah, didn't leave a message...figured you must be busy because I haven't heard from you. Hope things are fine with you, and we can see each other sometime soon. Did you get my e-mail? Is it okay? Well, talk later, bye."

She sounded angry, or upset, or sad, or a mixture of all those emotions. Not her usual peppy, flirty manner. Cheyenne; I'm sure it's Cheyenne. He doesn't stay in touch with her much when he's gone. He told me he didn't like to contact her on a regular basis because he's often in places where he has no access to e-mail or texting, and is afraid that if Di gets used to him staying in touch, and then he doesn't for weeks at a time, she'll worry. Just like before.

"She's a big girl, Cheyenne," I'd told him. "And you did this to her once before. She's going to worry one way or the other."

"I never know what to say. I killed a couple of Arab-Islamic-terrorists-bastards today? How would that be?"

"Just say you miss her, you fool."

"No, Rock, I'll contact you when I can, and you tell her."

Trouble is, the only messages I'd had from him weren't the kind Di'd care to hear. They were more in line with what Chey had said, "I killed some terrorists bastards today, etc."

And now, far as I knew, several weeks ago he finally had been able to call her and tell her he was coming home on leave. He sent me an e-mail but didn't say anything specific. Thinking of which, I've ignored Di's e-mail too, the one about her suggesting she come to San Diego for a visit, but she didn't say exactly when.

By now Cheyenne's probably back humping the hills of Afghanistan...or Pakistan, from what I gather from reading between the lines of his messages. I'd love to see them both but didn't want to bust up their time together. And from the sound of Di's message, maybe the reunion didn't go as smoothly as she'd hoped.

"What are you doing? Checking phone messages at three in the morning?"

Helen's voice startled me, made me jump. I felt guilty, sneaking in the night to listen to a message from someone I didn't yet want Helen to know about.

"Oh, jeez, you scared me! Ah, yeah, couldn't sleep so I was going over the messages I need to deal with in the morning," I lied easily.

"Are you worried about the show? Are you sure you don't need me there from day one?

"No, it'll be fine. I've checked on the product delivery schedule, and it's right on, and when I get there it'll be a bunch of guys catching up with each other's lies about our golf game. Meetings and lunches; you know, boring stuff."

"You just need me to help in the booth, is that it?" she asked, a bit slyly and fool that I am, I didn't catch the tease.

"Well, yeah, I'll need some help then."

"Oh? *Some* help? Like, anybody? You won't need me at night? Okay, I can take a hint." She turned and walked away. I heard the bedroom door shut.

What the hell is with her? It's my house and she shuts the bedroom door on me? I started to walk to the bedroom; I'd open the door and leave it open, but not go in. That'd show her. I stopped in time; what good would that do? And I did need her to help at the trade show. Actually, Dennis could help, too, but Helen convinced me she should come to San Antonio and we could take a few days for ourselves after the show.

At the trade show we are introducing sophisticated security system products, a new line for the company. Having a pretty girl always helps, although, quite frankly, this is not a car show or a electronic gizmo show with young babes wearing tight sweaters two sizes too small, or a bathing suit out of Sports Illustrated, to attract potential buyers. They can't explain crap about the product, but they look good. I should have invited Di to help me. She's young and good looking, and smart too; a quick learner. Kind of late to think of could haves and should haves.

If Di had accepted the job when I offered it to her, things might have worked out differently. Maybe I wouldn't have gotten involved with Helen, but if I had, she and Di would be friends and they could both be coming to San Antonio. Hmm, coincidence, that the show is in San Antonio. That's where Di and I really began to develop a friendship, those few days we spent wandering around old San Antonio waiting for Cheyenne to be released from the hospital. Fun memory.

I had cooled down some, but didn't want to go back to bed with Helen. I wanted her gone from my house. Damn! I should have kept our relationship on a business level. She hadn't been so damn sexy that night...sooo... after the show, when we get back from San Antonio...I'll break it off. If she wants to quit her job, that's her choice.

I decided then and there that I'd leave earlier than planned so I could stop in Tucson to see Di, and still get to San Antonio the day after in time for the first round of golf. Then Helen and I wouldn't need to stop in Tucson on the return trip. Helen doesn't need to know any more about Di than the little she does.

I went back into the den where I'd already placed my suitcase. I also packed an accordion folder in which I was keeping the messages from Cheyenne I've been planning to give to Di when I next saw her. They gave me my official excuse for going to Tucson. I still needed to get toiletries and a few other items, so I tiptoed into the bedroom, hoping Helen was asleep and that I wouldn't wake her. But I'd have to tell her I was leaving early; I can't just sneak out. Still, acting the coward, I was as quiet as a mouse until I was ready to leave. The digital clock next to the bed clicked 4:00.

"Helen," I whispered. Isn't that crazy? If you want to wake someone up, why do you whisper? It's not like I was in a library and there were people around I didn't want to bother. I shook her gently.

"Hmm. Are you back?" She mumbled. Or maybe she said, "Get off my back."

"Helen, I'm leaving for Tuc... for San Antonio."

For a few seconds she lay there, head half buried in the pillow. Then one eye opened and she turned her head. "Wha? You're leaving now?"

"Yes. I'm wide awake and keep thinking about things I have to do and I want to stop to see a friend in Tucson on the way." I didn't think she'd connect Di with Tucson; it's not like I ever mentioned Di around Helen, other than the one time I told her about my meeting Di and Cheyenne, and a little about our drive east. Come to think of it, I'm not sure I even told her that Di and I, just the two of us, had driven all the way back from Richmond, with me dropping Di off at her home in Dry Hole. I wonder why I never mentioned that?

"And you just decided this now?"

I shrugged. "Yeah, it's been on my mind and I can't get back to sleep now."

She slumped back into the pillow and said something that was muffled. It could have been, "Go to hell", or "So that's swell," I'm not sure.

"I had nothing on the docket at the plant today that you or Carl or Dennis can't handle."

"I'll see you Friday," I think she said. I kissed her on the cheek but she didn't respond. I think she was already asleep. I eased out of the room quietly.

In the kitchen I left Helen a note. 'Go out the front door; it'll lock automatically.' She didn't yet have a key to my place, and now I was glad we hadn't advanced that far. I added, 'Look forward to seeing you next Friday.' I wasn't sure if that was true, but it was prudent.

It was beautifully dark outside, a great time to be starting off on a drive. I could get out of the city without hitting traffic and be in Tucson before noon, or a bit later if I stop for breakfast. Then it's over nine hundred miles to San Antonio, but the drive will be good for me; alone time, just me and some great driving music. One thing I had already packed in the car was my collection of John Stewart's CDs; can't drive all that way without those.

I panned the skies before I got into the car, just in case the mother ship from *Close Encounters of the Third Kind* picked tonight to visit. I saw nothing out of the ordinary; darn. I wished the car to start quietly, a silly wish, as if I could explain to the dumb machine that it was four in the morning and we didn't want to wake anybody. It roared to life and I backed out slowly, and pulled away at a mere ten miles an hour, until I reached the end of the block. I pushed the CD button and John came on, singing about chilly winds.

One cynic, I had heard, said something to the effect that no one traveling on a business trip would be missed if he failed to arrive. So I preferred to think of the drive to San Antonio as a pleasure trip, in which case, if I should find something along the way that is so enticing, so much fun, so much more *more* than going to a series of business meetings, talks and a showcase of new products, I could say to hell with San Antonio and run off to whatever new adventure beckoned. Peter Pan, here I come, second star to the right, isn't it?

I made sure my cell phone was turned on and set it on the console between the seats. Then I looked at as if it were an alien device and thought, who's going to call me at four in the morning? It reminded me how we are becoming slaves to technology, with instant access to more information than we can possibly decipher and comprehend.

It's a generational thing, I realize that. People my age never got used to having information instantly available as an event was happening. We'd read about it the next day in the newspaper, or sometimes, several days later. Even the baseball scores weren't always available until the morning paper. Now we have ESPN telling us who made the last shot and how many tenths of seconds are left in a game thousands of miles away, or even on the other side of the planet.

If there was an uprising in a country we'd never heard of, did it matter that we didn't know about it until a week later? Now, it's on CNN or Fox and we have on-site correspondents to show us pictures of mobs and fires and tell us in clipped, dramatic prose that no one really knows what will happen next, but they'll be right there to show us. But is the news they're giving us necessarily accurate? Is it necessarily necessary? Why do we need to see and hear this right now?

Generally, realizing I sound like an old-fogey, knowing something, other than when you're taking a crucial test and you need to recall the answer this instant, other than a brain surgeon needing to know exactly where the tumor is and the patient's blood pressure this very second, other than that and maybe a few other cases that are vital to a particular person at a particular time, does it really matter a rat's ass if we know all the news all the time? Do we really need to know that our buddy who we see once every two or three months is having the best roast beef sandwich he's ever eaten, and he tweets to tell us? Or that he just made a birdie to break one hundred? Who gives a shit?

I shut the phone off.

In fact, after a few minutes I even shut the music off. I decided I wanted nothing but quiet; the hum of the car engine was enough. I didn't even want to think, for a little while, at least, about issues I did eventually need to give serious thought to.

Soon I was in the desert, and I reveled in the dark sky dotted with stars, thousands of them, causing me to grin at the thought that the sky looked almost as beautifully decorated with silver sprinkles as you can see at the Griffith Planetarium show. As I usually do, my mind spilled out memories of great old sci-fi movies of the 50s which take place in the desert.

Of course there was *It Came From Outer Space*! A good, basic, fun movie with a clear, solid title. Then there was arguably the best of the genre, *Them!* Are those eerie, tingly sounds merely the wind blowing over the bones of the desert, or could it be...giant ants! The mental image of ants big enough to pick up my car reminded me to watch the road carefully, not keep peeking up at the sky, for a meeting at seventy-five miles an hour with a coyote or even a jackrabbit could be costly. For several more minutes I drove without thinking, selfishly enjoying the quiet and the isolation. Eventually, I came back to those things I did need to ponder.

First of all, the trade show. My company designs engineering tools, but in the past couple of years we've expanded into security devices, geared towards the professional companies who sell and install high-end home security equipment, and to city and county police and fire departments. It was a bit of a gamble on my part, but I have good people advising me and early returns had shown that there was plenty of room in the marketplace for us, mostly due to the enhanced fear of terrorism.

I put on a CD of a book, some mindless mystery, wherein our hero is a near-Superman, one who can overcome all evil, despite his addictions and failings, his women-problems, his drinking like a fish.

These 'thrillers' run together any more. Our 'hero' is either a hard-drinker, who can down a quart of bourbon for breakfast to get himself primed for the day, or else he's a recovering alcoholic, filled to the brim with angst over how he can overcome his addiction, something we need to read about at least once a chapter, at the same time trying to emotionally connect with his pre-teenage daughter, who, while living with his ex-wife, yearns for the firm hand of a father.

Naturally he meets a young chick, the tech-babe, who at age twenty seven has doctorates in medieval history and thermo-dynamics as it relates to nuclear energy, speaks seven languages, was All-American on the college basketball and water polo teams, has contacts (former lovers), in the United States Senate, the New York mayor's office, several major corporations, (including world-wide ones), and the prime minister of a European power, contacts which allow her to obtain the most personal information on anyone in the world, all from a smile or a whispered come-on, has traveled the world extensively, enough to know where all the best restaurants are (and the unsophisticated, regular tourists don't know about), and is welcomed on sight at the major museums and art galleries from St. Petersburg to Rio de Janeiro. Oh, and she has a photographic memory of course, or he does, but one of them must, so they can remember all the incredible information they uncover, and that we, the reader, can't possibly keep track of. Naturally, she and our hero can't stand each other at first, but that doesn't deter them from jumping into bed shortly after an argument. I switched back to the music.

At one time I was disappointed that my son, Chris, had not opted to come to work for me. I'd hoped he might take over the company some day. But his interest was more in the line of software and he worked for a medium size firm specializing in financial analysis programs. He was confident a larger company would soon buy out his firm making he and everybody else a small fortune, after which he could start his own software development company, probably in the lucrative gaming market. His dreams are his own and I'm sure he'll do fine.

Me, I look in the mirror when I shave and I see sixty years of age coming at me like a runaway locomotive. I see age spots and wrinkles and gray hair and they tell me I'm not too many years from selling the company, or at least a chunk of it, and letting someone else run the show while I ease into retirement, whatever that will bring. Which brought me to the next item I needed to think about, and which I now found myself doing. Helen.

This was going to be difficult. Helen had quickly worked her way up the company ladder. She was extremely competent and ambitious. She'd been an acquaintance of Mary Ann, though I don't believe they were ever close friends. Helen's expertise was in marketing and sales and she was crucially involved in marketing our new line of products. For a while Helen handled personnel issues and was still technically in charge of hiring and firing, not a major issue lately because virtually every thing we were doing was being handled by people who'd been with us for years, and the only recent personnel moves had been the comings and going of temps, except for Dennis.

Which reminded me that a year ago I offered Di a job, in large part an outgrowth of the time she and I and Cheyenne had spent together. It was a short time but one filled with edginess, emotions, and adventure, a time in which all of us were brought to focus on the way lives are often ripped along, like an uprooted bush careening in the flood of a raging river; unable to stop and reach the safety of the bank, in need of a hand to pull it out of danger.

It was a period of time in which senses are intensified, a time when emotional intimacy develops quicker than it does during the mundane days that fill most of the hours and months and years of most people's existence.

But we had enough cool-down time on our drive back from the east to learn about each other. Different generations, yes, but people's character and ideals don't have to be in conflict just because of an age differential. Di seemed like a sharp, eager person who could learn anything she put her mind to. Despite growing up in the dustbin of the southwest she'd learned to manage a small business, make it thrive, and had found time to learn basic accounting and apply it in work she did for local ranchers.

I wanted to give her the chance to get some serious schooling, if she wanted it, and come to work for me. Not that I'd expect her to be a permanent fixture; I'll probably sell the company in a few years anyway. In fact, I had offered Cheyenne a job too, if he was interested, so it wasn't like I was trying to keep Di near and Cheyenne far away.

She sure looked good that night. It wasn't supposed to be more than an informal get-together for the staff, a way for people to toss out ideas in a casual atmosphere without fear of being ridiculed. Sometimes people are reluctant to express their ideas lest they be thought of as inane, yet some of the best notions have come from freewheeling brain storming sessions.

So we gathered after work at a comfy, but not fancy dinner house, a place people could wear their work clothes to without feeling over or under dressed. But Helen, she must have had an idea far different than what I was expecting, she changed clothes. From a business suit to a form–fitting dress, one that I'm sure was a size too small, and maybe not quite suited for her age, but she wore it well. She looked especially good after my second martini.

I don't drink a lot of hard alcoholic drinks; an ice-cold gin and tonic on a hot summer's afternoon is refreshing, or late at night on a crisp, rainy evening, a warm snifter of cognac. With dinner, it's wine. I hadn't been there a minute when Helen nuzzled up to me and offered to buy me a martini, and before I remembered we were there for dinner and conversation, I was milk for the kitty, if you'll pardon the expression.

Only via firm force of willpower did I manage to turn the talk to business, once we had all sat down in our booth, between everybody's second drink and the serving of the appetizers. By then Helen's hand was on my thigh and I couldn't have cared less if Hammond Tools had burned to the ground.

I'm not sure what it was, other than how she looked, how she acted, the two martinis...I was still missing Mary Ann; I still am. She must have sensed a weakness in me, the female knowing exactly when to strike. What was she after? She's divorced, no kids, has good looks (real good after two martinis and two glasses of wine), intelligent, dresses smartly, is competent, ambitious, and sexy...okay, I was easy pickins. Still, I should have known better. And I think everybody there saw what was happening...to the boss. What a jerk. I could have at least tried to keep it quiet.

What was that movie? Oh, hell, there's been a slew of them, guys getting caught with their pants down, and it's nothing but trouble. *Play Misty for Me*, for example, though I hardly think Helen is psycho. Maybe I am, for getting involved with her.

She ended up driving me home. After which I don't remember anything until morning when I woke up, to the smell of fresh coffee. I was only wearing boxer shorts and Helen was lying next to me, smiling. I didn't remember undressing, I didn't remember her undressing me, I didn't remember anything, which can be embarrassing.

She saved me, I thought at the time, when she said, "Tonight, don't drink so much, and it'll be better."

Now I'm not so sure what she saved me from.

"You're takin' my road away

Oh, road away" ---from the song, 'Roadaway', by John Stewart

***

FOUR

Calvera: "Why a man like you took the job in the first place?"
Vin: "A fellow I knew in El Paso, one day he took off all his clothes and jumped into a mess of cactus; I asked him the same question, why?"
Calvera: "And?"
Vin: "He said, it seemed like a good idea at the time"--
Dialogue from the movie, *The Magnificent Seven*, screenplay by Walter Newman and William Roberts.

"YOU LIKE BEING here, Captain?"

Cheyenne spat into the mud, then wiped his mouth with the back of his hand, which only served to rub dirt onto his lips. He cursed and spat again.

"I told you the fuck do not call me Captain, you hear me, Private?"

"Yes..."

"Nor Sir, neither!"

"Yes, I mean, okay..."

"Cheyenne is fine," the captain said, softly, a firm order and apology at the same time.

The private was quiet for several minutes, as was the captain, who continued to pan the valley with his binoculars. He saw no movement.

"So do you like being here...Cheyenne?"

"Sure, hell, what else could I be doing; be back at the base chugging a few cold ones?" Cheyenne offered, continuing to look through the binoculars.

"I mean here, as in Afghanistan. Do you think we're doing any good here?"

Cheyenne shrugged, lowered the binoculars and turned to lie back against the wall of the foxhole. He wiped his hands on his pant legs, and then rubbed his face, massaging the tiredness that permeated his skin. He opened his eyes wide and blinked several times, trying to cry the dirt specks out.

"I don't have a goddamn clue." After a pause, he added, "I use to think so, at first."

After Cheyenne didn't say any more, the other soldier asked, "At first? And later?"

"Later? There always seems to be a later. I don't know how many times I've been told, 'Cheyenne, we get this guy, it'll break up their organization'. So out I go, crawling through the mud and the dust; you ever notice that it's either hot or cold, wet or dry? Never anything in between?"

"I guess so."

"Hey, Jason, we might make a good team, Smith and Jones, incorporated."

"Yes, sir, I mean, Cheyenne."

"You're a Jones, I'm a Smith. Couple of common names for common folks, hey kid?"

Jason smiled. "Yeah, I guess so; I guess I am just a common guy."

"Hell, Jason, it's the folks back home are common. What the hell do they know about putting their lives up for grabs every day? Wake up in the morning, hot shower, orange juice and a cup of coffee, read the paper, check the body count. How much danger are they in? What's your morning like, Jason? Duck, dodge, piss in a hole in the ground, cold breakfast, some asshole's shootin' at you for no good reason. That ain't common, Jason."

Again the two soldiers were silent for a minute. Cheyenne turned to look down at the valley with the binoculars. He scanned the panorama slowly from end to end, up and down, taking several minutes while the only sound was an occasional distant squeal of a hawk.

"They say you've been back three times. I mean, twice to Iraq and now here, and you didn't have to. Seems you must like it." Jason said, in effect asking the question, why in the good name of anything are you here?

"Maybe I like the scenery," Cheyenne said.

Jason reached into a pocket and pulled out a packet of cigarettes. "Cigarette?" he said, offering the packet to Cheyenne, who shook his head.

"You don't smoke?" Jason asked.

"No. Smoke bothers my eyes. Need to keep sharp," Cheyenne said, nodding in the direction of the trail that wound about the side of the valley wall.

"Don't light up now, kid. A wisp of smoke could give our position away. Give me those."

Cheyenne grabbed the package of cigarettes and crumpled them, then smashed them into the dirt with his boot. Jason didn't seem bothered.

"I gave them up when I enlisted. Hell, cigarettes and training don't mix together very well, but then, out here, I started again."

"Nasty habit."

"You're not afraid it'll shorten your life span, are you?" Jason asked, a timid laugh in his voice.

"Life span? Kid, out here you don't have a life span. It's like, you know, suspended. You get out of here alive, you can think about life span. But until then, there is no life span."

Jason looked at Cheyenne and wondered what he had gotten himself into when he volunteered for special operations training. The selection process was brutal and there were times he only stayed with it out of stubbornness.

Usually the special ops units were organized as 12-member teams, smaller than regular Army units and appealing to guys who craved action. But then, like Cheyenne, there were soldiers who enjoyed even more independence, and the Army had found a place for them as snipers.

The terrain in Afghanistan, and Pakistan, for the record, not that the United States Army was at war in Pakistan, ha, ha, is full of crags and broad valleys, even deserts, where insurgents can hide and shoot from long distances. They jump in and out of caves and narrow troughs for years, skipping and sneaking from one to the other, taking a shot here, a shot there, laughing all the time. To counter them, and to take out the bad guys with minimal civilian casualties, the snipers had become an essential element in the counterinsurgency campaign. But all the training they get is nothing compared to live action in the field. For Jason Jones, as demanding as the training had been, with most candidates never getting close to the completion, nothing can prepare you for when the guy on the other side is *really* trying to kill you.

After finishing the scan, Cheyenne again turned to lie back against the side of the foxhole. He looked at Jason, saw a kid who was so young it made him feel like a grandfather, old before he was thirty.

"Do you shave yet, Jason?" He asked with a grin and a pat on Jason's cheek.

Jason smiled back, shrugged. "Every other day. Had to every day in training, even if I didn't need to."

"Kid, you wouldn't have volunteered for this kind of work unless you felt it was a necessary job. Or else you were like me, bored stiff. And you wouldn't have made it through training if you weren't tough enough, and intelligent enough. I been there; I know what it takes. But here's my advice, for what little it may be worth: use your intelligence and don't stay any longer than you have to. Go home as soon as they'll let you, go hide where they can't find you, don't come back. Don't be like me."

"Hell's bells, you sure didn't come back because you like being shot at, I wouldn't think."

"No, well maybe I like shootin' *at* someone, ever figure that?"

"Do ya?"

"Eh, I used to. Gung ho, macho crap; besides, I didn't have a regular job, didn't know what to do with myself. Parents gone, town a shithole, seemed like a good idea at the time, the Army, I mean. I wasn't thinking necessarily about goin' to Iraq to do any killin'. But I always had a good eye, even as a kid, and in basic training they said I was one of the best ever. Fuckin' Davy Crockett and Annie Oakley rolled into one."

"Hmmm. So that's why you got this plum assignment, hey? You must have killed a few people, haven't you?"

Cheyenne gave Jason a scowl, a mean look that scared the young soldier. Jason eased away a bit, afraid Cheyenne would reach out and grab him, maybe even hit him.

Again Cheyenne felt the anger rise, knowing it wasn't the kid's comment that irked him, but the fact that what he said reminded him of the truth. Yet, he knew he had done a job that needed doing. He knew, he truly felt sure, that everybody he'd killed not only deserved to be killed, but also, by their dying, prevented them from killing others, Americans, mainly. He let the anger flow and abate. Knowing that what he'd done was a job worth doing didn't make him feel good about it, and yet he'd come back to it. Did he really believe that what he did couldn't be done just as well by someone else? And even if it could, would his quitting make it someone else's responsibility, cause another to learn about killing and to have to learn to live with those deaths on his head? Besides, you kill one terrorist, another one pops up like a fuckin' duck in a shooting gallery.

No, shit, I'm not responsible for the deaths. Someone is, some asshole terrorist, or dictator, or a general or even a goddamn president, how the hell do I know? He wished Spiedel were here. That old fart had a way of dealing with his work that was gentle on the soul, justifying the killing without excusing it. I wonder where he is; must be close, because this is where it's all happening now.

In the attic of his mind Cheyenne knew the reason he'd come back. He could have easily stayed a civilian, what with the injuries he'd suffered in the fiasco at Samarra and afterwards, as a prisoner for several months with Johnny Bracken, that poor sonofabitch.

He and three others had gone out on a sniping mission that on paper looked like shooting fish in a barrel. But something had gone wrong; hell, everything had gone wrong— they'd been set up. Two dead and Cheyenne and Bracken taken prisoner. Johnny died in prison or somewhere; their captors had taken Johnny from the cellar of the house in which they'd been held prisoner, and the body had never been recovered.

Cheyenne had gotten his revenge: in the process of making his escape he'd killed the two guards who assaulted and beat on them for weeks and weeks, and also his original target, the emir Abd al-Talad, a traitor to his people and the Americans. But there was one more person Cheyenne wanted, and that was the reason he'd volunteered to return.

The mission then had supposedly been to capture al-Talad to interrogate him. Cheyenne, working for Col. Spiedel of Delta Force, had his own orders, that being to take out al-Talad, on the spot, no talking about it. But someone had leaked information about the mission and that led to the deaths of the three men Cheyenne had chosen to go with him. His guilt was like an itch in the middle of his back; he couldn't reach it and it kept pricking at him. Spiedel had determined the source of the leak, an interpreter who had disappeared moments before Cheyenne's team left on the mission.

Spiedel knew that the real reason Cheyenne came back was for the nearly impossible challenge of tracking down the traitor, one Mohammed (of course) ab-Hawsawi. It was unlikely Cheyenne would find ab-Hawsawi, but Spiedel was glad to have his best sniper back, whatever the reason. And Cheyenne had Spiedel's reluctant permission to go after the traitor, with a slight detour, which is why he and Jason Jones were laying in a damp ditch, waiting for their unsuspecting targets.

An operation on the leg that had been injured while a prisoner had made it nearly whole. Now, Cheyenne joked, I don't limp, and it only hurts when it's going to rain, is raining, or has just rained. His hearing in his left ear still wasn't a hundred percent, an infirmity he'd managed to disguise so far. I just want to get ab-Hawsawi—he has to pay for the deaths of Pecan Pete, Murzyn, and Johnny Bracken.

Cheyenne nodded in the direction opposite of the ditch in which the two soldiers huddled. He pointed towards the rugged hills to the west.

"You remember that sad excuse for a river we crossed a few miles back, the one running down towards the cliff?"

Jason nodded. "River? Some river, you couldn't get more than half a canteen of water from that creek; all mud."

"Yeah, now; but one good thunderstorm and it becomes the mad Mississippi."

"So?"

"That's the border, kid."

"Huh? What border?"

"Between Afghanisfuckinstan and Pakisfuckinstan, that's what border."

"You mean we're in Pakistan? Are we supposed to be?"

"Yeah, you and I are right where we're supposed to be for what we have to do."

Jason licked his lips, then chewed on his bottom lip. He tried to produce saliva in his mouth, in which a cottony sensation was developing. When he swallowed it was as if a lump of something left over from a bad meal was stuck in his throat.

"It felt like we'd gone a lot farther east than we needed to. I thought we were suppose to rendezvous near Khost, in Afghan," the private said, rather meekly, as if that would make them any safer.

Cheyenne nodded in the direction of the valley floor, miles away, towards a cluster of structures.

"That's why I kept the map away from you. You see that village down there?"

"Barely," Jason mumbled.

"That's a nothing village in itself, but it's on the outskirts of the town of Miram Shah, in the district know as North Waziristan, deep into Pakistan. The main tribal group there is the Turi. They're enemies of the Taliban and their big complaint has been lack of support from the Pakistani government. They've come under heavy pressure from the Haqqani."

"The who? The Hock..."

"The Haqqani. You weren't at that briefing. They're another group of assholes friendly with the Taliban. The Turi have had their own fight with them that's totally unrelated to the issues we have. I swear, kid, you need a scorecard. Anyway, the Haqqani go back to the days when the Afghans were fighting the Russians. Now they raise money by extortion and kidnappings in eastern Afghanistan, then they cross into safe havens in Pakistan. Lately they've been negotiating with the Turi to let them move into another enclave farther north."

"So we're here to..."

"You're here to watch my back and learn something about staying alive in these mountains; I'm here to take out the local leadership of the Haqqani."

"So when do I get to…"

"Get ready, kid. Less than a minute now," Cheyenne said.

Jason nearly jumped up. "What? Did you see something?"

"I saw them several minutes ago," Cheyenne said, lifting the binoculars. "They should be coming into position in a few seconds. Remember now, all you have to do is watch my back and pick up anything I happen to drop. Don't shoot, don't scream, don't talk, don't think. Just watch me, and when I get up and move, you follow me without a question."

"Yes, yes sir," Jason stammered.

Cheyenne quietly raised his rifle and rested it on the ridge of the foxhole wall, bracing it on the rocks he had piled there earlier, and brought his eye to the scope. Some snipers liked to use rifle braces, but that was one more thing to carry, and Cheyenne liked to travel light. The view was of a wall of rock, below which a narrow trail slithered along the side of the wall, and the scraggly shrubs and weeds that clung to the dirt path and the granite cliffs. It looked like nothing less than a mountain goat could travel that trail, probably why it's been so hard to find how these guys have been sneaking behind us.

He moved the scope to a point that stared out at the rocky wall of the canyon, a space that within seconds would be filled with a man as he came around the bend of the trail. Next to Cheyenne, Jason struggled to see what the sniper saw, but there was nothing yet.

Cheyenne was normally confident in his ability to complete his assignment successfully. He was slightly concerned this time because he was using a new weapon, the latest in men's toys. It was the 'Enhanced Sniper Rifle', or more technically, the XM2010, a modified M24. Its range was up to, and possibly more than, three-quarters of a mile. The scope was more powerful than previous models and the flash and noise were dampened to provide more protection for the user. As with every other weapon he tried, Cheyenne had excelled with the rifle in practice, but this was the first time he was using it on a mission. Now he could kill from even farther away than ever before.

It was a good day for his task; not too hot, not too cold. Hot days were difficult for sniping because one perspired more, making the fingers slippery, the gun slippery, the forehead dripping salty sweat into the eyes. Cooler days like this were better; not so cold the breath showed, but comfy, a day for football, a day for a walk in the woods or raking leaves in the back yard.

Through his scope Cheyenne saw the first man come around the corner of the rock wall. A second man appeared a few seconds later, not too close, the men keeping their distance to prevent exactly what Cheyenne was intending to do. Cheyenne pulled the trigger so quickly, so automatically, it was as if the appearance of the second man had sent a computerized signal at light speed to the rifle. Swifter than Jason could gauge what had happened Cheyenne moved the scope a fraction to aim on the first man, who now had no cover, but who knew even before his comrade had fallen that he, too, was in mortal danger. The man turned to retreat around the bend of the wall, but crashed into the other, who was already dead with a dark hole in his forehead, and whose body slumped against the wall of the cliff and blocked the trail. A second blackish hole appeared, this one in the back of the head of the man who had been first in line, now second to die. A third man could be seen coming around the wall, his mouth wide open in shock. His hesitation in retreating caused him to join his comrades in death as Cheyenne fired a third time. Before all three dead men had crumpled to the ground Cheyenne was up and running. Jason, his mouth agape in awe and shock, chased after Cheyenne.

The two soldiers ran over the bare ground, moving quickly but carefully watching where they placed their feet, for the rocky terrain was slashed with fissures that could twist an ankle in an instant. After a quarter of a mile they reached a grassy meadow, a yellowish-green oasis. As they squinted up into the sky a black object appeared, its rotors bringing a smile to Jason's face.

"Perfect timing, Spiedel," Cheyenne said.

"C'mon baby, set her down, take us home."

In less than three minutes, minutes during which Jason constantly scanned the surroundings, fearful they'd been followed, the chopper was hovering above the meadow, the pilot expertly placing his machine where Cheyenne and Jason could hop aboard, while also keeping it ready for a rapid escape. It took off while Cheyenne was still swinging his legs aboard.

"Got a beer?" Cheyenne asked.

The pilot pointed to the cooler setting behind his seat. Cheyenne reached in and pulled out two cans of cold beer. He popped them both and tossed one to Jason.

"Is this allowed?" the private asked in amazement.

"Whaddya worried about, that they'll send you to Iraq or something?"

Cheyenne and the pilot laughed. "How about Pakistan?!" chortled the pilot.

The Kiowa was originally designed for scouting duties, spotting targets for the more powerfully armed Apaches to attack. It carried a two-man crew, a pilot and a co-pilot who doubled as a gunner for those occasions when combat could not be avoided. In this case the sole occupant was the pilot, a veteran named Childress, so there would be enough room for Cheyenne and Jason. It was still cramped quarters.

The whistle preceded the bang by only long enough to say "Holy sh...!"

"Are we hit?" asked Jason.

"It just nicked us, but the controls are stuck; I'm losing altitude!" Childress reported, his voice steady. The Kiowa lurched, knocking Cheyenne and Jason on their backs.

The weird whirling sound told Cheyenne that the rotors were struggling. He regained his balance and looked outside to see if he could spot the source of the attack. Childress struggled to gain altitude, but the engine coughed and the stench of fuel and smoke gagged the pilot. The wounded Kiowa fought gallantly to gain airspace but began to drop, foot-by-foot, sputtering and then lurching to regain height, then spitting smoke and oil and losing more altitude than it had gained.

Cheyenne got a bead on the target, two men aiming another missile. He fired just as they did. Like the first shot, this one was also a near miss, but the projectile caught the tail rotor, a mortal wound. As the enemy on the ground collapsed from Cheyenne's return fire the helicopter gave up its efforts and slowly descended, the pilot now only attempting to make the landing as soft as possible and hoping there wouldn't be an explosion.

Even before the thump of the forced landing Cheyenne had pushed Jason out and followed him. Childress wasn't moving. Cheyenne yelled at Jason to move farther away and climbed back into the smoking chopper and tugged at the pilot. Childress had been unconscious for a moment but Cheyenne's shaking revived him. But the dazed pilot didn't seem to know what to do. Cheyenne took a firm hold on Childress and yanked him until they both tumbled out of the helicopter.

Cheyenne pulled Childress to his feet and dragged him away from the burning machine. Jason was waiting for them and Cheyenne waved at him to keep moving. The threesome dashed desperately to put distance between them and the dying chopper. They dove for cover a fraction of a second before the explosion.

Shrapnel flying through the air is indiscriminate in where it goes and whom it hits. Cheyenne had often said it was his Indian instincts that had protected him from serious injury more times than a cat has lives. The pilot and Jason were less fortunate as spinning hot metal sliced into their backs and arms and legs.

Before he tended to the wounds of his companions Cheyenne scoured the area for additional danger. Even if the men who had downed the helicopter were the only enemy in the area, the sounds of the explosion and the smoke from the fire would likely bring forth anyone else within sound and sight.

Cheyenne knew they were still on the Pakistani side of the border and to avoid hassles trying to explain who he was and what he was doing here, it would be best to scamper back to the Afghan side. First he looked at the wounds of Jason and the pilot. None appeared to be life threatening, but they required first aid. And they wouldn't be running any hundred-yard dashes for a while.

"Jason, Childress, we've got to move a few hundred yards away from here, at least to that crag over yonder, where we'll have some cover."

He nodded in the direction from which he had minutes ago assassinated the purported leaders of the local Haqqani, or whatever the local terrorist organization was calling itself; Cheyenne at this point didn't given a flying fart what their group was called. Seems they changed names every few weeks, probably more often than they changed underwear.

"Can you guys walk?" he asked.

The wounded men attempted to stand, Jason using his rifle as a crutch. "Yeah, yeah," Jason insisted. " I only got nicked."

Childress, the pilot, collapsed. "Damn; sorry Chief."

Cheyenne slung his rifle over his shoulder. "C'mon, we've got to move. Personally, I don't give a shit if we're in Pakistan or Fuckistan, but I know they'll be political crap flying if we're caught here. I really don't want to hear about how upset the Sec of State is."

Cheyenne forced Childress to stand, the pilot wincing as he did so, and taking most of his weight, practically dragging the man, Cheyenne began to move.

"Keep an eye out, Jason."

"Yes sir, I will. Sorry, I mean, Cheyenne."

They returned to the spot from which Cheyenne had made his ambush, and then Cheyenne insisted they continue on towards an outcropping of rock that would provide even better cover. From here he could spot anyone moving in on them. Childress groaned with every other step but Cheyenne wouldn't stop until they reached the ridge of the escarpment. He lay Childress down as gently as if he were setting down a stack of expensive china, and pulled out his binoculars.

"Here, Jason, scan the area for anything moving. I'll tend to his wounds," he said, pointing at Childress, "and then I'll see about yours."

Cheyenne traveled lightly when he was on an assignment, but he always carried the minimum necessities for first aid, though generally it was to use on himself. He tended to Childress and a few moments later checked on Jason.

"See anything?"

"Just some goats," Jason replied.

Cheyenne hastened to finish cleaning and dressing the pilot's wounds.

"Let me see," Cheyenne said as he grabbed the binoculars. "I told you to tell me if you saw anything moving!"

"Just some damn goats," repeated Jason, a bit squeaky.

"Where there's goats there's gonna be people. They might be friendly, but I need to know before we show ourselves."

A split-second later a sharp ping echoed and a fragment of rock was chipped off the ridge, mere inches from where Cheyenne was lying. He turned the binoculars in time to see a man aiming a rifle. Cheyenne ducked lower a microsecond before a second shot bounced off the ridgeline.

"Only goats, uh?"

Jason couldn't speak; he tried to swallow but it felt like a wad of old Kleenex was stuck in his throat. He gasped out a strangled, mumbled, attempted apology, which Cheyenne wasn't listening to.

"I...I guess they aren't friendly," Jason said when he recovered his voice.

"Not necessarily unfriendly, either," Cheyenne countered. "This part of the world, you shoot first, ask questions later. That guy may think we're out to kill one of his goats for food."

Another bullet, and then another, zipped overhead. "On the other hand..."

"I hate to do this," Cheyenne said. "Be tough to explain to the village chief."

He raised his rifle, had the man in his sights, seeing him as clearly as if the doomed goat herder was standing right in front of Cheyenne with a bull's eye painted on his chest. But Cheyenne hesitated, and then lowered the weapon.

"What's wrong?" asked Jason.

"I'm not sure he's nothing more than a peasant guarding his goats. It's like shooting ducks on a pond, I mean, I can zap him and every one of his goats from here, but when they hear about it in Kabul, or worse, in Islamabad, then we'll hear about it, not to mention the poor bastard will be dead."

"Damn, Cheyenne, you just wasted three guys, and you're worried about this one?"

Cheyenne turned and looked at Jason with anger and with sympathy. He slowly shook his head. "You think it's so damn easy, hey, kid? You kill one, two three, why not four? Fuck it, I don't have to explain anything to you." Cheyenne spat into the ground, as if that would expectorate his anger and frustration.

"Ah, kid, I shouldn't take it out on you; I've been pissed at myself for weeks, but it doesn't seem to do any good to yell at myself."

"Pissed about what?" Jason dared to ask.

A deep sigh and then nothing; Jason thought Cheyenne wasn't going to say anymore. After several seconds he spoke, softly and slowly, as if confessing.

"Had a fight with my...girl, before I left."

"That's tough. What about?"

Cheyenne shrugged. "Who knows? Me. Actually it wasn't a fight because I walked out before the fight started."

Again Cheyenne paused long enough for Jason to think he was finished. Finally the kid asked, "So what'd you do? I mean, where'd you go?"

"Huh," Cheyenne's grunt was almost a laugh, one of those laughs that identifies an ironic or absurd situation.

"I went to see another girl, how smart was that? And you know what?"

Jason shook his head.

"She told me she was engaged to get married in a few weeks. In fact, by now she is married, how's them apples?"

"Gee, I..."

"Let's move. I'll take Childress, you cover us."

Cheyenne knew they were moving deeper into Pakistan but he didn't have a choice now, as any other direction provided no cover if the goat herder decided to keep shooting, or if he had reinforcements nearby. They needed to find shelter. Chey scanned the sky and sniffed the air; rain would be falling soon. Childress was too weak to walk without help and by the time someone in headquarters figured out that the Childress wasn't returning, it'd be too dark to send another chopper.

***

FIVE

"...for I never yet met a man that I didn't like." ...Will Rogers, on Leon Trotsky, *Saturday Evening Post* (6 November 1926)

Dear Diary,

I HAVE TO CATCH up my notes a day late, while on the road again, without Rock. No, instead I'm with, get this, his *girlfriend*! How that came about is a story even I can't understand.

I slept late, peeked outside to be sure there were no cowboys laying in wait, and stepped lively to my car. I threw my bag in and peeled out. I drove for an hour before I stopped, now in California, for gas and coffee. I wasn't hungry and I calculated it'd be about noon when I got to Rock's office, so maybe I could wrangle a lunch out of him. If he even wanted to see me.

I timed my drive perfectly, pulling into the parking lot of Hammond Tools as the car's clock turned to noon. The company still carries the name of the former owner and founder, Rock's late father-in-law. Rock had gone to work for Mr. Hammond, and not knowing she was his boss's daughter, was at the same time dating a girl he'd met somewhere, I don't remember the entire story. So it turns out he married the boss's daughter, and when the Hammonds passed away, Rock and his wife Mary Ann inherited the business. Then when Mary Ann died in an auto accident, Rock inherited the whole shebang. I know it sounds like he couldn't have planned it any better, but I also know for a thousand percent certainty that Rock would give up the company in a heartbeat to have his wife back. I never met her, Mary Ann, but from the way Rock talked about her, once he opened up, she must have been something else. Guess that's why I'm always trying to impress Rock, because I think he compares all women to Mary Ann, and they don't measure up. Why not? Hey, I want a man to feel that I'm the greatest gal who ever walked the earth, even if some of it is in his imagination!

So I go in, a bit concerned because I haven't talked to Rock in weeks, and I'm not sure if he got my message telling him I'm coming, but eager to see him whether he's ready for me or not. The receptionist, who had to put down her magazine before acknowledging me, but not before she finished a paragraph—probably some temp, told me Rock wasn't in. To be accurate, she didn't call him Rock, I did, just to let her know I was somebody who knew the boss on a first name basis.

She moved the gum she was chewing to the other side of her mouth and said, "I'm sorry, ma'am, but he's away on business for the rest of the week."

I asked where he went, she said she couldn't tell me, and called me ma'am again; I hate being called ma'am! I insisted I was a friend he'd been expecting, but she wouldn't fall for that, so I asked to speak to the person in charge. That was how I first met Helen.

"That would be Ms. Harrison; I'll call her."

I waited, fuming because I had to wait, and even then I might not find out where Rock was or when he'd be back. What was I going to do now? There wasn't even a decent magazine to look at while I waited, just ones about engineering and tools.

She had light brown hair, cut short, but nicely done, framing her face like a museum piece, and the face was one that was probably beautiful when she was in her prime, and even now, I, a woman much younger than Ms. Harrison, would have to admit she was strikingly pretty. I write this because that was my original impression. I also felt an ache—it must have been a premonition—because I got this hunch that this woman was on friendly terms with Rock—*very* friendly. Why was she in charge when Rock's gone? I never heard him mention a Ms. Harrison. But, trying to be honest, I had to admit she was quite attractive and emitted an aura of competence and confidence. She also did not seem like Rock's type; what the hell do I know? I've known guys whose type was simply female. I didn't like her.

Repeating what the gum-chewing receptionist had told me, Helen advised me that Rock was away, gone to a trade show in guess where? San Antonio! He had left early this morning, can you believe I just missed him? I told Ms. Harrison my name and that I was a friend of Rock's from...and she interrupted.

"You're Dinah Russell? From...that town, what was its name, Dirty Hole, or something like that, Rock said."

When I want to I can dribble out a southwest accent, pure homespun country-cowboy. Or I can talk as sophisticated as a New York secretary to a CEO of a major bank, and I can hem and haw like a hillbilly from eastern Kentucky. Natural talent and lots of old movies.

Why I wanted to make Helen think I was a hick from the boondocks, I'm not sure. I guess so she would wonder how Rock and I could be friends. Diary, I can't even spell the way I talked, and it was silly of me, no doubt. I was being a brat, not unusual.

"Drah Hole, Ms. Harrison; it's Drah Hole, Arizona. Rock always gets the name mixed up." I said, forcing a laugh. I wanted info from her so I was making nice-nice.

"Mr...Rock didn't tell me you were coming," she said, slyly, pointing out that were I important, he would have mentioned my pending arrival.

"Ah, I've had problems with my cell phone," I lied. "My voice mail shows he's called, but the messages aren't getting through." I shrugged my shoulders. "Satellites... sun spots, who knows?" I smiled my widest, and most vicious, smile.

"So, you're second in command," I added, before she could come back on my obvious lie about my cell phone problem. I also wanted to emphasize, *second,* even tho second in charge to Rock was pretty good. I couldn't figure how she could have risen that high in the company when I'd never heard of her before.

"Yes, well, in a few days I'll go to San Antonio, also, to meet Rock." She smiled when she said it, pointing out that she, not me, was meeting Rock.

"You must have done well for yourself, I mean, you can't have been here very long. I know Rock would have mentioned you." After all, I speak to him every day, honey.

"I came on board six months ago. Rock was looking for someone who could handle daily operations when he's not around, or involved in other projects. It's a big job."

"Hmm, I'm sure." She's screwing Rock, I'm sure of it; bitch.

"Rock offered me a job a while back, but I've been tied up with some other things so it wasn't until now that I've had a chance to get to San Diego."

"Really? He hadn't mentioned it...please, why don't we go to my office where we can talk." Damn, she was taking charge.

I followed her down a hallway decorated with pictures of tools and engineering projects that Hammond Tools had been involved in over the years. I'd only been here twice before but I tried to act as if I was familiar with the layout. *Her* office? She took me to Rock's office. I couldn't imagine she would use his

91

office while he was gone, so I assumed she had deliberately taken me here to show she had access to Rock's office whenever she wanted it.

"Please sit," Helen said, an order, not an invitation. I purposely stalled, waiting for her to sit first. She did, in Rock's comfy chair, a leather, chocolate colored padded chair behind a huge desk that looked old, heavy, and functional. Rock told me the desk had belonged to the original owner, Mr. Hammond. It was big enough to play football on, but the top was mostly clear. I remember the first time I was here I noticed that Rock didn't keep a lot of things on his desk. He liked to move papers along and didn't care for knick-knacks.

The middle of the desk was covered by a desk pad with a calendar—Rock still liked to use an old-fashioned, paper calendar to quickly note what was on the day's schedule, or to add appointments, when he was in; his computerized appointment calendar he used when traveling. Off to the side sat one of the new iPads, first on the block. I assume Rock had taken his laptop with him, so this must be Helen's toy. On one corner of the desk was parked a two-tiered tray that held a few sheets of paper and a three-ring binder with the words on the cover, 'San Antonio Trade Show'.

A picture of Rock and his wife—his late wife, Mary Ann, use to have a prime location on the right side of the desk, but it was not there now. My devious mind suspected that she, Ms.

Harrison, had temporarily moved it. Or maybe Ms. Harrison has permanently replaced Mary Ann?

"You know, I handle hiring, and firing, when necessary; one of my several duties. I'm not sure what job Rock was thinking of for you."

She could have at least offered me a cup of coffee.

"I'm not sure what he had in mind for me either, Ms. Harrison. He did say I'd brighten up the office a bit, you know." Gag me.

"I see your accent has cleared up." Oops, she caught me fooling around. I smiled to cover my embarrassment.

"Oh, well, when I see him later this week I'll tell him you dropped by. But I don't see that we have any positions open right now."

"No, I guess not. I mean, you have such an efficient receptionist and all, so I'm sure there's nothing for me, but oh, I thought I'd drop by. You know, maybe I'll just zip on over to San Antonio and see Rock. I mean, we had such fun there last year, it'd be like old home week, you know, homecoming. Yes, we had quite a time."

"Oh, I thought he gave you and your boyfriend a ride to the east coast?"

"Oh sure, he did *that*, of course. Anyway..." I rose to show I was deciding when this interview was over. "It's always best to talk to the boss man, so maybe I'll bump into you in San

Antonio. Nice meeting you, Ms. Harrison." I turned and abruptly walked out of her—Rock's, office.

I was less sure of what to do next than I had indicated to Ms. Harrison. I really wasn't thinking of following Rock to San Antonio; my saying so to Ms. Harrison was silly talk. That's two days of hard driving, and to what end? I could wait here in San Diego for him to return; that would make more sense than driving over a thousand miles to get there, maybe find Rock not happy to see me, and then have to turn around and drive to Tucson with my tail between my legs. In the mean time, I'd be the extra person, once Ms. Harrison showed up. Then she, Helen, let's call her by her first name from now on, helped make my decision.

I was already out of the door, idly walking to my car, undecided on what to do next, looking for my keys which were buried somewhere in the bottom of my purse, when I heard a voice call me.

"Ms. Russell! Dinah?" She hurried out to meet me. I waited, making her come all the way to the parking area.

"Yes?"

"You know, I'm supposed to fly to San Antonio on Friday, and help Rock at the trade show over the weekend. I originally didn't want to ride with him because I don't like long drives, and he loves to drive. But if you're going to go to San Antonio, maybe I could tag along with you? You think you'd enjoy some company?"

I wasn't sure what I was going to do, but if I did go to San Antonio one thing I knew was that I didn't want her company. However, if I said no, I assumed she would change her flight and leave in time to get there before me, and, she'd surely tell Rock I was on my way. I'd feel like a doofus. And I still wasn't sure I wanted to go at all.

"We'd have to leave immediately. How can you do that if..." I was going to say, 'If you are second in command', but I held my tongue.

"Nothing going on that Carl Mendez can't handle. It might be fun, to get to know each other a bit."

Now why in the world did she want to get to know me?

She said she needed an hour or so to tidy up the office before leaving, and then would need to run home to get her things, most of which were packed already. I assumed she had to have her airline arrangements canceled, too, but that wasn't my concern. She graciously offered to let me wait in Rock's office, but I declined, choosing instead to run out for a sandwich. I told Helen I'd meet her back here in an hour.

Purposely I rushed through my lunch and returned in about forty minutes. The receptionist remembered me and I told her Ms. Harrison had said she'd meet me here.

"Oh, yeah, I guess you can wait here." She nodded to the chairs in the waiting area.

"Excuse me, but she said I should wait in the Rock's office." I deliberately used Rock's name as if he and I were bosom buddies (aren't we?), and strode past the receptionist and down the corridor to Rock's office. I sat in his chair and waited there for Helen.

"Oh, yes, Ms. Green said you had made yourself at home," Helen said a few minutes later, when she returned to the office.

I grinned and said, "You ready?"

WE STAYED ONE night at Aunt May's house—mine, now, in Tucson. When I suggested we stop in Tucson for the first night—which is a good haul of over 400 miles—Helen cringed.

"Tucson? I thought you lived in some little decrepit town in the desert."

Decrepit? Is that what Rock told her, decrepit?

"You mean Dry Hole? I did live there, all my life, but now I've moved to Tucson, though it's still in the desert."

"Oh." She stared straight ahead with her mouth half open. She was thinking, cogitating bits of info, like the possibility there are real cities in the desert. Duh, have you ever heard of Las Vegas, Helen? Phoenix?

Not that it was any of her business, but to be sociable I spent several minutes telling her about Mom's illness, my trips back and forth from Dry Hole to Tucson, about Aunt May, etc. She wasn't listening.

"That's why Rock said he was stopping in Tucson on the way, he was going to see you, wasn't he?

I felt like I was being accused of being accessory to murder, or worse, for Helen, alienation of affections.

"Helen, I don't know anything about that. He didn't tell me he was coming to Tucson. Would I have come to San Diego if I knew he was coming to Tucson? Huh?"

"Oh, I guess not. I just don't understand why he didn't tell me it was you he was going to see."

I had no good answer to give her, and right at that point even I, naughty as I can be sometimes, didn't want to tease her by giving the wrong impression about Rock and I. So we drove on for a long time in silence. I even lowered the sound from the CD player down to where you could barely hear it.

I was glad Aunt May's house—my house—was clean; I wouldn't want Helen to think I was a lousy housekeeper. When we had neared the border between Arizona and New Mexico I was cognizant (I'm trying to improve my vocabulary), that we would soon hit the turnoff, the state highway, that could take us past the ratty road (more like a wagon train rut) that leads to Dry Hole. The highway zigzags in and out of New Mexico and Arizona, and if one knows which dirt road to turn on, a thin line that doesn't show up on most maps, you can find your way to the dust bowl of the Southwest. Not that a sane person would have a reason to go there.

Of course, Rock did turn down that sorry excuse for a road, enticed by an old beat-up sign for my café, advertising 'the best pies in the Southwest'. You never know who might drop into your life at the oddest moments. I almost opened my mouth to point out to Helen that we were near to my hometown, and the place where I first met Rock, but I didn't say anything. The timing did not seem appropriate. On the other hand, she might want to detour to see Dry Hole, and where I met Rock is something I didn't want to share with Helen. There may be no logic to my feeling, but hey, I'm not Mr. Spock.

It's a good thing I didn't open my big mouth because only a moment later Helen started talking about how Rock and I had met, at least, the way she understood it.

"Wasn't it in some desolate spot around here that Rock found you and your boyfriend, in a car crash?" She nodded towards the outdoors, the forlorn desert that to her was nothing more than dirty sand, thirsty tumbleweeds, cowboys and Indians.

I was taken aback and delayed answering. I assumed Rock had told her he met Chey and me at the café in Dry Hole, and after meeting there, arranged to meet again in San Antonio, but then, the subject hadn't come up yet between Helen and I.

"Ah, we were in a crash, yes, but quite a ways farther east from here. In Texas, actually. Some crazy truck driver sideswiped us. Sent the car spinning and Chey was banged up enough to be hospitalized for a few days."

I was trying not to say too much, or anything that wouldn't coincide with what Rock had told Helen. I didn't exactly lie, but it sounded like Rock had, so I had to protect him, I rationalized.

"So you two were going to the east coast, too, uh? And Rock took you all the way. Nice of him," she said.

The sarcasm seemed to flow naturally out of her. Or was it jealousy? (I had the disconcerting thought that Ms. Harrison and I might be more alike than I cared to admit). I guess I could safely assume that Rock had not told her about my silly stunt when I climbed into bed with him, that time we shared adjoining rooms in the motel near the Alamo, while Chey was in the hospital after the accident. Ah yes, a nice memory, even tho all we did was sleep. I still sometimes wonder how...oh, never mind.

I suppose she might be jealous because I'm younger than she, and, quite frankly, I'm not bad looking, if I can be less than humble here, just between you and me and the jackrabbits. I mean, I won't win any Miss Universe contests, but I was Homecoming Queen at Coronado High. As I wrote earlier, Helen's pleasant looking, too. I'm sure most regular guys Rock's age would find her quite attractive. But she may see me as competition, tho I know I'm not, that is, not in the way she thinks. There's never been anything physical between Rock and I, other than hugs and pecks on the cheek that are mostly air-kisses. Not that I haven't wondered what it might be like to be more intimate with him, but Rock thinks he's too old for me, and when I met him he was grieving his wife's death, and I know I'm repeating myself; sorry, Diary.

So why is Helen doing this, traveling with me to meet Rock? She could have flown and arrived there long before me. Maybe she wants to go mano a mano with me for Rock's attention! Is that how you say it, spell it, mano a mano? Like a couple of bullfighters matching testosterone levels!

"What was it you were going east for?" Helen asked. My mind was inventing possible responses and she must have thought I was ignoring her when I didn't answer immediately.

"What? Oh, well, I was going to visit a friend, and Cheyenne, he had to report in Washington regarding some army business."

Not knowing how much she knew, I didn't want to go into detail about how when Cheyenne was reported as killed in action, I had received the insurance money, and after he escaped and returned from the dead, we worried about what to do with the money, because we couldn't find a way to give it back, and Rock had this friend, a general, in Washington who took care of things, etc. None of her business, actually, and I'm sure Rock wouldn't have told her about the money, because I asked him not to tell anyone.

Seems the general figured that for all Chey's heroics, and for how he'd suffered in the Iraqi prison camp, he deserved the money. Besides, the general explained, it's very complicated if not impossible to give something back to the Army after they insisted it was yours. They'd be admitting they made a mistake.

Of course there was another reason Chey was going east, and that was to see the sister of the soldier he'd been in prison with. Seems my dear boy became infatuated from his buddy's talking and bragging about his sister. Sadly, the guy died in prison, Chey felt guilty about it, since the guy was under Chey's command, so he went to visit the parents and the sister, became even more infatuated with the sister and began making goo-goo eyes at her, the bimbo! So despite his professed love for me, he went to see her again before he reported back from his leave.

Wait—that's not fair of me. I shouldn't call her a bimbo. I realize that Chey is all male, which means that whenever a pretty girl walks into the room his brain shuts off and control of the body moves south. But he'd never go for a bimbo. I'm sure she's a nice person, smart, and pretty. Tho I do wonder how big her boobs are, because I know Chey's weakness. It still bites me when I think of him and my supposed friend Marilyn, one of the other cheerleaders in high school, necking in the back of her Daddy's pick-up truck. Marilyn must have had some sort of glandular problem, because she was so top-heavy she could hardly walk and keep her head up at the same time. But the boys sure liked to watch her jump around leading the cheers. Go, Team, Go!

"What is that music?" Helen asked. "Is that the same guy Rock is always listening to?"

On the car's CD player a disc called 'Rough Sketches', by John Stewart, was playing. I thought it was appropriate music for the time and place of our drive. John was singing about some old guy who had a barbershop along Route 66 and wouldn't leave even after the Interstates were built and most of the traffic disappeared from 66.

Shortly after that John sang one of my favorite of his just-for-fun songs, about the alleged crash landing of a flying saucer in New Mexico back in 1945. I found myself looking out at the cerulean sky and searching for bright flying objects. Usually there is something in the sky; a high-flying hawk, the even higher-flying streak of an intercontinental jet, or the reflection from a loose piece of debris caught in the wind. People often see what they want to.

"You, too, uh? Is that what you learned from Rock, about this cowboy singer?"

I looked at her and frowned quizzically. "He's not a cowboy, he's a songwriter and singer. Or was. He died recently, Rock told me."

"He did? When was that?"

"I don't know exactly."

"I mean, when did you last talk to Rock?"

I felt like I was being interrogated. "Oh, not in a little while, like I said, I had no idea he was thinking of coming to Tucson."

"I suppose it was a spur of the moment decision," she said.

After a pause that took us past three herds of cattle, two corrals of horses and a dilapidated red barn that looked like it would fall over the next time a cow brushed against it, Helen asked, "Do you and Rock talk often?"

I *was* being interrogated. I actually hadn't talked to Rock in several weeks, not since before the last time Chey came home on leave. Last year I had been ready to take Rock up on his job offer, but then Chey called and I reneged and I think Rock was upset with me. But I couldn't let Helen know that.

"It varies," I said, a lilt in my voice and a shake of my head, the intent being to make her think we talk all the time and it's a normal part of our lives, which didn't fit with the fact that lately we had been missing each other along the entire Interstate system of the southwest United States. Maybe Rock said he hadn't talked to me in months and I'll get him in trouble if I say different.

Well, my, my, a little woman trouble might be fun for Rocky, old boy, especially if I could be in the middle! I thought of saying we talk every other day, or so, but I didn't think she'd believe me and I'd look silly later when she questioned Rock, which I was sure she'd do, so I left my answer hanging incomplete. Let her wonder.

Is she this way with Rock? I can't believe he'd put up with someone bossy and sassy like her. But maybe she's not that way with him. Like I said, she may be jealous, but damn, I just can't let myself make it easy for her! I know it's selfish of me—bratty, too! Really and truly, Diary, I don't expect anything to come of my relationship with Rock other than a long friendship, one that lasts, I hope, forever. There can be no romance (long-term, anyway, because he is more than twice my age). But I'm afraid that if he gets too involved romantically, or, heaven forbid, married, he wouldn't have time for me, for our friendship, even if it's a long-distance one. Again, not logical, selfish, if anything; so sue me. Maybe I'll have to protect Rock from his lady friend. For all I know, she's planning to stick her claws deep into him, trick him into marrying her, so then she can inherit the company. I started humming the theme song from *High Noon.*

The CD changed and now John was singing from one of his older albums. (I am getting to know his music, Diary. At first I listened because Rock liked the songs, but now I've become a real fan. I'm sorry I never saw him perform live. Rock said he used to go to Santa Monica frequently to see his act.) My humming changed to meld with John's singing; I wasn't sure of the name of this song, but it sounded nice, even if I didn't understand every word—isn't that the way it is with songs? You can listen to a song for years and get a phrase wrong because it's frequently difficult to catch the words, especially with singers who are drowned out by the pounding cacophony of their electronic musical instruments. But the incorrect phrase sticks in your mind the way you heard it, not the way the singer sang it. Eventually it becomes more fun to insert your own words when you hear the song. There's the one by Led Zeppelin, "and as we wind on down the road," that sure sounds like, "there's a wino down the road," as an example.

I had passed on recordings of the John Stewart music Rock had given me to Cheyenne, and I think he listened to please me, but then, like I did, he got hooked, too. I bought him a mini iPod to take with him and loaded it with his favorite songs of contemporary singers, lots of C&W, of course, but I also put on several albums of John's music. I don't know if Chey ever listens, but I'd like to think he does, and thinks of me.

(If he thinks of *her* when he listens, then I hope he drops the iPod in the mud!)

We didn't talk much for a long while. Helen dozed off and I was fine with that. I wanted to let my thoughts wander a bit, the road taking me along mindlessly, wishing the lure of this road I was driving on could help me figure out what road my life was traveling down, with Chey and otherwise, I mean, my entire life.

I couldn't figure—can't figure—if it's mere coincidence or some factor of fate, that a little over a year after I first went to

San Antonio, to meet Rock, with *my* boyfriend (for lack of a better term, like 'significant other', gimme a break) I'm going there again to meet him, this time with *his* 'girlfriend'.

Back then I was excited to be getting away from Dry Hole for awhile, stunned that Chey had come back after I'd been notified of his death, and flattered that this handsome guy with silver temples and age lines that only served to make him look distinguished, was fond of me (no, it wasn't just my delicious pies).

Back then I was worried about Mom, excited that Chey was alive, but totally lost as to where my life was going. Baking pies at the Only Café, trying to get some schooling part time, getting older every day, the biological clock ticking and me already wondering if I'm going to inherit Alzheimer's from Mom, Chey just as confused and in and out of love, or fascinated, with another woman, and me, admit it, fantasizing that Rock would lift me in his arms and carry me away on a dream voyage to the South Seas, or some place where there's more than a bucket of water, which is about all we see in Dry Hole. Fool that I was, I had no idea that Rock was bent out of shape over the recent death of his wife in a car accident for which he blamed himself. He had no more interest in romance when I met him than does a black widow spider on her honeymoon.

Now, I was again following Rock, for what reason I cannot put a finger on; chasing him, like a love-sick teenager mooning over the latest teenage idol. To get a pinch of comfort

106

from him, now that Chey had left me again? Maybe so, and how do I do that while I'm paling around with Rock's new girlfriend, Dinah Russell, you goof? I like to think it's because I trust Rock's judgment and I'm hoping he can help me get on track. I have no regular job (the one in Tucson I was only doing to fill my time), Chey is gone and I can't keep waiting on him, trusting that he'll show up alive and ready to settle down, I have no relatives, no real skills, and no future that I can see. Funny, I've got money, honey, and I'm not very happy. Goes to show. Yeah, I can bake pies that'd make Marie Whatshername, the one with the restaurants, jealous, and I have some computer skills, good enough that I did bookkeeping for a few of the ranches around Dry Hole, but who wants to do either of those jobs for the rest of one's life? Do I want to continue on some crummy, dusty road to nowhere? Or find a new one, one that probably won't include Cheyenne Smith?

Okay, Diary, here it comes: I want a loving husband, a nice house with green grass in the back yard, a gurgling fountain, just for the sound of flowing water, a store where I can buy clothes other than jeans and plaid shirts, and a couple of kids, cute ones, preferably. Is that too much to ask? Maybe it is. I'll get back to you.

***

SIX

"Just when I thought I was out, they pull me back in."---
Michael Corleone (Al Pacino) in *Godfather III.*

NIGHT FELL LIKE a piano dropped out of a ten-story building. Boom, it was dark. Cheyenne was ready for it and had found a small cut in the block wall of the canyon. Not exactly Mammoth Cave, more of a grotto, but protection from the coming rain and, hopefully, from anyone looking to avenge his actions of the day.

Childress was asleep and Jason Jones was watching at the entrance to the grotto, while Cheyenne rested with his eyes closed and his ears open. He'd instructed Jason to call him if he saw or heard anything, any movement or sound, no matter how faint or innocent.

I hate taking on a newbie, but someone has to train them. That's what Spiedel did for me, so I owe it to do the same. This kid will work out and he can have my job and I can go home. Home—when I'm home, I can't figure out what to do with myself, so I come back here; when I'm here, I want to be home, except I'm not even sure where 'home' is anymore. Do I have a home in Dry Hole?

The three men had taken shelter a couple of miles from the original rescue point. When the next rescue chopper came in the morning the men should be able to spot it; maybe have to send up a flare if they weren't able to get to the meadow in time. Cheyenne's GPS responder would give the rescuers a good fix, but there aren't many places a helicopter can land. And the last thing Cheyenne wanted to do was lead it into an ambush.

Cheyenne knew that if they weren't able to keep the rendezvous—or in this case, when Childress doesn't return at all, another attempt would be made early morning. And another twelve hours later, if necessary.

The cave, or grotto, they had found, was a cut in a semi-circular cliff on the west end of a valley that spread east as far the eye could see. A few yards outside the entrance to the grotto the ground sloped downward for fifty or sixty yards, ending in a narrow shelf hugging the side of the cliff that spread to the north. At the edges of the shelf the drop-off was sheer, hundreds of feet to the valley floor. To the south of the cave, a trail wound along the south cliff, ever downward, eventually reaching to the village Cheyenne had pointed out to Jason earlier.

It began to rain, suddenly and with force. Cheyenne's eyes opened and he saw Jason turn his way. "I hear it." He'd scared the kid enough so that he would have awakened Cheyenne to tell him it was raining—I told him, *any* sound at all. Cheyenne smiled in the dark. At the front of the grotto Jason was a mere silhouette now as the last gasps of daylight slipped below the horizon. No fire tonight, and only a small, quick one for coffee in the morning. Nowhere for the smoke to go inside the grotto and a fire might give away their position to anyone who inhabited these hills and glens and the village.

Cheyenne was sure that word of the deaths on the trail had spread far and wide, quicker than gossip on the Internet, and the charred remains of the downed Kiowa discovered. So *they,* whoever the fuck *they* were—the Haqqani, probably, or even the Turi tribe, ostensibly friendly but you never know about those goat herders—knew Cheyenne and his little group were out here somewhere. But there are thousands of little grottos and caves in the hills, and with luck, they'd be secure until morning. And with a little more luck, Childress would sleep through the night and be rested enough to move. Cheyenne knew he himself wouldn't sleep; he just needed a few winks now and he'd take over for Jason. He'd feel more secure being on guard himself.

Cheyenne dozed and awoke with a start, for a fraction of a second unsure of where he was. A flicker of a memory of Di pricked his brain; she was getting married, but Cheyenne wasn't sure if it was to him or someone else. Susan was there too, and Cheyenne had the weird feeling that he was supposed to choose between them, a thought that thankfully lasted for only a blip as he realized he'd been dreaming.

He took some water from his canteen, swished it in his mouth and spat it out, then downed several swallows.

"Jason?" Cheyenne whispered.

"Yeah. Have a good nap?"

Cheyenne crawled toward Jason's voice until he reached the entrance. It was almost pitch dark inside the cave, and as he reached the edge the only light was from the gazillions of stars that decorated the sky. There was no moon out yet.

It was too dark to see it now, but when they had first found the grotto Cheyenne noticed the steep drop-off on one side, and the tree and brush filled hillside that stretched above the grotto. Only the direction they'd come from, and the direction straight out, towards the trail that led to the bottom of the valley, were passable, which cut down the likelihood of anyone sneaking up on them. He hoped.

Cheyenne methodically scanned the canyon looking for any dots of light that might indicate a campfire, though with the rain continuing in full force he didn't expect to see any.

Anticipating, Jason said, "I haven't seen any lights, Cheyenne, none."

A professional sniper doesn't keep his job, or his life, for long, by being over-confident. Cheyenne attached an infrared scope to his rifle and repeated a scan of the surroundings. He took a full ten minutes to do so.

"Hear anything?" Cheyenne asked when he had finished.

"I think there was an owl, and some coyotes. I wasn't gonna wake you; you need rest, too."

Cheyenne nodded, glad the kid was getting some sense. "How're you managing?"

Jason shrugged and rubbed his leg, movements Cheyenne couldn't see in the dark. "Okay, a little sore. Nothing's bleeding."

"You'll stiffen up some by morning. I'll take over; get some food and then some sleep. Pee in the corner back there if you need to go."

"Cheyenne?"

"Hmm?"

"What you did, taking out three guys like that, so quickly. And then, saving Childress...you think you'll get something, I mean, like a medal?"

"Ah, kid, and here I thought you were learning something. You don't do this for medals. What the hell they teaching you kids these days?"

"It's just that, what you did was something else, I mean, I never..."

"Kid, you're gonna be out here a year or more, if you survive, and you'll find out pretty damn quick that just surviving from day to day, is pretty heroic. That is, if you're concerned with heroics. Besides, I've got enough goddamn medals to start an army surplus store. I'll give 'em to you, you want medals. Now go get some sleep."

Chastised, Jason slumped away.

Night came early here and so would morning. It wasn't yet midnight so Cheyenne had four or five hours to keep guard.

He hoped a chopper would show up at first light. But the friends of the three men he'd killed this afternoon might show up about the same time.

Trouble is, he wasn't sure if he could get Childress to the rendezvous site. By morning the pilot will be one big bruise and barely able to walk on his own, and I'm not sure how smoothly the kid is going to be able to move, either, with his leg all banged up. And from here to the meadow there's precious little cover. What was it the fat guy used to say to the skinny one in those old films Di's Dad liked to watch? 'Here's another fine mess you've gotten me into!'

Using his infrared scope Cheyenne again surveyed the valley below, the sides of the valley, and up and around, up the slope in back of the grotto, and did it all again, taking his time, slowly, the way he'd learned. He spotted a few goats, but no people; any herders were probably asleep in a cave or in a shelter, some simple structure adequate to keep out the worst of the weather.

Even the village, which he knew was out there in the dark, was totally black, except for an occasional wisp of gray as smoke seeped out of chimneys and mixed with the rain that continued to pour down. Probably cooking up some rabbit stew or soup, and keeping warm and dry.

The heavy rain told Cheyenne that the ground near the meadow, and the meadow itself, would be muddy in the morning, making it tough to move even if they could get close, and the chopper isn't going to want to put down if it's too muddy. Getting Childress aboard might be dicey.

Cheyenne continued to search the darkness with his scope. There appeared to be only one route that could be used to get close to them, should anyone want to. It didn't take a genius to suspect that three deaths of the Haqqani leadership were going to warrant a strong reprisal attempt. From here, and making careful, strategic withdrawals, Cheyenne felt he could hold off a small army until they could get close to the meadow. Chopper doesn't show up, we're screwed anyway, but we can't stay here come morning.

Cheyenne slipped back deeper into their temporary home. Both of the other men were asleep, though Childress tossed and mumbled, his wounds causing pain that was in turn causing disturbing dreams. Jason was out solidly; good, I need him to be well rested come daylight.

There was a little coffee left, nearly as cold as the rain. Cheyenne sipped it and cursed quietly. It was at times like this he remembered blurbs from those days in Dry Hole, when he'd while away the morning in the Only Café and nurse coffee for hours, just so he could be near Di. He'd keep an eye on the front door and if he saw his Dad coming, he'd skip out the back and be at the shop when his Dad returned. Who did he think he was fooling?

A slice of Di's homemade pie, any type, any flavor, and a cup of hot, dark coffee, fresh made, right now, and I'd re-up again. Ha, screw me, I'll probably re-up anyway.

He splashed the remainder of the coffee on the ground and went back to the cave entrance. The rain had eased off to a steady fall, pleasant sounding and stimulating the sense of smell. Even the scent from the dirt was not offensive, as it had been the times Cheyenne had his face pressed down in it. Plants he couldn't identify, nor see at this time of night, emitted aromas that reminded him of the desert. The smell of the rain itself was sweet and fresh, another reminder of Di.

Funny, thought Cheyenne, I think of Di, but I dream of Susan. He remembered that in his pack, which was in the interior of the cave, he carried a mini-IPod, given to him by Di. She'd loaded it with music, some of his old favorites and others that she liked. He hadn't had time to use it much but he carried it with him on his missions, an exception to his rule of only carrying essentials.

He slipped inside and found the IPod. A little night music to keep me company. He set the volume low so that he could still hear the sounds of the night. It was unlikely anything— read, any person, would try to get at them during the night, but Cheyenne had learned you can never be too cautious in enemy territory.

He set it at random and the first few songs were a mix of Di's jazzy pieces she insisted Cheyenne would enjoy, and a few western twangy songs that Cheyenne liked. Then came a song from Di's new favorite, ever since they'd met up with Rock.

'She believes the ships come home singing from the sea. She believes in losers, oh, she believes in me.' *

Yeah, how fitting; but I wonder, does she?

The rain continued and did not ease any more until near dawn. With the first hint of orange on the horizon the rain ceased completely. Cheyenne studied the panorama, first checking the one trail that he felt was the weak point of their position, then covering the entire valley and surroundings, as he'd done several times previously.

Faintly he heard the baaing of sheep, or was it goats? What the hell kind of noise do goats make? No people, no danger signs yet. He turned towards the interior of the cave.

"Jason! You awake?"

A mumble, a grumble, a moan.

"Make some coffee. That much I need before we skedaddle. And wake up Childress. Got to get him moving around, work out the cramps."

A few minutes later Jason appeared with a cup of coffee for Cheyenne, who took the cup in one hand while continuing to scour the valley with the binoculars.

* From the song, *"She Believes In Me,"* by John Stewart

"I can feel it kid; hell, I think I can smell them."

"Who? The goats?"

"Fuck the goats! It's the bastards who shot down our chopper yesterday, and who are going to hunt for us today."

"You think they know we're here?" Jason asked. The kid wanted to think that this morning they could simply walk out of the cave, saunter to the meadow, a nice walk in the park, and wait for a ride home; just hail a taxi. Who would believe they'd still be sitting here, in a cave in Pakistan, of all places, for God's sake?!

"Yeah, they know we're here. They know the chopper went down. They knew that goat-herder was shooting at us, they know we couldn't get far last night in the rain, in this terrain, pitch-black..."

"Goddamn it, I hurt," came a voice from the cave.

"Childress is awake," Jason said, stating the obvious.

"Here, keep watching," Cheyenne said as he handed the binoculars to Jason. Cheyenne went in to see Childress.

"Fuck, Cheyenne, I don't know if I can walk at all! I'm so stiff I feel like I've been rolled down a cliff and then dumped in a pot of starch! Oh, man!"

"Take it easy, take it slow. We'll help but you've got to help too. We may have to move quickly. So try to stand and move around a bit. Eat something, but hurry; we're out of here in ten."

Cheyenne turned on the GPS responder, which should have instantly sent a loud beep to Spiedel, loud enough to wake him if he wasn't yet astir.

They all had had a quick cup of coffee, peed in the corner of the cave, ate an energy bar, and gathered up their gear. Childress was trying to stretch out the aches but every movement was painful.

"If I can get these bones moving, Chief, I'll be okay," he said, hopefully but not too confidently. "You guys leave me behind if you need to."

"Not bloody likely, Childress," responded Cheyenne.

Cheyenne saw the scenario in his mind, as if it had already occurred. As soon as they moved out they'd be spotted and the chase would be on. He'd have to urge Jason to help Childress and head for the meadow while Cheyenne covered them, and pray that there weren't enough bad guys to circle around and cut them off from the landing zone. I hope they send an Apache or a Blackhawk this time.

"Let's go; Jason, give Childress a hand."

The lighting was still dim in these first few minutes of morning, and the men hoped they could get a fair distance away before they were spotted. But in the dark, walking on the rugged terrain was difficult, and Childress and Jason stumbled twice before they'd gone a few yards.

Below, in the valley, Cheyenne spotted movement. Headlights from a vehicle, or a fire, or a light from a shack as morning gently moved in to replace the night. Some of the movement was probably innocent—goat herders, farmers, the regular residents of a poor village rising to meet another day of scuffling for enough food to make it until nightfall and to the next morning so they could start all over.

But some of the movement would be the insurgents— even Cheyenne had taken to calling 'them' insurgents, for lack of a better term. The enemy, is what they were; his enemy, and he didn't want any philosophical discussion on who's the enemy here when he was the one invading their country. Self-defense reaches a long way.

Cheyenne motioned to Jason and Childress to move out. Together they looked like the crippled leading the lame. Cheyenne continued to scan the valley, first with his infrared scope and then, as the sky began to brighten, with his binoculars. Far below, where the trail up the side of the valley wall commenced, he saw movement. Six, seven, now eight figures, moving up the trail. He knew what they were looking for, and it wasn't their herd of goats.

Cheyenne pocketed the GPS and slung the binoculars around his neck and gingerly stepped as deftly as he could over the craggy ground to follow Jason and Childress. Thinking back to the Samarra incident Cheyenne was determined not to lose anyone else under his command. This is why I hate working with anyone else, he pondered; if I get it, it's me and only me. But if others get it, I feel responsible.

It didn't matter that the ultimate responsibility might lay somewhere else, like with whoever had ordered him on this mission, had ordered him to take the new recruit, and had ordered Childress to make the pickup.

It didn't take long to catch up with the two limping soldiers. Cheyenne tried to urge them on, calculating that at the pace they were moving the people following them—Pakistanis, Haqqanis, Al-Qaeda, whoever the hell they were, would be on top of them in a few minutes, and they'd be nowhere near the meadow.

"Jason! Here, take this." Cheyenne handed Jason the GPS responder. "Keep it on now—they'll find you."

Cheyenne stepped ahead of the others and motioned them forward, trying to urge a faster pace.

"Are you sure someone's coming?" Jason asked, nearly breathless. With Childress hanging onto Jason, the two men struggled to keep up with Cheyenne.

"They'll come. The colonel won't forget us, even if he has to steal a chopper and fly it himself. I may be late; don't wait for me if it's getting hot. Now move out and I'll catch up later."

"Whaddya mean, don't wait?" Jason stopped and turned as Cheyenne headed back in the direction from which they had come.

"Where you going?" the kid asked, his voice shaking with apprehension.

"They catch us in the open that chopper won't have anybody to pick up except corpses. I can hold them off from the cave. You've got your hands full with Childress. Now move your butt, soldier!"

"Then you should take this, so we can find you later!" Jason yelled, holding the GPS out.

Cheyenne waved him off. "No, get going! That's an order!"

He wasn't being stupid, nor heroic, or particularly brave, either. Cheyenne wanted Jason to get his ass moving because if they all tried to stay together, with no substantial cover between where they were and the meadow, they'd likely all die. But Cheyenne knew that the cave would give him a good opportunity to hold off an entire platoon, if not more, assuming he had enough ammo. A little help from an Apache gunship before his ammo ran out would be appreciated, so with a little luck, once Jason and Childress made it to safety, they would lead the Apache to find Cheyenne. It'll work, Chief, no? Yeah, keep telling yourself.

Back at the grotto Cheyenne reclaimed his position at the entrance and peered through the binoculars. The trail wound along the side of the hill like a desert sidewinder. And the people hiking up the trail were as deadly as any rattlesnake. Maybe worse, because they had a penchant for killing for fun, not only in defense.

He eagerly scanned the part of the trail he could see, estimating where the snaking group would be...the next bend, or...? He saw the first man, then the second as they appeared around the curve of the valley wall, hugging the cliffside, moving carefully but steadily along the narrow path.

It was the second man in line who caught Cheyenne's eye. The man looked familiar, but at this distance Cheyenne couldn't be positive. The group disappeared from sight as it reached the next bend in the trail. Cheyenne would have to wait until they came into view again. He used the time to search in other directions, just to be sure there were no surprises coming from anywhere else.

As the line of men came into view again Cheyenne stared intently until he was sure. There could be no mistake—the face he now saw in his binoculars was a face he had burned into his memory, a face he could never forgive or forget. It was ab-Hawsawi! The traitor who had caused the deaths of the three men under Cheyenne's command, many months ago, all those many miles ago, back when Iraq was the stage.

Cheyenne raised his rifle, the desire for revenge almost overtaking him. Then he stopped, realizing he'd give his position away too soon, warning the enemy and giving ab-Hawsawi's buddies a chance to take cover. He might get ab-Hawsawi, but not his comrades, and they would, with the patience of three thousand years of ancestral culture, outwait Cheyenne, get reinforcements, until one by one they crawled up the trail, and found a way to get behind him. No, he needed to wait until he could get them in the open, take down three or four of them before they knew what was hitting them.

My God, ab-Hawsawi! This is why I'm here, this is why I came back. Selfish, yeah, so sue me, he said, arguing the case in his head. This becomes my mission now, and it's going to be him or me, and to hell with the consequences. Spiedel will be both pissed and will understand; more pissed probably if I don't make it back and he's got to fill out a dozen reports explaining what the hell I was doing taking on a private war. But, shit, if I don't make it back, no one will ever know I was laying for ab-Hawsawi. Hey, Jason can put me in for one of those goddamn medals! Yeah, send it to Di with my love. Okay, man, be cool, concentrate.

Cheyenne checked his weapon one more time. The modified M24 wasn't scheduled to be issued en masse until late in the year, but a few had been procured to get some actual field use and for feedback. Cheyenne had already shown that he was accurate with it, and with the extended range he could shoot from a distance too far for enemy retaliation. But it wouldn't do any good if they had solid cover.

There was a wide section of the trail that opened into what was almost a glade, a circular recess, roughly twelve hundred yards away, Cheyenne estimated. At that point, if they are careless the entire group should come into view. That's when I'll hit them, Hawsawi first, if I'm lucky.

The rifle used five round detachable magazines. Not exactly what's needed for rapid fire against a far superior force, but Cheyenne was quick and could easily handle magazine replacement without looking. In training he was faster and more accurate than his instructors. He set several magazines next to him, though he didn't expect to need too many shots.

The sun was above the horizon now and the rays felt good on his face. He was still chilled and damp from the night's rain and the heat made him feel near human for a moment. In the sky he spied several hawks on the hunt for breakfast. Yeah, breakfast would be nice, like steak and eggs, OJ, and coffee; hot, dark coffee. This time tomorrow, with luck.

He looked back to where he'd last seen Jason and Childress, but of course they were no longer in sight. He checked his watch and calculated that the chopper should be arriving in about thirty-five minutes; he hoped the two gimps could get there in time.

You know, Cheyenne Smith, this could be your ticket out. Spiedel keeps telling me one more mission, and every time he gives me the chance to say, 'no mas.' But if I can get Hawsawi, I can leave, and not feel any guilt; not feel I've left something undone. Time to move on and make amends to Di for cutting out on her, if she'll give me the chance.

What an asshole I am. Got myself drunk again, started a fight. Hell, I have no idea how I got home, but I suppose Mac called Di and she came for me. Serves me right if she's gone for good once I get home again…once I can start a life span again.

A body appeared around the curve entering the wide section of the path, the most vulnerable spot for anyone attempting to keep their presence unknown. Cheyenne crouched back and down at the cave entrance and watched the lead man step into the opening and then halt. The man studied his surroundings, looked up at the ridgeline, down and all around, every which way possible.

The lead man, like all the others, was dressed in layers of clothing, bundled against the early morning chill. With scarves wrapped around their necks and what to Cheyenne always looked like a hat made of rags, (hence the derogatory nickname, 'ragheads'), they looked more like peasants than dangerous soldiers. That is, until one noticed the AK-47s they carried. More than likely they also each had another gun buried amongst the layers of clothes, along with a knife or two.

Cheyenne hunkered as low as he could, swiveling his hips and legs to move dirt, digging himself in until only the top of his head and his rifle poked above the rim of the grotto entrance. His hair was black, his forehead was dark from dirty sweat, his clothes were covered with dirt, and the rifle bore was granite gray. Even the sharp-eyed hawks floating on the currents above couldn't spot him. Cheyenne hoped the men weren't so cautious as to have each clear the area before the other entered. They had to worry about being in the open, but

125

also about the chance of an ambush on the other side, where one or two men handy with a knife could quietly take them out one by one without the following men hearing anything.

After a full minute of eyeballing the surroundings, the point man decided it was safe. He turned and waved his compatriots forward. They moved slowly, one, two, three...finally there were seven in the glade. They all stopped, and began to chat. The trail had been uphill to this point and it was a place to rest, have a smoke or a bite of cheese and bread, a sip of water.

Ab-Hawsawi was standing in back of one man and Cheyenne did not have a clear shot at him. He aimed at the man in front of ab-Hawsawi, made an estimate of the distance and wind, and made the adjustments automatically, without a conscious calculation. His finger squeezed the trigger ever so gently.

Cheyenne's aim was slightly off and the bullet entered the man's shoulder, knocking him down but not killing him. Worse, as he fell backwards he knocked ab-Hawsawi down, out of sight of Cheyenne's view. He had no shot at his primary target. The sniper instantly recalculated, adjusting slightly to compensate for having hit the first man lower than he'd intended, and fired again. This time Cheyenne's aim was perfect and he saw a second man take a hit in the chest, certainly fatal. A third target was also quickly disposed of by the .300 Winchester Magnum cartridge exploding in his chest.

Cheyenne had no time to relish his success; his main target was ab-Hawsawi, but he couldn't see him. If the traitor was smart, and Cheyenne assumed he was to have survived this long, he was crawling low to the ground. Cheyenne wanted ab-Hawsawi more than anything, but he also wanted to get as many of the seven as he could before they retreated. He fired again and again, changed magazines and aimed again but they were gone, except for three bodies that lay in the dirt. One had crawled off, the first man who had been wounded in the arm, and one bullet had apparently missed completely. So much for my perfect score, Cheyenne considered. Ab-Hawsawi had escaped, so far.

Three were certainly dead, and one was certainly incapacitated. That left three or four, unless they there are more of them working their way up the trail. Cheyenne doubted that they'd give up easily, but as long as he kept the glade in sight, they weren't going to be able to do anything soon. Cheyenne began to think that if his pursuers stayed back, assuming he is still there, he could leave now and reach the rendezvous point in time, before they realized he was gone. But then he wouldn't get ab-Hawsawi, and he might never get another opportunity. Then again, he might persuade the Apache to help.

The arms and head of a man appeared around the curve of the wall with a rifle pointing in front of him. He discharged several rounds but none of them came close to Cheyenne. They

127

haven't a clue as to where I am, Cheyenne realized, but are trying to get me to give away my position. No, sweetheart, not unless you stick your ugly mug out a little more, so I can send you to Allah-land.

The shooting stopped and Cheyenne continued to lay still. The man turned and appeared to be talking to someone in back of him, someone out of sight. Reluctantly the man entered the open space and gingerly stepped forward, fear tattooed on his face, his lip and mustache quivering. From behind him another rifle appeared. Cheyenne saw it all and knew that the first man was a sacrificial lamb; draw fire and the others will have a direction to aim at.

But they don't realize how far away I am. I doubt they have anything that can reach me even if they spot my location. So, lamb, here we go. First, Cheyenne fired at the curve of the wall, at the rifle sticking out. Chunks of rock flew off the wall, which caused the man hiding there to recoil, while the man in the open turned to run for cover. He never made it.

Now, Cheyenne decided, they should be scared enough that they'll stay hidden for a while, before they decide on their next move. So it is time for me to move my ass. Cheyenne crawled for the first twenty yards, tearing his clothes and accumulating dozens of scratches, but he wanted to be absolutely sure that if anyone was brave enough to stick his head out, they couldn't spot him. Then, Cheyenne stood up and broke into a run, his goal the rendezvous at the meadow.

Had he waited one more second to stand up he would have never stood up again. The bullet came so close it nicked the pant leg of his filthy uniform. Cheyenne hit the ground again, surprised more than injured. He recovered quickly as a second bullet kicked up dirt and pebbles just inches from his face. He dashed back to the cave as several more bullets rained down towards him, thanking his stars that whoever was on his ass was a lousy shot.

Glad these guys didn't get sharpshooter training like I did, Cheyenne thought as he scrambled to safety. The attack had come from above and behind him. Somehow, on a trail he could not spy from his position, the Haqqani, or whoever they were, had slipped behind him. Now Cheyenne was nicely trapped.

***

SEVEN

"I'm gonna die in Casablanca...it's a good place for it."...Rick to Ilsa (Humphrey Bogart to Ingrid Bergmann), in *Casablanca.*

Dear Diary:

WE STOPPED FOR the night at a motel off of I-10 a few miles west of Sonora, Texas, the town where Helen and I almost went to the big corral in the sky. What is it about Texas that keeps trying to kill me?

There aren't any decent-size towns after El Paso for over two hundred miles, until Fort Stockton, so originally I suggested we aim for there. Helen mumbled something and went back to sleep. I don't mind driving, especially since it's my wheels, but she could have at least offered.

When we neared Fort Stockton it was still light, so I kept on going, in the groove now and with Helen dozing I figured why stop and wake her. A couple hours later we neared Sonora; we'd covered almost 700 hundred miles and I had TB: tired butt.

Helen stirred from her nap, grumbling.

"Oh, God I'm stiff. I don't know why Rock likes to drive so much. It's so uncomfortable."

I looked at her as she opened wide with a yawn that reminded me of a hippo I'd seen on a nature program.

"Is that why you wanted to ride with me, Helen? To show Rock you were tough?"

She shrugged and rubbed her eyes. "Where are we?"

"Near Sonora, deep in the heart of Texas."

"I wanted to find out who you are."

"Say what?"

Helen hesitated, as if gathering her words into a coherent paragraph. For the first time she looked slightly fragile, not as assured of herself as when I first met her.

"I remember an incident, when I'd been working for Rock for only a few weeks. I was in his office, discussing something, when he got this telephone call. It was you."

"Me? Really?"

"I didn't know who you were at the time, but I remember him beaming as he said, 'Hey, Di, how are you?!' He seemed elated to get a call from you.

"He waved me out of the room. He said he had to take this call and to come back in few minutes.

"So every five minutes for the next half hour I peeked in. Each time he was still on the phone and the grin had not left his face. You two must have been having a great conversation."

I smiled, remembering how we had joked and laughed about our drive to the east coast, and the return trip, talking about the things that had happened, some of which hadn't been funny at the time, but were in retrospect.

"Finally he got off the phone and I went into his office. The way he was smiling you'd think he'd won the lottery. I didn't say anything, after all, I hardly knew him and his personal calls weren't any of my business. He grinned and said, 'Young friend of mine, in Arizona.'

"Then we went to work but his mind seemed to stay on the phone call for a long time. I knew he'd been talking to a woman; a guy doesn't smile and gush and talk so long to a guy buddy. But I also knew he'd lost his wife recently and I was sure he wasn't seeing anybody."

She hesitated then, maybe wondering what I knew about her relationship with Rock.

"That was long before Rock and I were...before we knew each other better," she said, turning to look at me, letting me know, Rock's is my guy, girl.

As we rolled into the motel parking lot Helen said it looked awful; to me, it looked a bit like home, sweet, home, Dry Hole, except with a lot more neon signs. The motel was brightly lit and there were dozens of cars in the lot, so it was either popular or, just as likely, one of the few places for miles around for weary travelers. West Texas is an awfully big place, and it can be many miles from one rundown town to the next.

Fortunately, Helen suggested separate rooms. I'd spent enough time with her today and the last thing I needed was to listen to her yak all evening while she filed and painted her nails.

Helen insisted on inspecting our rooms before we agreed to stay, a request that threw the clerk for a loop. The rooms looked clean and might even have been vacuumed today, so Helen was appeased.

We hadn't stopped for lunch so Helen and I agreed to go out for a meal before we settled in for the night. Hungry as I was, once I took off my shoes I didn't want to put them on again today.

Okay, grandkids, if you exist and are reading this, don't stop now, because this is where it gets exciting. It turned out to be quite an adventurous evening. Too adventurous; shoulda stayed in our rooms and called out for pizza.

As I write this I am sitting in a hospital room keeping Helen company. Well, not quite, since she's asleep and has no idea I'm still here. She has a probable concussion, possible broken leg, and a gash in the other leg where the bullet from her cute little gun nicked her (fortunately, the bullet didn't enter her leg), a sprained wrist, and multiple contusions, bruises and bumps. Reminds me of Chey when we got smacked by the truck last year. Me, I'm fine with only a cut lip, bruised ego, and a ruined blouse. I started writing this while I waited for the report on Helen, so I may as well finish before I go back to my motel room. Oh, and I probably should call Rock, even if it is late, and hope he'll take my call this time.

WE ATE DINNER at a coffee shop less than a mile from our motel. Nothing great, nothing bad, just something to fill the tummy without needing an Alka-Seltzer afterwards. When we returned to the motel I couldn't find a parking spot near our rooms so I had to park about twenty yards away, right by the stairs. No big deal, but as we exited the car I had this funny feeling, like a tingling...a sixth sense...a snap of a memory of when those two cowboys were standing by my room...but they were okay, so it must be nerves, right?

I had reached back into the car to grab my purse, and by then Helen was a few paces ahead of me. I heard her say something, a syllable, an "Oh!"

"What'd you say?" I asked. Then I saw her looking at something in the shadows under the staircase that led to the second floor of the motel. She was holding her hands in front of her chest, as if in defense. Two hulks came out of the shadows and towered over us. I'm not short, but these guys were basketball players.

One was blond, I could see from the curls hanging out from under his hat, with a mustache and a big grin, wide and toothy. He wore a gun and holster on one hip and my first thought was that we were going to be robbed at gunpoint. But he briefly reminded me of the tall blond guy I saw with his buddy, a stubby guy, at the pizza place, and they didn't do anything other than ogle me.

The other guy was a bit shorter, but wider, darker, and his grin was the kind you see on pictures of serial killers after they've been captured, and the people who knew him said, 'He was always such a good kid; wouldn't hurt a fly.'

The shorter and stockier one, still taller than me and with a mean face, not handsome at all like his partner in crime, the tall blond, moved to block us from going forward, while the tall one stepped right into my face and put his big paw on my left breast. Helen, standing besides me, grunted or something—I wish she'd burst out a wild scream, but how can I blame her when I didn't scream either—and tried to run, but Stocky grabbed her arm with one hand and covered her mouth with his other hand.

"What's the matter, honey, don't you want to have some fun with us?" He giggled like a maniac.

I reached towards Blondie and grabbed his ~~test..tects~~...oh, I can't spell that word!...his balls, and squeezed...he yelped and let go of me...he wasn't sure what to do...I think he was afraid that if he tried to grab my arm I'd squeeze tighter—and I would have.

"You like squeezin' my tits, buddy, how's this for squeezin', hey?" And I held tighter, not that I was enjoying it, mind you.

In the mean time Helen wiggled loose and began to run away, heading for the farther staircase (her room was on the second floor, I was on the first). I couldn't believe she was abandoning me!

With her gone Stocky turned his attention to me. He spun me around, causing me to loose my grip on Blondie, who sank to his knees on the pavement and let out a sorrowful groan. Stocky ripped my shirt and buttons went flying.

"Ooh, real nice!" he cackled.

He slapped me and I tasted blood in my mouth. Then he twisted my arm and held tight to my wrist, really hurting me. I'm not sure why I still hadn't screamed...guess I was too shocked.

Then Stocky pulled me towards him and shoved his evil snout in my face, getting ready to kiss me! Ugh, I could see the brown tobacco stains on his teeth and smell his sickening, bitter breath.

It reminded me of when Chey tried tobacco. First it was cigarettes, because that was what the guys were doing. But the smoke irritated Chey's eyes, so he faked it. He'd hold a cigarette like he was James Dean, let the ash get long, tap on it to knock the ash off, bring the cig to his face and pretend to puff on it, then let it burn some more. He got bored quickly so he gave up trying to fake it and didn't hang around when the guys went to their secret smoking place. He didn't care if they teased him; he was already the star pass receiver of the football team. Lucky thing too, because one day a whole bunch of them got caught and were suspended for one game. Chey had to play quarterback and threw three TD passes but we lost anyway.

Then he decides he'll be a real cowboy, a chaw-chewin', shit-kickin', ball-breakin', bronco-bustin' cowboy, and chew and spit tobacco. He got some from Bull, the old chief...now Bull, he could chew that stuff all day long and spit it ten feet like a laser beam and knock a horsefly out of the air...I swear, I've seen him do it!

But Chey's breath stunk and his teeth looked like they were all rotten with bits of tobacco leaves stuck in between so I refused to kiss him or even let him get close to me. Took him a whole month (which made me wonder how much he loved me), before he took me seriously and quit chewin'. Even then, I had to drag him to the store and make him buy a bottle of Listerine and gargle six times a day for a week before the stench went away and I'd kiss him again. He's never, far as I know, lit a cig or chewed a chaw since then, tho how the hell do I know what vices he's picked up in the Army—best I don't know, I suppose.

So anyway, Diary, where was I? Oh, yeah, Stocky tried to kiss me so I spat into his face, as a big a wad of goop as I could rustle up, right between the eyes! Shit, that made him mad!

For a second I knew I was going to die. I'd never get the chance to be jilted at the altar. I'm gonna die far from home and Chey won't even know it until my bones have crumpled to dust. Then came the clatter from the staircase, then the clunk of something falling, then the bang, like a gunshot! That got all of our's attention.

The bang was immediately followed by a scream, another clunk, and then groans. It was Helen who screamed...finally, one of us had the wherewithal to scream. But it wasn't out of fright...hey, she had run off, but to her credit she came back...it was because she tripped and came tumbling down the stairs, head over heels! Damn high heels!

"Oh, my God, oh, Dinah, help, I think I shot myself! God, it hurts," Helen called out as she lay crumpled at the bottom of the stairs, a gun lying by her side. She must have retrieved it from her room and was coming back to rescue me. I didn't even know she had a gun with her. She looked like a hundred pound sack of potatoes, lying there as helpless as a newborn.

The scream pierced the resolve of our attackers. It was like Janet Leigh in *Psycho*; scared the stuffing out of all of us! People in the next county must have heard it and jumped. Blondie, still kneeling on the ground holding his hands between his legs, squeaked, "Let's vamoose, Mick." Yes, he did say 'vamoose.' I hope he never gets his voice back.

The two varmints ran off towards the far end of the parking lot and I scurried over to where Helen lay moaning like a sick kitten. I mean, I knew she was hurt, but her groans were really obnoxious. Her left leg was twisted beneath her; she wasn't going to be frolicking on 'Dancing With the Stars' anytime soon.

I heard tires squeal and turned to see a mud-splattered pickup truck bounce over the parking lot curbs and into the street, then shoot away with a squeal and a roar. The side of the truck carried the name '...Hauling Service'...(I think...the truck was so dirty I couldn't read the first word...was it Mick? Or Nick? Didn't Blondie call the stocky one Mick?).

Someone must have heard the commotion and called the police because no more than fifteen seconds after the pickup truck tore away, a squad car careened into the parking lot, blue and red lights spinning and spraying a discothèque pattern on the walls of the motel. (I found out later it had been Helen who called the police from her room, so she wasn't as panicked as I thought). I waved to them and two cops came running over, with guns drawn! Geez, the Wild West again!

"For God's sakes, Marshal Dillon, they went thataway!" I yelled, pointing in the direction the truck had gone.

"She needs help," I added, in a more normal tone of voice, not wanting to irritate the policeman. I looked at the sad bundle on the ground.

"Would you please call an ambulance?" I asked, trying to sound forceful but not too angry.

I stood there in my most commanding posture, one hand pointing at the two cops, the other down at Helen. One of the cops hesitated, then tipped his hat and said, "Yes, Ma'am", and ran back to his car. The other just stood there and stared. Then I realized...

I was standing there, in charge, shoulders back, head high, chest out...oh, yeah, chest out, my shirt torn to shreds, doing my best Maidenform commercial!

"Ma'am, would you mind stepping back," the other policeman said, a polite order if I ever heard one.

I did, but I did it defiantly, more of a tactical redeployment rather than a retreat. I wanted to cover myself but stood there, two of my better features keeping him distracted; I hoped it gave me an edge, I mean, he wouldn't shoot a half-naked woman, would he?

Then I saw what had made him nervous. It was the gun lying on the ground next to Helen. It was a small thing, one of those 'purse pistols' with a small caliber, one that wouldn't do much damage except at point blank range. That was the source of the bang that had startled everyone, flustered our attackers and saved us from further damage. What I noticed in particular was that the darn thing was pink! A pink pistol!

The policeman stared at me, decided I wasn't dangerous, (or just liked what he saw), gazed down at Helen, looking pitiful, and at the same time he and I both noticed a dark, damp spot on her leg and something dripping onto the pavement. Helen had shot herself when she fell down the stairs and was bleeding!

"Uh, oh, excuse me, ma'am," the staring cop said. He put his weapon away and stooped down to help Helen, tho he did take one more peak before I was able to pull what was left of my shirt over my nearly bare front.

He was a young man, the policeman, not any older than me. His nametag spelled 'O'Keefe'. After he holstered his gun he took his jacket off and made a pillow of it for Helen. He appeared to scrutinize Helen's wound and must have decided it wasn't very serious. Using a pen from his pocket he picked up the gun by its barrel and put it a plastic bag—just like on TV!

"Are you in pain, ma'am?" he asked Helen. Probably a dumb question. Then to me he asked, "Did you see who did this?"

"She fell down the stairs. She ran off when those two hoodlums jumped us, then she was coming back...to help, I think. Looks like she shot herself. I didn't even know she had a gun. A pink one, too, isn't that cute?"

"Yes ma'am, it's a Taurus 738. Light weight, lots of women like to carry it because it fits easily in their purse."

""Hmmm. Maybe I'll have to get me one those, but not pink. Color doesn't suit me."

"Ma'am. You mentioned two hoodlums?"

"The two who took off in that dirty pickup; I don't know how you could've missed them. I think one of them was named Mick...or Nick."

"Did they...assault you, ma'am?"

I looked down at my tattered shirt and curled my lip.

"Do you need...are you hurt, other than..." he pointed at my mouth. I wiped a finger over my lip and saw the red. I'd forgotten my own injury once Helen came tumbling down the stairs and screamed.

"It's just a bruise," I said. "If it's okay with you I'm going to go to my room and clean up."

He nodded, but Helen mumbled, "No, wait with me Dinah."

Just then the ambulance drove up and two paramedics rushed out and knelt at Helen's side. They quickly went to work and I slipped away to my room. I motioned to Officer O'Keefe where I was going, pointing to the door of my room, a short distance past where Helen lay. He returned the nod and added a smile.

"I'll wait for you ma'am, and drive you to the hospital. I'll also need a statement...when you're ready, that is."

In my room, before anything else, I whipped off the remains of my shirt and threw it into the trashcan. I even wanted to throw my bra away since it'd been soiled by the grip of...that bastard...but it was the only one I had with me...bad planning, girl. I'll need to buy a new one in San Antonio. I didn't think it was a good idea to go braless to the hospital, especially with Officer O'Keefe keeping tabs on me.

I stood in front of the sink and examined my bloody lip, winced at mussed hair, and I began to sob. Then I got the shivers and broke out in goose bumps the size of marbles, I swear. I wrapped my arms around myself and squeezed until I forced the tears and shivers away. Needed several big sniffles, too, real honkers. I must have used up half a box of Kleenex. This wouldn't have happened if Cheyenne hadn't left me. Immediately I realized that was an unreasonable notion, because even if Chey hadn't run off in a lurch when he had, by now his leave would have been over and he would have returned to duty.

I'd hate to have to start carrying a gun everywhere I go; what the hell's going on out there? Maybe living in Dry Hole, away from civilization, is a smart thing to do. I can't remember the last time there was a crime in Dry Hole, unless you count spittin' on the sidewalk or when a few of those cowboys get their dander up from too many beers and throw a mug at the picture of Geronimo. And I'd stake that most of them are tougher than Blondie and Stocky, but they don't strut around like John Wayne rootin' for a shootin'.

I turned on the cold water and splashed several hands full into my face. My lip was swollen and sore, but the bleeding had stopped. I combed my hair and rinsed my mouth with warm water. I put on a clean shirt, blew my nose again, and went back to see how the medics were doing with Helen.

Officer O'Keefe (the cop who had fallen in love with my torn shirt) was standing right outside my door, waiting patiently, I assumed, for me, protecting me against further violations. Gary Cooper couldn't have been more polite.

"They've taken your friend to the hospital. My partner and I will drive you if you'd like, and we can take your statement there."

"How'll I get back?"

"We'll bring you back here when you're ready, ma'am."

"Please; I'm not your mother, nor your aunt; my name is Dinah...Dinah Russell, Officer. What's your name?"

"Ah, it's Jared O'Keefe, ma'am...I mean, Ms. Russell."

I laughed. "Okay, Jared, let's go."

Diary: I'm back in my motel room, sipping a merlot and writing more notes on this evening's activities. I even made Officer O'Keefe (Jared) stop at a liquor store because I knew I needed something to help mellow me. Now he probably thinks I'm a lush! I'm sure the storeowner was taken aback by a cop coming in to buy a bottle of wine at near midnight! Hope the poor dear (Jared) doesn't get in trouble.

While I waited at the hospital the police went looking for the guys who assaulted us. They stopped a truck that fit my description, and Jared said it was driven by a local rancher named Mick Canfield. Along with him was a fellow named Bud Johnsen, a blond long-drink-of-water.

"Did he speak with a high-pitched voice?" I asked.

"Huh?"

"Never mind." I hadn't mentioned what I'd done to Blondie. Officer O'Keefe might think it wasn't ladylike of me.

"They deny even being near the motel," Officer O'Keefe said. "They said they'd been at a pool hall on the other side of town, and their friends would vouch for them." He shrugged. "Probably so; Mick and Bud are cousins, and both their Daddies are fairly well-known and well-off ranchers. We bring them in and they'll have a lawyer there before you can drink a cup of coffee."

"You mean these juvenile delinquents can get away with assaulting two women?"

"No, ma'am...I mean, Ms. Russell, I'm not sayin' you shouldn't press charges, I'm just tryin' to tell you the realities."

"Which are?"

"Which are that if you want us to bring them in and put them in a lineup, we can do that, but you'll have to be prepared to stick around here, and then, if you ID them you'll have to plan on coming back here for the trial. And they'll probably get off anyway because they'll have friends who will insist they were playing pool at the time of the assault."

"What about their names? I heard the tall one call the other Mick, and you said one of them is named Mick."

"Yeah, and you also said it could have been Nick. And there are three or four Micks and Nicks I can think of, and certainly a few more around. But don't let me discourage you..."

"Oh, don't fuss, Jared, I understand. And I do have to get going. It doesn't seem right tho; those boys may go on doing the same thing until they hurt someone real bad."

"There's few things we can do, you know, to let them know we're on their case."

"Such as?"

"For one thing, I noticed that the license plate of Mick's truck was covered with mud. I didn't ticket him, but I could. I also noticed that one of the brake lights was out. There's another ticket. And I know Mick tends to speed, so I can keep an eye out for him."

"You think traffic tickets are going to reform these guys?"

"No, but that and a little conversation with Mick's Dad, who I happen to know is not happy with his son's philandering, might make the family take things more seriously. I mean, the old man would insist his lawyers get the boys off, but he'd have his own way of dealing with them, likely harsher than we can."

"Well, I don't want to interfere with the local police, Officer O'Keefe. You do what you think is best."

"Yes, ma'am. So, you're heading where? Maybe you can give us an address if I...if we need to get in touch, Dinah."

My goodness, he's flirting with me! Me, the champion flirt, and I'm getting it from some cop who can't forget the image of me standing in my bra giving him orders.

"We're heading to San Antonio to meet our, I mean her...Helen's boss. He's there at a business trade show."

"Do you work for this fellow in San Antonio?"

"Yes, no, I don't, not yet, but she does. And he's from San Diego, not San Antonio, and I'm from Dry...from Tucson,

146

but we, Helen and I, met in San Diego and we're on our way to San Antonio...well, it's a little confusing."

"Are you continuing on to San Antonio, or going back to Tucson? Or San Diego?"

"I guess I should call Rock first, find out what he wants me to do."

"Rock? Who's Rock?"

"My boss. I mean, her boss, in San Antonio, the guy from San Diego."

"Ah, okay," Jared looked confused.

"Sort of like a Cary Grant comedy, I guess."

"A what?" he asked.

"Never mind. Look, let me talk to you tomorrow. I'll be here to check on Helen."

He smiled, but I think it was a smile of confusion, rather than of fondness.

Anyway, that's the way I remember our conversation. Then he and his partner drove me here (my motel). I took a long shower, not because I was dirty, but I wanted to wash away the idea of those creeps touching me; it was as if the mere scent of them permeated my body, and I had to scrub to get rid of their essence

After toweling myself near raw I opened the bottle of wine and took a bigger swallow than I should have, and crawled in bed, and here I am. Then I realized, even tho it was past midnight, that I'd better call Rock. Might wake him up but at least he would probably accept a call from me at this time of night. Unless he'd shut his cell off.

I let it ring, waiting for Rock's message to kick in. But before the recording came on a blurry voice mumbled and grumbled.

"H'llo? Who's this?"

"Hi, Rock honey. Did I wake you?"

"Huh? Di? Di, is that you? What...where are you? Are you in Dry Rot? Are you okay? I stopped at your house in Tucson, but no one was there."

"You did? And here I thought you were avoiding me."

"Ah, heck Di, I was just dreaming about you, you know?"

"That's a crock, but it's a nice lie to hear."

"So what's happening? Wait a sec...hell, it's after midnight...I just got to sleep. Why are calling so late?"

"I'm surprised, I thought you conventioneers partied until the early hours of the morning."

"Nah, I've got a golf game at seven in the morning."

"I think you may have to change your plans."

"Why? What's up?"

"What's up is, let me tell you about Helen."

"Helen? Who Helen? You mean *my* Helen? You're with *my* Helen?"

"*Your* Helen, is she, Rock dear? Well, sweetheart, I hope you weren't planning a romantic rendezvous along the River

Walk in San Antonio, because your girl friend shot herself in the foot."

What a brat I am!

***

EIGHT

"If we weren't all crazy, we would go insane."[SIC]---from the song 'Changes In Latitudes, Changes In Attitudes', lyrics by Jimmy Buffett

CHEYENNE WAS A QUICK thinker when he was in the field. As he rapidly analyzed his present situation, the question came to mind, *why I am such a dullard in the real world?* Which was not entirely true, but lately it seemed that he did one stupid thing after another, like skipping out on Di without saying anything, just leaving a crummy note. *What a coward I am.*

But bullets zipping past one's head can force daydreams to take a back seat to more relevant issues, such as current survival. Cheyenne had backed farther into the shelter of the grotto. He figured he was still okay, as no one could get close to the entrance without him spotting them, but escape appeared to be a non-option now that the enemy was above and to the rear of him.

Of course, these guys don't seem to be the smartest tacticians on this side of town. They might band together and try to storm me; I hope they haven't got any grenades. Suicidal idiots! Trouble is, my firepower is actually less formidable than theirs is for a heads on battle.

Cheyenne's strength was from a distance, both due to the remarkable specifications of his rifle, and to his own special marksmanship skills. He needed to take out as many of the enemy as he could while he was still outside their range, and hope the Apache, assuming it had made its call at the rendezvous site, would come to his aid. If it's coming, it'll have to be soon.

He crept as close as he dared to the opening of the grotto, or hole in the wall, whatever, and spied through his riflescope in the direction of the trail. He couldn't detect any movement in the glade, so there was no telling whether the survivors had fallen back or slipped farther up the trail while he was dodging the attack from above. And he had no idea how many people were above him; could be one, could be a dozen, but that seemed unlikely.

Cheyenne's hope was that they would try to outwait him, and that should work to his advantage. If Col. Spiedel did send an Apache, it would have the firepower to knock these guys from here all the way to Islamabad.

He saw movement, a crouching figure hiking up the trail. It wasn't ab-Hawsawi, damn the luck. The man was still about 800 yards out, Cheyenne estimated, easily within his range. The baddies had AK47s, which have firepower that made Cheyenne's rifle a popgun in comparison, but their effective range was no more than 400 yards.

Cheyenne raised his rifle and sighted on his target. His intended victim disappeared behind some bushes but Cheyenne could pick out the slightest hint of a reddish color from the man's scarf. Not the best camouflage, Mohammed, Cheyenne muttered as he fired at the color. Contact! The shaking of the brush told Cheyenne he'd been spot-on. He instantly ducked farther back in the cave and as he expected, a fuselage of bullets came raining down. His worry now was ricochets.

The firing stopped after only a few shots—they probably don't want to use too much ammunition when they can't see what they're shooting at. Going to have to work your way closer, guys. Come on, Hawsawi, it's you I want, you bastard.

Cheyenne inched forward again and through the scope found the brush where his latest victim lay. He was hoping one of his buddies would come to check on him, but I think I've got them cowered now. They can't even begin to shoot at me from their distance so unless they want to crawl about a thousand yards on their bellies, they are going to have to stay put, or go back down the way they came. And if they do that, I won't get ab-Hawsawi. The thought that he should go out and force a confrontation passed through his mind, but even in his lust to avenge the men ab-Hawsawi had betrayed, Cheyenne knew that was not a smart idea. I'll be just as happy if the Apache gets him as if I get him, he told himself; okay, not *as* happy, but happy enough.

"Yeah, baby," Cheyenne muttered when he heard the sound of the helicopter, and it was an Apache, he could tell from the sound.

"They made it, yes!"

Now he needed to show his rescuers where he was without the sniper above him getting an open shot.

The Apache was a lethal weapon. It was designed primarily as an anti-tank weapon, but with its load of laser-guided missiles it was devastating against infantry, too, and could hover above trees and swoop in and out between rolling hills, ejecting its deadly load and quickly moving outside the range of enemy response.

In the sky, nearing the site of the cave, Jason directed the pilot, certain that Cheyenne would still be in the area, maybe even still holed up in the grotto. Then he saw him, Cheyenne peeking out to wave up at the helicopter. His wave elicited a response from the daring young men in the tree line above the grotto, who fired several shots at Cheyenne, at least one of which appeared to hit home, in Cheyenne's arm.

"There! You see them?" Jason called out.

"That's who we want," the pilot responded, nodding in the direction the shots had come from. The rocket exploded out from the Apache and deadlier than the surest arrow, found its target, that being the group of insurgents firing at Cheyenne. The explosion sent three men flying into the air and set the brush ablaze.

Jason was eager to jump down and help Cheyenne, but he was too high yet. Cheyenne looked up and waved, a grin on is face. His injury must not be too bad, Jason thought, smiling and waving back at Cheyenne just as the captain retreated into the grotto.

The Apache pilot circled above, scouring the hillside for more targets. The co-pilot pointed in the direction of the trail and seconds later a missile burst into the side of the valley wall, ten feet above the trail. Rocks and dirt rumbled down burying a section of the trail. At least one insurgent appeared to have gone down under the debris. Now the others would have to climb over a pile of rubble to continue on the trail towards Cheyenne's location.

With more trepidation than he cared to admit, Cheyenne stepped out from the safety of the grotto. To get ready to climb the rope ladder his rifle was strapped across his back, leaving him defenseless. He had wrapped a bandage around the wound on his left arm, not a serious injury, good enough to hold him until they got back to base.

The Apache circled and a rope ladder appeared. The chopper had to give itself enough clearance from the valley walls and the trees, so to get under the ladder Cheyenne had to step completely into the open. At this point that didn't seem to be a danger.

As the ladder unfolded in front of him, with the pilot working the controls to keep his machine hovering steady so that the ladder didn't sway too much, the co-pilot keeping a close eye for any danger from crazies foaming at the chance to take down a big bad American helicopter, Cheyenne crumpled.

No one heard the shot due to the noise of the Apache, and no one was sure where it had come from. Cheyenne tried to rise and grasped for the rope ladder, but he stumbled and fell, and began to roll down the side of the slope.

Jason watched, his mouth agape in horror, as Cheyenne rolled and rolled, unable to stop. With only one good arm he couldn't get a grip on a bush or tree limb as he continued to tumble down and down.

Cheyenne heard the swoosh of another missile, and the following explosion, and assumed the Apache had discovered who it was that had shot at him.

"There must have been at least four of those fuckers in the hills, we only got three on the first round," the co-pilot said.

"What about Cheyenne?" yelled Jason.

"We can't get to him, kid, I'm sorry."

"Set it down, I'll go for him!" Jason insisted; pleaded.

"No, no! There's no place for me to land, kid, and I can't take a chance of losing this machine and the three of us. Somebody will have to go in on foot."

"I'll go!" Jason reached for his helmet and started to climb down the rope ladder. The co-pilot reached behind and grabbed Jason.

"We've got our orders, too! To bring you back. Somebody can come back with a Kiowa—it's smaller and might be able to put down in there."

"By then it may be too late," Jason argued.

The pilot pointed at the fuel gauge. "Time to go."

"No!" Jason said, and again, but in a whisper, "no."

Cheyenne was not injured as badly as it had looked to the men in the helicopter. The bullet that knocked him down had only hit the heel of his boot.

As he was tumbling down the slope, unable to grab onto anything to stop the fall, Cheyenne worried first of all that his rifle would survive and that his ammo magazines would not fly off all over the hillside. Then he worried that the iPod would get broken; I'd hate to have to explain to Di that all her work in downloading those songs had been for naught.

Cheyenne was dazed for several seconds when he finally stopped rolling downhill. His foot felt wet and he thought it was blood. Then he realized one leg lay in water, and that was when he discovered that only the boot had been damaged, not his foot itself.

Cheyenne quickly studied his surroundings, saw nobody, and checked that his weapon was undamaged. It appeared so; he didn't want to let off a test shot lest he give away his position. Of course, by now everybody in the valley knew his position anyway, by the Apache that was still hovering above.

He waved goodbye, knowing there wasn't a place to set down, and he couldn't handle the rope ladder with only one good arm, and by now the chopper was low on fuel.

"Later!" he yelled, not expecting them to hear him, and watched the helicopter veer off and away.

The water was from a rill fed by mountains far in the distance. It wasn't much of a stream, a trickle, but enough to supply Cheyenne with a healthy drink of cold, fresh water.

The area near the rill was strewn with boulders and dead tree branches. Nearby, tall grasses, bushes and a few small trees could provide cover. He looked up the slope and gauged whether he could climb it, considering his damaged arm. The bullet had not penetrated his arm and the bleeding was negligible, but he knew the arm would not be as strong as normal. The slope was steep and rugged, and very much in the open; Cheyenne would be a pigeon in a shooting gallery if he tried to climb it in daylight.

His binoculars were gone, somewhere on the slope or still up by the cave, so he'd lost the edge they gave him in tracking his foes, although the rifle scope worked nearly as well. He didn't have much food, but the stream provided water, and if he guessed correctly Col. Spiedel would send help as soon as he heard, which he should have by now.

Without the GPS they won't know where I am if I move too far away from where they saw me fall, but I do need to find some cover. The best cover was a copse of trees a hundred

157

yards to the northeast, at a point where the stream came down from the hills. Trouble is, that may also be a watering hole for the goat herders.

The decision wasn't too difficult to make since staying put was like painting a target on his chest and saying, here, take your best shot. So Cheyenne began to hike to the copse of trees, his head swerving as he walked, watching for anything or anybody. The Apache may have forced the remainder of ab-Hawsawi's group to hunker down in a cave, but they could come skulking back once they realize I didn't get away. Ah yes, the life of a sniper.

I wonder what they'll say when I don't return? Missing in action again? Maybe Di can collect insurance on me a second time; at least I'm good for leaving her money, if nothing else.

The sun was large and yellow in the sky, and the heat it sent down warmed Cheyenne and began to dry his uniform, still damp from last night's rain. It was a camouflage fatigue uniform, and in keeping with Delta Force policy, it carried no markings on it of any kind. No unit designation, no rank, not even Cheyenne's name. He carried no ID of any kind and if captured he had memorized a phony name and ID number he was to give to his captors, that is, if they didn't shoot him first before they wasted time with questions.

Walking along the stream with the sun shining on him Cheyenne felt happy and secure, as if he hadn't a care in the world, a feeling he couldn't let exist for long lest he lose his concentration. Something in his memory banks reminded him of an old war film he'd seen, called, coincidentally, *A Walk In The Sun,* about a squad of soldiers in World War Two marching in the Italian countryside to a villa where the enemy soldiers maintained a stronghold. Just a leisurely walk in the sun.

The stream ran along the edge of the slope of the north side of the valley and high up on the slope, amidst the brush and wildflowers, Cheyenne could see the fading curls of smoke from where the Apache's missiles had landed. The brush and grasses were soggy from last night's rain so he wasn't worried about flames erupting.

Cheyenne stopped and scoured the slopes, ruing the loss of the binoculars. He stared at the spot from where the shots came down on him, and hoped the Apache had nailed everybody. But Cheyenne was concerned that there was a trail that led to somewhere he couldn't see from his position, somewhere from which other people who weren't big fans of Americans might pop up out of the ground.

In the sky Cheyenne saw more birds, bigger ones than the hawks. These would be the vultures, those ugly suckers who have a knack for finding carrion even before it's cold. Ugh, Cheyenne muttered, but it was an indication that the only bodies on the hillside were dead ones.

As he approached the copse he slowed his pace and listened carefully for any sounds. He heard a chirp of a bird, the faint echo of the caw of the hawks and vultures circling above, but heard no sounds of goats or sheep, any voices or dogs barking. The copse appeared to be vacant except for the birds in the trees. Cheyenne took another few minutes to scan the surroundings, especially the slopes of the hills, before he relaxed and sat down under a tree not too close to the stream. If anyone showed up he wanted to spot them before they spotted him.

All he could do now was wait and hope that if a chopper came looking for him they would search along the stream and maybe he'd get a pilot willing to get close enough to pick him up. There wasn't much room for a landing, but a Kiowa with an aggressive pilot might provide Cheyenne a chance to hop on. If he could muster the strength.

Cheyenne wanted to listen to the iPod but also wanted to keep his ears focused on the sounds of the valley, and the sky, so he simply sat still for a while and vacated his mind of any thoughts. It is difficult to completely empty one's mind of activity, so eventually fragments of memories seeped into his consciousness. He now noticed the ache from his wounds, but at least nothing was bleeding.

Right now I wish so much I hadn't skipped out on Di without talking to her. It was a thought that had been snapping at him for days, one he'd tried to ignore because it got in the way of his work, but it kept coming back, much like the yearning a gambler feels for one more bet, or the alcoholic for just one more drink.

Dinah, his friend from when they were infants, growing up and learning together, loving together, in the confined environment of a town so small, so irrelevant, that the mapmakers didn't even note it. So insulated were they that when they went off to Douglas, to them a huge metropolis of 14,000 people, for high school, it was culture shock to see so many kids their age, but kids who were so much more sophisticated.

Yeah, sophisticated; they knew all the four letter words, they knew all the popular songs and TV shows, they had steadies, knew where to get beer, and they teased Cheyenne and Dinah as being small town hicks, and in Cheyenne's case, some of these sophisticated kids didn't like people with Indian blood in them.

It took an entire year and a few scuffles before either of them felt comfortable. Until then they had clung to each other, and in a way, they became 'steadies', and an item among the other students. Cheyenne became a star athlete, and Di overcame her initial wariness of the crowded school to get involved in a variety of activities and eventually became as popular as any girl in the school.

All the guys were afraid to ask Di for a date because she belonged to Cheyenne. Heh, Cheyenne smiled to himself at the memory. I wanted to date other girls, but had to do it on the sneak, afraid Di would find out and have a shit-fit. I wonder if she ever dated anyone else behind my back?

161

But when it came down to it, they were always drawn back to each other. Children together, playmates, classmates, friends, companions, lovers (Cheyenne's first, and he was sure, Di's first, and maybe only), now supposedly fiancés, but hell, who knows any more?

Whenever we talked, it was always about the things we would do together—get married, have a family, la di da, what else is there? We never gave much consideration to where we'd live. We'd always been in Dry Hole, and until we visited any of the larger towns around, like, whoopee, Douglas, I don't think either of us considered there'd ever be any place to live but Dry Hole.

And then, one day, I looked around and saw that Mom and Dad were gone, Di's Dad was gone and her Mom had lost her mind, and Dry Hole looked like the worst possible, the most fucked up and dreary spot on the planet earth. It sucked big time and I had to get out, with or without Di.

And Dry Hole, for the most part, I can do without. But goddamn, I miss Di. I know, you big oaf, for a while there I felt I needed to get away from Dry Hole just because I needed to see what else the world had to offer besides sand and wind. And getting away from Dry Fuckin' Hole meant getting away from Di. So now I've seen it, and for the most part, it's more sand and wind, how smart am I?

So I got away all right, and what did I learn? To shoot people. Seems I've had this discussion with Spiedel a time or two. Some people need shooting, okay? He handles it better than I do, that's all. Hell, even if I don't get ab-Hawsawi, at least I can report where I saw him, let someone else go after him.

The world seemed peaceful with the hum of the wind in the trees, the song of the birds and the bubbling of the stream. Who'd a thunk I was stuck in a dysfunctional country so far from anything I care about that I have to wonder if I'll ever enjoy a home-cooked meal again; a grilled steak, or a slice of Di's pie? Will I ever get the opportunity to apologize to Di, and ask for one more chance with her? How many one more chances have I got?

Cheyenne decided it was safe to listen to the iPod. He set it to play John Stewart's songs, the better to think of Di, not that he needed a catalyst to think of her. Out of the blue Chey realized that Susan was suddenly gone. Not that I'll forget I knew her, as short a time as it was. But she's gone in that there's no more angst, no more infatuation, no more feeling I owe her for Johnny. I mean, I always felt it was only an infatuation, but I guess it was all caught in some weird way with my need to avenge Susan's brother.

I haven't done that yet, exactly, though for all I know the Apache may have taken ab-Hawsawi and his buddies out. But I'm okay with it, I really am.

Cheyenne put a plug in only one ear, so he'd have the other open to listen for any sounds that might signify danger.

"*You got a road of your own, your own*
You got a road of your own." *

Maybe this winding road I've been on leads back to where I left from, back to Di, back to a life with her. But no more of this life; no more soldiering once I get out of this fix. Cheyenne closed his eyes, mindful that he'd hadn't had much sleep the last three nights. The music played on in Cheyenne's head, not all of it registering as he began to doze, but enough to keep him from drifting into a deep sleep.

"*Oh, I treated you so bad, I was walkin' with my head in the clouds...*" #

He awoke with a start—that frightening feeling that he had let something happen while he was supposed to be watching, like letting the cake burn in the oven because he'd nodded off and didn't hear the oven chime.

"*Oh, I never knew what I had 'til I lost you...*" #

* from the song, 'Road Away', by John Stewart
# from the song, 'Runaway Fool of Love', by John Stewart

But a burned cake usually doesn't get one killed, unless someone else was in a particularly bad mood. Was it only a gust of wind? Cheyenne took the earplugs out and listened for sounds in the air. There, the faint sound of a dog barking, coming closer. It could be a goat or sheepherder bringing the flock to the water.

"And you can call me the runaway fool of love" #

Possibly he'd be perfectly safe but he didn't dare take the chance. Cheyenne moved deeper into the trees away from the water. He could only hope the wind would blow his scent away from the dog. Cheyenne lay down in the brush and waited.

"*Where did they go, all the good times I used to know?***

Cheyenne pulled the earplug out and shut off the iPod. He smelled the sheep before he saw them. He heard them moving closer, then heard the sound of the sheep lapping water. The dog came into view and for a second Cheyenne feared it had sensed him when it lifted its head and sniffed the air. But the breeze was blowing towards Cheyenne and the dog did not pick up the scent. One man came into view but Cheyenne couldn't know if he was the only sheepherder, or

** from the song, 'You Can't Look Back', by John Stewart

165

whether there was another. After a while the sheep were satiated, the dog was lying quietly, and the herder also sat still, his head nodding. Cheyenne let his head rest on his arm and closed his eyes. It was almost like sleeping, getting some needed rest, while his ears remained alert.

It was over an hour before Cheyenne heard the sheep stirring. He perked up and saw the herder rise, and the dog jumped up, yapped at the sheep and returned to his job of moving the flock.

Cheyenne watched the animals until they were out of sight, and after he could no longer hear the sounds of their baaing or of the dog yapping, he snuggled down into the brush and this time he allowed himself to fall into a serious sleeping mode. He'd be no good to himself later if he didn't get some solid shuteye.

At first Cheyenne interpreted the sound as a bee buzzing in his ears. He slapped at it but the sound was still there, louder now. His eyes snapped opened and at the same time he deduced the location of the noise; it was not buzzing around his head, but was in the sky. He didn't see the source yet but he knew it was a Kiowa helicopter. He didn't expect that it would be Childress again, not with his injuries, but some of these chopper pilots are wild and crazy guys.

Cheyenne stepped out of the brush slowly, his eyes searching for anything that might be a threat. He had his rifle at the ready and the holster for his .45 unsnapped. A few seconds and the Kiowa was in view, almost directly above him. Either Childress and/or Jason were there, or they'd given good directions as to where Cheyenne had last been spotted.

He waved and moved farther out into the open, almost to the edge of the stream. The Kiowa, which had continued to circle, spun around and made a diving feint. Then from inside he saw a hand wave—they'd seen him and were coming down.

The movement from the trail, the one that hugged the valley wall to the south, caught Cheyenne's eye and he froze. The movement could have been a bird, or a falling rock, even a lost goat or some other animal. He wasn't sure so he waved to the Kiowa in a motion telling them to back off.

At Cheyenne's wave gunfire sprayed the helicopter and only the fact that it had reversed its descent at Cheyenne's warning kept it from being pummeled with dozens of hits, maybe enough to bring it down.

Cheyenne hit the ground and in one motion had his rifle ready and aiming in the direction of the attack. He saw a stream of smoke and a hint of color. Those idiots with their colorful scarves make a nice target even when they think they're covered. Cheyenne fired and the shooting stopped.

Unfortunately, it started up again a heartbeat later and was aimed in Cheyenne's direction. He was too far off for their return fire to be effective and the rounds shot at him landed short, some diving into the stream or bouncing off rocks, or digging into the dirt. Still, it was prudent for Cheyenne to take the opportunity to dash back into the brush to gain some protection. He couldn't expect the Kiowa to set down under heavy attack and as long as the Haqqani kept their noses on the side of the valley wall that Cheyenne couldn't see, they could sit there all day and peck away at the Kiowa.

The helicopter was far from defenseless—it carried 7-tube hydra rocket pods and .50 caliber machine guns, and it quickly went into action. From Cheyenne's position he couldn't see the results but the Kiowa was vigorously spraying the trail and the rockets, if they did nothing else, were bringing rocks down and possibly blocking the trial.

Then he heard a burst of gunfire that he knew was from AK47s. Three men, suicidal, had run out into the open and were firing madly at the Kiowa. Cheyenne took aim and hit one of them, who went down screaming while his gun continued to expel deadly projectiles.

A second was taken out by the Kiowa, and as Cheyenne took aim again the third man turned to run. The bullet from Cheyenne's rifle hit him in the leg. He fell to the ground and Cheyenne could see the Kiowa finish him with a burst from the .50 calibers. But the helicopter had taken a hit and was spewing oily smoke at a furious rate. It began to spin and Cheyenne feared it would crash into the cliff.

Just when it looked like the rotors would scrape the cliff, which would have been deadly, the pilot gained control and spun away, the machine making an eerie, screeching noise, like the sound of fingernails on a chalkboard.

Cheyenne almost laughed at the absurdity of Childress getting shot down again, and he, Cheyenne, having to rescue him and Jason a second time. Fuckin' crazy war, I don't know how I've kept my sanity. Or have I?

But this time the pilot, be it Childress or someone else Cheyenne couldn't tell, was able to keep the chopper aloft, but it was obvious it could not attempt to land. The Kiowa had gained altitude and appeared out of danger, but as soon as it dared drop lower it was attacked by gunfire coming from somewhere, probably one of the many caves tucked into the cliff. The ugly smoke that had been spewing out had dissipated. Cheyenne didn't know enough about helicopter mechanics to know what that meant, but it seemed to be a good thing, and possibly the Kiowa could stick around and still try to pick him up. Would be nice to have a steak dinner tonight. My other choices are, water and an energy bar, or an energy bar and water.

The Kiowa climbed higher while moving west. Childress—Cheyenne had chosen in his mind to think of the pilot as Childress, even if it was someone else, wiggled a signal, which Cheyenne interpreted to mean he needed to get closer to the previous rendezvous point. Trying to land near the stream was too dangerous.

Yeah, there must be a bunch of them bastards out there. You'd think they had a personal grudge against me, just because I knocked off a few of their buddies. If they've got a nice cave to hide in, even the Kiowa's rockets won't reach them, other than with a lucky strike.

Cheyenne had a good location for any direct assault, and he had access to water, but he was almost out of food, running low on ammo, and getting awfully tired. He decided that he would attempt to climb the hill he had rolled down, hope that Childress can hang around to give him cover if he needed it, and then trek back to the pre-determined rendezvous point.

Cheyenne grasped the reality that the Kiowa would have to leave soon if it was leaking oil, and it wouldn't be able to give him cover while he tried to climb the slope, if he didn't get his sorry ass in gear, pronto.

High above him Cheyenne could see the chopper hovering, staying out of range of gunfire but hoping to be able to give Cheyenne cover if he needed it, because once Cheyenne started up the slope he'd be defenseless.

Cheyenne took a long swallow of water from his canteen, then threw it aside. He wanted to lighten his load as much as possible for the climb, so the only things he was keeping was the rifle and his sidearm and his boot knife. And of course, Di's iPod. If I'm gonna die here I want Di to know I kept her gift with me. He started up, wincing as he'd almost forgotten that his left arm couldn't take full pressure without causing pain.

The slope was steep and muddy, and there weren't many decent handholds. A scraggly little bush, a small rock, but with the mud Cheyenne slipped back a foot for every two feet he ascended. Still, he was getting there.

Already he was sweating profusely and wondered about the wisdom of leaving the canteen. If I don't make it up this slope, I'll be back down by the stream with all the water I want. Take a bath while I'm at it.

The first shot kicked up dirt mere inches from his face. For an instant Cheyenne wasn't sure if it was a bullet, or merely a falling rock. Then he heard the sound of the Kiowa's guns blazing, in the direction of the north slope, the area from which Cheyenne had been fired on previously.

At the same time he heard shooting coming from the trail, although he was sure he was still out of range. He turned to look and saw two men standing on the rubble that had been brought down onto the trail, firing their AK47s. Worse news, there were two others who appeared to be preparing to launch a shoulder-fired missile, something in the order of a Stinger.

Theoretically, Cheyenne knew, there should not be any more usable Stingers in Pakistan. They were supplied to the Mujahideen in Afghanistan during Operation Cyclone, in the 1980s, for use against the Soviets. But even those not returned would have run out of battery life long ago. Still, a version of a

Stinger missile was known to have been used by the Pakistani Army in the Kargil District of Kashmir in 1999 against India. It is thought that this homegrown version had brought down a helicopter and a Mig-21. Another possibility was that this was a version of the SA-7, a weapon fielded by the Soviet Union as far back as the 1960s. Many knockoffs of a later model, the SA-7b, have been built since then in several countries. They have been known to bring down large aircraft and could be deadly against the Kiowa. Unfortunately, nowadays, any crazy bastard could buy anything from a pistol to a goddamn submarine from some weapons supplier somewhere in the world; like a friggin' Saturday afternoon yard sale.

Unsure whether to continue climbing up or to let himself roll back downhill, where it might be safer for him, Cheyenne lay on the slope and watched the battle raging above him. The Kiowa had locked onto Cheyenne's attackers and the sniping had stopped, at least temporarily.

As the Haqqani on the trail prepared to fire the Stinger, the Kiowa spotted the danger and fired a rocket of its own and immediately swerved away and upward. The rocket found its target and Cheyenne smiled as he saw the two men and their weapon blown into the air and tumble down the side of the trail.

Cheyenne set forth to climb again but hadn't gone far when he felt a hundred bee stings hit him in his left thigh. But he knew it was a bullet. The shock of it caused Cheyenne to lose what meager grip he had and he began to slide downward. He cursed silently, using all the four letter words that came to mind.

When he hit bottom Cheyenne was dazed and couldn't get to his feet immediately. When he opened his eyes he saw the Kiowa hovering high above him and heard the continued clamor of the AK47s. The lack of heavy armor makes the Kiowa susceptible to even small arms fire so the pilot had to keeps his distance. The fact that the Kiowa was doing so and only firing back with the .50 calibers told Cheyenne it was out of rocket pods. The Haqqani could keep slipping back into their cave whenever the Kiowa got too close, then jump out, let fly a few rounds at Cheyenne, and prevent his recovery. And it appeared that each time the Kiowa backed off, one or two of the insurgents moved up the trail, getting them closer to Cheyenne's location.

Cheyenne had recovered his wits by now and he dragged himself to the copse of trees he had used as cover before. A few shots whistled through the air but did not come close to him. He was bleeding, did not have a first aid kit, it was getting dark, he knew the Kiowa was getting low on fuel, and in any case, there were obviously more Haqqani out there than he or the helicopters had estimated.

He heard a screech and looked up to see the Kiowa diving towards his position, its machine guns blazing. The rope ladder unwound and someone began to climb down. The

Haqqani had begun firing frantically as the Kiowa came into range, but with the Kiowa's .50 calibers blazing away and someone in the doorway working an M4, putting his life seriously at risk hanging out there like that, their aim was way off. Like the Keystone Kops running in mad circles in an old silent movie, the Haqqani scurried away to find protection.

The least I can do, Cheyenne decided, was provide some cover for this idiot hero. So he sprayed in the direction he'd last seen the Haqqani, even without lining up a specific target, as rapidly as he could. This gave the hero coming down the ladder an opportunity to do so without getting shot to pieces.

The man jumped the last few feet, waved up at the Kiowa, and then ran towards where Cheyenne lay.

"Nice to see you, but you must be crazy—Jason!"

"Hey, Cheyenne, how ya doin' old man?"

"God Almighty, Jason, didn't I tell you not to do anything stupid? Don't you listen to my orders?"

"You listen to me, Captain. Let's move to some cover so I can work on your leg. I brought first aid and more ammo and some food."

"Yeah, thanks, but now we're two targets instead of one. And it's getting too late in the day for another rescue attempt."

"The colonel says he'll send in a 'reconnaissance team in force,' to use his terminology, tomorrow. We just need to make it through tonight."

"You know, Jason, this reminds me of an old movie I saw once with my girl's old man."

"You mean the girl you walked out on?"

"Yeah, don't remind me."

"In this movie—it's before your time; actually, it was before my time, too. Anyway, I was only about twelve years old. Now Dinah's old man he loved movies, especially Westerns, but other kind, too. We sat at the counter of his café watching this movie.

"Until then, all the movies I'd ever seen the good guy wins. You know, the guy wearing the white hat prevails.

"One day Di's Dad shows me this movie about jet fighter pilots in the Korean War. Our hero is William Holden, a big star at one time. Mickey Rooney's in it, too. Maybe you heard of him."

Jason nodded but it wasn't a convincing nod

"No matter, they were our heroes. Cool movie; jet fighters taking off of aircraft carriers, flying high over Korea, bombing bridges; yeah, the name of the movie was *The Bridges At Toko-ri.*

"Now William Holden wasn't even supposed to be there. He gets called up out of the reserves. Sort of like Ted Williams, from what Di's Dad told me; you know, the ballplayer turned fighter pilot."

"Hmmm." Jason shrugged.

"But he goes into combat, a real citizen soldier. Now Mickey Rooney's job, he's like Childress. Flies a chopper to rescue downed pilots. They didn't have Blackhawks then, nor Apaches, not even Kiowas. But he'd fly right into a hail of bullets to rescue a pilot.

"Sure enough our hero gets shot down. He takes cover in a ditch. Meanwhile, a couple of jets are covering William Holden, strafing the commies; North Koreans, Chinese, whoever the fuck they were. But eventually the jets run low on fuel, so they've got to leave. They fly over William Holden and waggle their wigs, basically saying, 'sorry, pal, you're on your own.'

"But here's come Mickey to the rescue. Oh boy, I think, he's going to get our hero out of the fix he's in. Mickey's about to land to pick up Holden but he gets shot down, just like we did when Childress picked us up.

"Mickey has to scurry for cover and joins Holden in the ditch. Commies coming at 'em from all sides, all our boys have are '45s, and neither one of them can hit the water if they fell out of a boat. You know, they ain't infantrymen."

Cheyenne paused long enough for Jason to have to ask.

"Okay, so what happens?"

"I'm getting worried, you know. The movie's been on a couple hours so I figure it's almost over. I'm thinking the jets will return and swoop in to shoot the commies, and another chopper to the rescue; but no."

"No, what?"

"No, that's it, it's getting dark, no more rescue. Our boys get killed by the commies."

"That sucks all to hell."

"Yeah, let me tell you! It was the first time I'd seen a movie where the good guys die at the end."

"I'm just saying, I'm sort of reminded of it now."

"Great, Cheyenne. Do I say 'You're welcome,' now, or save it for later?"

"C'mon, kid, you crazy fool, wrap up my wound while I keep you covered. Then you need to stay awake while I catch some zees."

"Why is America lucky to have such men? Where did we get such men?"---Admiral Tarrant, "The Bridges at Toko-ri", by James Michener.

***

NINE

"The problems of three little people doesn't amount to a hill of beans in this crazy mixed up world"... Rick to Ilsa (Humphrey Bogart to Ingrid Bergmann), in *Casablanca*.

Dear Diary:

A FEW QUICK NOTES while I take a potty and coffee break at McDonald's. I'm only about an hour away from San Antonio so I wanted to stop and write a few lines before I get there, 'cause I don't know when I'll have time again.

I went to the hospital to see Helen this morning. She was feeling better, and worse. Better in that the shock of her fall had worn off and she was reasonably alert. Worse, because she was beginning to feel the aches and pains from her bruises and sprains. I hope she doesn't look in the mirror because she looks awful. Even her face has bruises. You name it, the color is there: blue, black, yellow, red, purple. Same with her legs and one arm.

She'll have to stay here a while and even though she's not my bosom-buddy I feel sorry for her. Bad enough to be hospitalized, but far from home and with no friends around.

"That was really something, Helen, what you did..."

"I...ah, I panicked, you know. I even forgot about my gun. I bought it for protection, and when I needed it I forgot it was there."

"You had enough sense to call 911, that's something. And you came to help me."

I sensed Helen was flattered by my showing understanding and appreciation for her actions, but was embarrassed by my attitude. I think she would have felt better if I was angry with her.

"Anyway, what you need the most is rest. And you shouldn't even be talking much."

"It's just a headache and some bruises. The doctor said the bullet wound isn't anything. Caused some bleeding but no real damage; the bullet only nicked me."

"Helen, for God's sake, your leg is broken!"

She waved at me as if broken legs were as common as headaches.

"The doctor said it wasn't a serious break. I just need to stay off it for a spell."

"By the way, the police officer from last night, Officer O'Keefe, he called and said they had found the bullet and could verify it came from the type of pistol you had. They wanted to make sure there were no other guns involved."

"Oh? Did he say anything else?"

"Yes, he asked me for my phone number."

"Dinah, you need to go to San Antonio and help Rock with the tradeshow," Helen said, her voice suddenly commanding, the near-timid voice of a few seconds vanished now that we'd done away with the formalities. A bossy lady.

"How can I help him, Helen? I don't know anything about..."

"In my briefcase is all the material you'll need. Get there today and study it. Rock can give you a crash course on our product line. You won't need to do much...did you bring some clothes other than jeans?"

"Of course."

I was insulted. I do have dresses and sweaters and blouses and I know how to wear them. I don't get many opportunities to dress like a lady, but I can garner a few wolf whistles those rare occasions I have the opportunity. Although after last night the last thing I want is to attract wolves.

"Alright, you just need to look good, Rock can explain and demonstrate all the products."

"Oh, is that it? Was that gonna be your job, to stand there and look sexy, to attract guys to stop and gawk at you, so then Rock can tell them about the latest in home security products?"

"Dinah, I am extremely capable of explaining the products myself. I don't expect you to learn how overnight, but yes, you...you're a nice looking young lady...you'll do fine. And later, if you decide to come back to San Diego, maybe the receptionist job will be open."

I lost track of how many times I felt she had either insulted me and/or patronized me. All she saw when she looked at me was a pretty good-looking young woman. Apparently she assumed I'd jump at the chance to help Rock, and if I did she'd repay me by giving me a job that even a simpleton like me could handle. Can you imagine if she and Rock got married and I was working for them, answering the phone?

"I'm sorry, Ms. Harrison is in a meeting. May I take a message please?" "I'm sorry, Ms. Harrison is on her honeymoon and is probably in bed right now with her boss. May I take a message?"

Wouldn't we have fun? Maybe they'd adopt me.

Here I am trying to express my thanks to her and she rolls over me as if I were her lackey, even as she's dealing with busted bones and a hundred bruises. I guess I should give her credit, she is a tough lady. Not Rock's type at all, but I guess he doesn't know that yet. Poor dear.

"Did you call Rock last night?" Helen asked.

"Yes, he was terribly upset," I cooed, drawing out the 'terribly' so that Helen wouldn't be sure if I was serious about Rock's reaction. He said he'd skip this afternoon's meetings and drive here to see you."

"No! Call him back...or...where's my cell phone, I'll call him."

"It's in your brief case Helen, in your room at the motel."

"Okay, you call him soon as you can. Tell him not to waste time coming here. The show is important; he needs to stay there."

She tried to sit up and groaned and held her hand to her head.

"God, where'd this headache come from? Water," Helen ordered.

I poured her a glass of water.

"Do you have any aspirin, Dinah?"

"Helen, I don't think I should give you anything. I'm sure the nurse will be here soon and give you whatever medicine the doctor thinks you need."

"Dinah, I need aspirin now. An aspirin's not medicine."

I guess if I really hated her I wouldn't have given her any, but bitchy as she was she was hurting, she had come back to help me, and for God only knows what reason, she was Rock's friend. So I gave her two aspirin.

"Concussions can be dangerous, Helen. You need to take it easy. Don't you watch football?"

She had barely gulped the pills down with a big slug of water when she continued with her orders of the day.

"My sister Sarah lives in Houston. I'll call her and tell her what happened. She'll come and stay with me until the doctor says I can leave the hospital. If they let me go before the weekend's over, Sarah will take me home. If I'm still here Monday Rock can pick me up on his way back from the show."

"Helen, I don't think you'll be leaving here for several days," I suggested.

"We'll see about that."

She may be right; the nurses might throw her out the window if she orders them around the way she's ordering me.

"You should get a move on, dear," Helen said. "You've got everything straight?"

I thought of asking her if I was on the payroll yet.

"Yes, Helen. I'll call Rock, I'll tell him not to come here, but that your sister will come to stay with you, I'll check you out of the motel, I'll take your briefcase with me, I'll go meet Rock, I'll study the trade show materials, and Saturday and Sunday I'll wear something sexy to draw in all the boys." And maybe I'll steal your man while I'm at it. No, no, Diary, I'm just being silly.

"Oh, and Rock better call Carl Mendez. And don't forget to bring me my cell phone and address book back here before you leave for San Antonio."

"Yes, right."

"Do you have nice legs?" Helen asked.

I did a double take, like, why do you care?

"Wear something with a slit, to show a lot of leg, and a low cut blouse. You've got a good figure, Dinah, show it off."

"I think I showed off enough last night."

She stared at me as if she had just realized that I, too, had been assaulted. "Sorry," she added.

I was taken aback again. I wondered if she'd ever used the word before. A sense of sadness came over me. Not only because Helen was hurt; that too, but because I think she's a lonely lady. A the same time, I also have the impression she's out to get her fangs into Rock and take his company from him. I hate it when I'm so cynical. I hate it worse when I find out I was right to be cynical.

"You sure you'll be alright here, by yourself, Helen? I could stay a while."

"Make sure you bring me my cell so I can call my sister. She'll come to stay with me."

Once Helen's sister gets her marching orders I was sure she would.

"Okay, Helen. You get some rest and do as the doctor says. I went to the side of the bed and held her hand and squeezed it softly. She pulled away.

"Don't hug me," she said. "My face feels bruised. Do I look awful?"

"No, no," I lied. "A little, but not bad." I better get out of here before she finds out she looks like she was the loser in a bare-knuckles boxing match.

On to San Antonio.

IT'S LIKE DEJA VU all over again! The first time I hooked up with Di someone was in the hospital. Then it was Cheyenne, her boyfriend, banged up in an auto accident, now it's Helen. Dumb broad, she shot herself in the leg! I knew Helen had a gun, nothing more than a popgun, and I wondered if she knew how to use it; I guess not!

So instead of sleeping I've got to figure out how to get her back home and still deal with my commitments here in San Antonio. Fortunately there's nothing too important in the morning; golf in the a.m. and a meeting in the afternoon I can skip. Tomorrow I'll need to do some final prep work for the show, but Helen was supposed to be here to help; what a mess.

I finally did get to sleep, still unsure of what to do when morning came. I awoke earlier than I wanted to because I had set the alarm so I'd be on time for golf. I felt like I'd only slept ten minutes. I delayed making a decision about what to do except to cancel golf, to the dismay of the rest of my foursome. Still, I didn't get myself moving very quickly. I wanted to speak to Di and Helen before I left for the hospital, a drive of close to three hours, just to know what was going on before I started the trip. I lay back on the bed and was instantly asleep. I didn't move for two hours.

Someone must have dropped a tray of dishes outside my door and the crash was louder than those mortar rounds that had nearly deafened me in Vietnam. I popped awake and felt dizzy. Not enough sleep, and I was blasted awake from a deep dream cycle. I sat on the edge of the bed for a minute, then called room service for a pot of coffee and toast and jam. I went to the bathroom and shaved. By the time I'd finished the coffee was here and I drank a cup as quickly as I could without burning my mouth. Then it was to the shower. I wanted to let

185

the water roll down my body for an hour but was afraid I might miss a call from Di. As I was drying off I heard my cell phone ringing, the chime the music of John Stewart's 'It Ain't the Gold'; it was Di.

She recited Helen's orders. Don't come to the hospital, call Carl at the plant (as if I needed to be told), find Di a place to stay in San Antonio, give her a crash course so she can help at the tradeshow, and, Di added in a squeaky, petty voice, 'Make sure that girl has appropriate clothes to wear to the trade show.'

"Yes, dear," I said. Who owns the business, I wondered.

"So you're driving here?" I asked, to be sure I understood what was happening.

"Dare I disobey '*She*'?"

"Now, Di, don't be snide. Helen was deeply involved in getting ready for this show, so I'm sure she's extremely disappointed."

"I just hope I can be of help, Rock."

"When are you leaving?"

"Right now; I should be there before noon. First I have to run back to the hospital to give Helen her cell phone and leave her suitcase. Maybe she'll have some more orders by then."

I ignored her last remark and proceeded to give Di directions to my hotel, then had her give me Helen's phone number at the hospital and Helen's room number, just in case I had trouble reaching her on her cell. It's awful to say this, and I was truly upset about Helen's accident, but I was now looking forward to having Di here to help. Still, I needed to call Helen.

First, I made an executive decision. I phoned the plant and asked for Dennis Willis. Dennis is a young man, not yet thirty, who came on board a few months before Helen, and knew as much about the new security systems we would be presenting at the show as anyone. He was the person I really needed, but Helen had convinced me that the two us, a man and woman, would look more affable in the booth, and that we could get along without Dennis. Besides, after the show was over we could enjoy a few leisurely days together. At the time, the idea was attractive, but it was an error on my part. Amazing how one's judgment can be clouded when making decisions while flat on your back in bed and a woman's hand is teasing the hair on your chest.

I tapped my fingers impatiently waiting for Dennis to pick up.

"Willis," he answered after the fifth or sixth ring.

"Dennis, drop what you're doing and get on the next plane to San Antonio."

"Rock? What's up?"

I told him what I knew about Helen's accident. I didn't mention that Di was coming to San Antonio; too confusing to go into right now. He didn't know who she was and I didn't have time to explain.

187

"Rock, I can't possibly get out until a late flight. I've got to meet with Phillips; you yourself said to handle him myself."

"Yes, I understand. That's fine, Dennis, take care of Phillips, but I need you here by Saturday morning to help me man the booth, so however you can manage it, just get here. Leave me a message as to your flight number and time and I'll arrange for you to be met at the airport."

Then I called the hospital.

Helen was more concerned about the show than she was about her injuries. I tried to sound upset and worried—which I was, I just didn't think I sounded like it, and the more she fluffed off my attempts to show my concern, the less I cared how I sounded. It's gratifying when an employee is dedicated to their work, but more and more Helen was beginning to sound like a co-owner, not an employee.

I wanted to end our conversation but Helen kept talking about the trade show, and what products I ought to emphasize, and how much help Dinah might be, and hopefully she won't screw things up, but if she does a decent job, Helen advised me, she might consider hiring her. Closed circuit television systems, wireless video surveillance systems, carbon detectors, flood detectors, panic buttons, laser shield systems, and of course, don't forget, dear, we want to push the systems for apartment and commercial buildings, too, more so even than the home systems.

Yes, dear, I said to myself several times. Like I don't know all this?

"And let me know how Dinah does, Rock, and don't make excuses for her. I told her she just needs to smile and look, you know, look sexy, I think she can do that, she's not a bad looking girl, and if she has on the right clothes, she'll draw a crowd and you can give your spiel...", yak, yak, yak, she went on and on.

I was sure Di was thrilled when Helen told her to smile and look cute. Some of the guys who come to these shows never sober up from the first night, but I'm sure if any of them say anything out of line to Di, or dare to accidently rub against her, they'll find out how cute she can be.

"Helen...Helen...hold on, please." After she finished one more long sentence she took a breath. I jumped in.

"Helen, this isn't a car show, it's a tech and engineering show. Di doesn't need to seduce anyone, she needs to be pleasant and friendly, and know just enough to keep someone interested until I can take over. And I think she can do that. I'll help her study all the brochures so she can at least fake a few big words, and she'll do fine.

"Besides, I already called Dennis, and he'll get here by Saturday morning."

"Oh, you did?"

It could have been my imagination but I swear she sounded put out that I—the owner of the company—would dare do such a thing.

"He knows this stuff as well as you or I. Between the three of us, we should be able to manage."

"I guess you don't need me, Rock; maybe things worked out okay?"

It was smart aleck comment and I almost replied in kind. But I clamped my mouth shut in time.

"Rock?"

"Yes, Helen, I need you here, and I'm sorry you aren't, but since you can't be, we'll do our best."

"I'm sure you will…" And she started again about how to present this, and that, or something or other.

"Are you sure you don't want me to come there?" I offered again, hoping she'd say no. I didn't want to, but truly, I would have gone right now if she had insisted. In a way, it was my fault. If push came to shove, I'd trust Dennis to handle the booth.

"Don't be silly! You have work there. I'll be fine until Sarah gets here. If they let me out of here before Monday, I'll have her drive me home. If I'm still here you pick me up on your way after the show."

"Of course, of course I will." Rats!

"I won't be very mobile for awhile, I'm afraid, Rock. Probably be on crutches, dear, I'm sorry."

Good, good, that'll make it easier to avoid intimacy until I get a chance to talk to her about us. I don't want to pull a Newt Gingrich and dump her while she's still ailing. I wouldn't do that to my worst enemy. Ah, crap, sure I would.

"Helen, from what I hear you're pretty banged up. You may be in the hospital longer than you'd like."

"I've already been here longer than I'd like."

I began to wonder about...things, and rued again how stupid I'd been to get involved with her. I wouldn't wish what happened to her and Di on anyone, but I found myself feeling relieved that I wouldn't have to see Helen this weekend. Maybe she'll go to stay with her sister in Houston until she's fully recovered. Of course, then she'd expect me to visit her there. And while she's recuperating it probably wouldn't be a good time to tell her our relationship needs to change back to what it was before, if that's possible. I know we can't go back to where we once were...it's sort of like trying to unring a bell. I'll need time to think of how to go about dumping her...I mean, telling her it's over.

Whatever Helen said for the last minute went over my head because I wasn't listening anymore. I started to recall how in the movie *Dial M For Murder*, one of Hitchcock's thrillers, a husband arranges for a hired killer to get into his house and kill his wife, played by Grace Kelly, while she's on the phone talking to her rotten husband. Why that thought occurred to me at this time, I can't say. I mean, who would want to hurt Grace Kelly?

Images of my friends on the golf course now interrupted. I waited for Helen to finish and prayed she wouldn't close by saying, "I love you", because I didn't want to feel required to respond in kind.

"Okay, dear, you take care and have a great show. Call me both nights and let me know how things are going."

"Yes, I will, Helen. But you take it easy; you're the one that needs rest...and quiet. Bye." I hung up, maybe a bit too quickly.

Peace and quiet for a moment, and I wished now I could make it to the golf game, but with Di on the way I needed to be here when she arrived. How I'm going to explain her is something else. My male friends aren't going to think as Helen does, that Di is kind of cute—Di is a traffic-stopper. Being objective, she may not be a ten, but she can hold her own. Nine and three-fourths?

I can hear the teasing already: "Hey, Rock, so you traded in Helen for a younger model!"... "'Hey, Rock, does she take dictation while sitting on your lap?"

Worse, there are people I run into at these shows who I don't otherwise see for a year or more at times, and they may not even know about Mary Ann. They may assume Di is someone I hired not just to look good in the booth, but for extracurricular activities, too.

Sure, a pretty smile doesn't hurt to influence someone to stop at your booth, but it won't make sales. Many of my current accounts, and a few potential accounts I had been in contact with before the show, would meet me at various meetings throughout the week, and they knew what they were interested in without needing a fancy lady to wiggle her ass.

But there are lots of customers out there who don't know every vendor, and Hammond Tools is still rather small, and the name certainly doesn't indicate we are in the security systems business. If Dennis and I are busy with a customer, Di could be an asset by encouraging lookie-loos to keep looking and listening long enough for one of us to move in and handle the more technical questions. If her smile helps to keep them interested, well, all's fair...

Actually, Dennis could do this stuff in his sleep, so I think we'll be okay. It's a tough way to make a living, trying to sell something, and there are days I feel like letting Dennis and Carl, and Helen, handle the whole operation and I'll go off and play golf or sail the seven seas.

A couple guys I know retired recently, but soon after said they made a mistake. They quickly tired of playing golf *every* day, and following the stock market wasn't fun on those days it dropped a hundred points. Every man to himself, but I don't think they cultivated enough interests outside of their job, so now they're bored. Anyway, what the hell would I do if I did retire, now that Mary Ann is gone? All those round-the-world trips aren't going to happen.

I should have promoted Carl. But Carl, good as he is, has a hard time making decisions. Helen had a great recommendation from her prior employer, and I knew her vaguely through Mary Ann—some mild friendship they shared that didn't involve me, and she's good, very good, at her job. She cuts to the chase, makes a decision, with no doubt in her mind that it's the right one. And, I must admit, they always seem to be good ones. I guess fooling around with that stupid gun may not have been her smartest decision.

Dennis is still young, but I need to talk to him about his future plans. Once I break the news to Helen that our dating days are over, I suspect she'll be mightily pissed, possibly mad enough to quit, so I would need Dennis and Carl to step to the plate. And I know I won't get romantically involved with either of them! I wondered if Helen's ever seen that movie with Glenn Close and Michael Douglas; sends shivers!

***

TEN

No man is useless as long as he's got a friend.---Walter Brennan character in the movie, *Bad Day at Black Rock.*

Oh what a tangled web we weave
*When first we practice to deceive!...*Sir Walter Scott (1771-1832), Marmion, Canto vi. Stanza 17

JUST BEFORE NOON Di called. She was nearing San Antonio, so I told her to meet me in the hotel restaurant for lunch. Most of the people I know here at the show, at least the guys, were out playing golf, so at least for now I wouldn't have to explain who the young beauty is. Your niece came with you, Rock? How nice!

Seeing her as she entered the restaurant put a smile on my face. Di can light up a ballroom just by walking in. We hugged each other for several seconds, holding tight. When we pulled away she leaned forward and for a blink of an eye I thought she was going to kiss me on the mouth.

"I'd land a smacker on you but you might have friends watching us, huh, Rock? Wouldn't want to embarrass you!"

We sat down at out table. "It might be safe now," I said, laughing. "most of the fellows I know are playing golf."

"Oh, did I mess up your game plans?"

"Nah, it's okay. I didn't sleep much last night after your call, trying to figure out what to do this morning, so I don't think I'd have been a good golf partner this morning."

"So what did you decide? You want me to help, as ordered?"

"Oh sure, I do want you in the booth. I should have planned on three people anyway, but Helen insisted she and I could handle it ourselves."

"She didn't want to share you with anyone that's all. So who's the third person?"

"Fellow name of Dennis, from the plant. I called him and he'll fly in early tomorrow morning. You and I can get things started until he arrives. Today, I'll give you a crash course on our product line."

"I know, just show a lot of leg and wear a low-cut blouse."

"No, no Di, it's nothing like that. I think Helen was teasing you in her peculiar way; I don't know. We're not selling bikinis here. I want you to be pleasant and friendly, and I know you can do both. The technical stuff Dennis and I can handle, but if it gets busy, and he and I are tied up, I want you to at least be able to maintain an intelligent conversation for a few minutes. I have all the material you'll need in my room."

"I have Helen's briefcase in the car, with her product material. She insisted I take it."

"Good, good. So, tell me more about your crazy

adventure. You said you're not hurt, but I see some swelling on your lip."

Di touched her lip and frowned. "Yeah, the big lug smacked me. A dab of makeup will help."

"Did the police find these guys?"

For the next hour and a half we enjoyed a leisurely lunch while we caught up on our lives. Di gave me all the details about the attack on her and Helen, the policeman who seemed enamored of her, Helen's condition, and how she and Helen first met.

"Yeah, that's one thing I still don't understand; why did she decide to ride with you? In fact, Di, why did *you* decide to drive all the way here?"

She smiled and shrugged. "I wasn't doing anything else, so...Cheyenne's leave was over and I seemed a little lost, Rock."

"How'd that go, Chey's leave time? You guys have fun?"

She told me about Cheyenne's last night of leave, and his abrupt departure to go see the girl on the east coast. Whatever fun they'd had for the previous ten days was wiped from her memory by Cheyenne's action on his last day.

"Sorry, Di."

Quickly getting away from that, Di told me she, too, was confused at first why Helen wanted to ride with her.

"She said we could get to know one another better. I hadn't a clue as to why she said that. After we'd been driving a while she told me a story about a time when I called you at your office, interrupting a meeting with her, and I guess she's been curious ever since about the voice on the other end of the line. You're not going to marry her or do anything crazy like that, are you, Rock?"

"Why, don't you like her, Di? After she saved your life?"

"I'll give her lots of points for coming back, even if she did fall on her ass and shoot herself." Di shook her head, and then laughed.

"Was it that funny?" I asked.

"Only in retrospect. I mean, me standing there with my torn shirt, her lying there looking so sad and beat up, Officer O'Keefe a little unsure how to deal with us, yeah, it's one of those, 'hurt so bad it's funny' moments.

"Rock, I think Helen felt some kind of challenge from me, as if I was a threat to her. I'll have to admit—you know how bratty I can be—I gave her the impression that since you weren't in San Diego I'd proceed to chase you down, so she made this instantaneous decision to go with me. I still don't understand it. Actually, I don't think I would have driven all the way here without calling you first to see when you'd be home. But, dearie, you haven't been taking my calls, so now's a good time to explain that."

"Hmmm. My bad. It's because I felt that by now I should have told you about Helen, but I didn't want to, so I avoided you."

"You can't avoid me, now, so what about you and Helen, or am I getting too nosy?"

"As a matter of fact, you are, but that's not unusual!"

She stuck her tongue out and I reached across the table and nearly grabbed it before she pulled back. We laughed and I looked around, hoping I wouldn't see anyone I knew.

"Let's get out of here," I said. "Let's go up to my room and look at the material for the show. You need anything from your car now?"

"No, I can get my things later. I need to do some shopping."

"For the show?"

"Yes, and some new underwear."

Dear Diary:

WE'RE BACK IN San Antonio. The first time, and only previous time, I was here, Cheyenne was in the hospital and Rock and I waited for him to be released before we continued our drive east. We did a bang-up job of playing tourist, visiting most of the city's major sights. Now, Rock's girlfriend, Helen, is in the hospital, but it's nearly a three-hour drive away. Thank goodness.

Rock and I had a long lunch and I hope I didn't come across like a teenager infected with puppy love. It was so good to see him I just wanted to hug him to death. Most of what we talked about I've already written down, so I'll go on to what happened after lunch, when we went to Rock's room. It's a mini-suite, suitable I guess for the boss and his girlfriend, who, ha! ha! won't be here to enjoy the comforts.

I surveyed the accommodations, the large bathroom, the balcony, and peeked in the refrigerator.

"A suite, Rock, business must be good."

"Help yourself to anything."

"Nothing now, maybe later."

As I turned around Rock handed me a brown accordion folder.

" I was going to give these to you in Tucson."

"What is it, Rock?"

"I received a few messages from Cheyenne," Rock said.

My mouth opened wide in astonishment, as if I was expecting someone to plop me a scoop of ice cream.

"I didn't know you and he had become such close friends," I said, rather tersely, hiding neither my surprise nor my ire. I hadn't heard from Chey since he left that cowardly note.

"A few is more than I've received. I hardly ever hear from him when he's over there," I said, somewhat bitterly."

Rock shrugged and didn't say anything. He looked at me with a silly grin on his face. The same grin I usually think is cute, but now it was plain silly.

"You're going to make me ask, Rock?"

Prefacing his next comment with a sigh, a hint that he understood I might think my two favorite men in the world were keeping secrets from me, but like, I didn't know that already? How dumb am I?

"I don't get messages from him often, and he doesn't get into anything personal. Some of these go back months. There's nothing recent."

Rock was telling me he didn't know anything about Chey's *other* love life. I'm not sure I believe him. He took the folder back from me, unwound the string that kept it closed, reached into it and pulled out the papers that were inside.

There were newspaper articles that had been copied and messages that Rock had apparently printed off his e-mail. I picked up the top paper and read it.

'Rock: Aug. 20, p.5a. Some of my buddies going home.'

Stapled to the message was a news article. It was the story about the withdrawal of US forces from Iraq, in particular the unit known as the 4th Stryker Brigade Combat Team.

"Is this his unit?"

"I'm not sure," Rock said. "The impression I got is that Chey is with a 'special forces' unit, but he may have worked with this combat team at some time or the other. I'm not sure we'll ever know exactly what the boy's been doing over there. By now, I think he's moved on to greener pastures. "

I looked at him with puzzlement until I realized what he meant: Afghanistan. "Oh. Maybe not so green."

I sat down on one of the twin beds and read the next e-mail...

'Rock...check p.23, 11-17.'

"How do you know what paper to look in?"

"He told me it would either be the New York Times or USA Today. I have to check them both. Obviously he's referring to papers from several days past. So I go online, find the story and print it out." Rock shrugged, answering my next question, 'why?', by indicating it was the type of secrecy that guys like Cheyenne get caught up in.

I read the newspaper article; the story was about the killing of two Taliban leaders and the capture of two others by NATO forces. The article gave the details about a raid that had resulted in the death of one man and the capture of the others. It said that the captured men and the slain man were known to have been involved in planting roadside bombs and organizing attacks on convoys. The story continued:

'NATO also reported that Haffiz el Jenen, a Taliban leader involved in training foreign fighters, was killed Saturday in Farah province.'

I read the e-mail and the article twice, then set them on the bed.

"So you think he was telling you that he was involved in these killings?"

"Yes," Rock said. "The one in the second paragraph, at least. It's his way of letting us know that he's still alive, what he's doing, and approximately where he's at."

"Us? He sent it to you."

"He sent me an e-mail not too long ago. Probably when he was on leave, staying with you in Tucson. Now I don't necessarily agree with him, Di, but reiterated that he didn't want to be in regular contact with you, because he's afraid you then would worry whenever you hadn't heard from him for a while. And he said with the work he does, he often is incommunicado for weeks on end, even with his own people. He said he would contact me when he could and that I should let you know that he's alright."

"So how often..."

"Not often at all," Rock said, before I could finish my question. "There are others," he added, pointing to the folder.

I read the third e-mail:

"Rock, Nov. 30, p.5a; I messed up."

"What does he mean, he 'messed up?'" I asked.

"Read the article."

The attached copy of the newspaper story was entitled, 'Bombs target two nuclear scientists', and reported on an attack by motorcycle assailants of two nuclear scientists in Tehran. The scientists were thought to be involved in Iran's nuclear weapons program. One of them was killed, but the other was only wounded.

"He did this? Chey; our Cheyenne?" I asked, as flabbergasted as I could be, and I didn't even know I knew the word. "I thought he was, like, a sniper."

"Branching out, I guess," said Rock, more sarcastic than humorous.

"He used to ride a dirt bike in the desert," I commented.

"Here's one from Dec. 9th in the USA Today, about a new rifle that the snipers are using in Afghanistan. It says the Army has 2,500 snipers receiving training with this new weapon, so we know Cheyenne's not alone out there."

Rock slid yet another article out of the folder.

"Here's one from about the same time on the special operations forces. Green Berets, Seals, etc. I'm sure the Delta Forces are there, too."

"Delta? That rings a bell," Di said.

"Does it? They're very secretive, Di. I suspect that's who Chey works for, but for all he's told me, he's never said anything specific about which unit he's assigned to. With those special operations units, he could go anywhere. Delta's a good bet, but I don't ask him."

"It sounds like something he said, or maybe he was talking in his sleep."

"Not good, Di. Don't say anything about it to anyone, okay?"

"Rock, you know I'm good at keeping secrets! It's so scary though, when I think about what Chey might be doing. He might even be dead, at this moment, and I wouldn't know it. And I'd be out having a good time."

"Di, there's nothing you can do about Chey right now. He seems to have a way of surviving. He's like a cat. Did I ever tell you about 'Splat'? "

"Who? Splat?"

"Yeah. A niece of mine used to work at a vet's. One day somebody brought in a kitten that had fallen out of a two-story building. The kitten landed on its feet, but broke three of its legs. It was going to need significant care to save its life, and the owner didn't think he could afford the cost. So the vet asked the owner to sign over the kitten to him because he wanted to take a stab at putting it back together."

"And?"

"He did, and my niece took the kitten home and it hobbled around on splints for several weeks and lived another eighteen years. Cheyenne's like that; he gets hurt, but lands on his feet and he'll outlive us all. He'll outlive me, anyway."

"And me? How I am suppose to survive not knowing from day to day, or even minute to minute, if he's coming home walking on his own two feet, or in a casket?"

Rock hugged me then, a gesture that I think is common for people when they don't know what to say. And what was there to say? I try to put it out of my mind, but in the background there is Cheyenne, and all too often a mental image of him being shot at, or sloshing in the mud or jungles or whatever the hell they have in those places he goes, crowds my head. Maybe that's why I love being with Rock, because I can tease him and pretend that everything is fine and dandy when I'm with him. It's a way of avoiding reality for a moment or two.

"Di, what did you mean when you said you're feeling a little lost?"

"Oh, I don't really know, Rock. Lost, useless, don't know what to do with myself."

"That doesn't sound like the Di I met, who was always busy and upbeat, always with a smile."

"You have selective memory, sir."

"Clue me in?"

"Rock, last year I was running the café, doing book work for some of the ranchers, flittering back and forth to Tucson to check on Mom; I was busy all the time. Then...you know, Chey came back alive and that was great, and I thought he and I were going to settle down, you know, in a real city, like Tucson. So I sell the café but Chey returns to the army. Mom gets worse, she dies, then Aunt May dies, and I don't know what to do with myself."

"This sounds like a topic that's going to need more than an adage or a hug. Hey, you said you needed to do a little shopping. A mall is right nearby so why don't we go there now, and get our minds off..." He pointed towards the papers we'd been looking at.

I nodded an affirmative, and Rock gathered up the papers and stuffed them in the folder.

Later: Diary: As I told you earlier I wanted to get new underwear because I still felt soiled by that creep who pawed me. I also bought a pretty white blouse to wear at the show. I have a blue one with me that would probably past muster with Helen, were she here, but I'm going to be working the booth for two days and don't want to wear the same blouse the whole time. When we got back to the hotel Rock said he was temporarily hiring me!

"Thanks, Rock, but you know I would help you this weekend for free. Besides, I thought only Helen could hire and fire," I said, the mischief in my tone all too obvious.

"You guys did have time to chat, didn't you?"

"Girl talk."

"Yeah, well, don't say anything to Dennis when you meet him, but there are going to be some changes after the show."

"Oh? May I ask what changes?"

"You may, and again it's none of your business, but Helen and I...yes, she's a fine lady, Di, really. I know she can be uppity and snarly, but..."

"She must be great in bed, Rock!"

"Di, don't start."

I stifled a big laughed, and Rock laughed, too. Even when he's mad, tired, or upset, I can make him laugh.

"I made a mistake getting involved with her. It wasn't a smart thing to do. I suppose if I was madly in love with her I'd find a way to make it work. But I'm not and don't think I ever will be."

"She's not in love with you, either, Rock."

"Oh? Did you two chat about my love life, too?"

"No, but I can tell. She's after you, Rock, but not for your bod, though I must say, I'm sure that would be a good enough reason, if she's as smart as you think she is."

"C'mon, wise-ass, you said you wanted to take a walk around the Alamo. Let's go."

The last time we'd been here we toured the Alamo. I didn't need to take another tour now but I enjoyed walking around the area.

"We going to dinner on the River Walk this evening, Rock? My treat."

"Your treat? Why so generous?"

"Dunno. You treated last time we were here."

We passed the Alamo where a sign stated, 'The Daughters of the Republic of Texas Welcome You'. Sadly, I had read recently that a serious rift had developed between the factions claiming they love the old mission and its remarkable history.

The Alamo has a leaky roof and recommendations that underground barriers be installed to keep leaks from destroying the famed limestone walls have gone unheeded. Instead, the Daughters seem more interested in building a proposed three-story annex to house the organization's library of historical documents, a recording studio, and office space. The building would cost $36 million. Have to sell a lot of coonskins caps and coffee mugs urging 'Remember the Alamo!' to raise thirty-six big ones.

"So go on, Di, you were saying what Helen wants."

"You sure you want my opinion?"

"Of course, Di. I trust your opinion...even if half the time I can't tell if you're flirting or teasing or being serious."

"That's why I'm so much fun! Hey, it's after five o'clock, buy me a drink now and I'll buy you dinner later."

"You're on."

We sauntered down Crockett Street until we came to a place by the name of the 'Original Mexican Restaurant,' which offers thirty kinds of Margaritas. I can't say if it is *the* original Mexican Restaurant—I have my doubts—but I love margaritas, so we went in.

Like someone who goes into an ice cream store that has over thirty flavors of ice cram and orders vanilla, I ordered your basic, traditional style margarita. Rock had a Dos Equis. I wanted another but Rock insisted we stop at one because he wanted me to study the brochures before tomorrow.

"Let's walk back to the hotel and I'll give you a crash course which should take about two hours. Then we'll come back for dinner, okay?"

I agreed and Rock either forgot to ask or decided not to pursue the subject of what my opinion was regarding Helen's long-term intentions. I didn't want to tell him, yet, that I thought her main purpose was to gain control of Rock's company, even if it meant marrying him. I didn't think this weekend was a good time to upset him with negative vibes.

So for the next two hours Rock briefed me on his company's line of new products, mostly the new selection of home and business security items, schooled me on key words to use, and reminded to be pleasant and confident.

"Act like I'm a know-it-all, hey?"

Rock opened his mouth and I'm sure he was going to say, 'you're good at that,' or something similar, but instead clamped his mouth shut, smiled and slowly shook his head.

I'll keep this short because I'm getting tired. But after my schooling, another jaunt to the River Walk area, dinner, and back to Rock's room, Rock looked at me with fear in his eyes, as if he suddenly identified me as the killer in thriller filled with plot loopholes.

"What is it, Rock?"

"Good God, Di, I didn't get you a room!"

"Oh, my Rock, is that a proposal?"

"Seriously, Di, I've had so much on my mind I never thought of it."

"Freudian," I suggested.

Rock wasn't amused. He called the desk and begged an pleaded for them to find a room, but they were full, or at least, Rock wasn't important enough for them to break out one of their extra rooms that most hotels have available for real emergencies for real important people.

"Rock, it's getting too late to be calling all over the city, and I don't want to be too far away from where you're staying. From here it's just a hop, skip, and a jump to the Convention Center."

"So what are you saying?"

I looked around his suite, basically pointing out to him how much room we had.

"What?" he asked, that tone in his voice that meant he wasn't liking what I was going to suggest, but he knew the practical solution.

"You have two big beds, Rock! I'll take the one on the right. And that's it, no more discussion. I'm tired and I need to get my beauty sleep if I'm going to knock 'em dead tomorrow."

"I'll sleep on the sofa in the sitting room," Rock said, a dumb suggestion.

"Don't be silly. I won't bite you, Rock."

I proceeded to open my suitcase, grab what I needed to take to the bathroom, went in and shut the door. When I came out, (wearing my heavy robe, Diary, so don't get any ideas), Rock was sitting at the desk writing something. Whether he was truly busy or pretending, he ignored me; you'd think we'd been married thirty years. He kept his back to me until he heard me crawl into bed. Still without looking my way he then went into the bathroom.

I was in bed, writing these notes, when Rock came out of the bathroom wearing a lightweight pair of gyms shorts and a tee that bore the unimaginative logo, 'Hammond Tools'.

"I don't have any regular pajamas," he said, a dead-serious look on his face.

"Is that what you normally wear when you're with Helen?"

"You sure have a way of asking questions that don't concern you. What is that you're wearing?"

I had on a long, dark blue shirt that belonged to Cheyenne. The logo said simply, 'United States Army'. I wore it a lot when he wasn't around. Even when I'm upset with him.

"That's for me to know..."

"Hmmm." Rock climbed in to bed, then said, "I'm going to read a while. Will the light bother you?"

"No. I want to finish some notes and then I'll be asleep in a minute."

"What are you writing?"

"My diary...it helps me clear my mind to write about what I've been doing and what's been happening. I told you I kept a diary."

"Yes, but I thought you meant you kept a diary when you were a kid, not now."

"You mean it's childish?"

"No, I didn't say that. Hey, you're in good company, you know?"

"How so?"

"Conan Doyle, the writer, he kept a diary all his life."

"Oh really? Old Sherlock, eh? He wrote mysteries, and sometimes I think this stuff is a mystery to me, and I'm the one writing it!"

"Great; if it works for you, I think it's wonderful. Sometimes I wish I had a diary from years back. It'd be fun to read, if I had the time."

"This isn't meant for anyone to read, it's for myself."

"Am I in there?" Rock asked, sounding somewhat childish himself.

"Maybe," I said, with a wink. "But don't you dare ever try to read this, Rock." I tried to sound forceful. "I mean it, this is something I'm adamant about. Even Chey hasn't read it. At least, not that I know of."

"I won't, unless some day you let me."

"Good night, Rock. Oh, and don't worry, I promise I won't climb into bed with you."

"You *promise*?" he said.

"Yes, really, don't worry."

"No, I didn't mean it that way. I mean, you shouldn't, that is, we shouldn't, and...I don't expect you to, but do you have to *promise*? Can't we just assume nothing like that is going to happen?"

"Would you rather I didn't promise? Leave it open?" I asked as I fluttered my eyelids quickly, several times.

"It's just that ...it sounds like you think I'm some old, reprobate...a used up old man...an untouchable." I think he was really hurt.

"You're anything but untouchable, dear. Good night."

I shut off the light on the table next to the bed and rolled over on my side. Then, without turning to face Rock, I asked, "Are you going to lie to Helen?"

"About where you spent the night?"

"Yes."

"The subject need not come up, does it?"

"She'll ask."

Rock was quiet. I assumed he was trying to think of an answer he could give Helen that wouldn't be a bald-faced lie, but that wouldn't unnecessarily alarm or hurt her.

"If she asks I'll tell her I got you a room nearby. How's that?"

"Our secret will be safe with me, you sneak."

"Tomorrow I'll get you your own room, even if it's in another city."

"Yes. I don't want you to have to lie too much when Helen gives you the third degree."

"The third degree? You think she'll seriously bug me about where you stayed?"

"I would if you were my guy."

"I'm not her guy...anymore...or..."

"Or what?"

"I don't know. I won't be, but I guess this isn't the best time to tell her."

"Then you'll have to lie."

Oh, I know I shouldn't be such a flirt, but Rock is so much fun to flirt with.

***

ELEVEN

"It is a good day to die."... Attributed to Tasunka Witko, a holy man of the Lakota Sioux (Tasunka Witko was also known as Crazy Horse).

THESE GUYS ARE amateurs, Cheyenne thought, his head resting on a pillow of Urdu-language newspapers, compared to Aziz al-Talad and his pals when Johnny Bracken and I were captives in Iraq.

When I got out of there I felt like I'd been rolled up and down a flight of concrete stairs a few dozen times. Come to think of it, I had been.

Can't figure why they are treating us so well. Good food—only two meals a day, sure, but decent and filling, plenty of water, and blankets at night. They even treated my wounds. Maybe they want to fatten us up for the kill?

They did take everything we had on us—weapons, GPS, first aid kit, and, worst of all, Di's iPod. Good thing for these guys she isn't here, she'd take their heads off.

A few feet away, on an adjoining cot, slept Jason Jones, who had come to rescue Cheyenne but now was a captive with him.

Fucked up again, Cheyenne said to himself, no one else being around to say it to. Got Johnny and those other suckers killed, now Jason's stuck with me, and will probably die with me, unless they plan to hold us for a prisoner exchange, which I doubt, because these characters don't ever seem concerned about their compatriots once they are taken prisoner. Should have blown themselves up and become happy martyrs, is the way these assholes think.

Damn, I told Jason to go back and forget about me. Hadn't been for him I would have fought until I was out of ammo, taken a dozen or so of them with me. Of course, if Jason hadn't brought more ammo I wouldn't have had enough to fight for more than a few minutes. I figured surrendering gives us a chance to live another day. You never know what might happen.

Realistically Cheyenne knew it wasn't his fault. The mission they'd been on had had more than its share of bad luck, that's all; shit happens. And no one said Jason had to be the one to come for me, in fact, I don't understand why Spiedel sent a rookie. Yes, I do—because knowledge of our missions in Pakistan is kept on a need to know basis, and there are damn few people who need to know. Goddamn President probably doesn't know what the hell we're doing.

The only thing Cheyenne was sorry about was that that traitorous bastard Mohammed ab-Hawsawi was still alive. Cheyenne was positive he had wounded ab-Hawsawi because he'd seen ab-Hawsawi with his arm bandaged. Cheyenne also suspected he and Jason were still alive because ab-Hawsawi was saving them for something special. It would be a real coup for one of these offshoot terrorists groups to show they had captured American Special Forces soldiers who had been illegally assassinating people in Pakistan.

Which posed the question, was there such a thing as legal assassination? I guess it depends on who's pulling the trigger. Or who's writing the law.

Cheyenne was wide-awake now, but it was still quiet and dark. Usually by dawn there were the sounds of vehicles, these walls not being as thick as the walls in the Iraqi prison he'd come to know so intimately, and of people moving about, hawking their wares, greeting each other and praising Allah for providing them with yet another sunrise. Those sounds suggested to Cheyenne that they were being held in the middle of a small village.

They'd been here three days and from what Cheyenne could tell they weren't heavily guarded. But that could be a ruse to see if the Americans tried to make an escape. There might be a whole platoon of guards just waiting for an attempt. And if they did get out, but are in the middle of a town or village, where would they go?

Three walls of the room in which they were held were stone, including the one facing the street, but the one on the building side, the west side, was nothing more than plasterboard, and a cheap variety at that. Sometimes Cheyenne and Jason could hear voices from the other side of the west wall, but they could not distinguish enough words to understand the conversation.

English is widely understood in Pakistan, and is in fact one of its two official languages, the other being Urdu. To further complicate things, the language most widely spoken is Punjabi. In any case, Cheyenne had learned enough words in several Pakistani languages to occasionally be able to follow a conversation with a mixture of Punjabi and English, and maybe some pig Latin thrown in.

Cheyenne had never heard any sounds coming from the next room during the night, so he assumed it was not used then. Cheyenne felt he could punch his way through the wall, given enough time and without interference. But that might be a tad noisy.

He rolled on his side and started to pick in the corner where the plasterboard wall met the floor, the fitting about as bad as could be done and still allow the structure to stay standing. What crummy crap; these walls are less than a quarter inch thick. I could build them a better wall in a day if they gave me proper tools.

Picking away Cheyenne found he could literally pull out pieces of crumbly plasterboard and soon he'd made a hole at the bottom corner where the wall met the floor, big enough to look into the adjoining room.

He couldn't see much, mostly the legs of a table and chairs. It did not appear that anyone was in the room now, and

Cheyenne did not hear any voices. It looked too easy. Maybe they think if we make a break we'll lead them to another rescue chopper, which they can then take down—that must be it. Fuck them, ain't gonna let that happen. After all the failures trying to extricate us, I doubt anybody's gonna look too hard for us.

But Cheyenne knew that wasn't true. If need be, Col. Spiedel would come on his own for Cheyenne and Jason. He might not have another chopper to spare but he'd take on this whole village single-handed if he had to. One thing about Spiedel, he was loyal to his men and never forgot them. Cheyenne had heard horror stories from some of the veterans about prisoners left behind in Vietnam. No one was sure about such stories, especially since by now they had been handed down, and it was difficult to know what was fact and what was lore.

As the sun slowly rose above the horizon and greeted the village, a few dim rays slipped through the slit that served as the only opening in the walls, about eight feet high, and lightened the room. At the same time Cheyenne began to hear sounds: a cart rolling by, a barking dog, a boy yelling, men and women chattering, hailing each other. Soon a guard would come with food.

Jason continued to sleep and Cheyenne let him. The younger man still didn't rouse when a guard jangled the keys and opened the door. The man had his trusty AK-47 strapped to his shoulder, and a second weapon, a rifle, which he braced against the wall as he entered. It was Cheyenne's new sniper rifle, the XM2010.

Damn, I wondered what happened to my rifle after we were captured! Cheyenne had tried to smash the rifle as the Haqqani had closed in on he and Jason. But one particularly ugly brute had made it clear that he would tear Cheyenne into a thousand little pieces with his AK-47 if Cheyenne didn't lay the rifle down gently.

One thing I have to do if it kills me trying, is get that rifle even if I have to destroy it. I escape and return without it I'll be up shit-creek. My sniping days will be over. Well, on second thought, maybe that wouldn't be so bad. Cheyenne knew his duty would compel him to make every effort to retrieve the latest in sniper's gadgets. Even if the fuckin' ragheads can't figure out how to use it, it'd be proof that we have special forces workin' where we ain't suppose to be.

The guard reached behind him and picked up a basket, which he placed inside the room. He nudged it forward with his foot, picked up the rifle, smiled wickedly, and exited. This time the jangling of the keys woke Jason.

The kid mumbled, turned on his side and lifted his head, looking around as if he'd forgotten where he was.

"About time," Cheyenne said. "I thought you were going to sleep away the day, princess."

"Shit, it's barely morning."

"Did you see the guard when he came in?"

"Oh, was that the noise that woke me?"

"Yes, and next time I want you to pay attention to what he does."

"Why? You planning something?"

"You want to stay here forever?"

Jason sat up and rubbed his eyes. "I gotta pee."

"Help yourself," Cheyenne said, nodding toward the bucket in one of the street side corners of the room. "I've already been."

"Wish they'd replace this bucket already, smells something awful."

"Whaddya think, this is the Ritz-Carlton? You want maid service, too? At least they feed us."

Cheyenne got up and went to get the basket. It contained bread and cheese and figs, two apples, and something that always brought a smile to Cheyenne, four plastic bottles of water.

"Hey, kid, Aqua Pakistani!"

"Even out here," Cheyenne said, "I wonder if they recycle?"

They ate their food without saying much. When they were finished Jason put the basket near the door, and then took the piss bucket, as he called it, and placed it near the door, too, hoping that the next time a guard came in he'd take the hint.

"Better hope he doesn't throw it at you," Cheyenne said.

"Beat his brains out if he does."

"Keep talking, kid, while I do something."

"Talk about what?"

"Anything," Cheyenne said, as he returned to the corner of the wall where he'd been picking at the thin plasterboard. "Tell me your life story."

Cheyenne lay down and looked through the small hole he'd made. It wasn't much bigger than he could put a finger in, but the possibilities intrigued him.

In the background Jason was saying something about a brother and a sister, and a farm in somewhere, South Dakota. Something about cows and pigs.

"You from a small town, too?" Cheyenne asked while he picked away at the plasterboard wall.

A chunk as big as the hole he'd already made came away in his hand. At the same time he heard the sound of a door opening, and he froze. At first he feared the guard was back for the basket and had caught Cheyenne red-handed. Then he realized it was the door in the next room.

"Psst, Jason."

"Yeah?"

"Listen for the guard...you hear those keys jangling say my name loudly."

Cheyenne got his head down as low as he could and peered through the hole. He saw the legs of the table and the chairs, and a little bit higher up now with the hole being larger.

Then he saw the legs of two people. The chairs moved, scuffling against the floor.

"Shuddup, kid!" Cheyenne whispered to Jason.

"I thought you wanted me..."

He crawled over to Jason "Not now...there are two guys in the next room. They might hear you and notice the hole I made."

Cheyenne moved back to his spy hole. He could distinguish two voices, though he had no idea what they were saying. One of the voices he recognized—it was ab-Hawsawi!

Son-of-a-bitch, my old buddy. We keep bumping into each other, don't we, old pal? Like kismet. Barely daring to breathe Cheyenne turned his head so that an ear was pressed as close as possible to the opening. The men did not speak loudly but Cheyenne could pick up a few words here and there.

Cheyenne sat up, his body covering the hole, just as he heard the sound of the guard entering. As before, the guard set Rock's captured rifle against the wall while casually cradling an AK-47 in one hand. He reached down and picked up the basket, and set it outside the door. He saw the bucket and jabbered a string of words, or noises, anyway, that sounded angry, like, what the hell you think I am, your fuckin' servant?

Cheyenne sat in the corner, his arms folded in front of him and smiled. Jason braced himself, fearful of what Cheyenne had suggested the guard might do with the bucket. But after his verbal outburst the guard took the bucket and placed it outside the room. He picked up the rifle, left, and locked the door.

"You think he was mad?" Jason said.

"Who can tell, doesn't even sound like a language, all that babbling running together. I just hope we get a new bucket before the day goes on too long, Jason, since you so wisely gave away the only one we had."

"Didn't think of that."

"You notice what he did? How casual he is with his weapon? I mean, *my* weapon."

"Yeah, I did. He doesn't even check closely when he opens the door. Sets the rifle down without hardly looking at us. Holds the AK as if it's a toy. Teasing us, almost. If one of us was by the door when he came in, on the side away from the opening..."

"He's either sloppy because he's overconfident that we will be meekly sitting around, or purposely so to see if we'll try something."

"What are you thinking, Cheyenne?"

"I'm thinking it makes no sense to keep us here, but make it easy for us to attempt to escape. Maybe I'm wrong, but I don't think these guys are too well-trained in security measures. The sloppy procedures may simply be their way. They may be able to live off the land and squeeze water out of a rock, and know how to handle an AK-47, but quite frankly, if we can't bust out of here, we don't deserve our paychecks.

"There's one thing you ought to know."

"What?"

Cheyenne nodded towards the next room. "I recognized a voice in the next room. Guy I've had an acquaintance with."

Cheyenne related to Jason the story of how ab-Hawsawi had betrayed a mission he and three others were on, a betrayal that resulted in Cheyenne's three 'volunteers' dead, and Cheyenne a captive and missing in action for several months.

"My girlfriend was told I was dead. Scared the crap out of her when I showed up alive."

"I'll bet you had a nice reunion, didn't you?" Jason said with a big grin.

Cheyenne couldn't avoid smiling but then he remembered the events of the next few days, concluding with the auto accident that put him in the hospital. He lay down in the corner and again put his ear as close to the hole as he could. He listened for several minutes. When he heard the men in the next room leave he sat up and the look on his face scared Jason.

"What'd you hear, Cheyenne? You look like you've see a ghost."

"Worse, I think."

"How so?"

"My language skills are only rudimentary, but if I heard right they were arguing about what to do with us. One guy wants to let us escape, and kill us in the process, while the other guy, my old buddy ab-Hawsawi, wants to execute us as spies. At least I think I got that right. He either called us spies or assholes, one or the other."

"Ha, ha, funny."

Cheyenne shrugged and stood up. "Exercise time, my boy. Don't want to get too lazy."

Except for those days when they were so beaten and tired they could barely move, Cheyenne had always insisted that he and Johnny, when they were in prison in Iraq, do a half-hour, twice a day, of calisthenics.

Back then they found it difficult to do any exercises after the first few weeks because they were so debilitated from abuse and lack of food. Here, Cheyenne insisted they work out until they'd broken a good sweat, and then go on for another half-hour.

Jason didn't forget the conversation they'd been having before exercising.

"So what's your best guess, a cold chop or a hot steak?"

"Don't tell me you watch the Three Stooges?"

"Classics are timeless."

"My best guess is ab-Hawsawi has enough pull to get his way. Which means the firing squad or the...what you said."

"Ugh. I suppose it's quick. Do you really think they'd execute us? I mean, wouldn't we, I mean, our guys, take retaliation?"

"I'm sure they would, seven-fold. Lot of good that'll do us."

"Okay, so what'll we do?" Jason asked.

Cheyenne stood silently in the middle of the room, still sweating, the drops rolling down his face and onto the floor. He had no towel to wipe himself. Jason likewise stood silent, waiting for Cheyenne to give him a plan. Outside the sounds of the village provided a background of civility and decent society, of people going through the motions of their day, working and buying and selling, making deals and planning meals. For a moment both men listened to the voices and noises outside their prison, only yards away. Take down the walls, set up some small, round tables with umbrellas, and you could be in a public square in any European town, enjoying a café au lait and reading the International Herald Tribune, instead of sweating in a locked room, trying to decide whether to run or fight. Or both.

"We can't wait any longer. When he comes with the evening meal, we'll take him," Cheyenne said, nodding towards the door, indicating the guard who came in with theirs meals each morning and evening.

"We sit here and wait, I'm afraid we'll become a news item that people will read about, anguish over and bitch about, maybe bring about a raid that kills our killers, but we'll still be pushing up daisies or whatever the hell they grow here."

"Sounds good, Cheyenne. Tell me what you want me to do."

AT BAGRAM AIRFIELD, about twenty-five miles north of Kabul, Afghanistan, three AH-64 Apache attack helicopters powered up for takeoff. Bagram is an Air Force facility run by the 455th Air Expeditionary Wing. NATO forces operating in Afghanistan against the Taliban also have been known to generate missions out of Bagram.

For the maintenance crews and others watching the choppers take off it was an awesome sight, these deadly machines swirling the dust and cutting the air, creating enough noise it would have scared off a herd of Tyrannosaurus Rex. With rocket pods carrying up to sixteen Hellfire missiles and its 30 mm cannon, the Apache could inflict devastating damage on an unsuspecting enemy.

A wing of Apaches suddenly rising up over a ridge, appearing out of the early morning mist or the early evening dusk could evoke memories of horror stories or legendary attacks. Swooping down on a rag-tag collage of amateur infantry, some of them teen-agers who, admittedly, know more about guns than they do about the alphabet, could be as frightening as it was for George Custer when Crazy Horse and his entourage of warriors materialized out of the clouds of dust, cutting off escape from the mound that became known as Custer's Hill.

The Apaches were slated for a mission to a suspected Taliban ammo storage facility and occasional hideout a few miles northeast of the Pakistani village of Alizai. The site had been on NATO's radar for several weeks. What the intelligence reports hadn't shown however, was that in recent days the Haqqani had ordered several dozen villagers from Alizai to evacuate and move to the storage site, which they thought had not been located by NATO, and was still a safe haven. The idea was to showcase a small village of poor farmers and deter NATO from looking closer. Unknown to the Haqqani leadership, ab-Hawsawi had other ideas.

At the same time, ten miles northeast of the Afghan town of Khost, Col. Eric Spiedel and two of his favorite volunteers boarded Kiowa helicopters for a delicate, not exactly authorized ride across the border into Pakistan—target, a collection of ramshackle buildings being used as a temporary staging area by the Haqqani. A third Kiowa carrying only the pilot followed. Spiedel had it on good authority, that being the homing device he had inserted into the heel of one of Jason Jones' boots before he went back to help Cheyenne, that amongst the clump of mud-baked shacks Cheyenne Smith and Jason were being held prisoner. Since he had not been able to get specific authority to mount a rescue mission—that wouldn't come, he was told, for several days, if at all, the colonel decided that a reconnaissance in modest force, for scouting purposes, only, of course, and not one that would violate territorial integrity, no, sir, absolutely not, was in order.

The Apaches from Bagram knew nothing of Spiedel's junket, nor did Spiedel's commander realize that the reconnaissance mission he'd authorized included the use of two Kiowas to inject Col. Spiedel's team to their destination, since their *supposed* destination was no more than a short walk in the park to the point east of Khost where three rivers merge, fifteen miles or so from the Pakistani border.

In the no-name, run-down collection of dilapidated buildings, that term being a generous description of most of the structures, including the one in which Smith and Jones were being held captive, the two American soldiers knew nothing about either mission, though Smith would not have been surprised to learn that Col. Spiedel had grown bored of waiting for official sanction to get his men out of Pakistan.

They send us here, where we're not supposed to be, then get caught up in bureaucracy and red tape trying to figure out how to extract us—it could have been Cheyenne Smith or Colonel Spiedel or any number of other soldiers fostering that cynical thought.

NORMALLY THEIR EVENING meal was delivered before it became completely dark. When night fell there was no light from the one slit in the prison room and Cheyenne and Jason could barely make out each other's form. There was nothing to do except talk or sleep. Neither was the chatty type.

The guard who brought the meals, the same one every time so far, had become so nonchalant about entering the room that Cheyenne and Jason were confident it would be a piece of cake to overcome him and take his weapons, though they'd probably have to kill him. How far they'd get after that was mere conjecture.

"Why is he so late tonight?" Jason asked. "You think he's still mad because I wanted him to give us a clean piss bucket?"

Cheyenne shrugged in the gloom, a movement Jason couldn't see.

"Maybe something's going on."

"Like what?"

"The fuck do I know?"

After nothing was said for several minutes, and they heard no sounds of any kind, neither from outside nor from the room next door, Cheyenne reminded Jason, "Keep your position, all night if need be."

Jason was sitting in the middle of the floor. Next to him the old newspapers that had been in the room when the two men were imprisoned, were wrapped up in the blankets and made to look, the men hoped, like a man sleeping. In the dark it would be hard to tell. Cheyenne stood next to the door, so that when it opened he'd be behind it.

It was nearly pitch dark when the door suddenly opened. The guard must have crept up slowly and quietly, but he could not temper the sound of the door and it scraped the floor upon opening. He stood at the entrance and flashed a light, the beam stopping on Jason's face. The guard swung the beam and stopped it on the lump on the floor next to Jason. Then he set his weapon—Cheyenne's rifle—against the wall, stepped back and picked up the basket of food he'd left outside. The AK-47 was hung over his shoulder. He set the basket down and reached back and brought in a bucket.

Cheyenne Smith had killed several men from long distance. It was his job. Circumstances had required him to kill a time or two from close range. He'd been superbly trained in the fine points of killing a man in hand-to-hand combat, with or without a weapon other than his hands. He now put that knowledge to use.

He pushed the door and it slammed shut before the guard could react. He was startled and stood looking at Cheyenne, only a shape in the darkness, his frightened eyes providing Cheyenne a target. The man tried to turn and reach for the rifle but Cheyenne was too quick.

It was done quietly and Cheyenne laid the man down as if he didn't want to hurt him any more than he already had.

Cheyenne picked up the XM2010 and stood at the side of the door waiting to see if anyone had heard the commotion and would come in. There was silence. Then a creak, maybe a footfall, maybe a mouse.

"Psst, Jason," he whispered. Jason was already at his side.

"Get behind me; let's go."

Just as Cheyenne began to open the door it was pushed open and a second guard burst in. He tripped on the body and as he fell his AK-47 sprayed wildly. In seconds dozens of rounds splattered on the walls and ceiling, sending chips of concrete flying wildly in the air like miniature meteors flashing through the night sky.

No need for silence now, Cheyenne fired one shot from his re-captured rifle. The guard stood as still as a statue for a second, his eyes wide in surprise. Then, dead, he fell. Jason picked up the dead guard's gun.

The alcove outside their prison was lit by a candle that set on a table, the only furnishing. A door to the right, at the far end of the alcove, appeared to lead to the outside.

Another door, to Cheyenne's left, must lead to the next room, the one in which he had often heard conversations, including the one in which he interpreted to be the argument about the fate of the Americans. Cheyenne opened the door no more than a quarter inch; the room was dark.

It was then that Cheyenne heard a humming, a rumbling sound, repeating itself like a bass drum in the smoky shadows of a jazz nightclub. The sound grew louder and nearer, and the rumbles clarified into the familiar whirling whumps of attack helicopters.

"Those are Apaches, Jason. What the hell's going on?"

A clamor reached them; the sounds of voices, startled, excited voices, jabbering and yelling.

"I just figured out where we are," Cheyenne said.

"Oh yeah? Can you figure how to get us out of wherever we are?" replied Jason.

"This is an ammo and re-supply depot we've had our eyes on for several weeks. We must have decided to hit it."

"Sounded like nothing more than a small farming village to me."

"Yeah, that's what I'm afraid of. The Haqqani may have moved villagers here thinking that would protect the depot from attack. But that only works as long as we known they've done it. On the other hand it could be a set-up...sounds like ab-Hawsawi's kind of work."

They pushed opened the door from the alcove and looked outside. It wasn't much of a village, more of a collection of temporary shelters and lean-tos lining muddy walkways and narrow cart paths. There were few sources of light—from some structures a slit of yellow escaped from behind pieces of plywood or cardboard, the glow emanating from candles or fireplaces. From around a corner of one building, a hundred yards away, twin beams of light flashed and a vehicle roared around the corner, headed in the direction of where Cheyenne and Jason stood. The Americans heard more yelling and heard the scuffle of people running and shouting, and now an occasional gunshot or a chaotic burst from an AK-47, probably some kid firing madly into the air because he didn't now what else to do. The thumping of the Apaches was closer and almost obscuring the shouts and screams.

Cheyenne and Jason ducked back inside the alcove as the vehicle, a jeep, roared past them. Three armed men were inside the jeep. The jeep bounced repeatedly and the men had to hold on dearly to keep from being flung out of their seat. They did not glance towards the direction Cheyenne and Jason had gone to hide.

ABOVE THE MAKE SHIFT village, which was, as Cheyenne had guessed, mainly serving as a resupply and arms cache for the Haqqani and their allies, but to which several dozen civilians had been forcibly moved, the attack helicopters homed in, rockets ready to destroy the armaments and any insurgents they could find.

"This is Apache Blue; we are in position over Objective Alizai West."

"Apache Red?"

"In position over Objective Alizai West."

"Apache Yellow?"

"Imaging shows no personnel."

" Is target clear?"

"So far, so good, Control."

"Depots in sight, confirm again Apache Blue?"

"Affirmative."

"Apache Red? Your status?"

"Target in sight. Looks deserted. One or two faint lights."

"Awaiting clearance."

"We'll have to make a second pass soon."

"Patience, my boy."

"We're passing over now; still clear of personnel. Hell, there can't be anybody here but bad guys anyway!"

"Make a second pass, Red; Blue, you too, until I get a positive okay."

"Apache Yellow, covering."

"Affirmative."

"Aye, going around."

ON THE GROUND, the sound of the helicopters faded slightly as they whipped past the arms storage facility and turned to begin a second pass. Cheyenne and Jason again dared to poke their heads outside. Their intention was to divine an escape route before their absence was duly noted. Not easy in this inky darkness, without any visible landmarks, where even basic direction finding was difficult.

Eschewing shelter Cheyenne trotted out into the center of the road. The limp he'd acquired when he was first injured, over a year ago, was back again, due to his recent wounds. Now he spotted the moon and recognition hit him.

"I saw the maps, Jason. The storage facility is that way," he pointed to their left.

Then, from several of the tumbledown structures people emerged, including several children being led by women. They began to run but appeared to be in a panic, seemingly without any idea of where they were going.

The sky lit up as the searchlight of the Apaches sought their targets. A woman screamed, loud and excited, something Cheyenne couldn't interpret exactly but knew its meaning. She picked up a small child, stumbled, regained her stance, and ran. Another woman duplicated the horrid screech as she, too, grabbed a child in one arm and nearly dragged another one by the hand.

Actually the women did know that there were two solidly built structures and in their confusion and desperation to find protection for their children, they ran towards the buildings that were the prime targets for the deadly Apaches.

"They don't know these kids are here!" Cheyenne screamed at Jason, meaning the helicopters, his voice now being drowned out as the attack ships neared, lower this time, their prehistoric whirling mind—numbing even to a disciplined soldier who knew exactly what was going on, much less to a panicked mother in a primitive country and who still believed in dragons and daemons.

"Those kids are going in exactly the wrong direction! The choppers won't see them from the angle they're coming in!

"You are cleared to engage, Red."

"Roger."

"You are cleared to engage, Blue."

"Roger. Targeting."

"Missiles away."

"Missiles away."

The swoosh of the missiles was barely audible amid the thumping of the helicopter's rotors.

"We've got to get to those kids, Jason!"

"Are you nuts? We'll get ourselves blown to hell and gone!"

"You got anything better going on right now, Private?"

Jason laughed, a bizarre reaction amidst the screams and the winds and whumps of the helicopters.

"No sir, Cheyenne, I guess not. Lead me on, Chief, into the valley of death."

∗∗∗

TWELVE

"People are crazy, times are strange..."---from the song, "Things Have Changed", by Bob Dylan

"As of Sunday, 4,417 U.S. servicemembers had been reported killed in the Iraq war. In and around Afghanistan, 1,259 U.S. servicemembers had been reported killed...---Statistics reported in USA Today, Nov. 8, 2010

THE DAY COULDN'T have started out worse.

I awoke early and tiptoed around so as to not awaken Di, who continued to sleep soundly even after I had finished in the shower. She lay on her back and I don't think she had moved since I first woke up and looked at her, very beautiful with her bright auburn hair spilling over the pillow.

I figured I'd get myself ready and go over to the booth while Di dressed and did whatever she needed to do, and have her join me for breakfast when she was ready. So far so good; then, I made the mistake of checking my e-mail, but why not, I do so every morning.

There was a message from Dennis saying he was taking the red-eye and not to worry about sending anyone because he had rented a car. On the company dime, he added, but he thought it would be more convenient then sending someone to pick him up. He said he'd get to the convention center in time for the show.

There were several other messages, most of which I deleted, and there was one I particularly delayed opening because at first I wasn't sure about the sender. It was from 'Col. S.', and the subject was shown simply as 'C'. Staring at the screen, it slowly dawned on me that I did know who it was from, but I feared reading it.

The message had come in less than an hour ago and read as follows:

"See attached message received thirty minutes ago..."

The attachment read:

"The international news agency Al Jazeera, based out of Qatar, today reported a message allegedly received from Osama bin Laden. Besides its usual warning to America and its allies, the message stated that 'Two American Special Operations spies were captured recently near a small village in North Waziristan and will be put on trial, and executed if convicted, for crimes against Islam, and against the nation of Pakistan.'

The alleged American spies were not identified and the Pentagon denies that they have any Special Operations soldiers operating inside Pakistan, nor are any American military personnel reported as missing. Pakistani officials said they had no knowledge of any American soldiers being captured in

Pakistan, and reiterated that American soldiers should not be operating inside Pakistan without clear consent from the Pakistani government."

Following the message was an addendum added, I assumed, by Col. S.:

"While the accuracy of the message has not yet been verified 100%, it is feared that the two soldiers referenced are one Cpt. C.S., and another soldier who was with C.S. on a mission inside P. I know Cpt. C.S. has been in contact with you. Please do not reply to this message; I'll contact you when I have more definitive info. Please advise others with prudence and delete this message after reading."

I was positive the message was from the man Cheyenne had mentioned to me, though not by name. I doubt even Cheyenne realized that this Col. S. knew about his contacts with me. I read the message again, but decided to not yet delete it. I fiercely debated whether to wake Di now and have her read it, or wait until after the day's work. I took the coward's way out and shut off my laptop.

For at least a minute I stood still in the middle of the room, looking down at Di, still sleeping the sleep of the innocent. At least, of the ignorant.

"Hey, sleeping beauty, time to rise and shine."

When she stirred but didn't open her eyes, I sat down on the side of the bed and nudged her shoulder.

"Hmm, what a nice surprise, Rock, to see you," she purred, here eyes open and then closing again.

"Did we have a good time?"

"Di, you wake up flirting, don't you? C'mon, dear, it's time to get yourself ready for your first day of work for Hammond Tools."

"I resign. I'm going back to sleep." She rolled over on her side.

I lightly whacked her on the rear end and stood up.

"You do love me, don't you," now she was laughing so I knew she was awake.

"I'll meet you in the restaurant in forty-five minutes; is that sufficient time to make yourself beautiful?"

"No, it isn't, but I'll show up as soon as I can. If I'm not beautiful enough for you, you can fire me."

"Okay, see ya later," I said, and left, feeling guilty for not having shown her the message. I justified it by remembering that Col. S. had said the accuracy hadn't been 100% verified yet. Still, I'd have to show it to her, but later, I decided was better than sooner.

Di met me in an hour, looking perky and happy and pretty. She smiled and greeted me with a firm kiss on the cheek. I was feeling even more guilty but it was too late to show her or tell her about the e-mail now, and then expect her to go to work like everything is fine and dandy.

I poured coffee for her from the carafe the waiter had left on the table and we ordered breakfast.

"Have you heard from the fellow who's flying in today?"

I nodded. "Yes, Dennis; he said he be here in time. You'll like him."

It dawned on me that Dennis was only a couple years older than Di, good-looking, single, good future. I hope she won't think I'm playing matchmaker because the notion never occurred to me until now. But, you never know. So now I felt even more guilty, because just the possibility I might have set up Di with another guy seemed like I was being disloyal to Cheyenne. But if Chey can't sit still long enough to ask Di to marry him, it's not my problem.

"I'm kind of nervous," Di said. "Maybe I shouldn't say much, you know, so I don't say anything stupid."

"You'll do fine. It won't get crowded until afternoon and by then you'll have a feel for what to say. Ask them to tell you about themselves, or their business, what kind of system they're looking for. The more they talk the less you have to. Then you suggest that 'our service expert' will consult with them, and nudge Dennis or me. I have confidence in you."

"Why, Rock, why do you have confidence in me?"

I pondered her question for a moment while sipping coffee. I remembered back to when I walked into the *Only Café* and saw Di, or Dinah, then, when we didn't yet know each other. Her physical attractiveness was certainly the first thing that caught my eye. But her pleasant personality and bubbly manner, her way of talking to the people, making every customer feel important, even her flirtatious ways, never mean or sly, made her sparkle. I wondered then and still do now, why she hadn't captured the heart of many a young man. I guess because everyone around the little town she grew up in, and even the surrounding towns, knew that she and Cheyenne had been basically betrothed since they were children, so Di was considered off-limits. Be interesting to read what she says in her Diary about her love life, or lack thereof.

"It's partially a hunch, based on my having worked up the ladder and then, where I am now, having to supervise other people. Your only fault is you're too cute, so I suspect potential employers see you as someone who can't be both smart and efficient."

"Too cute? You've got to be kidding. I still feel I look like someone who's barely survived an attack of the killer tomatoes, the way those ruffians went after us. My lip still hurts."

"The bruise is hardly noticeable."

"Speaking of which, have you called Helen this morning?"

"No, come to think of it, I haven't."

"Don't you think you should?"

"I thought you didn't like her?"

"Rock, whether I do or not is irrelevant to your responsibilities to her. She's your...friend, and employee, and she's all beat up and feeling sorry and angry and sullen, and who knows what else. I suspect she is extremely frustrated at not being able to be here."

"You're right. I was going to call her this evening, but maybe I should do so before we get busy."

"Yes, you should. Go now before breakfast arrives."

"I'll step outside and call her," I said, pulling out my cell.

"Tell her I look awful and you told me to go away, that'll make her feel better," Di said to as I rose to go.

I laughed and went outside. Dennis was coming in as I was going out. I pointed out the table where Di was sitting and told him to introduce himself. He looked at me like, you picked up a girl while you've been here?

I frowned. "It's kind of a long story, but she's an ...old friend, and she's going to help us in the booth."

He glanced over to where Di was seated and said, "Can't be very old."

"I'll be right back."

When I called Helen I got her voice mail. I left a message telling her I felt we were in good shape for the show with Dennis here and that I missed her and hoped she was felling better and I'd call her later, blah, blah. I didn't even mention Di. When I returned to the table Di and Dennis were laughing and getting along famously.

Suffice it to say, the rest of the day went better than expected. I was glad Dennis was here; it was the way I should have planned the event in the first place. Helen could get a little pushy; Dennis was competent but laid back, confident without being arrogant. Di performed brilliantly. It wasn't long before I heard her discussing 'line resolution', 'vandal-proof housing', 'zooms', and 'wireless access points'. Just enough verbiage to sound like she knew what she was talking about, but not too much to get her in trouble. She did as I'd suggested and encouraged people to talk about their business until they asked specific questions about installations, engineering problems, and costs. Then she turned to Dennis or me with a big smile and we took over. I was sure that in a few weeks I could teach Di enough that she could handle all the questions by herself.

The booths were open until late into the evening on this day, Saturday, so dinner was each person taking a turn to skip out for fast food. But finally, about the time our feet were yapping at us, we were able to close the booth and retire to the hotel bar for a well-deserved drink.

"This place is full. I had to get a room down the street," Dennis said.

I looked at Di and grimaced. "Ah, geez, Di."

"I forgot too, Rock."

'What?" said Dennis, wanting to get in on the secret.

"Ah, Di needs a room," I said. "Forgot to check on that today."

"Oh. I thought you were staying here," Dennis said, still not with it.

"I did stay here last night, but..." She looked at me and I looked at her and Dennis looked at us and said, "Oh, I see."

"No, Dennis, don't get carried away now. Are you at the River Walk Plaza?"

He nodded. "I called from the plane."

"Do you think you could call and see if they have another room, for Di?"

"Sure, I'll call right now, but I doubt they have anything. At first they said they had nothing for me but then found a cancellation." Dennis went to make the call and I grinned sheepishly at Di.

"Sorry. Di, hope I didn't mess anything up for you."

"Huh? Whaddya mean, mess anything up?" She mugged at me as if I'd said an especially stupid thing.

"What are you thinking? Oh, Rock, don't be silly, I just met the guy."

I shrugged. "Yeah, but now he thinks, or he knows, you stayed with me, and maybe if he was thinking..."

"You didn't do this to set us up, did you Rock? Tell me you didn't because if you did..."

"You'd be really pissed, wouldn't you?"

She folded her arms in front of her and stared daggers.

"Honestly, Di, I wasn't thinking anything. Heck, I didn't call Dennis to come here until after Helen had her accident."

"But you're thinking it now."

"Well, you two seem to be getting along like old buddies, and now if he thinks that you and I, and you know, he knows about Helen..."

Di laughed, which irritated me, but the more she laughed, covering her mouth to stifle the sound, the more it made me laugh, too.

We were still giggling when Dennis returned and we both guiltily turned stolid as he sat down.

"They're full up. What'd you expect, Rock, with three conventions in town and it's the weekend? You'd probably have to go a long way out to find place that's got a room."

"Alright, never mind, we'll work something out. Sorry, Dennis."

"What for? None of my business."

We went back to our drinks and eventually returned to small talk, and then moved on to what to expect tomorrow. We'd corralled several prospective clients today and already the show was looking like a success. Still, I felt bad because if Dennis was eyeing Di, he now was assuming she and I were shacking up, if he even knew the term, and wouldn't approach Di with a ten-foot pole, if he knew that phrase. Screw it, I'll explain to him later. Or not.

We broke up and Dennis left to go to his hotel and Di and I went up to our shared room. It was just as well, I realized, because had she left with Dennis I still wouldn't have a chance to tell her about the e-mail. The fact that I'd kept it from her for over twelve hours sent a shiver through my entire body. Talk about being pissed, she's gonna kill me.

In the room Di plopped down on her bed and took off her shoes, letting them drop with two clunks. She rubbed her feet and sighed as she did so.

"I've been wanting to do that since noon."

I excused myself to the bathroom and when I got out Di was lying on her back, her legs dangling over the edge of the bed. For a second I thought she'd fallen asleep.

"Did I really do okay, Rock?" she asked, without opening her eyes.

"Yes, Di, you did wonderfully. I couldn't have asked for more. You up to another day? Sunday's not as long."

"Sure, sure. Don't know why my feet are so sore, I used to stand all day at the café."

"The floor's harder here, I suppose. You should sit down more often when it's not busy."

She rose up, slowly, and began to unbutton her blouse.

"Like yesterday?" she said, pointing to the bathroom. "Me, then you?"

"Ah, Di, wait a minute. I grabbed her hands, stopping her from continuing to unbutton.

"Oh, don't worry, Rock, I was heading for the bathroom. I'm too tired to flirt with you tonight, sorry, dear."

"No, wait, there's something I have to tell you. To show you, I mean."

She frowned. "Why so serious? Don't tell me you decided to marry Helen? Have you talked to her tonight, by the way? How's she feeling?"

I nodded. "Yes, I called her, and no I didn't decide to marry her. She's feeling left out, but was glad to hear the show went smoothly and that you did fine, though I got the impression she thinks I was covering for you, but no matter, sit down." I eased her back onto the bed and took my laptop out of its bag.

Several times during the day, as I accessed information on the laptop, I thought of the ominous message waiting there.

"I hope you don't expect me to study tonight."

I didn't reply and said nothing until I'd accessed my e-mails. There were no new ones from Col. S. I set the laptop on the bed and turned the screen so Di could see it.

"I received an e-mail from someone who I believe is Chey's commander. Or at least he works with Chey."

"Oh, God, what?"

"Here, I'll let you read it."

She read the message, the attachment, and Col. S's addendum. She seemed confused, and read the messages again. Her body shuddered and I heard a mewl escape her lips, almost imperceptible, like gas seeping from a miniscule tear in a balloon. Her face screwed into such a scowl you'd think it was Diane Keaton screaming at Al Pacino in *The Godfather.*

"Godammit! Damn it all, all of you!"

"Di?"

She pushed the laptop, blaming the hunk of bits and bytes, and I had to practically dive over the bed to catch it before it crashed to the floor. Di pounded the mattress with her fists.

I folded the laptop shut and held it in my arms, uncertain what to say or do. Had Spencer Tracy been a woman he couldn't have done a better job than Di did of turning into a female equivalent of Mr. Hyde. She continued to pound the bed with both fists, and a primitive moan accompanied the pummeling. Her hands gripped the blanket and pulled it into a ball that she tugged to her chest.

"Fucking wars, and guns!" She stood up and looked at me as if I was evil incarnate. She swung her arms wildly but mostly hit the laptop as I held it in front of me. I feared she'd damage it more than I feared her hurting me, so I backed away and set the computer on my bed. She moved forward and continued to beat on my chest.

"You goddamn men and your wars and guns, and, and fucking cage fights, and dogfights, and kickboxing, and, and..."

The force of her fists began to slacken, just in time, too, because the repeated bashing was beginning to take its toll on me. I took her wrists in my hands, gently, not to frighten her, but she shook free of me and again hit me with both fists, but much weaker this time, slowing with each clout. One of her wild swings caught me on the cheek and I felt a scratch that shocked me by the ferociousness of Di's anger. She started to sob, a mournful cry more distressful than I'd ever heard from anyone, even in the most atrocious horror film. All the stress of the past year, of wondering and worrying about Cheyenne and the dangers he faced, dangers Di could not imagine, was finally too much for Di to contain. Like a string of pearls that has broken, her tears dripped and bounced along the floor.

I recalled how I felt when Mary Ann died, and I wanted to scream and beat on something. I wanted to throw a lamp through a window, or a glass at a mirror, or hit someone until my knuckles bled. I wanted to die. I did go to the pound where the totaled car had been towed, to retrieve personal possessions. I wished I could set the damned thing on fire, and maybe I would have had a guard not been with me. All I could do as I was leaving was spit on the car, my feeble gesture of defiance, blaming the dumb hunk of metal for an accident of fate.

Her energy drained, Di slumped to the floor, slipping downward in slow motion, as if her body were melting from the bottom up, like James Arness in the original *The Thing,* which only goes to show that in the most calamitous moments, my mind conjures up scenes from movies or songs to help me understand the incomprehensible.

This time when I took hold of her wrists she didn't resist and I slumped down with her, not wanting to tower over her in her torment.

We sat on the floor like two derelicts passed out after their last bottle of hooch had been emptied, and who didn't have the strength or the interest in ever rising again. Why face life when the fates keep kicking you in the face? An overly dramatic embellishment of course—neither Di nor I had very many bad licks in our lives, and less than most, truth be told. Even losing my wife in an accident was not something unique in world history. But when it hits the fan, people are tempted to ask, why me, as if we are special and don't deserve anything but good fortune.

I let go of her wrists and she stretched her arms around my neck and laid her head on my shoulder. The sobbing, which had eased, now morphed into a steady sniffling. I felt her tears run down her cheek and drip onto my neck. I wanted to wipe her eyes but didn't want to move just yet, and I don't think she wanted me to dry them anyway. The tears needed to flow freely to expel her anger and fear.

I know we all exaggerate the time that has passed during a notable or jarring event. People say the earth shook for at least three minutes, when in fact the earthquake lasted ten seconds. Had it lasted three minutes all the buildings in the city would have come down in a cataclysm of dust and destruction. But truly, I know we sat on the floor, entwined around each other, not moving, for at least five minutes, maybe longer. The only sound was Di's decreasing sniffles.

Finally, she pulled her head off my shoulder and rubbed under her eyes. I duplicated her effort, wiping away the remaining tears with my finger.

"I got your shirt all wet," Di muttered, the words slurring amidst the last gasps of her sobs.

"No matter."

"How could you not tell me, Rock? Just because you wanted me to work?" For all her recent rage, and her right to be angry with me, her voice was meek and pathetic.

I shook my head. "I was wrong to keep it from you, but was afraid how you'd react, and I knew I couldn't take the time to be with you this morning, if you needed me."

She nodded, agreeing, I think, only because the strength to be angry with me had oozed away.

"He might not be dead, Di. The addendum from this colonel said they weren't positive of the information."

Di nodded, but it wasn't a convincing nod. "I can't do this again, Rock. I joke and I flirt and kid around to cover up, but I can't go on for months wondering if he's really dead, thinking any day he'll come limping home again. I'll be an old maid and I'll still be waiting. Probably have Alzheimer's and not remember what I'm waiting for."

"Yeah, I know it's difficult."

She looked at me with watery eyes, the two of us still flopped down on our butts, too drained to get up off the floor.

"How do you know, Rock?"

"I told you Di, I've been there."

"Did you lose someone even before Mary Ann? Like when you were in Vietnam?"

I hesitated, not wanting to say the dumb, mundane reflection that came to me, but I did. "I lost whatever innocence remained."

"Sorry, Rock. At least with Chey there's a chance, but for you, Mary Ann is never coming back."

That was exactly what I was thinking. With a grunt I made the effort to rise, then reached down to Di and helped her stand up.

"One of the worst things about getting old, Di, is that it's harder to get up off the floor."

"I hope you mean that literally, not figuratively."

She laughed then, and her smile lit the room and nearly, but not quite, extinguished the gloom we both felt.

"Listen, I've got some e-mails I need to respond to. I'm going to take my laptop to the bar and work there for awhile. Why don't you take a shower or a bath, and get to bed. I'll be quiet when I come in so as not to wake you."

She nodded and didn't even tease me about whether I wanted to scrub her back, and I hoped that her despair over Cheyenne wouldn't shatter her spirit.

"We'll hope for the best, Di. Cheyenne's got nine lives so I'm betting he'll be back, and this time he'll stay home."

"Humph. Cheyenne will resign from the army when Brett Favre retires from football."

"I thought you didn't know football."

"I'm trying to learn," she answered.

"I'll see you later," I said. "I'll hang the 'Do Not Disturb Sign' on the doorknob.

"Tuck me in when you come back," she said as I went out the door.

That was a good sign.

***

THIRTEEN

A NATO air strike that appears to have killed nine children as they collected firewood drew strong condemnation from Afghan President Hamid Karzai, as well as an apology from the commander of NATO forces. ---newspaper article, Washington Post, Sacramento Bee and others, March 3, 2011.

THE FIRST EXPLOSIONS resulted in a fireball that was nothing less than a super nova going off in the blackest regions of outer space. Anyone looking at it was temporarily blinded. The first missiles hit dead-on to the main storage depot of rocket-propelled grenades, including a large cache of high explosive anti-tank rounds, home–made explosive materials for constructing IEDs, such as ammonium nitrate, and aging, unexploded Russian ordnance.

Cheyenne and Jason hit the ground a split-second before the shock wave blew past them and pummeled them with dirt, bits of wood and metal, and body parts. How many people died in that explosion may never be known. Village leaders and the Haqqani would later claim as many as ten women and children died while NATO and American forces would dispute that claim, but neither side would be able to provide definitive proof one way or the other.

"Hold on Apache Red, Blue"

"Say again, Apache Yellow?"

"Hey, it looks like there are people running *towards* the depot, Control."

" Apache Yellow, do you see any personnel on the ground?"

"Bull's-eye, Apache Red!"

"Too fuckin' late."

"Ditto, Blue, that's one."

"You are cleared for another pass if your second target is available."

"There are surely bad guys guarding the depot, but I think I see women and kids."

"Are we cleared, Control?"

"No, No! Make another pass, Red, Blue I'll be back with you."

"Roger."

"Apache Yellow, maintain surveillance, report any civilian activity."

"Roger."

EVEN BEFORE THE debris ceased raining down on them, Cheyenne and Jason had leaped up and started to run towards the villagers who were now frozen in disarray and uncertainly. Cheyenne quickly counted a dozen women and at least as many children, and a handful of men who looked too old to be fighting any more battles. They were stunned and terrified.

Cheyenne scared the already frightened villagers as he yelled at them to move back to their flimsy kalats, their homes, trying to convince them that contrary to what seemed logical, they were safer there than in the large wooden and concrete buildings that housed the weapons and ordnance. But then he also realized that the roaring flames might easily spread embers among all the other structures, so nowhere in the compound was safe.

The confused people huddled and shivered in fear as Jason and Cheyenne waved their arms and weapons and screamed at them. Jason yelled in English, which the people didn't understand, and Cheyenne called out in several dialects, randomly spitting out words he hoped someone would understand. He probably looked like a wild man, waving a gun in each hand and screaming at them while he ran clumsily.

Unable to encourage the group to begin moving, Jason and Cheyenne pushed the women and children and old men away from the buildings and along the road that led to the woodlands and the stream outside the compound. Cheyenne calculated that if the Apaches made another pass the spotter would recognize the group as civilians and not launch any missiles in their vicinity. There should be enough light from the burning depot for them to see what was happening. But as they moved farther from the buildings visibility again became an issue. The sun was long gone, and when the sun sank below the horizon here, the darkness came down like a wide swath of black paint over a window.

Seconds later the whir of the approaching Apaches again began to drown out most other sounds, including the crying of children and the shrieks of the women and the yelling of the two American soldiers.

"Control, I see a group of people running away from the compound. Looks like civilians...hard to see with the smoke, but...yes, definitely women and children there."

"Positive on the ID, Apache Yellow?"

"Roger. There also appear to be two men urging them away...away from the target area."

"What the hell? Hold fire Apache Blue, Apache Red."

"Affirmative. We'll be in position in a few seconds."

"You are not, repeat, *not* cleared to fire."

"Understood, Control."

"Apache Yellow, any positive ID on the two men you mentioned?"

"Hard to tell, but they look like our guys, tell the truth."

"I wouldn't think that likely."

"We shouldn't have any ground assets here."

"Okay, guys, call it off, you did enough."

"Easy pickins, Control."

"Can't take the chance, not if there are civilians around. We don't need that problem."

"Too dark to be sure."

"Okay, call it a day and come on home."

"That's an affirmative."

FROM ANOTHER direction came a new problem. Something was kicking up dirt at Cheyenne's feet as he continued to shove the people along. Jason was at the side of the group, waving them onward. The villagers seemed to get the idea now, to move away from the building they had intended to shelter them from the missile attack.

Bullets were splattering everywhere and they weren't coming from the sky. The screaming increased as the people recognized the sound of gunfire, more distinct now as the helicopters moved farther away. One woman fell and a child bent down crying and tugging at the woman.

Another projectile hit the ground near Jason, kicking up dirt and ricocheting, knocking him down. To his left, Cheyenne spotted the flash of the shots, coming from the building next to the ones which the terrified villagers had fled, a larger building, more of a warehouse than a kalat. He fired rapidly in return, not taking time to aim, then bent down to check on the fallen woman. She was dead. He picked up the crying child, a girl no more than three years old. More shots whistled past him and one nicked the child, fortunately no more than a flesh wound.

"Who the fuck is firing at us?!" Cheyenne yelled. Then he saw Jason, struggling to regain his feet.

"How bad?"

"I'm okay, just a scratch."

"Got yourself another Purple Heart. Here, take this girl, I'm going after whoever the hell it is that's shooting at us. Keep herding them away from the village."

Cheyenne handed the girl to Jason. With a rifle in one hand Jason hoisted the child against his left shoulder and she held on but continued to cry.

"I think the choppers are gone, Cheyenne."

"Just in case, Jason, move!"

Jason moved out as fast as he could, again calling out to the group to continue moving, although the danger from helicopter attack apparently was ended. Another risk was that the flames would spread to the other shacks, and the piles of dry wood, grass, and cardboard, and set the entire compound ablaze. Even the woods would be a dangerous spot, so Jason intended to take the people as far as the stream.

Cheyenne ducked behind a tree stump as two more bullets ripped into the dirt and kicked up pebbles that splattered against his legs. As he scanned the building in the direction from which the firing appeared to originate, a flare-up from the burning depot reflected off a window and he saw a face.

"By the spirit of Crazy Horse, it's goddamn ab-Hawsawi!"

Cheyenne shot quickly at the window but the face was gone. Then, from behind a grove of fruit trees that ranged from the building in the direction Jason was prodding the villagers, Cheyenne saw another familiar face.

"Spiedel! We've got to quit meeting like this, Colonel. Damn!"

Colonel Spiedel smiled—or grimaced; with him it was hard to tell the difference, his face faintly lit by the glow of the flames that still burned less than hundred yards away. He turned to speak to a man following him.

"Perez, you and the others move these women and kids out of danger. The wounded ones send back on the birds."

"Yes, sir."

Running in a stoop Jason Jones joined Cheyenne and the colonel.

"Place is getting crowded," said Cheyenne.

"I handed off the girl to one of the colonel's men."

"You go with them, Jason, that's an order."

"Cheyenne, sir, I want..."

"I don't care what you want, soldier. No need to risk your life. Nothing for you here."

Jason's puzzled face spun from Cheyenne to Spiedel and back again. Then he looked at the building from which the shots had been fired.

"Who's in there, Cheyenne?"

"My old friend, the one I told you about. I owe him. It's the reason I'm here."

"You sure he's in there, Captain Smith?" Spiedel said, the formality obvious.

"I'm sure, and if we keep gabbing here and he'll get away again. Now Jason, I haven't got time to argue. Move out."

Jason hesitated, then nodded. "Good luck, sirs."

ISLAMABAD...---Thursday's missile attack was carried out in North Waziristan, the region on the border with Afghanistan that is the focus of the drone campaign and the base of a menacing collection of militant groups, including al-Qaida and the Haqqani network, a ferocious ally of the Afghan Taliban. --- news article, McClatchy Newspapers, March 18, 2011.

"SO WHAT DO we have here, Cheyenne?"

"FUBAR, Colonel, and beyond."

"Way beyond recognition, uh?"

Cheyenne nodded. "The Haqqani moved villagers here, probably from Alizai, to make the arms depot look like a friendly food storage barn. Trouble is, our intel hadn't picked it up, at least, that's the way it looks to me.

"I think they knew."

"Who knew?"

"Not the poor saps running this place, but whoever commands the district operations. We saw three of them leave in a jeep, like the devil was chasing them. Only a couple of guards were left behind. It's like they knew a raid was coming and they cleared out. My thinking is, we were supposed to be found here, as evidence that we planned the attack."

"Set it up? Worth losing their ammo depot just to give us the bad publicity of killing civilians? You're a suspicious bastard."

"It's been known to happen. I think most of the stuff in there is old Russian junk, not much good anymore except for making a lot of noise and smoke when it blows up."

The colonel nodded. "You may be right. The shit will fly again; more civilian deaths. You think ab-Hawsawi's behind it?"

Cheyenne shrugged, stammered, his anger rising.

"You shouldn't take it personal, Cheyenne."

"Yeah, yeah, but you know what he did. Cost us three men, probably more. And this..." Cheyenne pointed at the burning building. "Could be his brilliant idea, too."

"You think he's still holed up in that warehouse?" Spiedel asked, nodding towards the building that was burnished in an orange-yellow glare from the flames still whipping at the depot.

"I haven't seen him come out, and your men should have seen him if he got out the back way."

"Up till a few minutes ago, yes, but now they're busy with the villagers."

"Then we go in and find him."

Cheyenne checked the AK-47 he had appropriated from the guard, made a 360 degrees scan of his surroundings, saw no one, but did hear faint shouts from a distance, and even fainter the sound of a vehicle, the rumble diminishing by the second.

"The rats are fleeing."

"Your ballgame," Spiedel said.

"Hey, rumor has it you're getting your first star," Cheyenne said to Spiedel. "Nice going. So I won't be seeing much of you anymore, hey?"

"Damn; last thing I want is a star. No more field work. Fuck it, let's go."

Cheyenne leading the way, his sniper's rifle strapped across his back, the AK-47 in his right hand, the two men commenced to crawl towards the building, trying to stay out of the glare of the fire. Every few feet Cheyenne stopped and surveyed the area. To their left, as the blaze found fuel and destroyed it, the flames would abate temporarily, and creep along until it discovered a new cache for the feeding, and it would erupt again. At this moment it was beginning to subside, the better to keep Cheyenne and Spiedel in the dark, but it also gave ab-Hawsawi protection. If the bastard was still in there.

As the flames faded the darkness gave Cheyenne confidence and he rose and dashed forward. Spiedel fired bursts at each of the several windows as Cheyenne galloped towards the building. He dove for cover against the side of the building, near one of the windows. He waited a second for Spiedel to stop, then jumped up and shot a burst through the window, then ducked down.

As Spiedel began his dash Cheyenne stepped back a few feet and sprayed at all the windows, most of which were on the upper level. There was no return gunfire.

Spiedel joined Cheyenne and they both plastered themselves against the building.

"I fear your friend has flown the coop," Spiedel said.

"Maybe. He was wounded. When I got a glimpse of him a few minutes ago I could see he still had a bandage on his hand."

"So? He doesn't run on his hands."

"No, I just point it out because the white bandage will give him away in the dark, if he hasn't torn it off."

"And if he's still in there."

"Other than the vehicle we heard a moment ago, I haven't heard or seen any others leaving, so I suspect he's still inside, being quiet like a monk, waiting for a chance to pick us off."

"Or hoping we'll go away."

'No, he knows I've been after him and he wants to settle this here and now, as I do."

"Fortunately we're too smart for him."

Cheyenne chuckled. "That may be the first time I ever heard you say anything even slightly humorous, Colonel. Are you getting soft?"

"Cynical, is more like it."

"You were born cynical. You still like this business?"

Spiedel didn't answer. The question was as odd as if he'd been asked to explain the physics of the Big Bang theory.

"I guess I don't know anything else."

After several seconds Cheyenne nodded and said, "Yeah. You're a good man, Colonel. Now let's go find this piece of shit."

From a few hundred yards away they recognized the whir of the Kiowas moving off, carrying the children injured badly enough to need medical attention, and the men who'd come with Spiedel. Jason Jones waved 'good luck' as the choppers flew off. He then moved out at a double-time pace towards where he'd last seen Cheyenne and Spiedel.

The burning depot was not much more than a large pile of ashes, but then the fire flared anew on the adjoining structure, which was to have been the Apaches' secondary target. Several small explosions suggested there'd been no need to use any more of their own ammunition.

The new illumination spread over the warehouse outside of which Cheyenne and Spiedel huddled. The glow warmed their faces for an instant and then they dashed through a doorway into the dark building. For a split-second they feared ab-Hawsawi would be there, waiting to blow them away. Then for the next several seconds Cheyenne rued that his quarry hadn't been waiting. Let's finish our business. At that moment Cheyenne truly felt fearless about death, as long as he could take ab-Hawsawi with him and avenge the deaths of the men that had been betrayed.

In the darkness he saw a face, but it wasn't inside the building, it was inside of him. The face was Di's and the one regret Cheyenne now felt was that he had left her the way he had. He knew, he promised, and knew it was a promise he could forever keep, that if he did get out of this he would make it up to her. Of course, she might not be interested in anything he had to say or do ever again.

Spiedel motioned to Cheyenne to sweep around the left side of the large room they were in. The colonel had told Cheyenne it was his mission, but his natural tendency to lead took over. Slowly they crept forward, the darkness enveloping them and after a few steps they could no longer see each other. The scrape of a chair caused Cheyenne to stop and stoop down.

"Me; hit a chair," came a whisper from across the room.

The smell of the smoke from outside mixed with the odor of dirt and hay, of rotting vegetation and grease. The building must have been used for storing food at one time, Cheyenne figured, maybe grain, and now fuel, or fertilizer. Again he heard a noise, this time coming from straight ahead, certainly not

Spiedel. He looked to his right, trying to find the shape of the colonel. He dropped to the floor, making himself practically invisible.

"Psst, Spiedel."

He thought he saw a hand move, then, as his eyes began to adjust and his night vision set in, Cheyenne saw the shape of the colonel as he moved silently across the room, a deadly silhouette.

At the back end of the room, directly opposite from where the two men had entered, was another doorway, a gray rectangle against the blackness. From the gray came another sound, the sound of footsteps, and they weren't from a cat or a rat.

Yes, it could be a rat, Cheyenne pondered.

A shape appeared in the doorway, and Cheyenne aimed, but held off as the shape did not look at all like ab-Hawsawi, nor did Cheyenne spy any white from the bandage. Of course if ab-Hawsawi's smart he took the bandage off or covered it with dirt.

Then Cheyenne recognized the figure standing there and he both smiled and was angry at the same time. "Hey, kid," he called out, just above a whisper.

Twenty feet to Cheyenne's right and several feet ahead of him, the form of Spiedel raised his rifle, but he, too, paused, unsure of his target. Then a flash from the shape in the doorway shot outward in the direction of Colonel Spiedel.

Cheyenne winced in surprise and heard a grunt come from Spiedel.

"No, kid!"

Spiedel stood fearless, like the clichéd hero in an action movie, and blasted away, one burst, then another. Jason, in the doorway responded in kind, until he fell with a thump.

"No! Stop, Spiedel, it's Jones!"

"Ah, shit!"

As Cheyenne started forward another arrow of yellow pierced the darkness, this time from above. He heard another thud and assumed it was Spiedel falling down. Cheyenne fired upwards towards the general area he'd seen the flash, no time to aim, and then crawled under a desk. Another burst of gunfire erupted and Cheyenne heard the splattering and dull whacks as bullets hit wood and dirt, and maybe a body, in the area Spiedel had last been. Another burst sent a salvo that ripped into the desk Cheyenne was using for protection.

Then silence. After a few seconds that felt like hours, without daring to come out from under the desk, Cheyenne called out, not bothering to keep his voice low.

"Jason? Spiedel?"

He was answered by another barrage and heard the bullets tear chunks of wood out of the desk and floor. Must be a good old piece of work; funny to find a solid piece of workmanship here in the boonies. Probably built by some old carpenter a hundred years ago, but ab-Hawsawi could sit up in his loft and rip it to shreds in minutes.

Cheyenne took several deep breaths, imagined his movements when he would leave his cover, then darted out and to his left. He quickly reversed direction, then dove, rolled, and as gunshots sprayed the floor, always a few inches behind him, he dashed for the doorway. He dove through it as bullets gashed the doorframe.

There was more light on this side of the door, coming from a small night-light bulb off to the side, just enough for Cheyenne to recognize the body of Jason Jones.

"Damn it, kid, damn it! I told you there was nothing for you here."

Cheyenne sidled up to the doorway, sitting himself to one side, away from the opening. Several shots flew past him, some hitting the body of Jason Jones. Ab-Hawsawi was taking a wild chance that he might get a lucky hit.

Bastard, Cheyenne said to himself. Risking another wild burst he crawled to the body and tugged until he'd pulled it away from the doorway. At least he won't get pelted anymore, not that it'd matter to a corpse.

Cheyenne called out, "Spiedel, if you're there, don't say anything to give away your position."

Another fusillade from ab-Hawsawi's AK-47 battered the doorframe and flew through the opening, most of the shots ripping into the floorboards. Cheyenne moved farther away.

There's a good fuckin' chance that Spiedel isn't just being smart by not saying anything, because he may have finished his last mission, Cheyenne reckoned. Well, hell, the old man didn't want to be a general anyway. He'd be no good stuck behind a desk, or sitting for hours in meetings drinking coffee and stifling yawns. Cheyenne decided staying where he was, pinned down, was not a good idea any more. It was hours until morning and it looked like his enemy was content to sit where he was until he smoked Cheyenne into the open.

Ain't no more cowboys coming to the rescue, I fear, least not until daylight, and by then I may be past rescuing.

Cheyenne stepped slowly across the room, doing his best imitation of a mouse, hoping ab-Hawsawi would think he was still ensconced near the doorway. What he was looking for was a stairway to the next level. And soon he found it.

The stairs looked fragile and Cheyenne feared each step would be a warning bell for ab-Hawsawi. He took off his boots. It might not make a difference, but maybe...from outside he heard an explosion.

The conflagration had reached another store of munitions and was gorging on new fuel like a dragon that had discovered a helpless stand of sheep. As another blast shook the night Cheyenne stepped up on the second riser. He heard a tiny creak but was sure it couldn't have been recognized by ab-Hawsawi over the sound of the explosion. With one foot on the riser and one foot held in the air, mid-step, he waited. At the next blast he took two more leaps and was near the top of the stairway.

Then he waited for several minutes, hoping there'd be at least one more opportunity for him to manage the last couple of steps. Suddenly it came, a lesser explosion, but enough to muffle the sound of Cheyenne's jump to the second floor. He stooped down and quickly scanned his surroundings. There were several windows and the ones to his left glowed from the burning buildings outside, but no light shone directly on him.

Cheyenne froze and listened. The explosions had ceased, but flames still licked at the sky. It was the dead of night, and the silence of the dead prevailed. He set his sniper's rifle down as carefully and quietly as if he was putting the baby Jesus into His hay-layered crib.

After several minutes muscles that had not moved from the crouch he was in began to whimper. But he refused to move. He suspected ab-Hawsawi knew he was there, somewhere on the second floor. Having sucked the life out of the second section of the ammo depot, the fire again was weakening and the feeble light it had sent through the windows of the second floor dissipated. It wasn't quite pitch-black in the warehouse, but Cheyenne could only differentiate faint shades of black, some shades taking the form of a chair, or a large basket, or a barrel.

It was ab-Hawsawi who blinked first. It could have been a rat, but it was only one creak and then nothing, like the footfall of a person trying to move quietly, but who stopped suddenly when his step elicited a squeak. Cheyenne counted to himself. It was two minutes before he heard the next creak, and it was closer to him than the previous one.

If he could see me, he'd shoot. In fact, the bastard might be purposely making a noise hoping I'll shoot at the sound and give away my position. Cheyenne felt a cold sweat develop under his armpits and on his forehead. A drop rolled down his side, a tickle. When Cheyenne had a target in his sights, sometimes from hundreds of yards away, there was no real immediate danger. He could take his time, prepare himself, wait patiently, press the trigger between heartbeats, watch his victim fall, almost silently, and without haste, but with a purpose, make his getaway. Usually it worked that way. The two times things hadn't worked as planned he'd ended up in a pile of horse manure deeper than the one old man Williamson used to keep on his ranch a mile outside of Dry Hole. Wind was right, you'd smell it all over town.

Cheyenne had trained himself to stand calmly, to not move for long stretches of time. The aching muscles were no more than a mild itch, discomforts that could be ignored by telling oneself, only a little bit longer, only a little bit more irritation, like one more step, one more step...

The third creak was louder, to Cheyenne's right and couldn't be more than twelve or fifteen feet away. Cheyenne didn't hesitate. Nor did ab-Hawsawi, who pulled his trigger about a thousandth of a second before Cheyenne did. Cheyenne fired the captured AK-47 and kept blasting away, straight ahead at first, then fanning to the left and right, and up and down, ignoring the pain in his side. He didn't even hear the fall of the body amidst the racket of his weapon. The gun was hot in his hand, emptied of every round.

Cheyenne was so sure he'd destroyed his target he stood still, defenseless for now, ready to die if that was his fate, and then walked straight forward until he nearly stumbled over the body. He dragged it by the legs closer to one of the windows. Even then it was difficult to tell, but by the light of the stars and the embers of the fire, Cheyenne recognized the face of ab-Hawsawi. Johnny Bracken and the others were avenged.

Cheyenne slumped down, the pain in his side noticeable now that things had quieted down. He felt the dampness in his shirt, along his ribs. He lay back and closed his eyes; I need rest, he said to no one. I wonder if I should get a message to Susan and her parents.

ISLAMABAD—Just one day after a CIA contractor was absolved by a Pakistani court of a double murder charge, Pakistan and U.S. relations were plunged into a new crisis over a CIA directed drone missile strike that Pakistan said killed at least 36 civilians.---news article by McClatchy Newspapers, March 18, 2011.

IN SAN ANTONIO Rock decided to ignore the suggestion from Col. S., who in his e-mail had said to delete the message and not reply to it. Rock hadn't deleted it yet and now he opened it, read it again, hit the 'reply' button and began to type.

'Thank you for the info you conveyed. While I appreciate it, I and at least one other very interested person are desperate to know more about the whereabouts and condition of Cpt. C.S. Is there anymore you can tell me, or is there another way I can find out? Thank you.'

A few seconds later Rock received the strangest response he'd ever received. His screen went blue and for a moment he thought his computer was experiencing a complete meltdown. Then the familiar screen returned, mostly white space for entering his message, with his list of folders to one side and options listed at the top. The screen blinked, then came back and the following message appeared, in bold and in a font much larger than what Rock usually used.

'You have responded to an address that no longer exists and to which you are not authorize to contact. Cease immediately and delete any references to this address. You are in violation of National Security Ordinances and may be subject to arrest, imprisonment, and fines.'

Rock stared at the screen and read the message again. How could I be not authorized to contact an address that doesn't exist?

KABUL, Afghanistan---*A NATO airstrike targeting Taliban fighters accidentally killed seven civilians, including three children...the NATO led International Security Assistance Force called an airstrike on two vehicles believed to be carrying a Taliban leader and his associates. A NATO team assessing the damage discovered the civilians after the airstrike.--*New York Times, March 27, 2011

***

FOURTEEN

"There's too many smart guys around here. I'm glad I'm a dummy."
---Walter Brennan character in the movie, *Bad Day at Black Rock.*

Dear Diary:

I DON'T HAVE much time to write this morning, as I have to work again at the trade show. I didn't sleep well last night and then when I finally did fall asleep I was awakened by someone running a vacuum in the hallway. Sounded like that giant German tank as it plowed through the rubble of the crumbled city, aimed right at Tom Hanks in *Saving Private Ryan.* You know how thunderous an unexpected blaring sound is when you hear it in your dreams. Not that I remember what my dream was; it instantly vanished as no more than a wisp with the howl of the vacuum cleaner.

I'm more worried, more upset, about Cheyenne than I was the last time he was reported missing. Maybe it's because since he survived and returned home, to my utter shock, I felt that he'd had his share of life-threatening adventures and he, and I, shouldn't have to worry about it anymore. Dumb concept, hey?

This time I won't accept the Army if they tell me he's missing and presumed dead. They're going to have to show me a body, I don't care if I have to go to Afghanistan or Iraq or wherever to see it. Maybe Rock's friend, the general in Washington, can help?

I'm tired, I'm sure I look like hell, with red eyes from crying and wrinkles from worry, so I need to shower and see if I can fix my hair and repair my face so I don't scare away the customers—it'll be a miracle if I look decent enough and have enough energy to help Rock and Dennis today, but I said I would, and it'll be better than sitting around worrying all day. So, later.

AFTER THE TRADE show ended I was as happy Gene Kelly when he was singin' in the rain. We lined up far more prospective customers than I'd expected, nailed down several solid sales and a couple of long-term contracts, and I'm invited to give a presentation at one of the largest commercial security systems manufacturer's annual meeting in a few weeks, in San Francisco. Dennis said he got the impression they are looking to buy me out. I'd have to think hard about the possibilities.

Di and Dennis and I went to dinner at a restaurant on the River Walk and celebrated. We also decided that Dennis would drive my car to San Diego, while Di and I would ride back together in her car. This proposal caused Dennis' eyebrows to rise in suspicion. I waved him off as being foolish and explained that I needed to stop to see Helen on the way, and Di wanted to see her, too, since they had been traveling together when Helen got hurt. Di kicked me under the table and I pretended it didn't hurt.

I also explained that if Helen isn't ready to be released, I might have to wait for her and Di could go on, then I'd rent a car for Helen and I. Di kicked me again and this time I scowled at her. She knew I was right.

I seriously doubt Helen will be ready to go home. I called her after dinner (and before I could say much she lambasted me for not calling as soon as the show ended, not wait until after dinner, because she was anxious to hear how things went—I didn't ask why she didn't call me, but I think she was waiting me out.) She was already as mad as Peter Finch in *Network*, (you know, I'm mad as hell and I'm not going to take it...), because the doctor said she needs to stay in the hospital until she gets a decent rest and her blood pressure stabilizes.

Monday morning, and the euphoria of last evening has dissipated and it's back to business. Dennis has already left, at least an hour ahead of us as we motor west. Dennis asked if I thought he should stop and say hello to Helen on his way but I nixed the idea by telling him I needed him back at the plant as soon as possible.

Apparently Helen hasn't rested properly due to her eagerness to get out of the hospital and worrying about the show, which has simply served to raise her blood pressure and given her nurses headaches. It'll be interesting to see who leaves the hospital first, Helen or the nurses.

"So what if they say she can't go home for a week; are you going to wait for her, or what?" Di asked.

I pondered on Di's question, an answer not obvious. "I'm not sure, Di. Maybe in that case I'll drive with you, and then fly back. It might be easier anyway to bring her home by plane. I don't know."

"Oh, fun, I could pick you two up at the airport. My first assignment."

I didn't find Di's attempt at humor at all amusing.

"So what else are you going to do?" she asked.

I played like I didn't know what she meant, and made no response. When Di didn't say anymore, I asked, "Do about what?"

She shrugged. "Ah, nothing, never mind."

I didn't pursue it. After a successful week of business, the fun of having Di involved, and the elation last night as we celebrated with fine food and wine, I suddenly felt depressed.

I did know what Di was asking. It was what I was going to do about Helen. That is, about where our relationship was going, and it had nothing to do with Di. But Helen will probably think so. And Di has her own problems without worrying about mine.

The hospital where Helen was at (incarcerated, she called it) was about a three-hour drive, including one coffee stop. We drove for half an hour before anyone said anything else, each, I suppose, waiting for the other to say something. Funny how fast dark clouds could move in when the morning was sunny and bright. I wasn't even sure why I felt blue.

"Coffee?"

Di mumbled what I took for an affirmative.

I pulled off into the parking lot of a building whose sign spelled in large letters, 'COFFEE SHOP'.

Not speaking, we walked into the coffee shop, sat down and each said 'yes' to the waitress when she asked if we wanted coffee. I was tempted to say, 'This is a coffee shop, isn't it?' like some smart aleck young Jack Nicholson. I wasn't in the mood for jokes, even my own.

I tried to lighten the air. "Probably don't have very good pies."

"Doubt it," Di said. I scanned the menu but didn't see anything that interested me.

"You want anything."

She shook her head. "No, just coffee."

"What are you going to do, Di?"

"I asked first," she said, continuing the conversation from over a half hour ago, when she asked me what I was going to do about Helen. Reminded me of the ten or twelve minute interruption scene in *Once Upon a Time in the West*, but it takes too long to explain if you don't know the movie. Suffice it to say that the coincidence is that a group of travelers in a way station are listening to this complicated tale from one of the patrons. They are interrupted by the arrival of a notorious outlaw, under guard. The sounds of horses neighing and guns shooting precede the entrance of the outlaw, free of his captors but still in hand shackles. No one dares make a sound, except for Charles Bronson, who begins to play the harmonica. The outlaw's gang shows up and we learn the leader's name, played by Jason Robards—Cheyenne.

"Remember in *Once...*"

"Yeah, Rock, I know the scene. I wasn't trying to be funny."

"You and me both."

"Okay," Di offered, "I'll go first. I don't know."

Dear Diary:

AFTER FIRST BEING delighted that Rock and I would drive back together, my mood quickly deteriorated to a sullen air, as if a dark cloud was parked over me, despite the sight of a spectacular blue sky as I gazed out the window while we sped along Interstate 10.

I tried to be rational and think through it. Worry about Cheyenne; the end to the fun of the weekend, a brief break from regularity; going back to see Helen, who I truly believed was plotting to stick her claws into Rock and hang on until she achieved whatever it was she wanted; yeah, reasons enough.

Still, understanding why I felt morose, I didn't feel like talking. Let the danger come, let the storm burst, come on, quit stalling.

Rock wasn't in a gleeful mood either, though he'd been positively ecstatic last night after the show ended. His aura seemed to change later, after he'd talked to Helen. Listened to, more like it, I'm sure.

He didn't say much about their conversation, either because he doesn't want to talk to me about her, or because she'd been her usual bitchy self. I guess I'm being presumptive—I haven't known Helen long enough to know what's usual for her. But I get the impression Rock isn't counting the minutes until he sees her again, but feels a responsibility to go to the hospital, and in a way, I think he's embarrassed to talk to me about her.

Why, you ask, Dear Diary? Because it's finally sunk into the foolish dear that Helen is not the girl of his dreams, nor even a poor substitute for his beloved Mary Ann. But he's too much of a gentleman to chastise her to me, especially considering the adventure Helen and I shared on our way to San Antonio, and because he has both employer and friend responsibilities to Helen. How and when he can rid himself of those obligations is a matter only he can figure out. When/if he's ready to discuss his options, he'll say so. Until then—I'm going to close my eyes and take a nap.

My eyes snapped open when the speed of the car diminished. As we slowed for the off ramp I caught a glimpse of a sign that announced 'Hospital'. I also saw a sign that advertised, 'Caverns of Sonora, 12 miles.'

"Gosh, Rock, guess I needed a nap. Sorry to leave you all alone. Beauty sleep, you know."

Rock smiled at me and for a moment I thought we had worked through our blues, me by napping, he by mulling quietly on issues he needed to deal with without feeling he needed to carry on a conversation. Fanciful wish on my part.

"This might not be fun," Rock said as he pulled into the parking lot of the hospital, a two-story, off-white building, only a few years old, set in an attractive setting amidst trees and grass that seemed incongruous in the dry desert sands of southwest Texas. I can't remember the name, somebody or other's Memorial Hospital, and it wasn't large, designed mainly to provide basic hospital services to the scattered residents of the county. Unless Helen was in urgent need of care I'm sure they'd want her out of there as quickly as possible.

This is another one of those instances, Diary, where I am recording my notes hours later and the best I can do is try to get the dialogue as close as I can to what was actually said.

First, I went to the restroom to wash my face and to do nature's business. I combed my air, brushed my teeth—you'd think I was getting ready to meet my prom date. For reasons I'm not going to waste time trying to understand, I wanted to look good when I saw Helen again. I can't get past this desire to best her, even if she is bedridden.

While I was freshening myself (have I made up a new word?), Rock found Helen's room and the nurse in charge. The nurse said she'd find the doctor and told us we were welcome to visit Helen. And take her, please, I think she meant, from the glaring eyes that backed up a polite smile.

Helen was slumped in the bed with the television on but was looking down at some papers she was reading. She appeared tired, not nearly as pretty as I remember her. When we entered she quickly took off her glasses. The bruise on one cheek and the lines under her eyes didn't make her look any more appealing. I suppose I'd look just as awful if I'd fallen down several steps and shot myself.

She sat up straighter when Rock walked in, brushed her hair with her hand, and smiled at first, but the beam dimmed as she saw me walk in after Rock. She put the glasses back on.

"Rock! It's about time. Oh, Rock you've got to get me out of here."

"Whoa, hold on, Helen."

"Come here," she commanded.

Rock went to the side of the bed, leaned down and attempted to kiss her on the cheek. With her hand Helen guided his head and they locked lips. It may have been the longest kiss ever between a patient in bed and a visitor bending over trying to untangle himself. Ugh. For my benefit, I suppose. Let me know who gets to kiss whom. Go ahead, flaunt it. This show was not going to make anyone forget Cary Grant and Ingrid Bergman in *Notorious.*

I stood there pretending to watch the television, considered humming or tapping my foot, but I didn't want to confirm that I was even noticing the action a few feet away. The idiocy on the TV is more interesting, folks. Finally Helen released Rock and deigned to acknowledge my presence.

"Hello, Dinah. Did you have fun at the show?"

"Hmm, yes, Helen, I did."

"She worked very hard, Helen. Caught on in a jiff and did a great job," Rock said in my defense, instantly sensing I needed a defense.

"I'm sure. Now, help me get dressed."

"Wait, Helen, you can't just walk out of here. We need to hear what the doctor says."

"He told me I could leave when you came for me."

"He did? Can you walk? What about your leg injuries?"

"The bullet wound was superficial; fortunately I'm not a good shot, even accidentally. The break isn't serious, but I will need crutches for a few days. You can carry me through doorways, Rock. It'll be good practice."

Helen's comment went over Rock's head. "Good practice?" he said, his face scrunched in confusion. What a dope.

"Dinah, be a dear and go find the doctor. If we leave right away we can get to Phoenix by night."

"Helen, you need to brush up on your geography. Phoenix is at least twelve hours away. Now take it easy; the nurse said the doctor would be here as soon as he can."

"If you help me dress we can be ready when he gets here. Go on, Dinah, find him, I think his name is Perez or Gomez or some sort of Mexican name."

"Helen, be careful," Rock said. Then he looked at me and nodded towards the door. I took the hint and left, so I have no way of knowing what he and Helen talked about, but I suspect it had something to do with reminding Helen that the Sonora area has a significant population of Hispanics.

I had no intention of going to look for the doctor. Doctors show up when they're ready, on their schedule, not yours. Being a small hospital it was easy to find the cafeteria so I went there and bought an iced tea and sat down and sipped it while gazing at the handful of other patrons. A large window gave a view of an unexpectedly attractive garden; unexpected I guess, because I think of hospitals as dreary places full of sick people. The view soon was lost in my mind as I wandered back to the current scenario that Rock and Helen and I were involved in, and I imagined how it would play out.

We've got two days ahead of us driving back to San Diego. Helen will sit in front and boss Rock around. I'll sit in back like some eleven-year-old kid forced to travel with Mommy and Daddy. Helen will tell us all about the convention she wasn't at, and how Rock's company will deal with the potential new business.

Rock will want to punch her lights out but he'll be polite because he won't want an incident in front of me. What I'm afraid of is that Rock will put off telling her that their relationship needs to eliminate one aspect or the other: the romantic or the employer/employee, because while she's hobbled he will feel it isn't the right time, and she will use her temporary disability to keep him on a short leash. Until he wakes up one morning and wonders how he didn't see the semi coming at him. Men, what ninnies.

Fifteen minutes later Rock came in. He had a cup of coffee he'd picked up on the way and sat down at my table. He set down a thick accordion folder.

"I don't blame you for hiding out."

"You told me to go."

He nodded and shrugged in one motion.

"So what happened to her sister?"

"She's in town, Helen says she's at her motel right now."

"Humph."

"What does that mean?"

I shrugged. "Nothing. I just wonder if Sarah's like Helen."

"I don't know her."

Our eyes locked. We were both thinking: Sarah can't stand Helen when she's being bossy any more than anyone else can.

"Did the doctor show up?"

Rock nodded. "Yes, and he got an earful, too. Helen can leave if she absolutely insists and signs out against the doctor's recommendation. However, he thinks she should stay a couple more days. It turns out the major concern is the concussion. Everything else is more bruises and contusions. One leg is badly sprained and she'll be hobbled for a few days. One wrist also is bruised so badly they may have discovered some new colors, and the doctor would like to see her blood pressure get to a more acceptable level. He put her on medicine which Helen perceives as a sign of weakness."

"Geez, she sounds like a man."

"Ha, ha!"

"Anyway, if she signs out against the doctor's wishes I think it could screw up the insurance. Besides, I think the doctor knows what he's talking about, so I told Helen I won't let her leave until the doctor agrees."

"You told her?"

"Yes, Di, I did. Come on, this is difficult. Give me a break."

"Helen said the doctor told her she could leave when you came for her."

"She was hearing what she wanted to hear. It's true, the wound from the bullet is slight, not a big deal, but she did suffer a break in her leg, also not a debilitating injury. I admit that if the hospital was full the doctor might be more amiable to letting her go today, but Di, I do have an obligation."

"To what?"

"What do you mean, to what? To Helen. She works for me, don't forget. She got hurt on company business."

"You don't watch yourself you'll be working for her."

"You come up with some weird notions."

"Don't be blind, Rock. You are not a stupid man, and I never thought you were naïve, either. But she sure has you wrapped up." I twirled my pinky.

"You're crazy, Di. She doesn't have me...anything. What do you expect me to do, leave her here to fend for herself?'

He had me there. We sat quietly for a few moments. I really didn't want either of us to leave the table while still angry with the other. I know I shouldn't bug him about Helen right now, but I can't get away from this feeling that she'll tie chains around Rock that he won't be able to unlock even with the help of Houdini.

My ice tea was gone, so was Rock's coffee.

"So what now?" I asked.

"I think I need to stay here with Helen for two or three days. There's no sense me driving home, and then have to turn around and come back."

"What about the idea of flying back for her?"

Rock shook his head. "I thought of it, but..."

"But Helen said no, you should stay here with her."

"Damn it, Di!"

We sat quietly for another minute. Then, firmly, without letting the anger show, the anger he felt at himself, Rock continued.

"I think you should go on and I'll rent a car when Helen's ready to leave. I'll give you a key so you can get into my place. I'll call Carl Mendez and tell him you are on staff starting immediately. I'd like you to take this material to him," he said, pointing to the brown accordion folder.

"What'll I do?"

"I'll tell Carl to start your orientation. He'll show you around, get you familiarized. There's lot to learn and you'll have barely started before I'll be back."

"And Helen?"

"Well? What about Helen? She does work for me."

"Rock, you dummy, do you really think you can carry on with her, and have her work for you, and not end up taking orders from her? Do you ever listen to the way she talks?"

"You know Di, the personal part of ..."

"Yeah, yeah," I waved him off. "Is none of my business. Come on, Rock, we've been getting into each other's personal lives since the day you walked into the Only Café. I'm just trying to give you some advice from a woman's perspective. Didn't you ever hear of female intuition?"

"I needn't remind you that Helen and I have several decades more perspective than you, sweetheart."

"Hmm. More experiences maybe, but I don't think age necessarily gives you a better perspective. But you're a big boy, even though the older I get—pardon my lack of experience—the more I see that big boys act like little boys when it comes to women and sports."

"This isn't getting us anywhere."

"Then I should get moving. If I leave now maybe I can make it to El Paso. Hope I don't run into any more fun-loving cowboys." I got up to leave.

"You'll need this," Rock said. He held out a key.

"Take it, Di. To my house. Make yourself at home."

I stared at him for several seconds, biting off the words that were forming.

"Rock, do you really think Helen would let me work there after you and she are married."

"Doggone it Di, I'm not going to marry her. I may be gullible but I'm not stupid. Besides, so what if I did marry her?"

"Smart guys do stupid things all the time in the name of love—or is it lust?" I took the key and started to walk away. I stopped and turned around.

"Rock, I once said I'd be happy to work under you; but not under her."

"Her...her name is Helen."

I ignored his jibe. "I'll have to go back soon to Arizona, to arrange for someone to check on the houses, and there are things I'll need, mostly clothes, so I'm not sure how long I can work before I'll need time off."

"I know the boss," Rock said. "He can get you whatever time off you need."

I walked away trying to think of something to say to ease the situation. I felt like I was arguing with my husband, even though I've never had a husband to argue with. This may have been worse, even tho Rock wasn't a husband or lover or parent, he was sort of a mix of all of those.

When you're a kid and your parents scold you for doing something you weren't supposed to do, you're angry because you got caught, and because it was something you wanted to do, but were told not to.

With a spouse, you're going to be in the same space so you don't want to let a heavy air hang over you for too long. And you can crawl into bed together later and make things right. Of course, how should I know? Chey and I have a snit and he packs up and goes to Afghanistan or some other place where it's not easy to even make a phone call.

"Di."

I stopped.

"Drive carefully."

I nodded. "You too. Give my...regards to Helen."

"Hey, and one more thing...call me after you are locked in for the night...please?"

I hesitated. "Sure, Rock."

"And save your receipts; the company will pick up your expenses."

I waved backwards as I walked out of the coffee shop.

I gassed up before I left so I wouldn't have to stop again, used the facilities at the attached convenience store, and bought some packaged food that would probably taste awful and I'd hate it, but once I found a motel I wasn't going out again until morning.

No crummy place for me, I drove into the busiest and well-lit section of town, and chose a large motel that looked like it would be safe. I know, looks can be deceiving, but I can't deny I was getting a bit antsy, considering my recent experiences while traveling.

So here I am, locked in, a chair propped against the door, nibbling on my picnic of cardboard-tasting sandwiches and a wilted salad, writing these notes before I proceed to a trashy thriller, which I hope will put me to sleep in five minutes, and being stubborn about calling Rock. I wanted to call him, but didn't want to get him while he was still in Helen's hospital room.

He gave in first. I admit I answered quickly, hoping it was him.

"Hello?"

"Di, are you okay?"

"Of course, why wouldn't I be?"

"I dunno, I was getting worried. No drunken cowboys on the loose?"

"Nah, the word is out, watch for a good looking broad with the little pink gun."

"You don't have her gun, do you?"

"No, but the bad guys might think I do."

"Hey, soon it'll be just a funny story to tell."

"I'm fine, Rock. I'm at a nice place, it looks safe, and I've locked myself in. Rock?"

"Yeah."

"I never used to feel afraid when I was in Dry Hole. Maybe I should never have left. Chey and I should have stayed there."

"It's a big world, Di. You can't ignore it."

"I can try."

"Is that what you want to do? Go back to Dry Rot and live out your life there?"

"At least I wouldn't have to worry about some goon with a six-gun strapped to his side trying to rip my blouse off."

"Probably not. Di, I tried to contact the person who sent me the message about Cheyenne. I couldn't get through."

"Well, you know, Chey is so secretive about everything, so I suppose even the messages they send have to be secured so nosy folk like you and I don't try to find out what's going on. Wouldn't want the government to let us know what they're doing with our money now, would we?"

"Your cynicism is noted, but what about Cheyenne?"

"I'm gonna start crying, Rock, if we talk about him. I've tried to put it out of mind, just like I did the first time I heard he had died."

"Sorry, I shouldn't have brought it up. Still, I think you have a right to know what's happened to him."

"I intend to, but I don't know what to do."

"I'll call my friend, you know, the general who helped us get Cheyenne's status straightened out?"

"Sure, I remember him. Chester Ostrowski; he was your friend from Vietnam wasn't he? And he figured out how I could keep the insurance money. Didn't he retire?"

"Actually, I'm not sure what his status is these days. But I think he still has connections, so it's a place to start."

"Would you do that, Rock?"

"Of course, Di. I'll try to reach him tomorrow."

"So, dare I ask, how's it going there?"

"To say I'm bored would be an understatement. There's not a lot to do in this town. I did connect with Helen's sister, Sarah, and we found a decent steakhouse. Sarah's, uh, not quite like Helen, if you know what I mean."

"Hmm. I think I get you."

" I thought about you and...how we, you know, shuffled around this afternoon."

"Yeah, well, we can talk later, Rock. How's Helen doing?"

"Doctor gave her something to relax, that is, to sleep better, thank goodness. She was driving me nuts bitching about being held as a prisoner of war. Geez, Di, I really got myself in a pickle."

"I'll try not to act smug."

"Ah, you will anyway, but that's okay."

"Goodnight, Rock."

"'Night, Di. Call me tomorrow, okay?"

"I will Rock, for sure...unless some crazy cowboys kidnap me. G'night."

Looking back, I think that from the moment I laid eyes on Helen Harrison she and I were going to be at odds with each other. But I fell asleep wearing a thin smile, knowing that Rock and I had softened the edginess that had cut a fissure between us earlier in the day.

***

FIFTEEN

"I'm aiming straight for your heart, Louie."
"That's my least vulnerable spot."--- Louie and Rick, from
Casablanca, 1942.

Dear Diary:

HAVE YOU HEARD the saying about 'things that go bump in the night?' Let me tell you about things that were bumpin' last night.

First, I should backtrack and catch up on the week.

I made the long drive from El Paso to Rock's house in San Diego (Lemon Grove, actually), in one swoop, and man, I didn't want to sit down again for a full day.

Rock stayed at a motel near the hospital and he and Helen's sister Sarah took turns visiting. I think they flipped coins, and the loser had to sit with Helen. The winner went off for a stiff drink.

Rock insisted he was firm with Helen: 'rest and don't talk much and the sooner you'll get to leave the hospital.' He didn't say whether he used duct tape or not. So by Wed. the doctor allowed her to leave (or gave in, or maybe the nursing staff threatened to quit en masse), and Rock drove himself and the sisters to Helen's home in San Diego, taking a day and half.

Rock said he was going to stay at Helen's on Friday night, which didn't make me happy, because I was hoping we could have dinner and talk about what my job at Hammond Tools is going to be. Actually I just wanted to be with Rock because I can relax with him, and I was envious of Helen having had him to herself the last few days. Not that she was in any condition to do anything with him, thank goodness. And since our last in-person conversation had been edgy, to say the least, I, and I think Rock, too, wanted to scour the memory out of our minds.

"Have no fear, my dear," Rock told me on the phone, "Sarah is here, too, to act as chaperone."

"Lucky you."

"Besides, I am totally beat. After a shower and a snifter of whatever I can find, I'm going to hit the sack."

"Alone?"

"There you go again, Di. Yes, alone. I'll be at the office tomorrow if you want to stop by."

I said I would and hung up.

The next day Rock decided he was going to stay in his office for the weekend. He's got a couch that pulls out into a bed, a washroom, kitchen facilities, virtually all the comforts of home, including a DVD player and a DVR. I almost wonder why he keeps the house. He claimed that with Sarah at Helen's house it was too crowded, but I think he welcomed the chance to be away from Helen for a few days, having had to babysit her all week.

I told Rock I was planning on going to the extended stay motel located less than a mile from his house, but he insisted he was going to be working late Friday and Saturday to catch up on things, so I could use the house until Monday and then I can go to the motel, and also start to look for an apartment. (I think another reason was that he could tell Helen, honestly, where he was and not have her wondering if Rock and I were staying at his house—together).

I didn't tell Rock that I wasn't yet ready to lease an apartment because for me, the jury's still out on how long I'll work for Hammond Tools. Maybe I'm being stubborn and pessimistic, but I can't see me staying on there once Helen comes back to work, if she does, and/or Rock does marry her. He seems to vacillate on the issue, but never mind, because last night something happened, which I'll get to in a moment—don't be impatient, Diary.

I finally saw Rock again on Saturday, at the plant. He looked like he belonged behind his desk, and the picture of he and Mary Ann was back. He saw me look at it and he smiled.

"You and Mary Ann would have gotten along wonderfully."

"I think we would have. I don't think I would have been jealous of her."

"Are you jealous of Helen?"

I shrugged. I would never admit to being jealous. And actually, while at first I was, I don't think I am anymore. What I am is worried for Rock and I feel sorry for Helen, even as I find it impossible to like her.

"Where was the picture?" I asked.

He looked at me uncomprehending. Then he remembered I had told him I had been in his office talking to Helen.

"Oh, yeah," he laughed, more of a snicker. "Helen put it in the bottom drawer. She probably intended to put it back before I knew. I guess I can't blame her."

We gabbed about what his week had been like, and it sounded so boring it made me yawn. He and Sarah had time to talk and Rock said he got the impression that Helen had always been bossy when the girls were younger. Sarah is a year older, but Helen's temperament overwhelmed Sarah. She, Sarah said, and Helen had never been very close as they grew to adulthood, but they have no other immediate family, so, when Helen called, Sarah felt an obligation.

We discussed my first days at Hammond Tools. Carl Mendez, Rock's plant manager, had been giving me a complete overview of the business, from sales to manufacturing, to distribution, to accounting., to where the rest rooms where. I'd barely touched the surface. Rock said he expects to have openings in several areas, including accounting and marketing, if his expansion plans work out, not a sure thing in this economy. He thought I might like the accounting end of it, since I'd been dabbling in that field, but I don't think I want to be shut up in an office all day long, especially on some of those wonderfully beautiful days they have here in southern California. And if Helen stays on I'm not sure how long I could deal with her hovering over me all day.

We ate a light lunch in his office and I spent most of the day reading manuals regarding Hammond Tools procedures and about the various products it makes and sells. Many of the items they design are unique with a limited demand. That makes them expensive, but they don't sell in large quantity. On the other hand, Rock insists on nearly anal quality control so that once they have a customer they can keep them, and hopefully provide other products, too.

We avoided talking about the two elephants in the room, Helen and Cheyenne, until we quit for the day and went for a drink and an early dinner.

"I did get a hold of Chester."

"Oh! What's he say?"

"He said he's technically retired now but has been working as a consultant for the Pentagon, hush-hush, of course, so he didn't give me any details on what he consults about."

"The Pentagon likes to think everything's a matter of national security, don't they?"

Rock shrugged, agreeing with my statement, I think, but not wanting to get into that discussion.

"He's checking on Cheyenne, but isn't sure what, if anything, he can find out."

"Does the general know who, or what kind of outfit, Chey is in? Some special operations unit or something?"

"From what I gather from what little Chey has said, and from what you said he let slip, I suspect he's in Delta Force. It's a secret outfit; the government won't even confirm they exist. It's one of those worst kept secrets, like the Israelis don't confirm they have nuclear weapons."

"So can the general find out anything?"

"He'll let me know as soon as he knows. I did some of my own research."

"And?"

"There's plenty of info on the Internet. How much is true and how much is speculation is difficult to know. But the basics are pretty clear."

The waitress returned to take our orders and as she approached Rock quickly turned the conversation to how nice the weather has been. After we ordered he continued on what he knew about Cheyenne's employer.

"Delta is a mix of soldiers from all branches of the military. In fact, they aren't even called 'soldiers', but are 'operators'."

"Hmm, more James Bond silliness," I said with a sneer (I think I did; I can be snide, but I'm not sure if I'm good at sneering).

"They usually wear civilian clothes, and if they are in the field, I mean *really* in the field, they don't wear anything on their clothes to indicate who they are or what unit they are with. They work in teams of twelve or less, and often they work solo, which is the way I think Cheyenne prefers to...operate."

"He never has developed real social skills."

Rock looked at me like, as if I have?

"Yeah, say it, has anybody from Dry Hole ever developed social skills?"

He mugged and sipped his drink.

"So, how long has this special unit been around?"

"Apparently it was originally assembled in the late 70s as a counter-terrorist unit. Soldiers were selected from Green Berets, Rangers, and airborne divisions and put through highly specialized training. One skill that is a must is marksmanship, and from what Cheyenne has said, hitting the target comes natural to him."

"Yeah, he could have been an Olympic shooting champion. You wouldn't believe some of the things I've seen him do with an old rusty rifle he found in the one of those abandoned warehouses. I can just imagine what he does with the equipment the military has."

And then I shuddered a bit as I realized that what he did with this sophisticated weaponry was kill people. Rock knew precisely what mental images were bouncing around in my head.

"It's a job needs doing, Di."

I nodded. "Yeah, but how much of it can he do without losing his heart and soul?"

Rock had no answer, not that I expected him to. Who does have an answer to such a question? It's like trying to understand why some babies are born already diseased.

"So anything else?"

Rock shook his head slowly. "Lots of conjecture. Some people claim they operate on the fringe of the law, even operating inside the United States when it isn't authorized."

"I thought the military was never authorized to operate inside the country?"

"It can under special circumstances. There's a law, passed over a hundred years ago, called the Posse Comitatus Act, which allows the law to be suspended temporarily by the president. I think it was done in Waco, maybe another time or two."

"But Rock, if Chey's in the military, don't we have a right to know where he's stationed? Or if he's been captured, killed or what? Dang it, how am I going to find out?"

"Like you said, the military likes to invoke 'national security' whenever it can."

"What about this guy who sent you the e-mails?"

"I suspect he was trying to do a favor for Cheyenne by touching base with us, but not by the book. Remember, I told you I tried to contact him and got this threatening message. I told Chester about it and he said I dare not try that address again. Said I could already be in trouble."

"The hell, you'd think we were the bad guys!"

"Ah, don't worry. Chester will find out something, and if not, we'll contact your congressman, make a fuss, okay?"

"Ha, I doubt there's a congressman or woman who knows Dry Hole exists!"

"Then we'll educate 'em!"

So we had a couple of drinks and vowed to raise hell, or at least heck, if we didn't find out about Cheyenne in the next few days, in between me learning my new job and Rock wrestling with his Helen dilemma.

I'm still tired from all the driving and the many hours I've spent at Hammond Tools this week, so after dinner I drove back to Rock's place, and he to his office pad, and in no time at all I was in bed. Rock had said he was going to crash early also.

TIRED AS I WAS there were still a few messages I needed to read and respond to. So I did that, sitting alone in my office, the building quiet with everyone gone except for old

Bud Biel, the weekend night guard. I wonder if all night guards at buildings like this are called 'old whatever?'

I don't think he was as old as me, actually, even if his hair is grayer. I'd told Bud I'd be staying the next couple of nights, not the first time I'd hunkered down in my office, so he'd know I was here. My office has all the facilities I need for the night so I wouldn't likely need to be prowling around anyway.

As my eyelids drooped I figured it was time to call it a day. Any work I did now I'd have to go over again tomorrow. I shut off the monitor and the only light was from the reading lamp on my desk. I made a quick visit to the bathroom, did what I needed to do, including a half-ass perfunctory brushing of my teeth, and pulled out the sofa bed. I suddenly felt so tired I hardly had the strength to yank the damn thing out.

I started to shut off my cell phone, then hesitated, considering whether I should leave it on in case Helen or Sarah needed to call. But what would they need to call about? Helen was doing fine now, limping no worse than Chester on *Gunsmoke,* and if she woke up with a headache I didn't want to hear about it anyway. So I shut the phone off, shut off the lamp on the desk, and crawled into bed. I think I was asleep the instant my head touched pillow.

Later I recalled seeing the clock display 12:40, but I can't be sure. The ringing in my ears reminded me of a train whistle. Sometimes at night, when it's clear and still, you can hear distant train whistles from this building. But it wasn't a train whistle. Or maybe it had been at first.

When I opened my eyes I wasn't sure where I was. You know how sometimes when you are awakened from a deep sleep and you are in a place that isn't home, and for a heartbeat, even several seconds, you aren't sure where you are? Once I remembered I was sleeping in my office, I recognized the ringing of the phone. Then it took another second or two to get my bearings as to where the phone that set on my desk was in relation to where I was. When I reached the phone, after stumbling in the dark, no one was on the line.

I figured it for a wrong number and went back to bed. Now I couldn't sleep and I wondered if it had been Helen calling. Or Di. Hell, maybe it was Cheyenne calling from a phone booth in Islamabad!

I worked my way in the dark to my desk, turned on the lamp and found my cell phone. I turned it on and sure enough, there was a message from a few minutes ago. I listened to it; it was Helen.

"Rock, are you there? Honey, it's me. Are you asleep? Hello? Oh, well, never mind. Bye, dear."

It didn't sound like anything urgent. So why was she calling at this time of night? Couldn't sleep? If it'd occurred to me what was going through her mind I would have called immediately. But it didn't, so I didn't. I left the cell on and took it with me to bed and set it next to me in case she called again. I went back to sleep.

Dear Diary:

THE CLOCK HADN'T yet hit ten when I crawled into the bed in the guest room of Rock's house. I call it the guest room but it use to be Rock and Mary Ann's daughter Janice's room. So it still retains the feminine atmosphere, with frilly pillowcases, pastel colors, and a whole herd of Janice's childhood stuffed toys piled on the bed. Some of them looked exactly like the ones I had when I was a child. The closet was nearly empty except for a rack of men's clothing, which I suppose was overflow from Rock's closet in the master bedroom, or maybe his son's leftover clothes. I only expected to be a here a few days so the room was comfortable enough for my needs. There is another bedroom on the side of the house opposite the main living and dining room, with a small alcove separating the two areas. The alcove leads to a bathroom. A cozy place, better than any motel. Hadn't been for Helen, Rock might have invited me to stay here until I found a permanent place of my own.

The next thing I remember was hearing a sound that reminded me of those bumps in the night I mentioned. But I wasn't sure if it was an external sound that woke me or rather the end of a dream. I thought it might be the newspaper being delivered, hitting the door. I glanced a the clock and it showed 1:15, which seemed too early for the paper.

I listened carefully, not even breathing for a few moments. All I could sense was the stillness; the hum of the night. Then there was a bark, and another, some dog maybe a quarter mile away upset about a noise it had heard and didn't recognize.

I relaxed and then heard another bump, this time like a thump; no, a thwack, like Long John Silver pegging his way along the wooden deck of his pirate's brigantine.

My heart skipped, or at least, it felt like it did. After my recent encounters I was beginning to get touchy, like an old woman scared of every creak and groan of an old house that is settling itself in its old age, or her own bones rattling. I didn't like being a wuss.

It must be Rock, I concluded. He's decided to come home. He forgot his toothbrush, or the mattress on the sofa bed in his office isn't comfortable. He's trying to be quiet and sometimes when you try to be really quiet you end up being noisier than you would otherwise. Like whispering in a library (which nobody does anymore—they just blurt out loud their conversations as if everyone else is interested. Which reminded of a time recently at a shopping center in Tucson; I was sitting on a bench rummaging through my purse and resting my feet after an hour of heavy duty shopping. Another woman sat down next to me while she was talking on her cell. I couldn't help but overhear her end of the conversation. Something she said sounded funny and I chuckled. She said, 'You shouldn't listen to private conversations'. I said to her, 'Then don't hold your conversation in public.' I stayed sitting on the bench, she got up and walked away, no doubt relating my bad manners to whomever she was talking to).

But what if it wasn't Rock? Maybe it's the blond cowboy whose voice I altered come looking for me to get even? Would he still speak like he'd been sucking helium? I realize that was a bizarre idea but so were the noises I was hearing. Another thwack, then a bump, then nothing for an entire minute, or maybe five, who can estimate time when you're alone and afraid in the dark? And I was becoming gosh-darned afraid!

I reached with my left hand to the bedside table where I'd put my cell phone. If it's Rock, and his phone is on, I should hear it ring, and he'll answer in the next room, and I'll sigh in relief, and he'll say why am I calling, and I'll say because you scared the dimples off my cheeks, and we'll laugh and I can go back to sleep.

Rock did answer but I hadn't heard the music of his ringtone.

"Hello?"

"Rock? Where are you?"

"Di? What's up? I can barely hear you."

"That's because I'm whispering?"

"Why are you whispering?"

"Is that you making those noises? Are you here, in the house?"

"What are you talking about? What'd you say? Speak up."

I was whispering because my instinct was telling me someone was in the house, other than lonesome me, and I didn't want them to hear me. On the other hand, if it's Rock who's in the house I should speak up, right? Or if it's a burglar I should let him know I'm awake and he'll run out, right? Or if I had any real sense I'd call 911, right?

"Rock..." I spoke louder now, almost in a normal tone.

"Are you in the house? I hear noises, bumps and, and thwacks."

"Thwacks? Di, what's going on?"

Just then I heard a shuffle and another thwack, and the doorway to the bedroom became even darker than it had been. A shape filled the doorway, the shape of a monster. It looked like a three-legged ogre, not tall, like Blondie, so it wasn't him come to square things.

I turned to reach for the lamp on the bedside table and as I did a tiny light flickered from the dark shape. I heard a thwapping sound (another word I've made up?) next to me, something hitting the pillow. I grabbed the pillow and threw it towards the doorway. I heard a surprise gasp and recognized the voice.

"God in heaven, Helen!"

From the phone I could hear Rock calling to me.

"Di! What the hell is going on?"

Then, as if he'd just eaten from the Tree of Knowledge I heard Rock say, "Ohmygod, Helen!"

Having been turning into mush a few minutes ago I suddenly felt the energy of the bunny on those commercials—can't stop me, gonna go forever.

I leaped up and charged towards the doorway, towards my attacker, who I could now hear and almost see making her getaway, thwacking along with her crutch and still bandaged twisted ankle. I heard a loud crash and a painful squawk, and a string of frightful language the likes of which I've never heard come from the mouth of a female person. Then there was the fall, a loud thump, and the metallic clank as something—I later realized it was Helen's cute little pink gun that she'd almost done me in with—slid across the floor.

I turned on a lamp in the dining room to see Helen collapsed on the floor, her face contorted in pain, almost as much as her leg, the one that hadn't been injured in her earlier fall. Two chairs were overturned and one lay on top of Helen.

I'm sorry, Diary, think of me what you will, but I laughed. Slowly at first, a giggle, then harder, until I had to sit down. Meanwhile Rock is still yelling at me in the phone I held in my hand.

"Rock, Rock, it's okay now. I'm fine."

"What happened? Who's there?"

"Three guesses, and the first two don't count."

"Di! Don't play games! Are you okay? Is Helen there?"

"See! You got it! Yes, dear, she's here and I think she broke her other leg."

"And you, are you okay?"

"Yeah. She took a shot at me with her little popgun. Should I..."

"What? She shot you?"

"She missed, not by much. I was lucky."

"Wait, Di, wait till I get there. Try to make her comfortable. I'll be there in twenty minutes."

"Make her comfortable? She just tried to shoot me!"

Then, after a sigh, I said, "Okay, Rock, I'll give her a drink. See ya when you get here."

I walked over to where Helen lay in pain. Or was it embarrassment? She glanced to the side and I followed her eyes until they led me to the gun. I walked to the cute little thing and took a picture with my cell. Then I kicked it under a sofa where I was sure Helen wouldn't be able to get to it.

Cruelly, I then took a picture of her lying there in a tangle. She gave me the one-fingered salute.

I sauntered back to where the pillow I'd thrown lay, took a picture of where the bullet had entered, and kicked the pillow to Helen. She set it under her head and lay back, groaning as the movement pulled on her busted limb. I stared down at the shattered form, not sure if I felt anger or pity.

"What would you care to drink, Ms. Harrison?"

IT WAS A PITIFUL sight I saw when I returned home. Helen lay on the floor, her head on a pillow and her legs on another pillow, which Di had generously provided her. It gave her some relief from the pain. The immediate impression, if someone hadn't known what happened, was that Di, the grinning young lady sitting quietly and sipping cognac out of one of my expensive snifters I'd purchased at the Murano factory outside Venice, Italy, had beaten up on this poor middle-aged lady and left her in agony on the floor.

I looked from one to the other. Even if Helen had shot at Di I thought Di was looking too catty at Helen's predicament. Until it struck me as to what had happened here in my house.

"You really tried to shoot her, Helen? Tell me it isn't so."

She remained quiet, her eyes pleading and sad.

"I kicked the gun under the couch and the bullet she shot off is in the pillow under her head," Di said, between sips of cognac.

I sighed and shook my head as I gazed at this woman who a few days ago I made love to. I felt nothing but pity for her now; and disgusted with myself.

"Are you in a lot of pain?"

Helen shook her head. "Maybe a little, but it's not bad," she squeaked. "I'm so sorry, Rock."

"Sorry? You must be crazy!"

I didn't mean to raise my voice or to call her crazy, but when it dawned on me that she could have killed Di, even with that little purse gun of hers, I felt like I wanted to pick her up and throw her out the door.

"I could have called an ambulance, " Di said, "but you told me not to."

I nodded. "The hospital's only ten minutes from here. We need to be able to explain this."

"I'll leave you two alone while I get dressed," Di said, and she went into her bedroom.

I looked down at Helen as if I was berating a disobedient child.

"I'm...I'm so sorry, Rock...I thought you...and Di...were together...here in the house." Her words were so broken by her sobbing and sniffling it was hard to understand what she was saying. I bent down and handed her my handkerchief.

She blew her nose and hen asked, "Do you...think Dinah will...you know...want to call the police?"

I shook my head, not saying no, saying I don't know.

"I'll talk to her. But, Helen, it's over. I was going to wait until you were...on your feet again, and even then I wasn't sure, but I am."

"What do you mean, Rock?"

"I mean everything; us, you working for Hammond Tools. I'll keep you on payroll until you're on your feet again, for insurance purposes, but you don't work there anymore. I'm sorry, this isn't the way I wanted to tell you."

She began to sob again. "You...can't do that to me, Rock...what'll I do? I'll be so embarrassed!"

"Embarrassed?! You almost killed someone and you're worried about being embarrassed?!

"Helen, you could go to jail, if Di insisted. But I think we can hold that in abeyance if you just agree quietly to what I tell you. In fact, I'll even keep you on payroll, technically, while you get some help; say, three months, sort of a going away present.. But you aren't to come to the plant again."

"What do you mean, help? Do you think I'm crazy?"

"No, but you're...I don't know, it's not for me to say. Never mind that for now. I'll go along with a story that you were staying at my house, you got up in the night and fell, of your own doing. I'm sure Di will agree to not say anything about what you tried to do to her."

"I didn't intend to hurt her, Rock. I just wanted to scare her."

"You did that, alright."

She nodded, and groaned, and I felt so sorry for her, and so foolish.

***

SIXTEEN

"Home is the place where, when you have to go there,
they have to take you in."---Robert Frost, *The Death of the*
Hired Man.

Dear Diary:

IT TOOK ME over an hour before the shakes hit me. First
it had been the two guys at the pizza place who scared me,
then the creeps who attacked Helen and me, and then Helen
comes after me with a gun! I might as well be with Cheyenne in
Iraq or wherever he is; can't be much more dangerous!

By then we were at the hospital, Rock and I in a waiting
room, Helen wherever they took her to examine her injury. I
don't think either Rock or I were eager to stay, but to leave
without talking to the doctor would look like we'd dumped
Helen off and didn't care what happened to her.

I agreed not to say anything about what Helen did, or
tried to do, but Rock said he gave Helen the impression we'd
hold it over her head. I just wanted to forget it. I really didn't
think it was something she'd try again.

Sitting there, waiting, occasionally whispering to each
other, me trying to convey how frightened I'd been by the
noises, I began to shiver, then cry, then leaned over and
hugged Rock and let drop a few tears. I'm sure the other

people nearby thought I was upset about the person we'd brought to the hospital.

When a nurse came and told us we could go in to see Helen, I declined the opportunity. I figured this was for Rock to do, and I didn't want to see Helen. Ever. Again.

While I waited I contemplated that even if Helen felt she was only trying to scare me, an inch or an instant one way or the other, and I could be the one in the hospital, or worse, the morgue. I was angry, scared, and relieved, all at the same time. When Chey comes home I can tell him, you ain't heard nothing yet, wait'll I tell you what's been happening to me.

Chey. When will I hear anything?

The excitement didn't end. Oh, for the next week after Helen's aborted attempt at assassination, life was sane and simple. I went to work everyday, my apprenticeship in high gear. Helen was past history for me and I prayed she stay as nothing more than a bizarre incident in my life, over and done with. Rock being Rock he was still in contact with Helen, because he felt he needed to see her through her recovery, but I didn't ask anything and he didn't tell anything, other than to say that Sarah had graciously volunteered to stay with Helen until she was mobile again. A medal to Sarah. Rock said he suggested to Sarah it might be good for Helen to have a change of scenery...get the hint?

Rock asked me if I would like to specialize in the new line of security systems the company was developing. I'd work with Dennis, the young man who'd come to San Antonio to work the trade show, until I knew everything there was to know about the products. Rock is obviously surer than I am that I will stay with this job long-term. It sounded fun and I dove into the task with more enthusiasm than I'd displayed since I sold the café.

In the mean time we waited for word from Rock's friend, Chester, the general. I wanted to start calling around, making some noise, but Rock suggested we wait until we heard from the general. Finally he called.

"YES, THIS IS Rock...oh, Chester, hey, we've been eager..."

"No good news yet, Rock, about your young friend. Delta is so hard to get close to, you know. Everybody pretends they never heard of it. Hell's bells, even I, with all the hush-hush crap I've experienced, I get sick of it. You may know this, maybe not, but these Special Operations folk are not merely another facet of the regular Army. They're 'special', and they aren't impressed by people who aren't like them, even generals with lots of stars. But I'm making some headway; cashing in some old favors due me."

"Any news at all?"

"Ever hear of the Haqqani?"

"No. Who are they?"

"Doesn't matter, except they aren't our friends. Rumor has it they claim to have killed three Americans who were captured spies. Said they were executed. And there's another rumor that an air strike killed civilians in Pakistan, a rumor which hasn't reached the press yet."

"Damn!"

"There's nothing conclusive yet. We get a lot of bullshit stories, some are true, some aren't, and most are half-truths. However, we also are hearing that the leadership of the Haqqani in the Waziristan region has been decimated recently, by the same operatives who are claimed as having been executed."

"Di's getting desperate. She's threatening to call her congressman."

"I don't blame her, I would too. But I'll keep digging."

"Thanks, Chester. Call whenever you hear anything, any time."

"Another thing, too, Rock, is some Pakistani civilians were brought into one of our bases near the border, for treatment of burn wounds."

"Yeah?"

"They claim two Americans were being held captive there, but they escaped and helped save the civilians during the air attack."

"What do you make of it?"

"I don't know...usually there's a kernel of truth to these stories. I'll talk to you later."

I related the gist of my talk with Chester to Di just before we left the plant at the end of the workday. I was afraid she'd lose it again, but by now her tear ducts may have dried up. She stood like Lot's wife and stared off into space for several seconds, as if she'd heard nothing worse than that a dinner date had been canceled. Then she looked at me with those big blue-green eyes.

I slowly shook my head. "I'm not sure what's the best thing to do, Di, but I suggest we wait until we hear again from Chester. Either he'll have something soon or he won't, then, if you want, I'll go to Washington with you, I mean it. We'll knock on some doors and we'll find Cheyenne."

"Dead or alive."

"C'mon, Di, be positive."

I think the knocks Di had taken in the past year or two were hardening her. Which can be good and bad. She thought she'd lost Cheyenne, he came back, she lost her Mom and Aunt May, sold the café because she thought she and Cheyenne were going to settle down, and now it seems Cheyenne might be lost for good. After a while it's difficult to cry or bitch or even get too upset. She was rolling with the punches but if Chey is really gone, I mean as in dead, dead, dead, I hope it's not a knockout punch for her. In defense she buried herself in the on-the-job training and wanted to work through the weekend.

"No teaching this weekend, Di; Dennis will be in LA. Take a break; go to the beach or something."

"It's almost winter, Rock."

"This is San Diego, Di. The ocean is still beautiful even if you don't want to sit in the sun. Take a walk in the sand, get your toes wet. Or go to Coronado; better yet, we'll both go."

"Okay, boss, I'll take you up on your kind offer," Di said.

Dear Diary:

THE DAY ON Coronado Island was a wonderful getaway. Rock picked me up at my motel around ten in the morning and we arrived at the fabulous Hotel del Coronado in time for brunch on the boardwalk.

By mutual consent, without having to vocalize it, we didn't talk about work, about Helen, about Cheyenne, or wars or guns, or anything that had happened in the last year. Mostly it was me doing the talking, jabbering away about places I wanted to visit, like Rome and Paris, Tahiti and Hawaii, without mooning over the fact that I had no one to travel with. I chirped about silly things I wanted to do, like ride the jet boats in the Bay of Fundy, walk up a waterfall in Jamaica, ride to the top of the Eiffel Tower and climb the Washington Monument.

"None of those are silly, Di," Rock said. "They are all exciting adventures."

We watch the Navy jets fly over, wandered throughout the hotel, enjoying the décor and the warmth it exuded. We scanned the exhibit about the movie *Some Like It Hot,* partially filmed on the property. We window shopped and browsed in the stores, and I bought a scarf and a blouse for myself and some baby clothes for Betty Ann's baby, who by my calculation is due in a few weeks.

"I'll have to go see Betty Ann when the baby comes," I told Rock, as we strolled towards where we'd parked.

"That's fine. I might want to go too. Maybe we can make it a long weekend."

On the drive back I did break the mood slightly by reminding Rock about Helen's gun.

"I kicked it under the sofa. Did you find it?"

"Yes, I did. I locked it in my safe. I don't intend to let her have it back."

"You think she'll give you a hard time about her job?"

"No, she knows she screwed up. A lot of it is my own fault, for getting involved with her. Stop, don't say it, I know."

"I wasn't going to say a thing." He punched me in the arm. I punched him back, harder.

"Hey, seriously, you gonna be alright?" I asked.

Rock shrugged, hemmed, hawed, mumbled under his breath, then nodded with vigor. "Yes, absolutely. I feel better already. I wish I could have found a way to break up with her that didn't put you at risk, Di. Geez, but I am sorry about what happened."

"Forget it."

"Yeah, but it still scares me to think what could have happened. If I had lost..." he didn't complete his sentence but I knew what he was trying to say.

Rock began to hum, than he sang, more to himself, barely above a whisper, "You can't look back, when you're movin' on...da de dum..."

"What's that? Sounds familiar."

"Something a songwriter wrote."

It was a good thing we took this day to relax because the next day the excitement started again.

The dream had ended, already forgotten, and I was stirring, minutes from rising, when Betty Ann called.

"Di, wake up, it's me, Betty Ann."

"Huh? Oh, Betty Ann! The baby...it's here?"

"No, no, Di. No, I...I'm sorry, but there's been a fire."

"The café? Oh dear God!"

"No, Di, not the café. Your house. There was a fire during the night. Jasper thinks it was kids goofing around. I thought you might want to come out."

"Is it gone?"

"No, but plenty of damage. I don't think it'll be worth fixing. Hard to say. Jasper wouldn't let anyone go in yet, not till he's sure the fire's totally out, and, he wants to look around, see if he can figure out what started it. But he said he thinks some kids were smoking. He doesn't think it was burned on purpose."

Jasper Littlebear was the chief of the fire department for Dry Hole, which consisted pretty much of him and a bucket brigade. He was also the town's plumber, electrician, and deputy.

"I'll get there today, somehow. If Jasper will let you inside, look for my diaries."

"Yeah, Di, I thought of that. I'm sorry, I hope they're...well, we'll see. Let me know when you're on your way."

I set the phone down and stared at the ceiling, not seeing anything there but in my mind's eye imagining the old house with no roof, charred walls, smoke rising from the ashes of my diaries, the clothes my mother had left behind that I hadn't yet disposed of, my old toys, but mostly, my diaries. God, if they are gone...I should never have left them there.

I called Rock and told him. I said I needed to go to Dry Hole immediately. He apologized for not being able to go with me but he had an out-of-town contractor he had to meet with, a meeting set up at the trade show.

"I understand. Probably nothing you can do anyway."

"Hey, keep in touch. I can fly to Tucson and meet you there."

"Okay, might work. I can kill two birds with one stone, I guess, since there are things I need to do at the Tucson house, too, like arrange for an agent to rent it for me. We'll talk later, Rock, thanks."

I showered and dressed in record time. I grabbed a banana and some clothes and was out the door before the sun was more than a tiny slice on the horizon. Back to Dry Hole. It keeps pulling me back, doesn't it?

It's over five hundred miles ('you can hear the whistle blow five hundred miles'); sorry, soon as the thought about the distance occurred to me, the song started to roll through my harried mind. That's okay, songs in my head helped to keep me from thinking about what I'd find when I got to Dry Hole. Anyway, even with a sunrise start I'd be hard pressed to get there before dark, and even I, born and raised in the heart of the desert, can find it intimidating to drive into the deep blackness that is often only broken by beady red eyes staring at your car as you pass, while you strain to avoid the ruts in the road that can bend an axle. Very few people drive outside the town borders of Dry Hole after the sun sets. So on the Interstate I drove like mad with one eye constantly on the lookout for the county Mountie, trying to cover as much distance as I could while the sun was high and bright. Geez, all I'd need would be to meet another one of those beady slobs like the sheriff Rock and Chey and I crossed paths with in Alabama last year.

With perfect weather I sailed east doing eighty most of the way, sunglasses on the whole time as the sun rose and bore into my eyes. I hit Yuma only a couple hours after I started out, but I knew from prior experience I'd need to slow down a bit in Arizona, where the gendarmes are a bit feisty at times if you exceed the sound barrier, even for one with Arizona plates.

The gentle warmth of the sun made me drowsy so I stopped for coffee and bought a book on tape of a Tony Hillerman novel, one of those situated in what he calls Indian Country. The story caught my attention and helped pass the time and keep me alert.

I ate my banana and stopped for gas, a call of nature, another coffee, and a Big Mac, and reached Tucson by one p.m., so I was doing fine. No time to stop at the house here. I decided to stay on I-10 instead of cutting down through Bisbee and Douglas, and with luck I'd reach Dry Hole before dark.

Now Diary, if you're thinking I'm setting you up for another horror story about some disaster that strikes somewhere on the lonely road home, haven't you heard enough bad news already? Tell the truth, even I was beginning to feel snake bit, so when I bounced onto the road to Dry Hole and saw the beat-up old sign I smiled. I was glad to see that the population hadn't been reduced in the short time since I was last here. I guess old Bull is still kicking and spitting.

I drove to the house first thing, not even stopping at Betty Ann & Jake's. I wanted to see it before it got too dark. With the sun now behind me, as low again as when I left this morning, the town looked gloomy and deserted. There's not much going on 'downtown' unless the cowboys are visiting. The few stores that still exist are closed by this time of day and about the only places open are the Boot Hill Bar and the Grande. Fortunately I'd topped off my tank in Willcox.

The house is a couple of streets off the main road, set back several lots away from any other homes, which is why I guess the kids found it a good place to party. They could be fairly noisy and no one would hear them.

The next closest house is three lots away, the one Chey grew up in, and it's empty these days, too. Don't know what will happen to it if Chey doesn't return. Sit silently until the windows are broken by kids throwing rocks, and when the wind blows at night the whistling wails will scare the dogs and cats, babies and old ladies. Same with my house in a few years, I suppose.

I'm sure Jasper wouldn't have a hard time figuring out who it was caused the fire, as there are only a handful of teens living in the town. Far as I know none of them are bad kids, but teenage boys (and girls, too, to be fair), can do stupid things. Ha! Like, don't we all, many times?

I didn't cry when I saw the house, only because I'd been shedding tears off and on all day. But it looked so forlorn I wondered if it'd been a good idea to see it this way. The roof wasn't totally gone, but the center of it had a big ugly hole, like one of those black holes in outer space that gobbles up everything it can suck in. The intact portion of the roof was seared black. The walls were still standing and I wondered if the house could be saved with a new roof. But as I stood there and looked at the old place with more objectivity now that I didn't live here anymore, I realized the house had seen not only its better days, but also its last days. My next thought was a brilliant one, if I may be so bold. I'd just have to see if Betty Ann & Jake agreed.

There was a ribbon of the yellow tape police and firemen like to put up around places they don't want people to go into, but it's my house and a little yellow tape wasn't going to stop me. The smell of old smoke and ashes still damp from the water Jasper had poured on the house was near nauseating. If the fire hadn't destroyed my diaries I was afraid the water had. I stooped under the yellow tape and opened the front door, which wasn't locked. The odor inside was even worse than it had been outside. The front room looked like a bomb had exploded. The walls were totally burned, the furniture unrecognizable, the carpet soggy.

"Oh, my Lord. I'm glad Mom can't see this."

I figured the electricity was out, and if it wasn't I didn't want to risk trying to turn a lamp on, lest I reignite the fire. So with it nearing dusk there was minimal light to see the damage, even with the hole in the roof. I stepped into the room, the carpet squishing under my feet.

"I figured it was you, Miss Dinah."

The voice startled me and for a millisecond I thought it was the kids who had caused this disaster. It was Jasper.

"Oh, Jasper!" I held my hand over my mouth to stifle a sob.

"Sorry, Jasper," I said, nodding in the general direction of the yellow tape.

"Oh, that's okay, Miss Dinah, ain't meant for you. The kids fessed up to what happened. They really didn't mean to start a fire, but you know, kids don't always think about consequences."

I smiled at him. Jasper was a nice man, is the best way I could describe him. About fifty years old, I reckon, hard working, quiet spoken, with a rounded face that gives him a babyish look, and hair black as the bottom of a coal pit. He believes he's about three-fourths Apache and one-fourth unknown heritage.

"This room got the worst of it. Course, the other rooms have smoke and water damage. I couldn't be too picky 'bout where I aimed the hose."

I nodded in understanding, thinking about my diaries but afraid to find out what condition they were in.

"What are you going to do to them?" I asked.

Jasper shrugged. "Dunno. I was sorta waitin' for you to get here, see what you thought."

"What did Bennie suggest?" Bennie was the police chief, but he's a sickly old codger and hadn't done much policing in a coon's age, however long that is. He's like the mayor; got the job sometime back in the Pleistocene Age because nobody else wanted it, and keeps it out of habit.

"Oh, hell, he don't even know about this. He's real sick these days, Miss Dinah. I've been handling most of the police work for the last year or so. There isn't much policing needed anyway, other than keep an eye out for a drunken cowboy or Indian now and then."

"Well, you gotta do something to them else they'll think it was cool to cause such damage and get away with it."

"Yeah, I know," Jasper said, rubbing a hand over his chin, as if pondering what to do, but stalling because he obviously didn't want to have to arrest the kids and make a big local commotion.

"How many were there?"

"Five, far as I know, a couple of 'em from one of the ranches. Jake's nephew was with them, and he came home smellin' like smoke. He admitted right off what happened. Jake said the kid was scared they'd all go to jail."

"A day or two to scare them might not be bad, but I've got a better idea. How about they tear down what's left and clean it all up?"

"You want the whole house torn down, Miss Dinah?"

"Why not? I'm not going to live in it anymore, and the old thing's not worth fixing."

"I guess that'd be okay, but we'd need a small cat and a bunch of trash bins. And some tools. Have to rent 'em."

"I'll pay for the equipment, you get the kids to do as much work as they can. Don't let them do anything that isn't safe. Hire one or two of the George's relatives who are looking for work to oversee; I'll pay for them, too."

We chatted for a few more minutes and then I told Jasper I wanted to wander through the house a bit more, to see what else was damaged and what wasn't.

"Sure, Miss Dinah, your house, look around all you want. See ya later."

The furnishings had all been old and worn, and none were anything I had planned on moving, so I didn't mourn the loss of chairs and tables as I looked around. It was definitely getting dark by now so I figured I'd better check the rest of the house while I could still see.

The kitchen was undamaged, but again, there wasn't anything much I wanted here. I'd been meaning to buy new appliances ever since I got the insurance money but hadn't gotten around to it because I was going back and forth to

Tucson and when I moved there, Aunt May's kitchen was amply supplied.

Okay, let's do it. Let's go to my bedroom and find out the bad news. I stepped lightly over pieces of charred debris and water puddles and stood in the doorway to my bedroom. *My* bedroom, as if it was waiting, and would wait eternally, for me to return.

Piercing the window an orange ray from the setting sun sprayed through and at first glance the room looked beautiful, tainted tho it was by the smell of smoke. When I took off my rose-colored glasses I saw that the door was covered with soot and the bed covers had obviously been burned, probably from embers sailing on air currents through the doorway. The bed was thoroughly soaked; Jasper must have charged in here and doused the flames in this room before it could spread and I would be forever grateful. I need to remember to send him some of those candies he likes.

As I looked to the shelves where my diaries stood, my miniature library, I let out a long sigh; I'd been holding my breath for several seconds from the moment I first saw the bedcovers blackened and burned.

The diaries were there, all of them, I'm sure. Must be a couple dozen volumes, simple books, the kind a little girl would treasure when she was nine years old, with the word 'My Diary' stamped in gold on the deep brown cover, and with a red ribbon for a book mark.

The first one I got was leather bound, and it must have cost my parents more than any gift they'd ever bought me. They probably thought it'd last me for years. But I filled it before my next birthday and I wanted another one. So they bought me another, but couldn't get the leather ones anymore, so I had to settle for simulation, but I didn't mind.

The last few years I had to search high and low for similar volumes, as I wanted all of them to look the same. About a year ago I found an antique store in Silver City, New Mexico, that had the exact same books. I bought all they had so I'd have enough to last me.

It looked like some water had splashed on the books but otherwise they were undamaged. I felt only slightly silly at how joyful I was. We all have our guilty pleasures, so this is mine, and I don't care if anybody thinks it's juvenile.

I opened one at random and read the entry, in my young girl's perfect penmanship. I always took my time when I made my entries because I wanted what I wrote to be beautiful.

'Dear Diary:
Carrie and I went to the park by ourselves today. I had Ginger on a leash. It's the first time Mom let me take Ginger for a walk by myself. He tried to chase the birds in the park and once I fell down because he tugged so hard.'

I smiled at the memory of my dog Ginger. Later I had a horse by the same name. I opened another book, one from when I was in high school.

'Dear Diary:

Cheyenne scored the winning TD today and I was so proud of him. The other girls are envious of me because they know he and I are steadies. I think we are. I did notice a couple of the cute sophomores giving him the eye and he did smile back. I tugged on his arm and gave him a look. We had time to go with the gang for pizza before the bus took us back home. There are only eight of us for Dry Hole, so we always kind of hang together. The bus drops us at the road that cuts off the main highway. The driver says the road is so bad he can't risk driving on it. So the eight of us start walking or if we're lucky, Bull, the old Indian, picks us up in his battered VW bus, the one on which he's painted, 'Sitting Bull 7, Custer 0'.'

I wasn't going to leave my diaries here, in case the fire flared up overnight. Caressing each one in turn, I filled my arms and carried the diaries to my car.

I quickly examined the rest of the house. My stuffed animals had survived, but they smelled smoky; time to donate them. Mom & Dad's room hadn't burned, but did have smoke and water damage, tho the only things in there were the a few pieces of ancient furniture that I could probably donate to

Consuela, the elderly Indian widow who owns an antique store in town. I don't know when she last sold anything. She says she sells antiques, but mostly it's old junk. Who knows, maybe some lucky scrounger will find something of value, if they are ever fortunate enough to stumble onto the road to Dry Hole.

My bed, minus the ruined coverings, I'd have the boys dismantle and I'd take to California with me, if only for nostalgic reasons. Other than that, there was no looking back.

I drove to Betty Ann & Jake's and was greeted by smiles and tears. Betty Ann was huge. She looked like she could have her baby any minute, but she said, no, probably a few more days. They had found out that the baby was going to be a boy.

"Little Jake," said Jake, beaming.

I decided I'd stay until the baby came, even if Rock was unhappy with his new employee taking so much time off so soon after starting work.

The plan was to close the café day after tomorrow and go to Douglas and stay at a motel until the birth was imminent. Tell it to the baby.

Jake carried my diaries in from the car. Having salvaged them, I wasn't going to let them get too far from me until I decided where their new home would be.

Over dinner I explained my idea to Betty Ann & Jake. The house they lived in was tiny, and they were going to need more room once the baby was walking and running, and that would be sooner than it might seem to them at this moment.

I'd lease the land to them for a nominal amount, with an option to buy at a time to be determined later; the exact language we'd work out. I didn't want to commit to selling the land in case they ever decided to pack it up and leave Dry Hole. I might keep it as a fallback position.

I even offered to loan them the money to build a house on the land, or, if they preferred, I'd pay to build a house and rent it to them. They were excited about the idea and we agreed to work out the details while I was still visiting.

I crashed on the sofa in the living room and cried myself to sleep. I cried for Cheyenne, I cried for the house, and I cried tears of delight that my diaries had survived. With Mom & Dad gone, Chey missing in action, and my only other best friends in Dry Hole, Betty Ann & Jake, moving to a life which will be more and more focused on their family, my diaries were about all I had left of my life in this dusty, tired town. I cried happy tears for Betty Ann & Jake, because they were so happy together, and I cried a little for myself, because I wondered if I'd ever have a baby.

I wasn't asleep long before I heard voices and clatter. Jake was rushing around like a chicken that had its head chopped off, bumping into things and wailing about where'd he put this, where'd he put that...calmly Betty Ann told him to not get crazy. The baby had decided it was time.

Jake was frantic. He and Betty Ann said they had practiced their routine in case the baby came early, but the plan went awry when Jake lost his composure.

"Where are the bags?" he pleaded, as if I should know.

"They're already in the car Jake," Betty Ann said. "You put them there two weeks ago."

"Oh, yeah, good! Where are my keys?"

Tired of driving though I was, rather than help Jake find his keys (which turned out to be in his pocket), and trust him to drive us in his wound-up state, I decided I'd drive my Range Rover while Jake sat in back with Betty Ann. At the last minute I grabbed a bunch of towels from the bathroom and threw them in the back seat. You just never know.

So now the dash to Douglas was on, in the dead of night, me trying to hurry but not wanting to blow a tire or crack an oil pan on the road out of Dry Hole. You don't dare go faster than 20 MPH at night on this road, lest it turns into Mr. Toad's Wild Ride.

Every few years the county discovers that there's a town out here and they come along and pour some sand and gravel in the potholes and claim they've fixed the road. There have even been times when the folks of Dry Hole have gathered together and tried to repair the road on their own. But once a year when this area gets ninety percent of its rain in one fell swoop, the muddy water comes running down from the mountains and washes the road away, leaving nothing but rocks and ruts. The rain that does fall on the town comes down hard, tho not for very long; sort of like God emptying a bucket. Most of the water in this part of the country comes roaring down the road until it hits the creek bed. Then it is diverted away from town, the only reason we haven't been washed away a century ago.

"I think it's coming, Dinah! What'll I do?" pleaded Jake.

"No, it's not," cried Betty Ann. "He'll wait till we get to the hospital."

"Are you sure?" I asked, not daring to take my eyes off the road.

"Drive faster, Dinah," called out Jake.

"Jake, you know I don't dare go faster on this road."

"No, I'm not sure!" said Betty Ann, still the calmest one in the car.

Diary, I can't remember for sure what everybody said. I think we were all talking just to keep ourselves calm, and we all three ended up jabbering at the same time. Jake exhorted me to drive faster, Betty Ann tried to assure Jake that she was fine, and I kept looking in the rear view mirror trying to see what was going on in the back seat. I didn't dare take my eyes off the road for more than a wink.

Every few minutes Jake would plead with me to hurry. Betty Ann was humming to herself, with an occasional soft grunt.

"Oh, it might be!" Betty Ann cried, her voicing sounding more frantic now.

"Might be what?" I asked. The last thing we needed for was the little guy to decide that the middle of the night in the middle of nowhere was a good time to be born.

"Don't panic!" I ordered. Who was I telling, Betty Ann, or Jake, or Little Jake?

"Oh, oh! Ah, never mind, it's okay, Di, just keep going."

"We're almost there!" We weren't but a little lie was okay, I decided. Even a big lie.

"Di, you ever help deliver a baby?" asked Jake.

"Heck, Jake, I never even played with dolls!"

I was a tomboy through and through. True, I had been involved in the births of calves, dogs and colts, so birthing was not an experience that was totally alien, but I'd never delivered a human baby.

From the time I was nine years old, whenever anybody in town or at a nearby ranch had an animal giving birth, Dad took me to watch. Sometimes I could help in bringing water or towels or whatever was needed. At first, I didn't make the connection that people were born this way, too. Eventually the concept set in, without anyone having to explain the details to me.

Once I had maneuvered our way around the ruts and potholes and hit State 80, it was about forty miles to the hospital. I drove like I was racing in the Daytona 500, praying that a deer or coyote didn't appear in the headlights.

I'd glanced at the gas gauge, then at the road, then in the rear-view mirror. If I didn't hear anything I called out to the back seat.

"Everybody okay?"

"Hmmm," from Betty Ann, "Yeah, hurry, please, Dinah," from Jake.

I made the stretch to the hospital in less than thirty minutes and took 10,000 miles off the life of my tires when I squealed into the parking lot, one hand laying it on the horn. I practically parked the car in the Emergency Room and jumped out before it had completely stopped moving.

"It's coming!" screamed Jake. "Help!"

"Ohmygod!" A yell from Betty Ann, the first words she'd uttered in fifteen minutes.

I hesitated; I'd intended to dash into the hospital to get help. Jake's bellowing changed my mind. I ran around the car and opened the door on Jake's side.

"Get out, Jake! Let me in!" I grabbed him by his belt and yanked. He readily backed out.

"Go get help!" I ordered him.

"How you doing Betty Ann?"

"Not too bad, Di, but it's coming!"

And it was. I could see a round, damp object working it's way towards me. I grabbed the towels and shoved them under

Betty Ann. The doggone kid was going to be born right here, in my car! Maybe his name should be Ranger, or Rover?

"Ohmygod!" This time from Jake. He was still standing at the side of the car.

"Jake! Go get help!"

Stunned by my ferocity Jake took off and ran towards the hospital entrance and crashed smack into a nurse who started to yell at him for making so much noise.

"She's having a baby, right now!" Jake cried, pointing at the car.

Luckily the nurse caught on quickly. She ran back in, called for help, and two men rushed out with a stretcher. They knocked Jake down in their rush to get to the car. The nurse helped Jake up and then set him on the curb. Not that I saw see this happening, but Jake told me about it later. He was so confused and disoriented that I have to accept what he says with a grain, you know, but I suspect his tale is close to fact.

"Dinah!" screamed Betty Ann.

It was too late to move her. I was afraid of doing something wrong. I put my hands under her and supported the head as it kept probing farther and farther out as Betty Ann pushed and grunted. Betty Ann was pushing, the baby was pushing, and I was pulling, but only slightly; I didn't want to hurt the little guy. Where in tarnation are the nurses and doctors? The baby kept coming out, inch by inch, so I figured that was good.

I was surprised at how much hair there was. Betty Ann's face it was contorted and looked like she'd been caught in a rainstorm. I thought the process would take much longer but suddenly, like toast popping up, he was out. No, *she* was out!

"Betty Ann! Who said you were going to have a boy?"

"Huh? What? Is he okay, Di?"

"*She's* okay, Betty Ann! You are the mother of a beautiful baby girl! I hope you're not disappointed."

Oh, no, no! I'll love her, and so will Jake. Oh, Di we have to think of a new name! What will we call her?"

"Anything but Helen."

"Ma'am, can I take over for you?"

It was one of the paramedics. He eased me out of the car and a nurse took my place, preventing me from doing any harm.

I was relieved to be relieved. A few minutes later they were able to move Betty Ann out of the car and into the hospital. Betty Ann's face was drenched with perspiration but it glowed with joy. Jake was sitting on the curb, his face one of stunned amazement. The baby was swaddled and the nurse carried her in.

"She's my niece," I bragged to the nurse as she passed me.

I walked over to where Jake sat and joined him. I took his hand.

"Hey, Papa, you've really got yourself a family now."

He nodded, then looked at me and smiled.

"Yeah, yeah, ain't it somethin'?" He shook his head in wonder.

"Let's go inside and see your daughter, Jake."

***

SEVENTEEN

*"You once thought of me as a white knight on a steed,
Now you know how funky I can be."*---from John Stewart's
song, 'Daydream Believer'

Dear Diary,

SO IT'S YOU and me, alone again, naturally. I keep
thinking I don't need to write to you anymore, but you deserve
to know how this ends, that is, about Chey.

I stayed overnight in Lordsburg at a motel while Jake
stayed with Betty Ann in the hospital room. Jake said he was
going to splurge and when Betty Ann and the baby were ready
to leave the hospital, he was going to hire a limo to drive them
home.

"Don't tell them about the road into Dry Hole, or they'll
charge you extra."

I offered to get up early and drive back to Dry Hole and
open up the café. It would be a treat for me to do it.

I awoke even before the sun and sped back to open up
the Only Café in time for the early birds, just like the good old
days—which weren't so long ago. It was fun but I had to hustle
my buns the first few hours. It seems practically everybody who
lives in town or within twenty-five miles came to the café.
They'd heard about the fire and somehow, who knows how

word gets around so fast, they'd heard about our mad dash to the hospital and the baby being born in my car.

I had to scuttle a few rumors. One was that Jake delivered the baby while I was tearing along at a hundred mph; another was that Betty Ann gave birth to twins, a boy and a girl; another was that I stopped the car in the middle of the road to help deliver the child, and a helicopter took us the rest of the way to Lordsburg. I thought the true story was exciting enough. Mostly, people wanted to know that Betty Ann and the baby were healthy, a fact I could confirm. I also had to nix the rumor that I was coming back to run the café.

Eventually, when I repeated what I knew about Betty Ann and the baby and our adventure last night, and about the fire many times over, people began to ask about Cheyenne. How's he doing? When's he coming home? Did he nail Osama bin Laden yet?

By the early afternoon, when I closed down and cleaned up, I was a mentally and physically exhausted. Little sleep, hard work, and just when it seemed I was busy enough to put Chey in the background, someone would ask me about him.

I was so tired I didn't think I could sleep, if that makes sense. I went for a walk and knew where I would end up without consciously making the decision.

Diary, I have to seriously consider the possibility that our boy has done it again; got himself shot to pieces and captured or even killed, this time for real. Went off to fight those terrorists, or his own demons, whatever, or maybe it was his way of not committing to me, or staying out of Dry Hole, or making up for his Dad, or because he really liked what he was doing better than anything else. I may just have to accept it; I did the first time, I can do it again.

Rock's friend, the general, called him and again had no good news. He didn't really have any news, but he says there is a lot of static—static, he calls it, about American special operating forces being executed by some group called the Haqqani. Taliban, Al-Qaeda, Hezbollah, I'd heard of all of them, but I guess there's always a new club starting up.

I hiked to the cemetery, again, third time recently. Most of the tombstones placed here have fallen over, from wind and lack of strong soil, and the ones that are standing have been sandblasted to where it's near impossible to read the engravings. Unless you know exactly where someone is buried, the grave's not easy to find. A few more years and the town will be gone and the wind will be free to blow wild, as if it doesn't already, and the buildings will fall over and the sorry excuses for roads will be cracked and weedy, and before long no one will know a town had ever existed here.

Whoever's buried here, including Mom and Dad (you know, I had Mom buried here after she died in Tucson, so she'd be with Dad), will be lost to history, or posterity, but will anyone care?

To the west the lower part of the sky was a blend of orange, red, and coral hues, spreading from the blue background, almost brushing the tips of the mountains. The sun was silently easing its way down to the horizon, the heat it had radiated over the land all day long already dissipating. The rocks and sand glowed with these last flings of color as the desert prepared itself for a chilly night.

I wrote the above paragraph to see if I could be a better poet, and possibly think of something classy and original to carve on a new headstone for Chey. My previous attempt seemed trite when I read it in the dimming light.

> 'Cheyenne Smith
> Dear son, loved one
> Died in battle, in a faraway land
> Now he's dust in the wind'

Guess I'll never make it as a writer, but at the time it was all I could think of. Of course, as it turned out, Chey hadn't been dead then, so my clumsy words were premature. Now, what do I say for a man who's died on me twice? I couldn't even think of anything silly to write, or something with finality, to close the book on Cheyenne Smith, to help me forget him once and for all. I mean, how long can a girl wait for a guy who keeps getting himself killed?

How about this…?

> 'Cheyenne Smith went to war
>
> Shoulda stayed home to mind the store
>
> Fought the bad guys in some far off 'Stan
>
> Left me alone without my man'

God, how corny, I know! I promise I won't have that engraved. I'll just stick to something basic.

I heard the footsteps before my mind processed what they were. At first I thought, the wind is picking up and blowing sand and the sagebrush are starting to wander. As the sound came nearer I felt a lump in my throat. The footfall was familiar, a slightly heavy step, each one a shade off key. Like the limp of someone who's had a bad injury. Then I remembered that surgery had fixed Chey's leg so he didn't limp anymore. I smiled.

"Hello, Rock," I said, without turning around.

He put his hand on my shoulder and I reached over and covered his hand with mine.

"Hello, Di. I figured I'd find you here. Or if I didn't, I thought I'd like to come here anyway."

I nodded, nothing to say.

"I flew to Tucson and rented a truck, to move your things."

"What are you doing here, in Dry Hole?'

"Couldn't find anything to do in Tucson."

"There isn't much to move from here, Rock. The bed frame and my books. Any clothes I still had in the house probably smell like a campfire. There are some clothes in the Tucson house I want, and small appliances. I don't think I want to move the furniture."

"Not ready to commit yet, are you?"

I shrugged and mumbled something like, 'I dunno.'

Rock nodded.

"Obviously you got my message."

"Yes, and I called Jake to congratulate him and Betty Ann. She's ecstatic about the baby but she's worried about you."

"Hmm."

"We still don't know for sure."

"Oh, Rock, come off it. It's like the last time. What is it with the Army, they keep losing Cheyenne?"

A slight chill was developing and I shook my head slowly and crossed my arms in front of me to ward it off. Or was I closing my arms against the dim hope that Rock tried to keep simmering?

"I'm trying to decide if I should put up another stone. See how many he'll have before we know for sure that he's dead."

"What would you write?"

"My mind's a blank. If you can think of something, be my guest."

After a few seconds he responded. "No, Di, I don't think it's for me to say anything."

"So why me? Who was I to him?"

"You're very special, Di."

"Oh, so that's why he kept leaving me? For Iraq, for the girl on the east coast, for Afghanistan, for the girl. Who knows who else?"

"Don't be bitter, Di."

"I'm not the type to get bitter, Rock. I guess I'm feeling a bit sorry for myself when I should be feeling sorry for Chey.

"It's funny, I call you to tell about a new life, Little Jake, —who turns out to be a girl—and how happy I am for Betty Ann, and then you tell me there's no word about Cheyenne, and like a snap of the fingers, my delight is whisked away."

"Yet I sense you have a faint hope. Why else would you keep the Tucson house?"

"Hope's got nothing to do with the house in Tucson, Rock."

"No?"

"Okay, faint, but I've been through this once before."

"And you survived, and Cheyenne came back."

We stood there for a minute more, enjoying the breeze as it strengthened, watching the suns lose its grip on the sky, a half globe now, falling from us and rising in some other part of the world.

"I wonder if Chey is somewhere where the sun is rising now."

A picture of Cheyenne sitting on a mountain top watching the sun rise as I watched it set came to mind, the two of us on opposite ends of the world separated, and protected, by the warmth and safety of the sun.

"Sometimes I get such corny thoughts, Rock," I said between sniffles.

Then I fell apart and bawled like a baby until the sun was just a sliver over the hills. By the time the tears stopped flowing the air was making me shiver and the sun was gone. Rock took his jacket off and wrapped it around me. He guided me away from the grave and we started to walk. I stopped and looked again at the tombstone that marked the empty grave. I shook my head and smiled.

"Di, in trying to get a line on Chey, and since we really aren't sure of anything, I got in touch with his friend, the girl in Maryland...the sister of the guy who was captured with Chey?"

"You did? Why?"

"To know, Di, for sure that he...well..."

"That he hadn't shacked up with her?"

"Ah, just to be sure."

I stopped walking, grabbed Rock by the sleeve.

"Well, dang it! Tell me, Rock, what'd she say?"

"She saw Chey. He came to see her. She said he seemed uncertain why he came to see her but spoke about avenging her brother's death."

"So he didn't stay with her?"

"No, in fact, she told him she was getting married soon."

"Oh! You mean she told him she was getting married to get rid of him, or ..."

"No, she said it was true. In fact by now she should be married. She told me Chey was fine when she told him she was getting married soon. She said he almost felt relieved."

I didn't know what to think.

"Did he tell her where he was going?"

"Like I said, she said Chey told her he was going back to get even for Johnny, her brother."

"So we're back to knowing he's in...somewhere in one of those damn 'Stan countries."

"Yes, I think we can assume so."

I turned around to look in the direction of the tombstone that set over the empty grave.

"I'll be back, Chey," I said.

"How often are you going to do this, Di?" Rock asked.

I shrugged my shoulders. "As often as he keeps dying, I guess, Rock."

"When the legend becomes fact, print the legend." ---
newspaper editor in the movie, *The Man Who Shot Liberty Valance.*

CHEYENNE SMITH'S eyes flit beneath his closed lids, trying to finish the dream before the daylight forced him to awaken. It wasn't a particularly happy dream, something about Cheyenne not being released from his commission until he captured or killed the traitorous spy, Mohammed ab-Hawsawi. But I killed him already, didn't I, Cheyenne's sub-conscious suggested.

Suddenly the dream ended in a flash. The bright light that brightened the otherwise dim surroundings of the warehouse in which Cheyenne had spent the night, was from sunlight, not flames. Cheyenne instantly recalled the events of the previous night—overcoming the guard, the escape, the attack by the helicopters, the explosions and the fire, the kids and women screaming and running in wild panic, helping them get clear, then finding ab-Hawsawi, Jason returning, Col. Spiedel showing up to help in the rescue, and the battle in the warehouse. Jason and Spiedel were dead, as was ab-Hawsawi.

He remembered his newest wound, one to add to a growing collection, a going-away present from ab-Hawsawi. He touched his side and winced. A bit sticky but the bleeding had stopped. He'd lost enough blood to weaken him and Cheyenne remembered now that as he was drifting off to sleep last night he hoped that Di had forgiven him for his pathetic note and cowardly departure. He remembered a word, a funny word he'd heard when he was young, and always wanted to find a way to use it. Pusillanimous—yes, that was how I acted. Damn idiot. Then he'd passed out, his last flickering thought being that he might never see Di again.

With a skip of a heartbeat Cheyenne looked over to where he'd left the body of ab-Hawsawi; it was still there, still dead. Now he heard sounds, footsteps and indistinct voices coming nearer. He clutched the AK-47, and then remembered that he'd emptied it on ab-Hawsawi and he had no more ammo. The sniper's rifle, lying next to him, only had one round remaining. Ah, shit, I'm too tired to fight anymore.

Cheyenne heard footsteps coming up towards the second level. He pointed the gun toward the stairs. Maybe I can scare the intruder off.

The dirty and bruised face of Cheyenne Smith broke out into a smile, one that hurt his face, when he saw who had come up the stairs.

"Fuckin' A, Lieutenant Perez! What in the hell are you doing here? Didn't get enough last night?"

"Come looking for you, captain. Looks like you had a time of it."

Cheyenne shrugged, looked over again at the body of ab-Hawsawi. "Yeah, it was a busy night." He could smell the smoldering ashes of the arms depot the Apaches had destroyed. He thought he could also smell the putrid aroma of dead bodies, but that might have only been in his memory.

"Quite a mess out there," Lt. Perez said, pointing with his rifle towards the outside, in the direction of the depot.

"Yeah. Haqqani moved civilians into this village. Some of 'em ain't moving this morning."

"Captain, we need to get you out of here. The IASF will be along soon. We don't want to be here when they arrive. We've got a chopper a quarter mile from here. You think you can make it?"

Cheyenne nodded and grunted as he pushed himself up off the floor. Yes, the United Nations International Assistance Security Force would be nosing around soon enough. Fuckin' Haqqani probably called them to complain about the horrific attack on civilians. In Pakistan, yet. Fuck it, let the diplomats straighten it out.

"Him we can leave," Cheyenne said, nodding towards ab-Hawsawi. "Downstairs, though, we've got to find Spiedel and Jason and take them out with us."

"Only one we found was Jones, the poor son-of-a-bitch."

"That poor son-of-a-bitch, he talked about medals; well, he deserves one or two. Came back to help me, and helped those kids get away. You know anything about the women and kids, and the old men?"

Perez nodded. "Yeah, a few wounded ones came in, the rest we found huddled up near the pond east of here. Scared shitless but okay. A few wounds and minor burns, we're trying to patch them up quickly so we can get our asses out of here before the ISI arrives."

Wonderful; the Pakistani Inter-Services Intelligence. Don't want to talk to those creeps.

"What about Colonel Spiedel?"

"Don't know where he's gone. Last I saw him was when he met up with you. I was busy taking those civilians out from then on. Had a bitch of a time getting a chopper to come back for you guys this morning."

"He was here, in this building with me, I saw him get shot."

"Don't know about that, captain."

Cheyenne moaned as he stepped down the ladder and Perez realized that the captain's injuries were worse than he'd realized.

"How's that wound, sir?"

Cheyenne held his hand to his side and when he pulled his hand away it was bloody.

"Might need a new band-aid soon. C'mon; did you find my boots down there?"

"Yes sir, we did find a pair. Didn't know they were yours. Hell, we didn't know you were up here. You want me to take those, sir?" The lieutenant nodded towards the gun Rock still held and the rifle on the floor.

"This you can have," Rock said, handing the AK-47 to the lieutenant.

"This I'll keep, " he said as he picked up his XM2010.

All the aches from crawling over rocks and tumbling down hillsides, of being shot and knocked down, all the old aches from his first imprisonment, the wounds, the lack of food and water for long stretches of time, all these affronts to his body seemed to coalesce at this instant, as Cheyenne gingerly made his way down the stairway, assisted, to his dismay, by the young lieutenant.

My whole body hurts, my head hurts, my side hurts, my whole fucking brain hurts. Spiedel, you brought me back for one last job, you've got to get me out of this. But I saw you dead, didn't I?

"Where the hell are you, colonel?"

"Sir?"

"Huh? Oh, nothing." Cheyenne realized his last thought had been vocalized. He eased down the final step where Perez handed him his boots.

Cheyenne sat down and struggled to pull his boots on, while Perez stepped back, not wanting to embarrass the captain by helping him with his boots.

"Uh," Cheyenne said as he pulled one boot on, the action pulling also at the wound in his side. He touched at it.

"It may have started bleeding again, Perez. You think you could find that band-aid now?"

"Yes, sir," the lieutenant replied. "We do need to move fast, sir," he said as he walked off to find a first aid kit.

I used to go three weeks without hot food or a bath, sleep on a pile of rocks, shoot people from hundreds of yards away, and now I'm all tuckered out from putting my boots on, Cheyenne pondered.

Perez returned and knelt down to dress Cheyenne's wound. Cheyenne raised his shirt and let Perez go to work, first wiping the dried blood off.

"How far you think it is from here to Dry Hole, Arizona, lieutenant?"

"Never heard of it, sir."

"Quit calling me sir. So what about Phoenix, or Tucson; how far to there?"

"Well, sir, I'm no geography expert, but I'd say it's about halfway around the world, you know, twelve, thirteen thousand miles or so."

"Long way home."

"Is that where you're from, sir? Phoenix?"

"Dry Hole son, Dry Hole. You ever come through there, you look me up. I owe you a drink for this little band-aid."

"Yes, sir, I will. Now, please, we need to hustle."

Perez helped Cheyenne stand up and didn't get any resistance.

"One more thing we have to do."

"Sir?"

"Don't call me sir. Across the way, that building where we were held captive, I have to look for something."

"What is it? I'll have one of my men look."

"It's an i-Pod, Lieutenant, I need it back or my girl is going to be mighty angry with me."

"Sir, we can get another…"

"No, I need that one. It has all her favorite songs on it."

"…the boy kept walkin'
Without a road of his own…" *

Cheyenne was tottering on his feet and Perez held on to him.

"One other thing…are you sure you can't find Spiedel? I was with him, in this warehouse; I saw him go down; he was shot full of holes." What did I really see?

"No, sir, the colonel's not around anywhere."

Perez grabbed hold of Cheyenne as the captain slumped down, passed out.

"Peavy, Atkins!" Perez shouted. "Get you sorry butts over here and help with me with the captain. We may have to drag him to the bird. Let's move, people!"

"You're takin' my road away
Oh, road away…" *

* from the song, 'Road Away', by John Stewart

***

EIGHTEEN

"On my way home
I remember
Only good days..." ---"On My Way Home", by Enya

Dear Diary:

CONVENTIONAL WISDOM has it that you shouldn't have a friend for a boss. Either the boss will be stricter with you, to make sure no favoritism is shown, or he/she will be easier going on you, which will be noticed and resented by the other employees.

Rock and I struggled with that at first. He would have let me come and go like I owned the place, similar to the situation I believed had developed with Helen. So after our one-day holiday in Coronado I told him in no uncertain terms to treat me like any other employee. We had a stare-off then as we each bit our lip, swallowing the smart-aleck comments that were begging to spill out. Finally he shrugged and said, "Sure."

So then I dart off for Dry Hole when I get the news about my house burning. Now I'm staying to help at the Only Café until Betty Ann gets adjusted to her new life style. Which involves waking up in the middle of the night, and again, and again, and breast feeding when the baby wants to eat (not just when business is slow), changing diapers, and changing more diapers...yech!.

I called Rock and told him I may need to stay here for as long as two weeks, until Betty Ann, or me, I guess, can find someone to work at the café, at least part time. I thought of my old friend Carrie, the home-school teacher, so we might give her a tryout.

Rock wasn't happy and apparently Dennis is even less enchanted with me. How the hell am I supposed to train her when she's not here more than two days in a row, he supposedly complained to Rock. I don't know if Dennis said it exactly that way, but I see his point.

Still, I told Rock when he first hired me that I'd need time off when Betty Ann's baby came; she just came sooner than anyone expected. I told him he could can me if he wanted to; he grumbled and muttered, "Yeah, sure, just get back here as soon as you can." And he hung up. In the mean time, some things don't change. Guess who walked in on my first day opening up?

"Whoopee! Lookie here, Kyle! Guess who's back! Hey, Dinah, need some help in the kitchen?"

"Hello, boys, set yourself down and I'll pour you some hot coffee. How ya all been?"

Yes, it was my favorite over-sexed, acne-faced, flirtatious young cowboys, the James brothers, who work on their Daddy's ranch some twenty-five miles south of here.

"What'll you have, boys, the usual?"

"Yes ma'am," said Kyle

"Colt?"

"Coffee, tea, or you, Dinah?"

"Ah, you need to get a new line, Kyle. Two usuals, comin' up."

The usual for the boys was a tall stack of pancakes, two or three fried eggs, several links of sausage, toast and jam, coffee until it's leaking out of their ears, and topped off by a slice of whatever pie I've had time to bake. They are growing boys, after all, and they do work hard out there in the sun and wind.

Actually, some things had changed, as they can quickly with young people. In the few months since I'd last seen them the pimples had cleared up and both Colt and Kyle looked rather handsome, tho they're probably just as horny as ever.

I've known them all my life and they've always been harmless. I thought of those creeps Helen and I ran into, and I wondered if Kyle and Colt could ever do what those two had done. I didn't think so; their Daddy was a real gentleman, and known to be rather strict. The sons were handsome young men, barely out of their teen years, and still sowing wild oats, as immature men of any age will do. They were big talkers, especially Colt, but I've never known them to cause any real trouble. Kyle was the eldest but only by eleven months. He wasn't quite as rascally as Colt, and sometimes he helped to rein in his younger sib. They looked close enough alike that some people mistook them for twins. They ever did anything to a woman that wasn't desired by her, I think their Daddy'd whip 'em over his lap, no matter what age they were.

There's a call for you, sir...on line one."

"I'll take it in my office."

"Hello...this is Rock...how can I help you?"

"He's at Reed."

"Chester?"

"He's in a private room, reserved for VIPs. You can't find it without a map, and you can't get near it without an escort."

"How is he?"

"They gave him blood; he spouted like the Fountain of Trevi."

"But he's going to be okay?" Chester was fond of hyperbole.

"Far as I know. He was at Landsthul until they got him patched up and stabilized, and then they sent him here. I'm told he'll be discharged from the service once he's reasonably recovered from his wounds. No way he can do the kind of stuff he's been doing.

"They offered him a desk job but he turned it down. I haven't seen him yet, but apparently he's pretty beaten up. He's must be tough; hell, all these Delta guys are. Stuff he's been through, I can hardly imagine."

Neither spoke for a moment. Rock knew that the Landsthul Regional Medical Center was a military hospital and the largest American military operated medical center outside the territory of the United States. It serves as the first treatment center for soldiers badly wounded in Iraq and Afghanistan.

"Yeah, hell, I guess I can. Sometimes I forget."

"Me, too," I agreed.

"You know, Rock, in the daytime, I forget the bad things. But at night, they come back."

"Tell me about it."

"And we weren't in as good a shape as these young studs! I still smoked, can you believe?"

I laughed, briefly remembering how when I was Cheyenne's age I too, assumed I was immortal and that the bullet with my name on it hadn't been cast yet.

"Can we see him?"

"I can arrange it, but I'll have to be there."

"When?"

"Make it soon. I'll be in D.C. all week. Let me know when you're coming and I'll meet you."

"And Di? Cheyenne's girl?"

"Yeah, that's fine. But I have to stay in the room at all times, even if he and his girl want to go at it."

"I'll make sure she knows the rules."

"You can't ask him anything about where's he been, or what he's been doing, Rock.

"No problem, Chester, I don't want to know. Hey, what about this other guy, colonel somebody or other?"

"Don't ask. Some kin of superman, way I hear it. A legend in his own time. He's even harder to get a line on than Cheyenne, but the people I talked to seem to think he's so tough that bullets bounce off him."

"Does Cheyenne have access to a phone?"

"I'm told no, but I can't be sure. I know you can't call into his room, I don't know if he can call out. You thinking of his girl friend?"

"This is very hard on her, Chester. Second time it's happened."

"You can tell her what you want, make up some story about how he's being debriefed and can't contact anyone yet, or some such crap."

"And I'll need some info. Sorry, Rock, but I need your complete name—first, middle, last, and your social. Hers too. And birth dates."

"Sure they don't want a DNA analysis?"

"Don't laugh, they might."

"I can give you my info now and call you..."

"Get it all together at one time and call me."

"What number?"

"Let me give this one to you. Don't call me at my regular number for this."

"Yeah, okay, I'll be in touch as soon as I get Di's info."

I wrote down the number Chester gave me.

Dear Diary:

THE LAST FEW days have been like old times; rising before the sun, getting the kitchen going, making coffee quickly because there are always a few insomniacs who knock on the front door before the café is officially open, desperate for a cup of strong, hot coffee. Long ago I developed the habit of unlocking the front door as soon as I had a pot of coffee going, and setting some cups out along with a carafe so the early birds could help themselves. Often I'd hear the door open, then the sounds of someone moving around and pouring coffee, hear the door open and close again, and would find money on the counter left by whomever had come and gone. Usually it was Bull, or Clyde, the mayor, or one of the ranchers who'd spent the night at the Grande.

Jake dropped all his other temporary jobs to work at the café and help Betty Ann with the baby. I needed Jake to do the short order cooking while I minded the pies, set the tables, and served the patrons. While it was fun in a nostalgic sort of way, I soon realized why I didn't mind not doing this every day. It is tiring, hard work, and with all the food around I'd find myself hungry because I hadn't had time to feed myself.

I asked Carrie if she'd like to work a few hours in the morning, before her home-schooling started, but for the three days she worked she never got there on time, and she broke more dishes than old Bull has adages. She spilled coffee on two customers and constantly got the orders mixed up. Fortunately most everybody knows most everybody else and they could laugh at her and exchange plates when Carrie brought the wrong order. Soon they were joking and teasing her and she felt embarrassed and so did I, because I was used to running an efficient café. Before I could talk to her she quit and suggested her seventeen-year old daughter would love a job. Cassie took to the job eagerly and in no time at all was collecting tips as good as any I used to get. See what happens when you get old and wrinkled? The cowboys right away are swayed by a prettier, younger thing. Oh well, it's the way of the world.

Oh yes, Diary, because I'm sure you want to know: the baby is fine and healthy and eating and growing. Betty Ann loves being a mother (tho I can't wait for her to come back to work full time. I gently reminded her I do have a job in San Diego). Cassie is enthusiastic about her job and learns so fast I have even started to share my not-so-secret-anymore pie recipes so she can take over that task. Lots of kids her age tend to be lazy, but around Dry Hole you learn to pull your weight soon as you can walk and talk.

Friday night: Diary;

Rock called and said he was flying to Tucson after work, and would rent a car and come to Dry Hole for a visit. Said he was eager to see the new baby. It sounded like he had something else on his mind but I didn't pursue it. The only thing I suggested was that he put off driving from Tucson until morning.

"You have no idea how dark it is on that old road, Rock. You could hit a pothole that'd suck you down halfway to China. You'd be stuck in the dark all night."

I finally persuaded Rock it would be safer to wait until Saturday to drive here and I'd bake a special pie for him. He relented so I'm looking forward to seeing him when he gets here, and a little concerned about what else he wants to talk about.

Betty Ann & Jake took baby Sally (named after Betty Ann's grandmother) on her first outing tonight. We (the new parents and the baby, myself, Carrie and her husband Jimmy, and Cassie) went to dinner at the Grande.

Friday night is a busy night because many of the ranchers come in for a big meal and some of them stay over. The hotel is generally full up on Fridays. Saturday gets busy too, mostly from the locals who don't have to drive far to get home. So it was show time for Sally and she and mother were nearly overwhelmed by the attention they received. The star attraction slept through most of the hurrahs she received. In a town where the population isn't even a rounding error to the census takers, a new baby is truly a reason to celebrate. I think most of them cowboys had a difficult time finding their room after they'd toasted Sally several dozen times. I wished Cheyenne could have been here.

Amidst the cheers and laughter the thought hit me— where is Cheyenne at this exact moment? — and gloom threatened to ruin the evening for me. It took great will power to push away the sadness I felt from ruining the evening. I glanced at Betty Ann and she caught my eye and I knew she'd noticed. She mouthed, 'He'll be okay, you'll see.' I blew her a kiss, smiled, and raised my glass to drink another toast to the newest resident of Dry Hole.

Rising as early as I needed to was tougher now then when I had to awaken before the birds to catch the bus to Douglas for high school. Seems it wasn't that long ago I had the energy to rise early for school, cheer for the football team, help at the café, go horseback riding on the weekends, bake pies, do my homework, run from Cheyenne until I let him catch me, and get up bright and early the next day and do it again.

Rock arrived before the first pot of coffee was consumed. It wasn't very busy; Saturday mornings generally are slower as even the old timers who have nothing else to do tend to sleep a half hour later. The ranchers and cowboys who stayed over at the Grande will sleep the sleep of the dead, probably the only morning they can sleep late. If they're home, there are chores to do, but if they found an excuse to stay over the night in Dry Hole, they take advantage.

Business picked up by eight o'clock, but by nine, with Jake cooking away and Cassie hustling, I had a chance to sit back and talk to Rock.

First I fed him and kept gabbing so he couldn't say much. I feared he had bad news about Cheyenne and I didn't want to hear it yet. It didn't occur to me that if Rock did have bad news he wasn't going to spill it here in the café, in front of other people.

When the crowd thinned out Cassie and Jake were enough to handle things so I took Rock over to Betty Ann's so he could make goo-goo-eyes at baby Sally. He'd brought presents, having decided he was an honorary uncle and thus, needed to bring goodies for the baby, a couple of outfits that Sally would outgrow in about two weeks, and squeaky toys that I wondered if he'd bought at the baby story or the pet store. Whatever, they were appreciated by the baby and the mother.

Then Rock asked me if I was free the rest of the day and whether we could take a drive somewhere. Here it comes. I suggested we drive out to the national forest, a drive of less than an hour. The scenery there includes wild flowers and cold, running mountain streams and seemed like a better background for absorbing bad news than the kitchen of the café with burgers frying and dishes clashing.

I packed a picnic lunch and we drove out in Rock's rental car, neither of us saying much. It was a perfect late autumn day, with blue skies and just enough fluffy clouds to draw the eye towards the imaginary shapes they conjured in the mind. The temperature was in the low 60s, not bad unless a breeze comes up. While still comfy we were getting close to the time of year when snow can be expected at the higher altitudes.

Our families, mine and Chey's, use to come here frequently when we were kids for picnics and hikes, fishing and overnight camping. This area is called a 'sky island', because of the towers of colorful rock formations that jut up abruptly from the surrounding plains of grass.

We parked a short distance inside the park boundaries near a stream fed by the Chiricahua Mountains. The sun felt good on the skin. I laid out a blanket and sat down and raised my head to the sky, closed my eyes and soaked up the sun for a few minutes while Rock arranged our picnic lunch on the blanket. A slight breeze rose and I knew it wouldn't be long before I needed to put on my sweater.

I nibbled on a sandwich and Rock opened a small bottle of champagne. Champagne? Are we toasting Cheyenne?

"Okay, Rock, tell me already...I can take it."

He poured champagne in a plastic cup and handed it to me. He raised his cup and said, "Cheers."

I nodded and took a sip. "What did you hear from the general?"

Rock looked at me and took another sip of his champagne.

"You don't really think I believe you came here just to take me on a picnic," I said.

"He's alive, Di. He's at Walter Reed. He's waiting for you to come and see him."

I stared at Rock to see if I could discern a lie; he wouldn't joke about this, he wouldn't lie about it, either. I downed the champagne.

"Don't make me pull it out of you bit by bit, Rock."

"Chester says Chey's doing fine, just banged up a lot. He was taken to a hospital in Germany and they wouldn't have sent him to the States if he hadn't been recovering from his wounds."

"What kind of wounds?"

Rock shook his head.

"Don't know, didn't ask, actually. He has to be debriefed about his mission, so he's somewhat in seclusion..."

"An excuse not to call me," I said.

Rock shrugged. "Eh, I suppose he's uncertain about what to do, you know, regarding you."

"Or maybe he thinks it'd be cute to show up again on my doorstep, months after I think he's dead, and smile like the Cheshire cat, ha! ha!, here I am!"

"I thought you'd be happy, Di."

"Oh, I am Rock, I'm just a bit numb right now. Relieved, unbelieving, worried when you talk about 'injuries', like, can he walk, talk, did he lose an arm or a leg. But, I want to go see him."

"I've already made reservations. We fly out of Tucson tomorrow."

"Oh, my!"

"You said you hired someone to help Betty Ann at the café."

"Yes, yes, that's fine. It's just...so sudden! All these weeks I've had Chey in the back of my mind constantly; everything I've done has been shrouded by Chey—where is he? Is he alright? Will I ever see him again? Is he being tortured in some rat-infested prison? There's always this fuzzy picture of how things will be once he returns, or how they'll be if he's never coming back. I even wished he'd run off with his east coast girlfriend instead of going back to the Army; at least he'd be alive. Now, it's...I don't know."

"Let's finish our lunch," Rock said.

"Thanks, Rock, and thanks to Chester, too," I said, and gave Rock a smack on the cheek.

"Ah, Di, Cheyenne would have shown up sooner or later!"

Dear Diary:

I'M WRITING THIS several days after the events noted...
I haven't had time to keep current.

We drove to Tucson in Rock's rental car. Then we flew to
Washington, D.C. arriving late in the evening. Chester said he'd
meet us at the airport. Rock had already told me it would be
too late today to see Cheyenne, so I was prepared to wait until
tomorrow.

"But he knows we're coming?"

"Yes, Chester told him."

"And Cheyenne didn't say no?"

"Of course not, Di."

As we neared the baggage claim we saw Chester
standing there, a big smile on his face. In one hand he held a
cell phone he was talking into and with the other hand he
waved to us.

Rock reached out to shake hands with the general and I
opened my mouth to greet him when Chester handed me the
cell.

"This call is for you, Miss Russell."

"Wha...?"

Chester smiled at me, then at Rock as I took the phone
from him.

I truly expected it was Betty Ann with bad news.

"Hello?"

There was no answer. "Hello," I repeated.

"Di? It's me, Cheyenne. Hey, Di, I ain't dead again, you know? No insurance money for you this time!"

"Cheyenne? Oh, my, it is you! Are you...are you okay?"

"Oh, sure. I'm a bit bruised but all body parts function normally, although a bit slower than usual, is all. I won't be going horse back riding any time soon."

"I'm so glad you can talk. I had this fear that they'd...you know, did something awful to you in prison."

"Ah, bunch of pansies didn't hurt me much."

"When can I see you?"

"They tell me tomorrow. My debriefing is nearly over, I just have some papers to sign and the day after I have to meet with...with some other people, and then I'll be free to go. Can't wait to see you, Di. And Di...?"

'Yeah, Chey, I'm here."

"I'm really sorry."

"Okay, soldier, this one time."

"I'll see you when you get here. I've got to go...it's not my phone. Love you."

"Love you, too."

Rock and Chester were standing next to me, silent but grinning. I mugged at them and said, "You shouldn't listen in on private conversations!"

"Then don't hold them in public!" they both replied.

I can't remember where we ate dinner or what I ate; not much, if I recall; too nervous. Rock and Chester gabbed like teenyboppers while I daydreamed about what would happen tomorrow, and the days after. I knew I still loved Cheyenne, but I also knew he had to make some clear decisions. I also knew that if he told me he was staying in the army, I'd tell him I would no longer wait for him. I had a new job, and I wasn't going to pine away hoping he'd call once in a blue moon. This was it, absolutely, positively, for sure, no maybes, no ifs, ands, or what nots.

"Penny for your thoughts?" one of the guys said.

"Huh? Oh, heck, cost you at least a dollar."

"Worried, Di?" Rock asked.

After a moment's reflection it dawned on me that while I was concerned, worried wasn't the proper description.

"No," I said forcefully.

"I don't think I can say I'm worried, Rock. I think I'm mentally prepared to deal with whatever Cheyenne decides he's going to do. It seems everything I've done for the last two years has been a reaction to what he's done, or hasn't done, even though he hasn't even been around most of the time. That's kind of a goofy way to lead one's life, don't you think?"

No answer.

"Rock, as far as I'm concerned I work for you now, if the job is still there after all the time off I've taken, and when we get back to San Diego I'm going to look for a place to live. Chey has to decide if he's with me or not. I'm not going back to live in Dry Hole, that's for sure."

"Tucson? You still have the house there."

"I'm going to rent it."

"Not sell, hey. A backup?"

"No, Rock, the market. I'll be lucky if I can rent it much less sell it. And in Dry Hole I'm going to build a house that I'll rent to Betty Ann and Jake."

"Becoming quite the entrepreneur. And if Cheyenne doesn't want to come to San Diego?"

"His loss, sweetheart, his loss." I hoped I'd could be as positive as I sounded.

Diary: the next day...

Despite having talked to Chey on the phone, I was petrified that when I saw him he'd be bandaged like the mummy, and his arms and legs in slings, like Spencer Tracy at the end of *It's a Mad, Mad...World*. He did have a number of wrappings, but when we walked into his room he was standing upright, as if he wanted me to know right off that he was not bedridden.

I remembered how skinny Chey was when he came back from being a prisoner-of-war the first time. This time, even wearing an oversized robe, give him a stovepipe hat and he would have been as thin as our 16th president.

"You look like you need some home cookin', soldier," I said.

"Know where I can get some?"

Okay, Diary, we hugged and kissed but with Rock and Chester standing there, big grins on their faces, our reunion didn't get past PG-13.

Chey wouldn't say anything about what he'd been doing or where'd he been. I don't know if he ever will. But he did have a surprise that caught me like a pie in the face.

"How angry were you when I left, Di?"

"You're lucky I didn't chase you down and shoot out your tires."

"Yeah, I'm really sorry."

This wasn't easy for him; big tough special forces soldier apologizing in front of two other pretty tough guys.

"Forget it, Chey. I'm over it. Although I think the note I wrote you is still on the kitchen table."

"Oh, I don't even want to guess what you wrote!"

"I'm still tweaked at you for not calling, not once, since you snuck out."

"The places I've been, Di, cell phone reception isn't so good."

Yeah? How come that bin Laden guy's always sending propaganda messages when he's holed up in some dirty cave in the hills of ...wherever?"

"Cave, my ass. I think he's got his own satellite system over his comp...never mind."

"Hmmm."

"Di, I want to ask you something personal even if it's in front of these two lugs, because without them..." Cheyenne grinned and mugged, a bit sheepishly. "Ah, these guys are good to talk to; they understand things."

I looked at Rock and Chester, and they both shrugged. I sensed that they knew something I didn't. I looked at Cheyenne and he shuffled his feet and ran a hand through over his head, smoothing back what little hair he had.

"I was so dirty and banged up, they just shaved me so they could look for wounds," he said.

"Now you're stalling."

"Yeah, well, what I was going to ask you is, did you know they have a chapel here in the hospital?"

"A chapel? Well...I guess... lots of hospitals do. Why are asking me...?

"Chey...what are you saying?"

Diary, I don't want to bore you with all the details. Rock and Chester said they had no idea what Cheyenne wanted to say to me.

The actual proposal was less than romantic, not at all like I had imagined when I was a silly young girl. No, Cheyenne did not ride up to me on spectacular white steed, white breath pulsating out of his nostrils (the steed's, not Chey's), rearing up on its hind legs like Silver used to do for the Lone Ranger. Chey did not then jump down and kneel before me, bow his head and beg for my hand in marriage, lest he be doomed to a life of misery and loneliness.

Anyway, after my quick acceptance (in my imagination I demurred, causing my knight in shiny armor to plead and promise undying love and devotion, until I began to giggle and feel sorry for the poor guy) we all went to lunch, my impromptu engagement party. Cheyenne had to return to Reed for the night (he was still too sore, he claimed, to get personal with me, anyway), so the party was, again, less than it had been in my imagination, and the next day he had meetings and reports to complete at Ft. Belvoir. The poor guy didn't even have a chance for a wild stag party, ha! ha!

I went with him to Ft. Belvoir and waited for several hours reading old magazines. I can't imagine why he needed to spend so much time on reports when he's getting out of the Army in a few days.

"That must have been some big shot you killed over there," I said when we were in the car, returning to Washington.

"Damn, Di, don't say anything like that, even in joking! Never talk about what I do."

"Okay, okay."

The next day was a day I'd often dreamt of, except when it came it came when I hadn't been expecting, and didn't have time to prepare for. It was exhilarating and disappointing at the same time. How to make sense? Instead of being able to spend days drooling over wedding magazines, and weeks with my friends shopping for the perfect dress, I had to rush out and in a few hours find a trousseau that would be classy and something I'd feel good about when I looked at the pictures years from now. Chester's wife, Paula, knew some shops in Silver Springs, Maryland, and she spent the morning running around with me and fortunately we found everything I needed by three in the afternoon, enough time for my 6 p.m. date.

When I was nine or ten, Betty Ann, Carrie and I used to play like we were being married. Carrie's Mom owned a used clothing store in Douglas, and one day, in a weak moment, she took in several young lady's frilly dresses. She gave one of each to the three of us.

They were different colors: I had pink, Betty Ann, blue, and Carrie had a yellow one. But we pretended they were white, because in all the pictures we saw of brides they were wearing white. Somewhere we heard that white indicated the bride was a virgin, which we thought meant they were very beautiful. So of course we wanted to be virgins and very beautiful.

We'd play in one of our houses and pretend we were in church, or sometimes we'd play at the park and pretend we were getting married outdoors. We did this until we outgrew the dresses and the game.

We agreed to be each other's maids of honor, the details to be worked out whenever. One thing we got right was our intendeds: I pretended I was marrying Cheyenne; Betty Ann, Jake, and Carrie, Jimmy. So far, two out of three got it right. And I was Betty Ann's maid of honor, as she was when Carrie and Jimmy married.

One thing I never imagined in my game was that I would get married in the chapel of a military hospital!

I was disappointed that Betty Ann & Jake couldn't be here, and some of my other friends from Dry Hole, and Mom and Dad, and...well, some things never happen the way you imagine them, and anyway, Carrie's and Betty Ann's weddings both ended up different than we'd ever imagined, but Diary, I wrote about those years ago.

In Dry Hole, most of the wedding guests wear their cleanest jeans as a way of dressing up, so being married in a new dress was like being invited to the marriage of an English princess. Even with his shaved head Chey was never more handsome, garbed in his fancy dress greens, adorned with what he described as a Combat Infantryman's Badge and a Ranger's Parachutist Badge and several other badges and medals. I'm afraid to think what he did to earn them.

Rock was best man and Paula graciously stood in as my matron of honor. Chester was also in full uniform, with a chest so full of medals it would make a third world dictator envious. Betty Ann will cry that she couldn't be here, but she'll be happy for me anyway. Rock hired someone to take a video of the ceremony so we'll have it to look at later. And Chey agreed that later we would have a duplicate ceremony in Dry Hole. The plan now is to take a honeymoon, so I pleaded with sorrowful eyes to my boss for yet more time off.

"I don't think I can keep the job open much longer," he said.

I gave him my sad puppy look.

"Much longer than two weeks."

Chey suggested Bermuda and I said anywhere but the places he'd been would suit me fine. We spent a couple days in a Georgetown hotel (I won't go into details about our wedding night, Diary, I'm too shy to get technical, but so that I'll recall it years from now when I read this to jog my memory, it was heaven!) Then the plan is to fly to Bermuda for a week, back here to Washington where Chey has stored his car, complete one more round of final processing, drive to Dry Hole to get my car and introduce my hubby to the town, and so forth and so on, and then to San Diego to look for a place to live. I did make it clear that I was keeping the job at Rock's company and Cheyenne is fine with that. One problem occurred. One tiny problem. Actually, one big problem. One, big, stinking problem.

Chester and Rock met us at our hotel to take us to the airport. When I looked at Chester there was something in his eyes that frightened me. Actually, it was the way he couldn't look me in the eye. I knew something was up and I knew I wasn't going to like it.

Diary, I can't write about it now...maybe later...much later.

CHESTER AND I went to pick up Di and Cheyenne to drive them to the airport. Chester had a manila envelope with him but he didn't say what was in it so I didn't ask. When we got to the hotel where Di and Cheyenne were staying Chester ignored Di at first, but when he inevitably glanced at her I could see there was something wrong. Di picked up on it too, and the new bride glow disappeared in a wink. I couldn't imagine what was in the envelope but I sensed it was not going to make Di happy.

"One thing I thought you'd want to know, Cheyenne, before you leave."

"Yes, sir?"

"You know this man?" Chester pulled an 8 x 10 picture from the envelope and handed it to Chey.

Chey stared at the picture and it was obvious he knew the man.

"Yes, I do. I'm not authorized to reveal his iden..."

"I know who he is; Colonel Spiedel, the man only kryptonite can kill."

Chey nodded. "Last I saw him was in a warehouse...near where I was held prisoner. I know he'd been shot up, but I never had a chance to check him out. I was involved in..."

"You don't have to give me the details."

Chey look down at the floor and stared for several seconds, as if seeing again what he remembered seeing in a place none of us could go to.

"I was sure he was dead. But the next morning there was no sign of his body."

"He's alive and we know where he is."

"Are you sure?"

"He had an implanted transponder."

"Ah...he'd talked about doing that, but I didn't know he had. So, where is he? Is he a prisoner? Is someone going after him?"

"It's on a need-to-know basis, Cheyenne."

"Well, sir, I need to know. I need to get to him; I owe him!"

"Cheyenne, what are you saying?" Di asked, the desperation all too obvious.

"Di, he's saved my ass more times than I can count! I can't leave him."

"No, Cheyenne, no more!"

"Di, I have to!"

I don't know if the look on Di's face could best be described as amazement, or surprise, or shock, or some combination. Her eyes bulged and her lips quivered. Her mouth opened but no sound came out at first...it was as if her scream was stuck in her throat. Finally she found her voice.

"Rock!" Di pleaded as she grabbed me by my shirt collars, her eyes as wide as a surprised tarsier. "Talk to him!"

***

www.ingramcontent.com/pod-product-compliance
Lightning Source LLC
Chambersburg PA
CBHW020509020726
47493CB00001B/258